WHITECAPS
ON THE
LAKE

A NOVEL

ALICE LICATA

Relax. Read. Repeat.

WHITECAPS ON THE LAKE
By Alice Licata
Published by TouchPoint Press
Brookland, AR 72417
www.touchpointpress.com

ISBN-13: 978-1-952816-44-4

Editor: Kimberly Coghlan
Cover Design: David Ter-Avanesyan, Ter33Design
Cover Image: © Meredith Licata Grogan Moore
Author Photo: Meredith Licata Grogan Moore

Connect with Alice Licata
@alicelicata.author @ readalicelicata @alicelicata.author

First Edition

Printed in the United States of America.

For my father, who was the epitome of the Greatest Generation,
and the best dad a girl could have asked for.

And, for my mother, a kind and gentle soul who
still makes me laugh on a regular basis.

Acknowledgements

Stephanie Hanson, my terrific agent, who saw potential and made it happen; Kimberly Coghlan, my editor, who was a breeze to work with and wonderfully supportive; Sheri Williams and the team at TouchPoint Press, so fortunate to publish with them; Barbara Brownell Grogan, whose early reads and cheerleading made all the difference; My amazing daughters, Meredith and Caroline, whose unwavering support, love and laughter enrich my life beyond measure; My four siblings and my dear friends for always being there for me.

PART I

CHAPTER 1

THE ORANGE JUMPSUIT was half hanging off her now. It'd been choking her. She had clawed at it—she couldn't breathe. All her nails were throbbing nubs. Her hands were rubbed raw from gripping the bars until her knuckles turned white. Her cheeks were chafed pink and stinging after trying to stick her head partly through, over and over. She desperately needed to breathe the air outside the bars. She pulled hard through her nose.

She yelled out. "Please, please, please, I need air. I can't breathe! There's no air in here."

A voice from outside rang out, "There's air in there; shut the hell up."

"Please, please, I'm going to die!"

"Just shut the hell up; you're not going to die."

"Please, I'm claustrophobic. I can't stay in here! I have to get out, I can't breathe! I'm claustrophobic! Please, let me out. I can't BREATHE!"

"Let you out? Now that's rich... *really* rich. For the last time, just shut the hell up!"

She glanced at the thick, concrete walls surrounding her, and up at the tiny, barred, square window, placed far too high to provide any outside view. She tried to take a deep breath, but it stopped short. Her lungs screamed for more air, but they wouldn't fully inflate. *Oh my God. I can't breathe.* Her heart pounded like a jackhammer inside her head. Her skull felt like it was about to split wide open. *Oh my God. My head is exploding! My heart is stopping! I'm going to die! I have to get out of here! I can't breathe...*

She snapped awake then with a start, drenched in sweat and shivering. Her heart raced, punching her ears with every beat. Her insides churned. She felt sick. She stumbled down the hall to the bathroom, tripping on the bath mat in the dark. She reached out for something to break her fall but went down hard against the commode. The porcelain felt like ice on her cheek. She hoisted up and slung herself over the bowl, heaving and heaving until there was nothing left. Then, she heaved some more.

A Couple Weeks Earlier

She'd only gone to the window out of curiosity, her nosy-neighbor-Gladys-Kravitz move. Peeking through the drapes, anticipating something perhaps mildly interesting—who didn't enjoy a little harmless spying? And then…

Wait… what?

Her stomach dropped like a bowling ball off a steep cliff. She wanted to buckle over, collapse right there on the hardwood floor, and curl up tight in fetal position. But like the pathetic moth to the flame, she had to keep watching… she had to *see*…

"Is that a bod—?" Her voice caught sharply in her throat.

Whoosh—she could feel herself starting to burn up from the inside out. She knew the image of this day would end up seared into her brain. It's how it always went with her. Things singed her, left marks—indelible, like a Sharpie.

This turn of events was a tad ironic: the very night before she'd gone to sleep feeling so satisfied, so blissfully oblivious—yes, even pleased with herself. She was actually happy again, a minor miracle in itself. She'd only recently been truly lower than low, barely able to crawl through the incessant moments of her life, as if heavy sandbags were attached to her every limb.

Her world was about to shatter into smithereens—yet again.

And like before, the universe hadn't tipped its hand a bit. She had sensed nothing out of the ordinary.

Daybreak had crept silently as usual—no fanfare, no hoopla, just here comes the sun again—trusty molten ball, pregnant with possibility, lingering below the horizon, ready to blaze yet another path through time on the planet it had faithfully cradled for eons. Then, like always, said planet dutifully rotated.

The sky had shimmered with pale pinks and soft yellows, signaling uneventful weather ahead—no-red-skies-in-the-morning-sailors'-warning for this day. Another bit of irony since there was, in fact, a fierce storm brewing. Only not the kind with thunder and lightning, high winds or torrential rains—it was to be a disturbance of an entirely different nature.

A vicious tornado might have been sincerely welcomed in its place.

The ordinariness of the day's beginning indeed belied a grim reality soon to engulf her, that unsuspecting speck of a soul quietly watching out the window. Someone who'd tried hard to live a decent life—a respectable, well-intentioned, never-wanting-to-hurt-a-flea sort of life. Sure, a little misguided at times and flawed, even occasionally a bit of a mess, but still a *good* life—or at least, not a God-*awful* one.

Her hand trembled now as she peeked through the tapestry drapes of the home where she'd grown up—the sprawling red brick ranch house sitting up on a hill, with glossy, forest-green shutters, bright yellow, double front doors, and old-timey, bronze rooster-weathervane cheerfully perching on the roof. The house seemed to say, "No worries; all's well here!"

But the ashen face and bleary, black eyes peeking out—wide, unblinking pools of panic and dread—would certainly have said otherwise. What she'd seen only moments before had sent piercing alarms and snapping bolts coursing through her brain—pinging every terror switch, zapping every corner, vibrating her every nerve. One glimpse of the outside world that morning had hit her like a monster Mack truck. She was instantly stricken and left teetering over the edge, about to career off into a deep, dark pit—a bottomless, greedy hellhole.

***

At the window that morning was Imogene Louise Mussomeli. The shock to her system would be nothing short of cataclysmic. She was hardly used to the shit hitting the fan. She wasn't somebody who dealt well with calamity, let alone impending doom. She felt sick.

Up to this point in her life, she'd mostly skirted catastrophe. Terrible misfortunes happened to *other* people, she'd thought. She'd actually come to feel blessed. She was undoubtedly a success story—a stand-out even. The girl who'd gone far.

Her parents had been especially proud. Her father used to beam—his daughter had a Ph.D.! Was "Dr. Mussomeli!" A professor at a prestigious university! She'd note this with embarrassment, though deep down, she'd loved being a source of such pride.

Yes, that doctorate degree had impressed. Wasn't she just *all* that?

Well, look what 'the professor' had done now. She knew the unexpected swivel her life had suddenly taken would not fuel any pride. Her father would have been appalled.

Although unexpected, she wasn't completely surprised. She'd had a sense that her life might eventually take a turn—some sort of pivot. It'd been only a tiny kernel of belief, a small inkling, buried in the recesses of her mind—unseen yet irksome—like a pea under a mountain of royal mattresses. Something was coming. Here, perhaps right on schedule, was that twist—the unequivocal justification for the inkling.

The turn, she figured, was that last piece in the jigsaw, proving once and for all, she was basically a misfit. Before, she'd sometimes entertained the notion that maybe she was just an "outlier," like those described by Malcolm Gladwell in his book. Famous "good" outliers like Bill Gates or Albert Einstein had changed the world. *Ha,* she'd thought; maybe *she'd* do something great.

Now this.

Transfixed, peering out the window of her childhood home, she wondered how she could have miscalculated so badly, been so cavalier, so *idiotic.* Finding herself in the midst of such an unthinkable crisis, she couldn't help but wonder, *How the heck did I get here?* She'd never expected her life to turn out like a Norman Rockwell painting, but now...

Her old-world, Sicilian-Italian grandmother used to speak of cursed people—hexed by someone who'd put the evil eye or "malocchio" on them. Supposedly, an Italian horn charm could ward this off. Imogene used to wear an 18 karat gold one on a necklace, literally 24-7, as a teen. Having the little gold charm on made her feel especially cool around her friends. Why had she ever stopped wearing it? Buried deep in an old jewelry box somewhere, it was obviously no good to her now.

Had Imogene simply been "cursed" all along? It sounded so unscientific and irrational, and *yet...*

All the way back to when she was merely a tiny girl, the little outlier was like an old worrywart. So many things would rock her. She'd immediately get a bad feeling in the pit of her stomach. But perhaps this trajectory had been inevitable since day one because, as it happened, Imogene's parents had essentially misnamed her. She was one of six girls born about two years apart, named (in descending order): Michaela ("Mic"), Melanie ("Mel"), Monica ("Mon"), Mallory ("Mal"), Imogene ("Im"), and Maria ("Mar").

All the other sisters also had the incidental treat of the initials "M.M." (M&Ms were an especially popular candy at the time—"M&Ms, they melt in your mouth, not in your hand!") They loved to call themselves "the M&M girls."

At some point, Im had asked her mother about not getting an "M." Her mother replied, "Oh, we just liked the name 'Imogene.' Besides, the second letter is an 'M'... we figured that was close enough, pretty much the same thing."

This in particular galled Imogene. It seemed so reckless. And why had they reverted to an "M" for the youngest?

Mrs. Mussomeli replied, "Oh, I don't know, we didn't think it would really matter."

Um... wrong, Im had thought. When ticked off with her sisters' names, Imogene's would sound out like a flatulent tuba.

Someone would invariably say, "Wow, Imogene, you're the oddball!" or "What happened to Imogene? Why didn't she get an M?" Or it would be, "Mic, Mel, Mon, Mal, Im, Mar." Then, "Wait a second... Im... I-M? Shouldn't that be M-I? What, is she dyslexic? Ha, ha!" Or even, "Maybe she was adopted! Ha, ha!" And so on.

Im would crack a small, half-smile and lift her shoulders in a shrug without uttering a word. Eventually, she internalized that maybe she *was* odd. While the reasons were trivial, a little girl really didn't know the difference. She heard, "You're the oddball!" or "Maybe she's adopted," and it would reverberate rudely in her mind.

In time, Imogene stuffed her feelings away, pretending not to be bothered, willing herself to act like everything was fine. A person's name wasn't such a big deal, right? But her brick and mortar exterior had its holes, and a free-floating sense of angst set-up camp within her. Feeling misaligned in the world, like in those early sister line-ups, she wondered if she'd always be that one apart.

Compounding this (and perhaps related to it) was Imogene's tendency to be easily rattled and spooked as a girl. Fears could spring up willy-nilly like creepy clowns at the circus. A harmless drawbridge near their home had terrified her. Naturally, the bridge had a joint right down the middle and lifted for vessels to pass under. From her little girl eyes, it looked so precarious. With such a big split in it, how could the bridge not collapse with all the heavy cars going over it? Sitting in the way-back of the family station wagon, she'd picture their car plunging into the murky water below with everyone trapped inside, petrified faces and hands flattened against the windows, banging to get out. The sound of the car's tires bumping over the ribs of the steel bridge as they traveled over would vibrate her with fear. Eyes squeezed shut, she'd silently pray, waiting to hear the smooth sound of the solid road when they made it to the other side.

Im had also been freaked-out by the *Wizard of Oz* movie. It used to air on TV every year. Most kids love it; the whole family would gather to watch. While the Wicked Witch of the West and her winged monkeys gave her the total creeps, for Im, the twister was the real monster. *Was a tornado going to come to their house?* During inclement weather, she'd watch the skies like a hawk—on the look-out for any twisters or whatever awful weather might be headed their way.

Along Lake Ontario in New York where the family first lived when Im was very young, squalls could indeed whip up quickly. In winter, lake-effect snow would blanket their home and street, smothering trees, enshrouding cars. Her father would completely disappear, shoveling the driveway, surrounded by huge walls of packed ice and snow. She imagined an avalanche could even bury a small girl (alive!) in her own yard.

And the nearby Great Lake would often grow wild, spawning frothy whitecap waves, furiously bashing the rocky shore. Imogene knew that big whitecaps on the lake usually meant something bad was on the way: a storm, thunder, lightning, heavy rain, hail, gale force winds, a blizzard. Pummeling the rocks, the ferocious surf seemed eager to engulf anything in its path. No one could survive the giant lake's wrath. And it was right *there*, practically in their backyard—vast and looming—poised to swallow up anything or anyone that got too near or fell off the cliff.

The Mussomeli's Rochester home had, in fact, been on a street running along a steep bluff on Lake Ontario—actually the highest point on the lakeshore between Syracuse and Buffalo. Local history deemed it a favorite spot for bootleggers in the 1920s, waiting for their whiskey to arrive from Canada. The elevation made it the ideal location to look out for the boats shuttling the booze. But it could also be treacherous.

Before Im was born, a man in one of the houses abutting the cliff had fallen to his death there. Suicide was at first suspected, but it turned out there had been unseen erosion under the craggy edge. Insidiously, it had looked completely solid.

The man's old house was a Spanish-style mansion with gloomy windows and tall spires that taunted her every time she innocently rode by on her little bike. The house seemed to whisper, "I eat little girls like you for lunch." Im had imagined it having tendrils, suddenly reaching out to snatch her. A cold shiver would run down her spine. She'd heard about the guy who used to live there—that he was leisurely strolling out in his own backyard when the ground suddenly gave way right under his feet, no warning, no sign—just one misstep, and he was dead.

Death. Even as a tiny girl, Im knew it was very bad—*the worst thing.* And it seemed it could happen any time in the big world out there, a place that might instantly give way, suddenly erupt, swallow you whole, bury you alive, or whisk up your house and drop it down in a scary foreign land where an evil witch tries to steal your dog and kill you, *dead.*

Indeed, when Im was small, the Mussomeli family was abruptly uprooted from their Northeast home. As it happened, many industrial companies were expanding at the time, and Mr. Mussomeli's automotive one needed engineers at a brand new plant in Ohio. When moving day arrived, a huge Allied truck appeared, and strange, large men walked through their house, boxing and loading up all their possessions. Imogene remembered sitting in a corner, clenching her favorite stuffed animal, as their home was being torn apart all around her. Finally, they said goodbye to their cozy neighborhood in Rochester, New York and boarded the airplane for Ohio. It was her first time on a plane. Her stomach was full of butterflies as she peered out the tiny round window. She'd seen photos on TV of the aftermath of a plane crash—debris scattered, and white, bloated bodies floating in the dark water. *Would they be flying over any water?*

Of course, they made it safely to Ohio, landing in the sprawling suburbs of Dayton. Situated in the southwestern part of the state, it was quintessential Midwest. Land-locked and drab, it could have been another planet. It felt like being in the boondocks. None of the girls was thrilled, but being that outlier, Imogene was thrown for a major loop.

In Rochester, Im had begun to feel happy, even secure. Now she suddenly felt out of place. In fact, her entire Italian-American family stuck out in their new town like a giant, greasy thumb. Nobody looked like them. Nobody acted like them. Nobody talked like them.

Everyone had a funny, southern Ohio accent, saying things like, "Have you got a pin?" when they meant a "pen." Or saying "git" instead of "get." And the Mussomeli girls laughed at the rampant bad grammar, as in "I'm gonna git me some," or "I seen him yesterday," and the double negatives, "He don't want none," or "I ain't gonna tell nobody nothing." Or ending a sentence with a dangling "at," as in "Where is it at?" or "Where's the party at?" It all seemed so hickish.

Plus, most of the Ohio girls were fair-haired and light-eyed, with translucent skin, rosy cheeks, and cute freckles. The Mussomeli girls had complexions that tanned deeply in the summer and faded to a sallow, olive tone in the winter. And they all had deep mahogany eyes and full dark eyebrows, along with thick heads of inky, brown-black hair. Where *had* they come from?

And then, what about the twisters? Tornadoes were much more likely in hot, humid, flat Ohio than Upstate New York. After all, the setting for the Wizard of Oz, Kansas, was in the heart of the Midwest, just like Ohio. Plus, Im had overheard her parents discussing a place called "tornado alley" in Ohio. *Was this anywhere near their new house?*

Im soon had the Ohio National Weather Service phone number memorized and dialed it on the black rotary phone in their basement multiple times a day to hear the forecast. She proclaimed that she wanted to be a "weather-girl" when she grew up and studied the daily newspaper weather map.

At 4:30 each afternoon, she'd be sitting on the driveway waiting for the evening edition of the newspaper. She also had developed a secret crush on the paperboy, so her heart would skip a beat as soon as his bike rounded the bend. It was the best part of her day! Then, newspaper in hand, she'd race into the house, spread the paper out on the family room floor, and turn directly to the weather page. Inspecting the large map of the country, she'd check the local forecast, taking note of low pressure cells or storm fronts headed their way. When she saw the big "H" for high pressure hanging over Ohio meaning no storms, no lightning, no thunder, surely no tornadoes—she got a warm, good feeling; she could breathe easier for another day.

In retrospect, maybe the weather fixation gave young Imogene a small sense of control in the midst of a world where she felt so little. Vulnerability and lack of control are inherent in childhood, but, for whatever reason, Im became acutely aware of this—along with her smallness and insignificance in the universe, the fragility of life and, in turn, the absolute dreadfulness of death.

Religion and God might have been of some solace to her, in this regard, had she been able to get her mind around it. But her precocious little self secretly questioned it all. *How could it really be true? How do you accept it without question?*

Yet, most around her seemed to. Sunday mass was a must for the whole Mussomeli family. And Im's Italian grandmother walked to church at least three times a week with her lady friends and prayed the full rosary every morning and every night. The rosary beads held such power for them, making worries disappear, calming nerves, keeping loved ones safe. Im wished she could have bought into all this, too.

Of course, being part of a Roman Catholic family, Imogene still received all the holy sacraments—although even in this, she proved to be the outlier. When it was time for her to go to the Saturday Communion preparation classes (CCD), she flat-out refused.

"I can't go, Mom!"

"Why not?"

"I don't know...I just don't want to go!"

"But, Im, your sisters have all done it..."

"I know, but I just can't, Mom. Please don't make me go!" Tears flowed. Heels dug in. What the heck was wrong with her?

Finally, an emergency, one-on-one meeting with the Mother Superior of the church was arranged. As she was led alone into the nun's austere office, Im's face grew hot, her eyes watered, and her throat clamped shut. She stood still and silent as the nun hugged her for what seemed like an eternity. The rustling of the nun's habit and the feeling of the stiff, starched collar against her nose were forever etched in her brain. Was the nun trying to hug the devil out of her? There could have been no other explanation for Im's insubordination.

Petrified, she never spoke a word to the Mother Superior that day. The nun couldn't have understood that her obstinate refusal to attend CCD had nothing to do with getting the sacraments or being possessed by the devil. It was only that she was terrified of the parochial school, a place she'd never been, full of children she didn't know. She'd already just been there and done that.

When the Mussomelis moved to Ohio, it was smack dab in the middle of her first-grade year. Going through the heavy wooden doors at the new school for the first time felt like walking the plank. All eyes fixed on Im as she scooted into her seat in the last row by the door. She wanted to melt into the wall. Her stomach clenched in tight knots; everything seemed foreign and strange. Even the school building itself scared the bejeezus out of her: spooky high ceilings, huge dark rafters, thick old plaster walls, clunky gray metal desks, heavy glass-block windows—nothing like the bright, airy modern school she'd left behind in Rochester.

Her first day at the new school also turned out to be picture day. School portraits back then were usually in black and white; the children were explicitly told not to wear white shirts or blouses—presumably to prevent a floating-head photo when the child's white-clad torso disappeared into the background. Having not received this instruction, Im wore an all-white knit top with a red, blue, and green plaid, pleated skirt. The teacher tried to calm the rest of the students, but there were whispers and snickers about her being in white.

And later, whenever Im tried to speak out in class at the new school, her cheeks burned and her windpipe constricted; she could barely produce a sound. Thankfully, she did, in time, make friends with another little brown-eyed girl, and she was overjoyed. But then, without warning, the girl's family abruptly moved out of town. Standing alone in the middle of the playground, Imogene watched, a huge lump in her throat, as her new best friend climbed into the back seat of her family's sedan and disappeared—whisked up and gone for good.

***

Eventually, a year later than usual, Imogene did receive her first communion, to the great relief of her parents and family. And she tried to be a good Catholic: praying hard at church, kneeling in the pew, gazing up at the cross, going to confession, asking God for forgiveness, dipping her fingers in the holy water, signing the cross and genuflecting. But something inside her was hedging. And ultimately, lack of attendance at mass and confession left her dangling.

Still, she would never really be a non-Catholic. She certainly had her fair share of Catholic guilt. For better or worse, as much as she might have wanted to shake it, the imprint of the Catholic Church was not really expungable. And maybe as a cradle-to-the-grave Catholic, she could yet be in the good graces…

Only *now*, finding herself in the midst of such an unspeakable crisis, such a monumental moral mess—all bets were essentially off. Yes, when the knife of fate had seemed to slash right through her that morning, she could only have been termed a lapsed Catholic, at best. She felt doomed.

Before, though she'd obviously not lived a saintly life, she'd not been overly concerned about her own death or where she would be going in the so called "afterlife." Notwithstanding white-knuckling her armrests occasionally on an airplane—praying they weren't going down and imagining herself being sent to purgatory as a fallen Catholic—she'd still wound up feeling pleased that she, former worrier extraordinaire, had finally become mostly comfortable in her own skin.

But all of that was *before*.

Before unforeseen events had unfolded right under her nose. Before the unthinkable had apparently happened, something her own hare-brained and reckless actions had set into motion.

She'd thought the recent sudden loss of her father was to be the nadir of her life—but far worse had yet been awaiting her.

Watching out the front window from the home where she'd grown up, it was as if the floor was collapsing right under her feet, and the years were rapidly falling away all around her. Instantly, she was that scared little girl again. The sister who never fit in. The one with the wrong name. The one with a plethora of fears. Ridiculously obsessed with the weather. Terrified of tornadoes. Afraid of First Communion. Deathly afraid… of *death*.

And within her, a massive implosion was taking place.

Im knew now that the thing nagging at her all along about her own mortality was ultimately going to come true. Peering out through the drapes, as the ambulance slowly crept away, down the street she knew so well—a place where she'd always felt safe and loved—she had a horrifying realization. It gripped her like an iron vice, thrashing every fiber of her being, crushing all hope, snuffing out all plans. She was left a quivering pulp of despair.

Cardinal sin.

She was going straight to Hell.

CHAPTER 2

THE MORNING AFTER the day all hell broke loose in her life, Imogene snapped awake at first light. Her eyes blinked wide open—but she didn't move a muscle. There, on the same single bed where she'd slept as a girl, with the tall, maple wood posts and pink chenille bedspread, she stared up at the familiar pattern in the ceiling plaster—cheery, overlapping swirls that now made her feel slightly dizzy. She tried to steel herself for the storm ahead. Every sickening tick of her little bedside alarm clock inched her closer and closer. The chartreuse clock had been a Christmas gift she'd asked for as a teen, the wind-up, round metal-case kind with a pair of shiny silver bells on top to ring the alarm. Why she had wanted it so badly was a mystery, but it had lived happily next to her bed for decades. Its constant ticking used to calm her. Now it only felt harsh and nagging.

She shoved the clock under a pillow and buried herself under the covers. She didn't want to move. Maybe if she didn't budge, somehow, time would stop, and it wouldn't be true.

A million thoughts raced through her head. She couldn't get the scene from the previous morning out of her mind... it could only mean one thing. One unspeakable thing. She wouldn't even let her mind fully go there, but it *knew*.

She shuddered. In the past, she'd wake from a bad dream and feel awash in relief, realizing it had been nothing more than a nightmare. If only she could have that now—all of it only being a bad dream. She desperately wanted to go back in time to the *before*. Before yesterday. Before that "wait-what" moment at the window. Before she was going to end up in Hell. Even all the way back to being that tiny scrap of a girl all over again, scaredy-kitten-self and all. Anything would be better than *now*.

The ambient light in her room was dim, but she could still make out the objects there, once so inviting and comforting: the knotty pine desk where she'd done her homework, written letters, confided in her embossed gold, latch-key diary. The neon-green lava lamp perched on her dresser, a present from her high school boyfriend. The mod hanging globe light she'd bought from Spencer's gifts at the mall. The vintage poster on the wall of the Beatles movie "Help!"—John, Paul, George, and Ringo standing on top of the block letters spelling out the word help. It read, "Stop Worrying, HELP is on the Way!" *If only.*

The previously friendly items now seemed to be jeering at her: 'Look what you did.' *Look. What. You. Did.*

Though she had little hope of redemption, she wondered if God would understand...hadn't she only just lost her father? Hadn't that seriously unhinged her? And maybe she'd even been warped by her "outlier" childhood—how could she be blamed for that? She had no say.

She suddenly felt supremely sorry for herself. She'd probably been doomed from the start. So many wrong things about her. Her name. Her nervous system. And what about that stupid dark, peach-fuzz mustache she had as a girl? Girls weren't supposed to have little mustaches. How could she have ever turned out normal? It felt like a calamity.

She'd spent hours in the sisters' bathroom, kneeling up on the long countertop, peering closely into the large vanity mirror—every angle revealing the flaw. It was so noticeable in her eyes. Ergo, potential mortification lurked all around her. The school's florescent lights were especially the bane. Inevitably, some nasty boy sitting in front of her would turn around and loudly point out, "You have a mustache!" or "Imogene has a mustache!" Her face would immediately flame ruby red. Her ears would burn. She'd try to act as if nothing happened, but she'd be quietly devastated for days—not even telling her sisters, who all had varying degrees of tiny mustaches as well. But she thought hers was by far the lushest, and for this, she felt severely cursed. Alas, being an Italian girl meant dark hair in wrong places.

Although Im couldn't really see it, in reality, she'd always been attractive by most standards. She somehow escaped the Italian/Roman nose (i.e., "it roamed all over your face"), had big chestnut eyes, a bright smile with naturally straight teeth and matching deep dimples. With her slim, athletic build, most would have described her as pretty. And yet, she always felt unattractive because of her fatal hair flaw. In some ways, it may have been worse coming close to beauty only to fall short.

But still, any reflection she did on her life and childhood offered no valid excuse for where she'd found herself. So what if she was named wrong? That didn't mean anything. Who cares if she felt totally out of place when they moved to the Midwest? She got over it. So she had a little mustache; come on, it wasn't really such a big deal. Afraid of all kinds of stuff? Should have just made her more careful—that wouldn't have been a bad thing. Overly concerned with death? Well, *that* was ironic.

So what if all this had made her a little nervous Nellie—how was any of it relevant now?

Besides, in her heart of hearts, she knew she actually had a good life all along. There'd been no trauma, no real hardship, nothing that was ever *that* bad. Im knew many who had it far worse. She never had to do without; not even close. Her life had been chock-full of happy, even giddy moments when she felt wild and free—ecstatic just to be alive.

Racing barefoot across the manicured golf course, stretching out from their back yard—how lucky to live right *there*—doing cartwheels and handsprings across the soft, smooth greens, sprinting through the sprinklers that popped up every night. Gliding down a long hill on her metallic-midnight-blue, banana-seat bike with monkey handlebars—the *coolest* kind. Plunging off the high dive into the gleaming pool on a sizzling summer day. Playing Red-light/Green-light in the street after dinner. Gazing up at the sky full of stars, marveling at the vastness of the Universe. Snagging the front car on the Racer Roller Coaster at Kings Island—cruising back to the station with arms up, showing off for all those in the cue. Catching fireflies in a jar on a balmy night with her sisters.

Running with sparklers on the Fourth of July, little American flags woven into their braids. And spectacular fireworks right over the golf course, like their own private show.

And simple things like enjoying special treats: Sweet Tarts candies and Blow Pops from the corner King Kwik store...Twinkies in her lunchbox... big Hershey bars, sans almonds, after Sunday dinner at their grandmother's house... white sheet cakes with thick, crusty white icing on birthdays... tangy lemon Italian ices from the neighborhood stand in Rochester. Or when she and her sisters had gorged themselves on potato chips and Cokes in front of the TV on a Saturday night.

Watching television at all in the Mussomeli household had been a treat in itself. Objecting to its passivity and increasing offensiveness, their mother called it the "idiot box" and deemed it the likely downfall of society. Some might say this was prophetic. Being allowed very little TV time, the Mussomeli girls practically lived for their favorite sitcoms like "Bewitched" and "I Dream of Jeannie." The powers those two TV women wielded went beyond their wildest dreams—if only they could twitch like Samantha or blink like Jeannie and have anything they wanted; make whatever was wrong all right again.

If only she could blink herself out of her mess now.

And with no cable TV back then, their measly allotment of television was often marred by lousy reception. With only a VHF and UHF rabbit-ears antenna to catch the analogue broadcast signals through the air, the Mussomeli TV viewing was essentially left to the whims of the weather and their wobbly aluminum antenna, stuck willy-nilly in the chimney. When the picture got fuzzy or doubled, or the vertical hold gave out and the frames cycled up and down mercilessly, Mr. Mussomeli would climb the ladder, crawl out on the roof, and adjust the antenna for his girls. They'd yell up to him through the fireplace when the TV station started to come in clearer. "OK, STOP! That's good right there! R-e-e-e-ally good there!" Then, "No, no, now it's bad, BAD, go back! Go back to where it was before!"

The girls envied the neighbors who had a brand new 27-inch color, console Zenith television along with an antenna perched high up on a tower outside their house. They could rotate it with a flick of the control dial sitting right there on the TV set and even receive the Cincinnati channels. The Mussomeli's TV only got a paltry three local channels, at best, on a clear day. Those neighbor kids had it made, living in the veritable lap of luxury afforded by an antenna tower and remote adjuster.

If only she could go back to that innocent time, when her biggest concerns had to do with bad TV reception... or even just dark little mustache hairs...:

Back when everything was in front of her, and she'd shown such promise. In spite of her "outlier" quirks, she'd always been clever and resourceful, determined and focused. Capable. Her competencies had sometimes even outpaced those around her.

She was the sister who would get things done, solve little problems—fix whatever it was—things that might leave the others spinning their wheels. Imogene had always just been so willing to step in. What better way to prove her worth and demonstrate she was not an unwanted oddball? And besides, things usually came easily to her. As far as her sisters were concerned, why not let Im do the heavy lifting? She *wanted* to do everything anyway. "Go ask Imogene; she'll know how to do it," they'd say. Or "Give it to Im; she'll do it." Im never said no; she liked being helpful.

Seeds of this can-do competence may have been sown early on when she was the only one who could understand her little sister. Toddler Maria's speech was virtually unintelligible to everyone except Imogene who could instantly translate every word. Maria chattered on endlessly, all sounding like gibberish and gobbled-gook; no one could decipher it. Someone would call out, "Im, what's Maria saying?" or "What does Maria want?" Without missing a beat, she could tell them, and she'd grin inside. It felt so good to be needed.

Im ended up the go-to for her sisters for all kinds of things: cutting and styling everyone's hair or doing a quick trim of bangs or split-ends. Making needed birthday or anniversary cards with cute poems inside, along with homemade gifts. She was the one pasting up the new purple-flowered wallpaper in the bathroom or hanging the frilly, lace pink curtains in their bedrooms, or painting a mural on the wall. The one with her nose to the sewing machine making Halloween costumes or repairing the rip in the Prom dress or even altering it for a different sister as a hand-me-down…

Im loved doing all this. Being valued by her sisters felt like the best thing ever. Who cares if she didn't have an "M" name—she was still one of them and she could do stuff!

In time, Imogene came to believe that maybe those early inklings deep down about being cursed or innately wrong for the world had been unfounded. Maybe they were only little girl insecurities, which could be chalked up to feeling like the odd one out. Perhaps this had even been an advantage—had motivated, even driven her to prove her worth. She had pushed herself and done exceptionally well. She'd even felt proud sometimes. Maybe all would be okay!

But now… Little Miss Smarty Pants—the sister who was so clever, so capable, so skillful, who always seemed to know so much (a doctorate degree, no less!)—had finally done herself in. The fixer was apparently in quite the fix.

She thought she'd always land on her feet like a cat. Assumed she'd always be able to control the horizontal and the vertical in her life. But here, in spite of all her competencies and talents, her successes and accomplishments, and all those happy, even blissful times in her childhood and beyond—after everything she'd actually done so right… it was all leading up to one thing:

Unspeakable doom.

***

No doubt, it had been her father's sudden, unexpected death—only weeks before—that had initially set the wrecking ball swinging in the saga that would become her life.

She'd never been able to stand the thought of anything dying—let alone a person she dearly loved. As a kid, she practically wept over a smashed chipmunk or squirrel in the road, not able to get the image out of her mind well past the "tragedy." She felt bad even killing a bug, squishing a spider, or swiping away its elaborate web—its life's work after all! No creature had been too small or insignificant.

Once out jogging with Maria, a prowling Tomcat snatched a fledgling dove that was learning to fly. Maria just stood screaming, but Im gave chase, frantically swatting at the feline with a stick. The cat finally dropped the poor dove from its mouth, but the tiny bird was severely maimed— wings snapped and sticking out at wrong angles—and apparently dead.

Maria screeched, "Don't touch it, Im!"

But Im rushed home and returned with a shoebox to pick up the birdie-corpse to bury it. When she got back, she was surprised to see the little creature nestled in the grass, upright and blinking its shiny bead eyes, downy wings still all askew. Though immobilized, it was still very much alive.

Im quickly tore some grass to make a soft bed in the box and carefully scooped up the tiny creature. She was amazed at how it seemed to weigh virtually nothing at all. She raced home with the box and began an urgent search. Finally, she found a wildlife rescue center listed in the yellow pages, which would take the little bird—but it was nearly an hour's drive away. No matter, she convinced Maria they had to take it there. Hopping in one of the primary-colored Vegas Mr. Mussomeli had bought for his daughters, Maria sat holding the shoe box on her lap, refusing to look at it, while Im raced up the highway to the rehab center. The rescue center's workers weren't sure the injured bird could be saved, but they handed Im a business card with a case number on it so she could call and see. Im never learned what happened to the little dove—she couldn't bear to call and find out. *What if it had died?*

When death came like a thunderbolt to her own father, Imogene was shattered. It didn't matter that he'd lived a long life. In fact, he'd already beaten the odds in his own estimation. "Look, the average for a guy of my generation is only about 78," he said when he turned 80. But Im couldn't embrace the glass-half-full notion. He hadn't seemed that old at all to her. Why shouldn't he have made it to 100?

Whenever her father had spoken about his eventual demise, Im basically tuned him out. He'd said, "Of course, your mother is going to outlive me by a mile!" referring to his wife's longevity genes—many of her relatives, including her father, had indeed lived to be more than 100. When he tried to drag Im into the den to go over what was in those big, black spiral binders, lined up and looming there on his bookshelf, she always made an excuse. "Oh, Dad, I can't right now." She was never busy at all, merely evading.

Discussing what to do with the financial affairs after her father died was an excruciating thought. She passed it off as an aversion to anything "morbid." But clearly, she was avoiding the idea of a world without her father in it. Later, seeing his black financial binders up on the shelf crumbled her with guilt. She never even let him show her what he wanted her to know in the end.

When the end came one day, without any warning, Imogene was inconsolable. Naturally, daughters love their fathers, but it seemed her father had been a compass, still somehow centering and grounding her. Although in her mind, he'd been just her dad: far from perfect, even fairly aggravating at times—their relationship would hardly have been described as warm and fuzzy. As an adult, out of habit, she still bristled slightly when he reached for her hand as she walked by him, instantly tensing up like when she was a teenager.

Her relationship with her father had perhaps followed a typical course. In the first decade of her life, she'd been quite attached. During those years, her four older sisters had formed something of a pack, and there wasn't room for Imogene. They told her she was "in the way!", "get out!" or "go play with Maria!" But Maria was still essentially a baby then— theirs was the largest age gap, in fact. Maria couldn't talk right, didn't even potty train on schedule, and seemed so far behind for so long to Im.

So her father was her first real pal. She followed him around like a puppy, watching while he worked around the house, handing him nails or the screwdriver. Or they'd go outside and rake leaves, dig in the garden, plant flowers, even laying the sod in their new Ohio front yard. And they spent hours at Ping-Pong in the basement after dinner or playing chess on the card table. She knew she never really challenged him at either game, but he never seemed to mind.

Then, by the time she hit puberty, in predictable teenage girl fashion, it was suddenly not okay to hang around her father. Telling him anything about her day, sharing any of her personal business—out of the question. Nightly Ping-Pong and Chess had long gone by the wayside, too.

After he died, Im rued those early teen years when she completely pulled away from him. She always hated herself for having done this. She pined for one last chance to 100%—no holding back—hug him tight and tell him how very much she loved him. Of course, she never got that chance. One day he was there, apparently perfectly fine, and the next he was gone. *Poof.*

The harshness of this left Imogene stunned and sent her instantly into a state of deep shock. The grief counselor at the hospital emergency room expressed amazement at her composure after her father's death, but it was only because Im was too numb to feel a thing. Robotically making the dreaded phone calls to all her sisters, in that little peach and lavender "bereavement" room with the soft lighting and multiple Kleenex boxes, Im choked out those awful words, over and over:

"Mar, Daddy had a heart attack... Um... He didn't make it." Instant shriek on the other end of the phone line.

"Mic, it's Im. Dad had a heart attack today... He's... um... gone." A wail, then the sound of the phone dropping.

"Mal, Im... it's dad... he had a heart attack... no, Mal, he's gone...." A gasp, then cries of "oh no, oh no, oh no!"

Each call was forever stamped into Im's memory.

Her poor mother had looked like a tiny wounded bird when Im first saw her sitting in the hospital ER waiting room that day. Her eyes, shining with tears, had the most pained expression. "He's gone!" she'd simply said. Then, sobbing, "Oh, Im, it's so final! What am I going to do without him?"

Imogene knew her mother was indeed going to be utterly lost without her husband of over 50 years. He was her everything. Her world had revolved around him for the majority of her life. Visitors to their home would find it funny how much she waited on him, but he never dared step foot in her kitchen. He was essentially banned. She wouldn't even have allowed him to help her wash dishes. This was strictly her domain. Not that she always relished being the "chief cook and bottle washer" as she called herself; it was just the way it was.

Roles for a husband and wife were well-defined when they married, and Mrs. Mussomeli was very much a product of the times. Wives were to raise the kids and be homemakers. Still, she'd been more than that: a bona fide live-wire in her day, she became a Yogi in the Sixties, complete with a guru from India. She taught yoga to lady prisoners at the local jail and held classes and mass meditation sessions in their basement. Eventually, the Mussomeli home became the hub for all her new age and kooky friends with wild parties in the living room and séances around the dining room table.

And Mrs. Mussomeli adopted vegetarianism well before it was a thing. She made her own whole wheat bread, yogurt, granola, and health nut cookies. She stocked wheat germ and carob bars, black strap molasses and bran, soy nuts and veggie burgers. White plastic containers cultivating active yogurt cultures and lime-green plastic pans with perforated lids for growing alfalfa sprouts lined their refrigerator shelves. Im always felt compelled to over-explain to her visiting friends, apologizing for her mother's obvious "weirdness" and the unappetizing foods in their fridge.

Her mother was decidedly not like other mothers. At one point, she had a large collection of wigs in virtually every shade—including platinum blonde. Im and Maria used to sneak in and try them on. They were displayed on Styrofoam heads in a line atop her bedroom bureau. Mrs.

Mussomeli could be anybody. Im suspected that her father enjoyed all this. Life with his wife was never boring.

Not threatened by her antics, he didn't feel the need to hem his wife in. She brought color and spice to his life. During the yogi phase, a turbaned, white-bearded guru straight from Bombay actually lived with them for an entire summer. Expecting to be waited on hand and foot, Mrs. Mussomeli even had to butter his bread. Dr. Singh held nightly meditation sessions at their house with wall-to-wall supine people carpeting their basement floor. The average man of Mr. Mussomeli's generation would not likely have tolerated such. It's part of what made him such a stand-up guy in Im's book.

His sudden death clearly left her reeling. The grief was excruciatingly intense. And made worse because of her sense that his death could have been staved off, postponed somehow. This was irrational, but something like it had happened before.

In the summer prior to his last, her father had very nearly died from complications after a routine surgery. He, ultimately, pulled through, but this seemed partly due to Im's dogged efforts at the hospital. After he suddenly "crashed" and was on the brink of death, the nurses seemed to be dropping the ball. Im went into overdrive and got him emergency intensive care just in time.

But the following summer, there would be no days of praying and bargaining with God, planting herself at the hospital, reprising her role as the aggressive advocate, making sure he *lived*. His death from sudden cardiac arrest had been immediate. No begging for the ICU. No bedside vigils. It was over in a second. She never even had a chance to say goodbye.

The year he lived after the previous summer's close call took on a bitter-sweet note. It was only borrowed time. The end was near all along, and she never even knew it.

Nothing could have changed it, but Im was still plagued with guilt: she should have seen it coming, should have known his heart needed help before it was too late. How could she have so easily accepted his proclamations that he was in "perfect health," that there was nothing wrong with him? Right, she believed him because she wanted to believe him.

Imogene felt completely lost after his death. Naturally, the same was true for her mother, but being the widow, she seemed to know instinctively how to navigate through her grief. Her collapse was legitimate, socially-sanctioned. And it would take its expected course. Healing would begin in its own time. Imogene, on the other hand, was just the adult daughter. Surely, she ought to be strong enough to withstand the loss of her father. The feeling that she was over-reacting, that she wasn't entitled to her profound grief, that there must be something inherently wrong with her, left her unhinged.

Why was she the only one of her sisters who was literally falling apart? Was it because she had been the one who, at least for a time, wholeheartedly was "Daddy's little girl?" Had this been that one thing which she clung to, relied on her entire life—without even knowing it? She didn't get an "M" name, but she did get to be her dad's best pal. After he was gone, she wasn't anybody special any more. She was filled with regret. How could she have been so awful to him as a teenager, distancing herself so completely, never to fully return?

Compounding the problem, she grew unable to sleep. She might doze off to late night TV, but then she startled awake with the image of her dead father in her mind. When she did sleep, a recurrent dream had her father lying in the ER. She'd reach out to touch his shirt sleeve, but when her fingers contacted the fabric, the shirt would deflate rapidly—as though he wasn't there at all, only his clothing pumped up with air.

Indeed, Im had seen and touched her father right after he died at the hospital. After racing there when her mother called, she was ushered back to a curtained cubicle. Her father was on a gurney. The plastic end of the intubation tube was still sticking out of his mouth, connected to nothing. His eyes were fixed and open, and she cursed the nurses or whoever for not closing his lids. She tried to gently do it herself, but they stubbornly stayed wide open. It turns out the eyelid muscles relax in the open position after death and then quickly stiffen that way. This explains the action so often seen in movies and TV where someone immediately closes the eyes of a person who has just died. For Imogene, seeing her father this way had been horrific. Her worst nightmare. She couldn't get it out of her mind.

Years later, Imogene ran across the specific symptoms of post-traumatic-stress-disorder, which include flashbacks, hypervigilance. and insomnia. She found she could check off each one about herself after her father's death. You didn't necessarily have to go to war to be post-traumatic. If you had the right kind of nervous system, many other things could put you into "post-traumatic-stress."

The heightened awareness and vigilance associated with PTSD may have been adaptive at one time in an evolutionary sense—eons ago—when staying highly vigilant and alert to further threats after a predator attack increased survival odds. But anxiety and unrelenting insomnia nearly took Im over the edge and certainly did nothing to increase her survival odds.

She was forced to take a leave of absence from her job at the University because her brain essentially became mush. Without REM sleep, the mind turns on itself, like a snake eating its tail. It gets totally stymied. All of Imogene's sisters rallied to support her in one way or another. But when they tried to connect with their sister—who seemed to be lost in a dense fog—their eyes would fill with fear. They were terrified of losing her now, too.

Not returning to the University and her career, Imogene spent the long days with her mother, attempting to regain a foothold in her life. Although she could not have functioned at her job, being home surrounded by so many reminders of her father was probably counter-productive.

Finding the book he was in the middle of reading before he died, waiting there next to his favorite chair—bookmark in place—sent her sobbing. It was a book she picked out for him at the local library, a mystery she thought he'd like. He had said he was enjoying it, though she knew it was nothing great. She wished his last book had been something more significant or meaningful. When she went to the library's return desk with his last unfinished book, the clerk recognized her and said she had a couple "holds" for her to pick up. In the summers when she was home, Im regularly requested books to bring to her father. They knew her at the library. One book waiting for him was "Cold Mountain." She knew he would have loved the historical fiction story set in the Civil War. Now he would never read it. Holding back her tears, she could barely speak when she told the clerk that she wouldn't be needing the reserved books any more. The library lady looked up at her, and Im choked out, "See, my father died."

Roaming around the house in her haze, she also found her father's last crossword puzzle in his bedroom. He left it sitting on top of the old TV stand he used as a makeshift bedside table. Her father always recycled and re-purposed things this way. The sight of it gave Im a pang. Nearly completed, the puzzle was fastened onto a homemade clipboard—the board a scrap left over from when he paneled their family room back in the Seventies. The Mussomeli girls thought the walnut paneling, along with the new avocado green Naugahyde couch, made their house look so cool. They dreamed of having thick, wall-to-wall shag carpeting also, but Mr. Mussomeli was too practical for that. They got a durable gold and brown Berber instead.

Because she knew her father loved doing the crosswords in the Sunday Washington Post magazine, Im would save them for when she'd visit. Like his last mystery book, the puzzle she found in his room was one she'd brought him. His little gold #2 pencil, with its worn down eraser, was there clipped on the board, too, at the ready. She could hardly bear to look at it.

The title of the puzzle was "Conic Relief," obviously a play on the phrase "comic relief," which struck Im as mildly ironic given that she hadn't laughed in days. She wondered what the title meant. Reading some of her dad's answers, in his easy-to-read block letters, she realized it had to do with things related to cones. One clue was "Net surfer's way to eat an ice cream cone?" (Those who do many crossword puzzles know the question mark means the answer will probably be a play on words or a pun.) Her father's surely correct answer was "POINTANDCLICK." Another clue was "Song for ice cream cones on 1904 Louisiana purchase exposition debut?" Answer "EATMEINSTLOUIS." Perfect. Im did find an error or two. For the clue "Otherworldly reading," her father had it only half right with "SCIRE." It should have been "SCIFI." This tiny thing gave Im another pang. It seemed everything made her sad.

Imogene might have worked through her grief better had she been able to be distracted, had she not been faced everyday with so many of her dad's personal things and the new emptiness of her parents' house. But she couldn't drag herself away. It was like there was a huge magnet under the floor, pulling, keeping her there long past the time she should have tried to get away—just to save herself.

CHAPTER 3

IM REMAINED FIRMLY in the grips of crushing grief and shock after her father's death. Zombie-like numbness and searing sadness took turns within her psyche. Barely holding herself together, on the surface, she might look more or less okay, but underneath, she was a writhing mess, about to crumble at any second. She felt more at-sea and alone than she'd ever felt in her life.

Yes, she'd lived and worked hundreds of miles away, had been on her own for years, yet there was a tether to her father, which had seemed to ground her no matter where she was—though it wasn't that she directly involved him in her life. While he was typically on the telephone's extension when she called home long-distance, it was mostly her mother's voice on the other end. Still, what he did say usually had weight.

While he was alive, Im had not truly realized the extent of the bond with her father. Having turned away as a teen, she felt mostly like a horrible daughter, never thinking of their relationship as especially close. She always regretted how she behaved as a snotty teen, even though in the big scheme of things, her father surely understood and probably took it all in stride. It's what teenage girls do; most fathers know this. Even so, around her father, she still sometimes felt like that awful, adolescent girl.

Regardless, the centrality of Mr. Mussomeli in his second to youngest daughter's life was often apparent to others. A boyfriend or two had sensed that he was the person by which they and all other men were measured. Most felt the bar was set unrealistically high and gave up trying. Besides, it didn't take much for Im to be off and on her way, leaving yet another guy in the dust. Better to exit before being exited upon.

Now that her father was no longer alive, Imogene felt a gaping hole within her. Its appearance was abrupt and jarring. She could feel herself slowly being swallowed up, leaving her flailing, grasping for anything to keep her from being wholly sucked into the abyss.

It was in this context that Im went through something that left her even more emotionally battered than she'd been before.

Although certainly misguided, it wasn't surprising that Im's reflex was to try filling the void left by her father with a man. Had she been her usual self, she likely would have seen the flaw in this impulse. But she was not at all herself—that independent, no-desperate-need-for-a-man woman she had been before seemed worlds away now.

However, being at her parents' home left her with few means to meet anyone new. She turned to the only place offering a sliver of connection: the internet and a dating website, which promised that true love was only a click away. Im perused the profiles with abandon. Soon, she lost herself in it. It was a relief to have a distraction, something to think about besides the loss of her father.

With her usual zeal, she clicked through dozens of local guys' profiles, carefully attempting to read between the lines and get past the pretense. She made copious notes and scrutinized what they said, their photos, their interests. Finally, she decided to take the plunge. What could it hurt to make electronic contact? Besides, being immersed, exploring the list of eligible men, the "merchandise," had lifted her slightly from the chasm of her grief and given her the tiniest glimmer of hope for the future. If she found the right man, wouldn't he be able to make her life feel right again? Couldn't he rescue her somehow?

Im figured she might have to kiss a few frogs before finding any real prospects over the internet, but then again, maybe her painstaking methods and intuition would guide her to a winner right out of the gate. It could happen!

In spite of not having had great luck choosing men in the past, she wondered if she still might be better equipped for this than the average person. Maybe she'd just been going about it the wrong way before. The format afforded by the internet-dating site could be exactly the system that would give her an edge—after all, she'd been studying human behavior for so many years. Academic psychology, while often dry and removed from the trenches of life, did have its direct applications. It was probably what had drawn her to the field in the first place.

As a college student, her first psychology class had been the one that completely enthralled her. The idea that there might be explanations for so many of the intense feelings she experienced in her life—there were actually labels for such things! This felt so liberating to her. And once she had a name for an emotion or fear, it seemed to lose a bit of its power. Social anxiety—something she'd always felt on some level—well, it was a common thing! Fear of tornadoes?—it was just a childhood phobia!

And that death anxiety thing. Though her erstwhile Catholicism had offered some comfort, existential psychology led her to finally turn a corner on this. Reading the book "The Denial of Death," she thought the author had to be the smartest guy on Earth. Becker's theory was that practically everything is a defense against mortality. That merely being alive and aware creates anxiety and stress, sometimes even worry and panic. That being mortal, by definition, meant *death* was always a looming possibility, and ultimately, of course, an inevitability. So her childhood fears and obsessions made sense—it was simply existential anxiety; she was naturally just afraid of death! At last, the angst faded into the background.

For Imogene, it was immediately clear to her that psychology was the only subject really worth studying. The inner workings of the brain seemed endlessly fascinating. How the brain could produce such a thing as consciousness seemed fantastic. The magic of this compelled her during college. Granted, all this was a bit telescopic, but she was young, and it was all so new. Not surprisingly, she ended up with a secret crush on the professor who taught her neuroscience "Brain and Behavior" class.

Young, attractive, and single, she fantasized about a life with him, bathed in knowledge about the brain, making ground-breaking discoveries about human behavior, finishing each other's sentences. But he never seemed to notice her at all. In spite of her best efforts at dolling herself up for class, wearing her tightest jeans and cutest tops, accentuating her voluptuousness (one perk of being Italian), he didn't seem to give her a second glance. It would have been inappropriate to have done so anyway. Im knew this but still found him irresistible.

While many of the college boys did find her alluring, Imogene foolishly pined away for her unattainable professor. Lingering around the psychology building, she occasionally ran into him, instantly quickening her heart. A hello might be exchanged, but that was the extent of her student-professor romance. Not surprisingly, she had only her bachelor's degree in hand in the end—no serious college boyfriend with whom she might ride off into the sunset.

Actually, she had remained peripherally attached to her high school boyfriend back home all along. While she didn't see Craig often, they had a bond that had survived the distance and all her antics. But she finally broke it off for good—and obliterated his heart—when she decided she wasn't ready at all for the engagement he proposed and ran off to study psychology in graduate school.

Since her early infatuation, some of its luster had worn off, but the field still held a solid place in her heart. It had lifted the veil on so many aspects of her own experiences and emotions, allowing her to finally feel some inner peace and understanding. Insight—it was a beautiful thing. She'd forever be grateful for this.

And with this psychology background, Im imagined herself poised to make a smart selection from the plethora of choices on the internet dating site. Surely, she would have honed a skill set, allowing her to see through the phonies and find that diamond in the rough, that one high-quality candidate among the mediocre masses.

Finally, after much deliberation, she found a good prospect. His name was Ted, and his headline read, "Nice guy seeking nice girl to take home to mom." (Doesn't seem to be looking for just quick sex, and who doesn't like a guy who loves his mother?) He was only a couple years older than Im (check), had never been married (check), but admitted to coming close a couple times, including a long engagement, which had gone south when his fiancée got cold feet (check, not a commitment-phobe). He was an engineer in upper management with a large company and had clicked the box for a salary range, which was far beyond her measly college professor stipend. More information was listed, but what really hooked her was his description of the perfect day: "Deciding to stay in together on a gray, rainy Saturday and watching all three of the Godfather movies." This was essentially hook, line, and sinker for Im; her all-time favorite movie was the first Godfather film. Ted was also not bad on the eyes, if his uploaded photo could be believed. She thought there had to be a catch but decided it couldn't hurt to get in touch with him.

New to the internet dating game, but savvy enough not to give out any personal information over the web, she decided to make email contact from an anonymous account. In the electronic exchanges that followed, Ted seemed wonderful. She couldn't believe she might have hit pay dirt on her first try: genuine, funny, irreverent, down-to-earth, and not too overly anything—Ted seemed like he could be the real deal.

Im decided to be up-front about her current struggle with bereavement and that she normally lives out of state. She was amazed when Ted wrote back saying that he'd lost his own father just a few years earlier and completely appreciated what she was going through. She told him about her life, and he told her about his. He had two older brothers and grew up in a small town in Connecticut. He came to Ohio to attend the University of Dayton and ended up landing a job in town, which was too good to pass up. Although he missed his family, he said he liked the pace of the Midwest and hoped to lay down roots. This all sounded great.

Yet, there was a little voice in her head telling her to be careful. She knew she was still reeling from her father's sudden death. Could she trust herself in this kind of situation? Desperation and desire for a lifeline eventually won out. She agreed to a face-to-face meeting. They'd rendezvous at a nearby Starbucks, a public place in the daytime (check).

In-person-Ted looked just like his online photo. She'd heard stories about guys showing up with bad toupees or huge beer bellies obviously not disclosed in the teaser shots they'd posted in their profiles. Apparently, some guys even put up photos either decades old or possibly not even of themselves. Im figured some women most likely did the same thing, but still, *the nerve.*

Fortunately, Ted was as advertised. Medium height and build with remnants of being a high school athlete (he'd said he played baseball all four years), clear blue eyes, a warm smile, good teeth (a must), slight cleft in his chin (something she'd always been a sucker for), and dark, curly hair that was a bit receding—but this didn't bother Im at all. She knew a balding tendency was linked to healthy levels of testosterone, so she'd take it. Her type was always a bit on the macho side, though not overly. She certainly didn't go in for the brutes. Her cup of tea was masculine but also intelligent, and maybe even slightly sensitive—at least enough to make him accessible.

She thought that too many "real" men were emotionally unavailable duds. Ted seemed to be anything but a dud; in fact, he seemed to be exactly her type. How was this guy still available? She couldn't believe her luck. But she told herself to remain skeptical and cautious—he could easily end up being too good to be true, as are so many things in life.

Standing there next to him at the Starbucks counter felt so natural, though she'd met him only seconds before. Im ordered her favorite Chai tea latte and was floored when he ordered the same thing. It was apparently his favorite, too. She and Ted sat for hours talking about everything and anything and nothing at the same time. Their eyes felt glued together; her cheeks hurt from smiling and laughing so much. It was the first time she'd actually laughed in weeks. And the first time she hadn't thought about her father's death for any stretch. It felt like a minor miracle.

Imogene didn't really believe in love at first sight, but what she experienced sitting there with Ted that first day, sipping on lattes, felt real and rare, and her heart danced a little jig. They were seriously clicking. It was obvious! Finally, after three hours, she found herself telling him she had to go. She didn't want to go at all, but she knew it was the thing to do. Moving too fast would certainly be a mistake. She knew this in her head, though every other part of her was starved for more time with him. It was the first time in weeks she'd felt like a person again, the first time she'd seen a glimpse of life on the other side of the loss of her father. The first time she felt a tinge of happiness...and hope.

He walked her out of Starbucks to her father's parked Cadillac. She'd taken to driving it rather than her own compact car. She could still sense her father's presence in the Cadillac. It made her slightly sad to drive it, but she knew he would've wanted her to enjoy the car.

Ted reached for her hand and said, "I feel like my life has just been changed forever..."

Imogene smiled and said something a bit less committal. "Yeah, I'm really glad we met..." She knew better than to seem too easily conquered.

Ted asked for her phone number, and she decided to give it to him. She wanted nothing more than for him to call her—multiple times a day! But she didn't say that. She just told him her cell phone number and gave him a solid hug when they embraced. She didn't want to let go.

He called her that very night and told her how much he'd enjoyed meeting her and that he wanted to see her again soon, but that he had a business trip the next morning to Boston and would be away for a few days. He said he'd call when he got back. Imogene could hardly contain her excitement, though she only said, "Sure, get in touch then." She wanted to tell him to call her every night while he was away, but again, she checked herself. She didn't want to scare him off.

The intervening days before she heard from him next felt like years. Back at home with her mom, she again felt the crush of the emptiness without her father. But now, when she began to dwell on her father's death or feel pulled down into the well of her grief, she would think of Ted, and a sliver of hope would shine, like a beacon on a dark sea. Yes, maybe she would get through this after all.

When Ted called three days later, her heart was singing once again. Although the thought of him had carried her through, a part of her had still been afraid that he might disappear and never contact her again.

Their next date was an afternoon at the Dayton Art Institute. While it was no Metropolitan Museum of Art, it was a respectable offering for a place like Dayton, Ohio. Ted had suggested it, and though Im wasn't sure how she felt about it for a first real date, she was happy just to be seeing see him again.

It turned out to be an amazing day. When they met in the parking lot, he came to her with a single rose. Then he did something no one had ever done to her before. He kissed her hand. She tried to remain cool, but she was swooning inside.

Strolling in the museum, she showed him all the Impressionist paintings she loved so much, and she led him to one of the jewels of the place, Claude Monet's 1903 Waterlilies. Imogene actually knew a fair amount about art, and Ted seemed genuinely interested in all she had to say. He didn't try to compete with her in conversation and appeared to enjoy listening to her every word. It was as if all he cared about in that moment was seeing the museum through her eyes. What girl wouldn't fall for that?

After a couple hours of wandering through the place, they sat down in the little museum cafe and ordered fresh-baked sugar cookies and a pot of hot tea. It felt perfect. They watched people going by in the lobby, and he made her laugh with his witty quips about each one. She was wildly entertained, and the time flew by. It was four hours later when they finally parted, and it was all Im could do not to fall into his arms and be swept away.

This time they kissed, and Im felt fireworks going off within her. Yes, her raw emotional state must have contributed to the intensity of it all, but no matter. For Im, it felt like she was being saved from a dark and lonely life—that her ship had finally come into port, that she wouldn't necessarily be dying all alone in a dreary room someday. She knew she was getting ahead of herself, but she couldn't help it. She had a good feeling about Ted.

They spoke on the phone a few times before he asked her to go out to a movie and dinner. Im was ecstatic and almost called one of her sisters, but decided against it. If she told one, she'd be telling them all; she didn't want to jinx it. Besides, her sisters would not have approved of an "internet hookup." She didn't want to put up with their judgmental comments or unfounded concerns. It was so easy for them; they already had their husbands and families.

Imogene dressed carefully for the date, going for an effortlessly sexy, but not too eager look. Her black, ultra-soft leather, mid-thigh jacket with tight blue jeans and a crisp white blouse was just right, she thought. When her mother asked where she was off to so dressed up, Im murmured something about meeting a friend for a movie, that it was no big deal. She felt bad fibbing to her mother and leaving her all alone for the evening, but no way was she going to pass up a date with possibly the man of her dreams.

Ted offered to pick her up, but she didn't want to confuse her mother, so they met at the movie theater. He was waiting patiently for her at the doors when she arrived, and the mere sight of him sent a thrilling jolt through her. They saw a good independent film, but it was hard to keep her mind on the movie. Having Ted right next to her felt electric; it was all she could do to keep her hands off him. Fortunately, he took her hand and held it throughout, so she could continue to mostly play coy. But his touch sent tingles through her, and her heart swelled.

After the movie, he said he made a reservation for them at a nearby Thai place he really liked. Im was glad to let him lead the way. Ditching her car, she climbed into his late model black Mercedes SUV—she was impressed. It took only a few minutes to drive to the restaurant, but she wished it was longer. When they were totally alone, it felt like no one else existed in the entire world. Before exiting the car, he leaned over, and they shared a long, sensuous kiss. Walking hand-in-hand into the restaurant, Im's heart was bursting.

They were given a table off in a quiet corner and Im floated through the meal—though not much real eating went on. It was mostly hand holding and gazing into each other's eyes in the glow of their table's candle. It would have seemed obvious to anyone watching that they were very much in love. Im never wanted the night to end.

Ted said, "Imogene, I feel like I've been waiting my whole life for you."

Im practically melted on the spot. How could this be happening? It was all so fast and right on the heels of losing her father and the very lowest days of her life. It felt like an emotional roller coaster, with the dizzying highs now leaving her giddy. She didn't want it to end. *Ever.*

The two of them were still grasping hands across the table, looking at the dessert menu, deciding whether they might share some Thai tapioca or mango pudding... when it happened.

Suddenly, there was a small commotion up near the front of the restaurant. Ted's back was to this, but Im had a full, clear view. A petite, but very pregnant, young woman with short, shiny, platinum blonde hair was talking excitedly with the hostess and gesturing toward their corner of the restaurant. What happened next transpired over just seconds, but for Im, it was like a slow-motion train wreck. The woman began to march/waddle across the room in the general direction of their table. And then, there she was, standing right next to them, hands on her hips, glaring.

"So this is your idea of working late, Ted? Dinner with some slut?"

The words stung Im's ears. She quickly withdrew her hand from Ted's and immediately felt nauseous. In an instant, she knew exactly what was going on—as did everyone else in the place. Ted went ashen, with one hand rubbing his forehead, and his face contorted into a grimace, which said it all.

It was a sickening, surreal moment. Im sprang up from the table and blurted out, "I'm... my God. I'm so sorry. I didn't know... I'm... I'm... just... um... so... so...sorry, really, really sorry!" She knew there was nothing else she could say or do in that moment. Meanwhile, Ted was mute, not even a peep. He didn't even look at her. She wanted to disappear.

Imogene grabbed her purse and ran out of the restaurant; then realized that she'd left her father's Cadillac in the parking lot back at the movie theater.

Did she even know the correct way back there? And how was she going to get there without a car? Calling and waiting for a cab was out of the question; she wanted to get the hell away from there as soon as possible. She would just have to walk. Unfortunately, she had chosen a pair of high-heeled suede boots to complete her "effortlessly sexy" look. It was going to be murder on her feet. But she didn't care. It's what she deserved anyway. She kept hearing Ted's wife's voice in her head. *Some slut!*

The trek back to the car felt like the quintessential walk of shame. *Some. Slut.* When she finally saw the movie theater, she was shivering in the cool night air, her teeth chattering like castanets. Seeing her father's regal black Cadillac parked under the glow of the streetlight, all by itself in the lot, stabbed her heart. She slowly climbed in, sank into its soft leather seat, and let out a long, anguished wail. Tears streamed down her face. Glancing up in the mirror, she saw how all her careful makeup was now streaked, black lines of mascara running down her cheeks. She was a literal mess. *Some slut. Some. Slut!* She sobbed, then, guttural, heart-wrenching sobs.

Im knew that she wasn't just weeping over some lying scumbag she'd met on the internet. Yes, she was mortified beyond belief and now emotionally shattered to smithereens, but it was of course more than that. The loss of her father felt even more raw and excruciating than before. Her heart, which had only hours before been soaring, was now in complete tatters.

CHAPTER 4

IM'S ILL-ADVISED attempt at a quick romantic fix had definitely set her back. The despair that crept in after her internet-dating debacle felt darker and deeper than any she'd ever known before. She was left barely crawling through her life, the unrelenting weight of despondency and grief weighing down her every move, practically suffocating her.

Now, days of nearly no sleep were creating a precarious emotional situation, complicating any natural ability to recover. It didn't help that she'd been publicly called a slut by an extremely pregnant wife, while she was on a date with the woman's cheating husband. Her self-esteem was not only in the toilet; it was all the way out to the sewer.

And exacerbating this, Im was hopelessly stuck like a broken vinyl record, rehashing the events leading up to her father's death, playing the do-over and if-only game. It usually involved some failure on her part: if only she'd insisted he call his doctor in those days before it happened, if only she'd been with him the morning he'd died, if only she'd paid more attention, noticed his heart was in distress... Hadn't there been subtle signs? It was an endless, agonizing loop in her mind.

Indeed, it may have been her father's close call the previous summer that set Im up to feel especially defeated after his death a year later. He seemed to be in fine health back then, too. Mr. Mussomeli had delighted in repeating that his doctor said he was in "excellent shape." Im had glommed onto this.

But when he suffered a gall bladder attack, things went south fast. Though the offending organ was safely in a heap of medical waste, complications ensued. Post-op medications had prevented his blood from coagulating, and he began to bleed-out profusely. Massive amounts of blood pooled within his body. Now all blue and purple from chest to toe, his blood pressure dropped like a stone. It was horrifying. And a sense of resignation seemed to be creeping in among the nurses. It was not looking good for the Italian octogenarian.

Appalled and panicked, Imogene immediately went into high gear—her father would not be dying on this day. Fired up and resolute, she stalked the resident acting on behalf of his now on-vacation surgeon. It was the peak of summer when all the brand new interns and residents were starting rotations—not an ideal time to be in the hospital. Many attending physicians were off on vacations, and apparently there wasn't a lot of experience lingering around.

In any event, without a physician's order, the nurses could do little for Mr. Mussomeli. His blood pressure had plummeted to a dangerous level; his face was as white as a sheet. Im couldn't believe what was happening. Finally, it was Mrs. Mussomeli—watching her husband of more than 50 years apparently on the brink of death—who'd had the presence of mind to blurt, "What about the ICU, Im?"

Yes, Imogene thought, that is exactly where he has to go or he'll die! Still, nothing could be done until they had "orders."

Imogene was enraged. It was so clear that her father was about to die, yet hospital protocol, and who knows what else (at 80-some years old, were they thinking let nature take its course?) wouldn't allow an immediate move to the critical unit.

"There's a procedure," the nurses had said.

Well, you can shove your damn procedures, thought Imogene. How many die in a hospital bed because of their stupid protocols? She barged right into the nurses' station—always off limits to the "lay" people. "I want to talk to a doctor! NOW!" she shrieked. The nurses looked shocked, but quickly got her the doctor. Then she stood right there in the office, listening to the calls made, refusing to move two inches from the doctor until her father was taken to the ICU. She knew they all thought she was crazy, but she didn't care.

Imogene was a fixture in the ICU lounge after, waiting for the short, on-the-hour visits allowed for family members. Her heart would thump wildly in her chest walking down the hallway to her father's room. There he would be, eyes closed, tangled tubes sticking out every which way. To Im, he looked dead already, and she'd be in a momentary panic until she saw some sign of life. Finally, her father's eyes would flutter open, he'd smile weakly, and she'd exhale in relief.

In the end, of course, her father survived the harrowing close call in that second to last summer of his life. The sisters thought Im's aggressive intervention at the hospital saved him. She'd been brazen, broken boundaries, refused to back down—basically threw a fit. But being passive in such a situation wasn't in her DNA. And the idea that she might have had some control over the outcome was reassuring to her. Perhaps this small sense of omnipotence the previous year is what made the following summer's events that much more devastating. She'd made a difference once, why couldn't she have done it again?

Naturally, everyone likes to think they possess some modicum of control over their own fate and that of loved ones. It can be a small comfort in a world where it seems anything can happen at any time, especially awful, immutable things.

After their father's death, while all were bereaved, the other sisters each had the support of their husbands and families. Glaringly, Im was alone. From the outside, she looked like a successful, well-adjusted career woman—strong, competent, and independent. But she was the only sister on her own, no husband, no family. Her father was undeniably the only man in her life who had always been there, her touchstone and rock—even more, her boulder.

He had indeed remained a substantial part of her life. She'd made it back to Ohio for most holidays, and with the college schedule, she was free to spend her summers whereever she liked. "Summering" in Dayton, Ohio, while not exactly a sought after sojourn, was a replenishing oasis for her, something she always looked forward to after another grueling academic year at the Ivy of the South (which will go unnamed). It was home to more than its fair share of in-love-with-themselves professors, constantly jockeying for position and status.

Yes, she held a prestigious faculty position at a high-powered university, yet Imogene, by her own estimation, was very low-powered. She figured she mainly got the peach of a job after getting her Ph.D. because she was at the height of her beauty—prime ripeness, if you will— and the place was like the old boys' club back then. Not to say she wasn't capable, but she certainly didn't have the academic chops or credentials normally required to reach the upper echelons of academia. She had one or two measly publications and had no intention of putting out any more. Her position, in fact, was the sole non-tenure track spot, mainly a teaching job. While she suspected she'd end up feeling like a fish out of water, she took the job—who wouldn't?

Im soon learned that non-tenure track meant more or less indentured servitude. The "department" could dump any and everything in her lap, and she couldn't say a thing. She was expected to teach classes no one else wanted to teach, handle the students no one wanted to bother with, and generally clean up pesky messes. The department Chairman even asked her to counsel a grad student who was "claiming" that her advising professor had been hitting on her. Things had supposedly not gone very far, apparently nothing beyond the prof touching her hair and the buttons on her shirt, but the student was clearly traumatized. Imogene hated herself for caving to the pressure to see if maybe the student had been "mistaken" about the whole thing. The girl was a hot mess of emotions, so it wasn't hard to convince her that she might have misinterpreted the situation. The girl dropped her complaint, then dropped out of school altogether. Imogene later regretted her part in this and realized that she certainly should have supported the girl. It would have been the right thing to do. She'd been more concerned about keeping her job. She felt like a sell-out.

There were also some wildly inappropriate faculty parties where everyone would get naked and jump in the hot tub. At first, Imogene hung back, but she was new and wanted to fit in; she eventually joined the mass of bodies. She was appalled when she thought about it later. All of them stark naked, shoulder to shoulder, brushing against each others' thighs. It was sort of disgusting, and yet she went along with it because she wanted to be liked, to belong. She wasn't even thirty years old, one of only a few women at the old boys' club. She was in way over her head—she needed to play along.

After the hot-tub shenanigans, it was virtually impossible to look any of her colleagues in the eye without imagining them standing there with their junk exposed, large or small—hanging down, sideways or trying to stand tall. In hindsight, she figured she could have created a firestorm if she wanted to call it sexual harassment and make a thing of it. She could have blown the roof off the place. But she wasn't that kind of girl. She actually enjoyed the naughtiness of the whole thing. Nothing untoward had happened. And she felt in-control the whole time. No one had twisted her arm.

Yet, if she was being honest, hot-tub parties aside—she hated her job. She always felt like the outsider. The highlight of every year was the summer she could spend with her parents back home, escaping from everything she'd grown to loath and surrounded by the unconditional love of her parents—not the smarmy kind, but the kind that ran deep and strong and was never questioned. For Italians, Sicilians especially, family is everything to the nth degree. It was the only place where she ever truly felt at home. Im had considered herself lucky to still have those months at home with her aging parents; she was the only unmarried, unencumbered daughter that could.

How was it going to be now? She couldn't imagine spending the summer in Ohio without her father there. Although nothing else about her life had really changed, she felt completely derailed, and everything about the future seemed dim to her now.

Her sisters did try to help her. While all lived a distance away, they made endless phone calls home, sent neighbors to check on her and her mother, repeatedly called her doctors, and generally meddled with a vengeance. Imogene knew it was all well intentioned, but she resented their intrusions.

Maria, who lived closest at an hour's drive away, would sometimes show up unannounced, obviously on the orders of the older sisters. And she'd get all mother-hen with her, which annoyed Im to no end. She hated feeling like the pathetic, problem sister, especially since she'd been the dominant one with Maria. There'd always been a pecking order; she'd never been on the bottom. It was humiliating.

Indeed, Maria would report back to the sisters about Imogene's desperate state. She hated to see her big sister in such pain and so incapacitated. She always looked up to Im and admired all that she was. What was going to become of her now?

The sisters all agreed. Things were getting dire. They began to see Im as walking wounded. Was she ever going to be herself again? They worried she was truly losing her marbles. The phone lines were burning up with calls among them, wishing they could do something to help her, wondering what was going to become of her. Im knew they were constantly talking about her, clucking their tongues. She could just hear it! They meant well, but it made her feel that much worse.

And Imogene was frequently haunted by thoughts of her father having his heart attack while he was out shopping. He'd fallen right in the middle of the grocery store aisle. A clerk told her that at first, he was joking about suing the store for having slippery floors, but then he went into full cardiac arrest. Though the EMTs were there within minutes, he was essentially gone already. The ambulance rushed him to the hospital anyway—the one practically within sight of her parents' house—but it was too late, of course.

Im kept picturing him there all alone, his grocery cart full. Maybe the coupons he'd been looking at in his wallet had gone flying, scattering on the floor. Her dad's coupon thing always tugged at her heart. He certainly didn't need to use coupons. Mr. Mussomeli had plenty of money thanks to many years as an automotive executive and shrewd investing in the stock market.

He had, in fact, amassed a small fortune. Still, he was that quintessential "millionaire next door" made famous by Stanley and Danko in their best-selling book. He saved and lived modestly. And as a child of the Great Depression, he religiously cut out coupons; no amount was too small.

Finally, the sisters convinced Im to go see a doctor. Clearly, what was happening to her wasn't normal. She was prescribed the usual medications, but her nervous system did not respond in the typical fashion. They either didn't work at all (powerful soporifics left her wide-eyed and dry-mouthed) or produced some sort of unwanted side effect (racing heartbeat or skyrocketing blood pressure, limbs that seemed to weigh 300 pounds or drenching night-sweats). She was left with a stockpile of pills, a veritable pharmacy's worth. Why had the doctors not been concerned that they might be arming her with a perfect suicide method?

Mrs. Mussomeli, too, felt helpless in the face of her daughter's fragile state. She'd sit on the edge of Imogene's bed while Im ruminated about how she might have saved her father if she'd only acted in some way. Hadn't his ankles looked swollen the week before he died? Couldn't that have been a sign of his impending heart failure? Hadn't he seemed more tired and drawn than usual? Naturally, hindsight was always 20-20—everyone knows this—but Im's ability to be logical had deteriorated to near imbecilic levels. She stubbornly held onto to the irrational notion that she could have impacted the outcome somehow. And Mrs. Mussomeli, the only one there with her daughter day-to-day, could do little to console her.

In fact, there were small signs that Mrs. Mussomeli's own mental status was beginning to slide. She was becoming easily confused and forgetful, losing her ability to keep track of events from one moment to the next, or suddenly finding herself lost in a familiar place. Once when she was driving home from the local library—a place she'd driven to scores of times—she became so disoriented that she apparently drove in circles for nearly two hours, finally stumbling onto their street and making it home. She was flushed and out of breath when Im met her at the door. "I don't know what happened," she said. "I just couldn't find my way home!"

Imogene initially chalked this up to the aftermath of losing her husband of over half a century. Maybe this was normal for someone her age, grieving such a huge loss. She felt pangs of guilt that she was perhaps making her mother's emotional state worse by being such a basket case herself. But Im was in no shape to just "snap out of it," as a neighbor, known for her bluntness, had suggested. So the two of them—walking sad-sacks—tried to feel their way through the grief together.

The only happy one was her mother's yappy Chihuahua, Marvin, who adored both of them. The thing about the dog—and Chihuahuas as a breed—was that he was fiercely protective of those he loved. Although he weighed less than nine pounds, he would attack—literally try to maul—anyone who went near them. Even Mr. Mussomeli attempting to plant a small kiss on his wife had resulted in an eruption of growling, snarling, and biting that would send anyone on the receiving end recoiling. He lived every moment of his little doggie life primed to pounce on any would-be attackers, ready to reclaim any lost inch of ground, or mangle an errant hand that had foolishly attempted to pet him at the wrong time. Everyone (except Mrs. Mussomeli, who thought he was an angel) called him "The Devil Dog" because he could instantly appear demonically possessed, with no warning and without any provocation—at least none that could be discerned by the human eye.

The dog was perhaps certifiably insane. He'd actually been a fourth or fifth-hand lemon, passed around from owner to owner—people who had at first been charmed by his unqualified cuteness only to find out in due time that his temperament could only euphemistically be called problematic. It was likely that he received more than his fair share of kicks and who knows what else. Mrs. Mussomeli, always a sucker for a pathetic case, animal or human, accepted him sight unseen after she heard about him from her nephew in upstate New York. This nephew arranged the "adoption" while the dog's current owners likely danced a jig to be getting rid of him. The long-haired Chihuahua (with papers, no less) was sent by way of another cousin willing to make the trip to Ohio, and much to the chagrin of the rest of the Mussomeli family, the devil dog had found his forever family.

For some reason, Marvin loved Imogene. Mr. Mussomeli used to marvel at the sheer ecstasy the dog would experience every time his daughter would walk into the house, yipping wildly and running in circles. All Im could think now was how much her father had enjoyed watching the dog's exuberance upon seeing her. Marvin's boundless fervor used to make her smile, too. But it only gave her sharp pangs of sadness now, another reminder of her father's absence.

She remembered the adorable way her father could hold the dog all in one palm. Yes, the dog was small, but it was more than that. Her father's hands had been huge—so large that they'd even been used in a commercial print ad once, holding a component his automotive company wanted to look especially miniature. The image of his massive hands lying limp and motionless at his sides on the ER gurney that awful day was one of the flashbacks that plagued Imogene. Recalling this would always send her into new paroxysms of grief.

In any case, Marvin's wildly enthusiastic greetings (i.e. rolling on his back in submission, including, for some gross reason, an extension of the shaft of his shiny pink member—he was castrated, so go figure) whenever he saw her only accentuated how her father was no longer there to exclaim, "He sure is happy to see you!" She doubted her dad ever noticed the dog's tiny penis coming to life, since he was always sitting off in his easy chair glued to CNN or CSPAN. So no, his comment did not insinuate that Marvin was hot for her—although the dog apparently was.

***

Finally, during one of the sleepless nights after her father's death, Imogene happened upon something that ultimately did what none of her sisters or the doctors or medications could do—lift her up from the vast hollow of her grief.

On this particular night, after tossing and turning as usual, she finally schlepped out of bed and went into her father's den. It was the place where she still felt his presence the most. A big oak teacher's-style desk took up a great portion of the small room, along with old-style gray file cabinets and over-stuffed bookshelves, leaving little floor space for moving around. Mr. Mussomeli had actually built the large desk himself from a kit popular in the 1950s. Its massive wooden drawers were bursting with years of miscellaneous personal stuff.

After his passing, the other daughters had swooped into their father's den, attempting to purge and dump—part of "helping" their mother with the house. This was typical. They'd done it at various times before. It wasn't unlike them—usually operating in pairs, emboldening and fueling each other—to assault their parents' home from time to time, throwing out anything they deemed to be useless clutter, "junk." Imogene was furious when she discovered that her beloved "Tony the Tiger" stuffed animal had been shucked during a purge of the basement, orchestrated by a couple of her sisters when she wasn't there. She could imagine the planning conversation they would have had about this "project" to make their parents' home more to their liking: "We have to do it when Imogene isn't around or we'll never be able to get rid of anything!" Now, with her father gone and Im basically incapacitated, they attacked the house with abandon. If hoarding was a disorder, Im thought there ought to be a name for the exact opposite thing.

Im's sentimentality left her reeling with every discard of her father's things. There was screaming back and forth with her sisters as she retrieved large trash bags chock full of stuff, which she hadn't had a chance to thoroughly inspect. Yes, they would have to get the house ready to sell. Yes, there was too much junk piled up. But no, nothing was going out that she hadn't completely examined and released. For Im, this was simply *not* negotiable. Her sisters scolded her, accused her of being a hopeless pack rat, and scoffed at her silly "melodramatics." But in the end, given her fragile state, they wisely let it go, though not without clucking their tongues and shaking their heads. "Poor Imogene, look how she can't even let go of the junkiest stuff. Why is she like this?"

There in her father's den that night when she again couldn't sleep, Im sat on the floor with a large black trash bag in front of her, one that had been destined for the garbage by her sisters. She began to sort through the heap. She had to know exactly what was in it before it got dumped.

It turned out to be stuff seized from the den closet where Mr. Mussomeli had kept a stack of frayed, old cardboard boxes, full of ancient college notebooks from classes like physics and electronic circuitry. None of it would have been of any value to anyone really, but Imogene felt she had to touch each thing, just out of respect for her father. He held onto the items for so many years. How could they be unceremoniously tossed out without the slightest consideration?

But she eventually forced herself to chuck them all back into the bag, cursing her sisters for having been essentially right about the stuff. Then she noticed a little composition book lying there that looked like some sort of daily journal. The faded blue cover was beat-up and the corners all worn down with disintegrating cardboard filling sticking out the edges. Her sisters had refused to open any of the notebooks in the grungy cardboard boxes, saying they were likely full of slithering silverfish bugs. Some were. But Imogene couldn't resist looking at her father's handwriting on the pages from so long ago when he was just a young man, his future still all ahead of him.

The tattered little blue notebook contained mostly empty pages. Only the first few had been written on as though the intent was to start a journal that never got past week one. She remembered doing this, too, as a kid. A nice new journal full of clean white paper, which would eventually be forgotten, abandoned in a drawer with only a few pages at the beginning filled in, offering a snippet of her earlier consciousness. Nowadays, kids barely even consider handwriting on the page. It's all digital, the remnants possibly found years later on a hard drive or memory stick, but maybe not—files can be corrupted, a proper program and power source are needed to open them. Hand-written diaries are extant, still just sitting there years later for anyone to see—if they don't get shucked out in a purge.

She wondered why her father had kept the little notebook for so many years. She imagined because it had so many blank pages remaining; if he ever needed a little notebook, it could have come in handy. Mr. Mussomeli, like Im, hated to discard anything that might be of use or had some life left in it. Although, in reality, these sorts of items usually languish undisturbed, gathering dust or bugs, eventually to be thrown out once they started to yellow and fall apart with age—gross and not willing to be touched by anyone.

When she opened to the first page of the notebook, she noticed that the printing was not in what she knew to be her father's normal adult hand, but appeared much more juvenile. She realized that her father must have written it as a young boy. The first page announced, "This book is the private property of Guiseppe (his official given name, Italian for "Joseph") Mussomeli & Anthony Scarpelli." Tony Scarpelli was her father's boyhood best friend. The second page had "Back Room Club Rules" in a list and the rendezvous time and place for club meetings. "4:00 on the stoop outside the backroom door."

Imogene knew this would have referred to the "backroom" of her father's childhood home in their little Italian neighborhood in Rochester, New York. Her paternal grandmother had kept this backroom off the kitchen, which was a cheaply constructed addition to the very end of the house, serving as a storage area as well as a general kitchen workroom. Imogene remembered an old, top-loading ice box in there along with a big, gray metal safe, and various wooden tables stacked with this and that—vegetables pulled from the garden, extra pots and pans, dishes, various sundries. She could still picture her grandmother in her usual "housecoat" emerging from the backroom with Hershey bars or Juicy Fruit gum for her grandchildren after Sunday dinner.

During the time the Joe Mussomeli family lived in Rochester before the big Midwest move, Sunday dinner right after church, approximately 1 p.m., was customary—actually mandatory—though no one would have argued. The feast was to die for—mountains of steaming pasta (usually ziti) al dente, plump meatballs and juicy sausages, "red" (tomato) sauce—stewed all morning, and crusty, fresh-baked Italian rolls, along with Coca-Cola for the kids. It was the one time the Mussomeli girls were allowed to have this drink with a meal. To this day, Imogene could close her eyes and conjure up the mesmerizing aromas greeting them as they all marched into their grandmother's house after church on Sundays: the sweet scent of sauce bubbling softly on the stove and the lingering smell of sautéed garlic and freshly baked bread.

For all the grandkids, their grandmother's backroom was a wondrous and mysterious place, stocked full of goodies and unknown treasures. Allowed to play in there on occasion as long as they didn't "get into anything," they'd spend hours pretending to be famous safecrackers with their ears glued to the old metal safe, peeking into various drawers or boxes looking for lost treasures, or playing "house." Imogene would always remember the creaking of the room's floorboards and the scent of aging parmesan cheese.

The second page of the little notebook Imogene had found in her father's den also listed a few other boys' names that her father and Tony were apparently thinking of asking to join their "club." Jimmy Salamoni, Marco Mirabella, Billy Palombo, Charlie Scaramucci. Who knows if they ever got around to doing this. The next page listed a book title, "On the Origin of Species" by Charles Darwin" and then under this in big block letters, "Club Motto: Survival of the Fittest!"

The page after that showed a little sketch, which Imogene immediately recognized as a crude diagram of her grandmother's backroom. It showed the two doorways (one to the kitchen and one to the backyard), the ice box on one wall, the safe in the far corner, and then an arrow pointing to an area next to the safe where there was a brick oven/fireplace, labeled with an "X." Then a notation next to the X that said "Hide book up in here. Wrap it in cloth." There must have been a ledge or hollow behind there, under the lip of the fireplace—probably a nook large enough to hold the book.

The old brick fireplace in the backroom had long ago been rendered useless since any attempts at building a fire would supposedly fill the place with thick smoke. A story was told about the fire department arriving once after someone had attempted to use it. That might have been a tall tale, but regardless, whoever built the thing must not have known how to design a proper chimney, which was too bad since the extra oven would have been useful. In any event, Imogene remembered that the fireplace hearth had made a nice seat for a little kid.

All the rest of the pages in her father's old blue notebook were completely blank. Not that it really mattered very much, but Imogene felt a twinge of regret. With her father now gone, and Tony Scarpelli as well (her parents had returned to Rochester for his funeral years before), she would never be able to learn more about his and Tony's little venture. Although, she could tell from the handwriting and drawings that her father had likely been under ten years old at the time, so it probably would have long been forgotten. And perhaps their interest in the "club" and Darwin's book had only lasted a tiny morsel of time. Still, Imogene and her sisters had always loved getting her father to talk about the old days and his childhood in the little Italian neighborhood. Naturally, in her morose mood, all she could think about was how it was yet another missed opportunity.

Nonetheless, it seemed very cool to Imogene that her father has been interested in Darwin's theory of natural selection and evolution at such an early age. She herself had only discovered the theory in college. It fascinated her to no end, and she believed it was valid, but she knew it was still a bit controversial for its implications about traditional religion. It would have been even more so when her father was a boy.

His mother was a devout Catholic, and she made sure her son attended mass regularly. But as an adult Mr. Mussomeli went to church only rarely and mainly for events like a baptisms, weddings, or funerals. It wasn't that he was opposed to Catholicism; he just seemed content to have it only on the periphery. Regardless, he'd been a man with a strong moral code and had instilled this in all his children by way of example, rather than explicit religious teachings. Even so, he was fine with all of his kids going through the Catholic paces, as he had done himself.

Imogene wondered how her father came to have the Darwin book at all, and whether the apparent hiding of it was due to any prohibitions against him having it. It was unlikely that either of his Italian immigrant parents would have read it, given their level of education and relatively unsophisticated grasp of the English language. They may have heard about it, though, and perhaps had been primed by the church to reject its evolutionary idea of how mankind came to be.

Im recalled her father expressing support for the theory of evolution, but he hadn't thought it actually contradicted a belief in God. Who knows? Maybe the natural forces of evolution were all part of a grand creation plan anyway.

If nothing else, Imogene's discovery in her father's den that night had sufficiently distracted her. In fact, she slept soundly for a few hours that night afterwards and woke the next morning amazed. For the first time in weeks, she felt rested! And just that bit of real sleep seemed to lift her ever so slightly out of her self-loathing and the pitiful pit she'd been living in.

A feeling crept in that day—a long lost one, like a sliver of clear, blue sky finally peeking out from behind the dark clouds. Maybe her life wasn't completely awful and not worth living after all. Those few hours of deep sleep gave her what none of the pills could: the hope that she might get back to being something like the person she'd been before the devastating loss of her father—not the same because she was forever changed, but at least something near a fully-functioning human rather than a completely broken down one.

CHAPTER 5

FINDING HER FATHER'S old notebook with its reference to Darwin's seminal work left Imogene in an intense state of wonder. Her father had never spoken of an early interest in Darwin's theory of evolution. Had it been introduced to him at school? This seemed unlikely since the writing in the notebook was only grade-school age. How would he ever have had a copy of this book? Her father talked of having very few possessions as a boy. He dreamed of having a bicycle, and his father finally bought him a second-hand one for his twelfth birthday. He was thrilled, but after a month or two, it had already broken down. There weren't funds to buy him a new one.

The family had owned a grocery and dry goods store attached to their house, so they were considered well off compared to many others in the neighborhood. But it was the time of the Great Depression; there was very little in the way of discretionary money. Her father had told her about working at "the store" as a kid, how he'd pile some extra slices of cold cuts on the stack for a family in especially dire straits. It warmed Im's heart to know her father had been kind and generous, even as a young boy. He also told of customers sometimes bartering to pay off their bills at the store. Perhaps someone had offered some books that his parents accepted for payment. While they would not have had much use for such themselves, maybe their young son would someday. Purchasing a book outright—especially Darwin's book—seemed very unlikely.

So what had ever happened to her dad's copy of "Origin of Species?" Something like this always sparked Im's natural curiosity, and it was like an itch on her brain—she had no choice but to scratch it. She looked through all her father's old books, some even dating back to Jefferson High in Rochester. She couldn't believe he'd held onto them for so long, but it was like him. Books were not things you threw away.

But none were the Darwin book.

Wherever the book had gotten to, it had to have been a very old copy. And the more she thought about it, the more she wondered. What if it was an especially early edition? It had to have been printed around or before the 1920s, since her dad had been in possession of it as a young boy. A habitual Googler, she looked up what an old copy of "Origin of Species" might be worth—just for the heck of it.

She ran across a *New York Times* article by a Darwin scholar on how a number of first editions were still unaccounted for—a relative rarity in the book world. Typically, a book as famous as "Origin of Species" would have very few early editions still in unknown places. But Darwin had written the book for a mass audience, and it was known to have been purchased by many non-elite, homegrown intellectuals. In other words, many copies could have originally been in the hands of everyday folks. The records of the printing and distribution history of the book also showed that of the 1,250 books in the first printing, some could still be unrecognized and in obscure places. Further, the article reported that a first edition had recently sold at auction for over a quarter of a million dollars. And that book had its share of significant flaws.

Imogene's skin erupted in goosebumps. What if her dad's copy was first edition? The *New York Times* article also told of the definitive way to determine if a copy was one of the rare first editions: On page 20, the word "species" would be misspelled as "speceies." Apparently, the error was corrected in all the "first edition" printings thereafter. All of this had Imogene feeling incredibly energized, and for the first time in weeks, she didn't feel like returning to bed to adopt the fetal position.

Where was her dad's copy of this book? It could be worth a quarter million dollars! Maybe even more if it was still in good condition! Sitting there on the floor in her father's den, staring at her laptop, she thought she could feel her father peering over her shoulder. She said aloud, "Dad, where's that book?"

Her mother called from the other room, "What did you say, Im?"

"Nothing, Mom. I was just talking to myself."

It was a wild idea that Im couldn't get out of her head. Her father could have had a first edition all those years ago. *Of course* she had to try to find it. Where had it gone? Was it long gone or had it been given away in a box of books taken to Goodwill by her sisters or even simply dumped in a purge? Books weren't necessarily sacred to them. They certainly could have done this without their father knowing. *Damn them, anyway!*

She decided she had to look through every box, every drawer, every shelf, every closet…every single inch of her parents' house. If it was there, she'd find it. For days, she attacked the place like a banshee. Her mother kept asking her what she was looking for, over and over because she had, sadly, begun to incessantly repeat her questions.

"Just a book, Mom. It could be valuable."

"Looking for a book of Dad's, Ma."

"An old book, Mom, it might be worth something."

"Looking for something, Ma, don't worry about it."

"Oh, just a book!" Im tried not to get impatient and short with her mother, but it wasn't easy.

Regardless, Mrs. Mussomeli was just happy to see her daughter coming back to life. She cheerfully reported to her other daughters that Im was doing better and even sleeping again. And Im herself was amazed that the heavy cloud of doom and gloom, which had gripped her ever since her father's sudden death, had begun to lift. Yes, she was still incredibly sad and missed her father terribly, but it felt somehow more bearable. Having some modicum of mental health back felt like a miracle. What a gift. She knew she'd never take it for granted again.

Now she just wanted to find the old Darwin book. She wasn't one to buy into the supernatural, but she thought she could feel her father there with her. Watching, wanting her to find the book, perhaps even guiding her in some unknown fashion. So even after days of coming up empty, she didn't give up.

In fact, this may have been one of Imogene's most predominant features: sheer persistence. She literally never gave up. Once she was on a mission, she stayed with it, whatever it was, like a dog on a bone. Her sisters often thought she went too far, but she could point to any number of instances where she got something done or made something happen, which most people figured was a lost cause. Yes, instances when most people would have surely given up.

Once when Im's laptop computer went on the fritz, her resoluteness was in prime form. The particular brand of computer was hyped as the best of the best. The company (which will remain nameless) had practically cornered the laptop market—and was poised to essentially take over the world (an exaggeration, but not that far off). Yet her wondrous computer suddenly began to malfunction. The entire top line of letters on the keyboard had stopped responding. Fortunately, it was under an extended service plan, which was supposed to cover anything and everything for a full two years. She bought the extra $200 warranty only reluctantly, as she thought such plans rarely paid off in the end. But when the thing glitched, she was glad to have sprung for the Cadillac of service plans. At just over a year old, the machine was outside the manufacturer's regular warranty. Vexing, but at least she had the extended service plan. Whatever it was, they'd be fixing it for free or replacing her computer.

At the computer store, she marveled at the beautiful design of the place, such a clean, sleek look—much like their product line. Everything white and gleaming as though the company was so pure and good. Even the air felt pristine. After the orderly check-in, she was told to expect a call soon with an update on the status of the repair. Great, this should be easy, she thought. But when the call came, she was informed that *unfortunately* her computer had water damage—all warranties and service agreements were now void. It was going to cost a small fortune to repair the thing!

Im insisted water damage was impossible. The guy offered to send her photos of the insides of her machine showing the evidence, including the telltale sign: water indicator button changed to pink. Outraged, Im went into overdrive. She demanded to speak with a supervisor. "Nobody will tell you anything different," he said. Her blood boiled.

She went into her "equalizer" mode: she was going to level the playing field against this huge, all-powerful corporation! She wondered if a scam was in play so they could squeeze yet more money out of their loyal customers, most having drunk the Kool-Aid.

Now on a mission, Im spent hours on the library computer researching whom to call in the corporate office. Pouring through countless online issues and complaints forums, she finally came across some direct phone numbers at the corporate headquarters. Remarkably, she actually had a voice answer her call. Explaining the situation, she added that she suspected the so-called photos of her "water-damaged" machine were not of her own laptop's insides at all, but rather stock photos they kept on hand for hoodwinking customers. Naturally, the corporate guy tried to convince her otherwise, that she could go into the store and see it for herself, and so forth. She persisted. How was she ever to know they wouldn't have just switched out the guts of her laptop with another, which were water-damaged? Im heard it in his voice—she was gaining ground.

Finally, she mentioned that she was considering starting a class action lawsuit for breach of the service agreement contract. She knew there were many others like her out there. She could sense the guy sweating a little then. Abruptly, he said he'd have to call her back. Within an hour, she got the call. Sounding conciliatory, he informed her that, while it was highly irregular, her computer would be fixed free of charge. Im was elated. When she hung up the phone, she pumped her fist. Score another one for the equalizer!

While some might question her tactics, Imogene always felt she was righting a wrong, settling a score, and winning one for the little guy. Large powerful companies, long entrenched systems, red-tape/bureaucracy, whatever it was, she shifted right into gear. The little guy might be herself, but there were occasions when she went to bat for friends she perceived were being cheated or scammed. Once she took on a major car dealership, which had obviously taken advantage of an immigrant family she knew.

Another time involved a health insurance company's arbitrary denial of services for a friend in desperate need. Rotten policies? She was on it. Unfair fees or charges? She was on it. No injustice was too small. Yes, it took a lot of energy, but her stores for such were practically limitless.

But it wasn't that Imogene was an activist. She was too reserved for anything that public. It was more about standing up when many people would shrink because they felt intimidated or powerless. This compelled her—being the random ombudsman, if you will. Never giving up while there was still a good fight to fight.

Or... a potentially valuable thing to find.

The top-to-bottom search of her parents' house for her father's old copy of "Origin of Species" was not going to end until she knew, without a scintilla of doubt, that she had looked in every possible nook, corner, cranny, and crevice.

CHAPTER 6

IM'S DOGGED SEARCH of the house for her father's long lost book lasted days—her mother closely in tow, frequently asking what they were looking for again. The sisters would surely have told Im to forget about it already; it was a fool's errand. Of course, they'd say that, she thought. This only made her dig deeper, especially in the basement, home to so much of the family's past. She liked to think of it as the Mussomeli Museum, valuable repository of history and memories, but she knew her sisters were probably right. It was mostly only useless junk that had seen better days, all going to have to be dumped sooner or later. Naturally, Im chose later. The chorus of clucks from the sisters would be deafening.

She was amazed to run across old boxes in the basement, which looked nearly undisturbed from when her grandmother had moved to Ohio to be near her son. Filomena had sold her Rochester home back in the little Italian neighborhood, which had been gradually diminishing over the years. In fact, her timing was very good—she'd still been able to get a "pretty penny" for the property before the neighborhood went completely downhill, which it did later, sadly.

The property was now apparently owned by a slumlord. When the Ohio Mussomelis returned to bury Filomena in the plot next to her husband's, the funeral procession drove by her old house. Things had clearly declined. The Rochester cousins had warned them of this. It was shocking to see everything on the once lively, prosperous street so dilapidated and ghetto-like.

Back again for their father's funeral years later, the sisters were more prepared for the state of the neighborhood, though it was worse. Despite cautions of the cousins, they stopped on the corner for some Italian Lemon Ice—a ritual dating back to their childhoods. Amazing that Al's Stand was still standing and that it looked exactly the same; not one iota of renovation. The pit stop was a beautiful moment: the whole family gathered on the street corner in the old neighborhood, enjoying Lemon Ice at the very same place Joe Mussomeli had done himself as a kid. It felt like a celebration of his life. They were even bouncing to the beat of a lively Earth, Wind and Fire tune blasting from the car stereo, "September."

Everyone was bouncing, that is, but Imogene. She could barely eat her Lemon Ice; there was such a huge lump in her throat. Her stomach had been clenched in a tight knot for days. Food basically tasted like wood pulp. Her grief at that time was still so raw and intense; she couldn't begin to lose herself in the moment—any moment. She knew her father would have wanted her to be better, stronger, but she felt utterly lost.

All she could think about was how they needed to get the heck out of there—a bunch of well-to-do white people. They were so conspicuous dancing right there on the street, alongside her dad's gleaming black Cadillac. She wanted to scream. A number of suspicious looking characters were lingering nearby too, clearly eyeing them, probably laughing at their sad white peoples' dance moves. The Rochester cousins had tried to dissuade them from making the stop at all, repeating that the neighborhood was no longer the safe place they remembered, when they could comfortably stroll down to the corner for Italian Lemon Ice after Sunday dinner.

Back in those days, the neighborhood still had its share of undesirables, but then, being Italians would have been an asset. Her father used to tell the story of when, after his own father had first opened the family store, the local gangsters known as "The Black Hand" tried to make him "an offer he couldn't refuse." They grabbed him by the scruff of the neck in a back alley, insisting he ante up and pay his "dues." The elder Mr. Mussomeli threatened them right back, saying that he had three brothers Upstate who could easily shorten their "careers" should any harm come to him. He was left alone after this. It was obviously a source of pride to Joe Mussomeli that his own father had been so morally upstanding and brave, going against the status quo of the day. The son had himself been cut from this same cloth and had done his best to instill this in his own children—with relative success: None of them had ever been in any real trouble. *Yet.*

Many of Filomena's stored possessions, moved with her from her Rochester home, were still in their original boxes. Household items— dishes, trinkets, linens, sewing notions. There were some old books there, too—though nothing by Charles Darwin. Im also found a large oblong box, which held her grandmother's cherished Infant Jesus of Prague, an elaborately clothed baby Jesus doll. Making replicas of the figure was in fashion back in the 1960s. Devout Roman Catholic woman, with a penchant for sewing, would design and sew the costumes for the dolls. The legend was that the Infant of Prague held miraculous powers.

Filomena was especially talented with a needle and thread and made ornate clothing for the wax-coated, 18-inch baby Jesus dolls. Each would entail careful sewing of the gowns and robes, embroidering them with gold thread, sequins, and lace. All her neighbors wanted them, and Im remembered Filomena made one especially for her son's family. Their Infant Jesus wore a gold crown, a white satin gown edged in sparkling gold lace, and a pale pink velvet robe with a gold and silver sequined collar—it still stood watch over their family home, perched high atop a curio cabinet in the living room. As a girl, Im had found the doll a reassuring presence, but now only a reminder of what she was destined for… What would Filomena think of her granddaughter now—lapsed Catholic going straight to Hell?

After moving to Ohio, Filomena first lived in her son's Dayton home, but eventually got her own apartment when it became clear that Mr. Mussomeli and the two Mrs. Mussomelis were one too many Mrs. Mussomelis. Not that there'd been any sort of altercation, but Imogene's mother had a way of getting her message across. Everyone felt bad about this turn of events, but in the end, it wasn't a tragedy, as the elder Mrs. Mussomeli mostly enjoyed the cute little apartment of her own, just a couple miles away. Besides, no one had blamed her for wanting to be close to her only son.

As it happened, she'd lost her only daughter in a tragic, heart-wrenching way.

Aunt Geneva had been one of the first people ever to have open-heart surgery to replace a valve damaged by childhood rheumatic fever. The surgery was initially thought to be a terrific success, and Geneva was the talk of the Rochester medical community. Im's search of her parents' house had turned up an old letter from her aunt amongst her father's things. In it, she'd described how she was even being shown off by her cardiologist at medical presentations. But the surgery was still in its infancy; the doctors didn't fully grasp the post-surgical risk of blood clots. They didn't know that Geneva should have been prescribed blood thinners. Just shy of a year after her famous surgery, Filomena's beloved only daughter died suddenly and instantly from a blood clot, right in the car, as her frantic husband was rushing her to the hospital. The fact that Im's father had kept his sister's letter for decades spoke volumes. Im wondered how the loss of his only sibling had affected him.

Geneva's passing was Imogene's first real experience with a death, even though her paternal grandfather had also died suddenly when she was three years old. While she didn't have any conscious memories of her grandfather's passing, maybe it had impact—outside of her awareness, but powerful just the same. Im knew, especially now, that her grandfather's sudden demise after a heart attack must have devastated her own father, and the whole family for that matter. The little ones would have been sheltered, but they likely would have felt the loss through the adults around them. Perhaps Im's early fears about death had origins in her grandfather's untimely one.

When Aunt Geneva died, though they were older, she and Maria never stepped foot in the funeral home. They were considered too young to endure the traditional Italian three-day vigil with an open casket. Regardless, Im would never forget the way her grandmother had been virtually inconsolable. She'd apparently screamed hysterically and thrown dishes across her kitchen when she'd been told the news of her daughter's death. Imogene could still picture the bald spots on her grandmother's head where she pulled out her hair in violent paroxysms of grief.

Had her daughter been alive, Filomena would have surely moved in with her. Instead, she left Rochester and all her friends to live with her only son. It was just the way it had always been done in Italian families. And it might have been fine had Imogene's mother been a bit less insecure and equipped with thicker skin.

Imogene felt bittersweet pangs as she went through her grandmother's boxes, marveling at how neatly everything had been packed away. This had been Filomena's way; everything "nice and neat," as she'd say. A highly skilled homemaker and cook, she rolled and cut fresh pasta, made homemade sausages with a grinding machine, baked her own Italian bread, and canned tomatoes and peppers, grown in her own backyard. And a talented seamstress, she crocheted blankets and doilies, sewed aprons and dresses, including matching shift dresses for her six granddaughters, and even made her son's bride's wedding dress—designed by her daughter, who had also been a gifted artist. Perhaps it was the efficiency and competence of her husband's female relatives, especially his mother, which had always left the second Mrs. Mussomeli feeling somewhat inferior. Most would have agreed Kate Mussomeli was hardly the meticulous housekeeper, wasn't spectacular in the kitchen, and scarcely knew how to sew on a button. Granted, Kate did have her own interests and talents, but none of them were domestically oriented. As the wife of an Italian man, this was not a good thing. Not that Filomena ever said a word. But her frequent presence and constant tendency to help out and do things in ways that invariably, though unintentionally, showed up her daughter-in-law, must have led to piles of built-up resentment, justified or not.

Take the simple task of making beds. When Kate Mussomeli made them, the bedclothes would look thrown on, leaving untidy folds and wrinkles, even a sheet corner jutting out and skirting the floor. It was obvious when Filomena had actually made the beds. You could literally bounce a penny on the smooth bedspreads—which was, in fact, the test Filomena had used when teaching her granddaughters how to make the bed "nice and neat." None of the beds made by Kate Mussomeli would have bounced any pennies. While it made her sorry for the way her grandmother had ended up displaced from her parents' home, Im could understand how her mother had been unable to make the mother-in-law-permanently-under-roof living arrangement quite work. It was just one of those things.

***

Not finding her father's copy of the Darwin book anywhere in her parents' house left Imogene slightly crazed. She found herself going back again and again to places she'd already looked, like a mad hamster on a wheel, hoping she might have missed it somehow. The frustration was killing her. Her father had kept practically everything else from the old days, especially books, and yet the one book she wanted so desperately to find was nowhere in sight.

The only good news was that she clearly turned a corner on her medication-resistant depression/grief/insomnia. She refused to think of it as any run-of-the-mill, garden variety, depressive mental illness, although it probably was textbook. Regardless, everyone was thankful for this welcome turnaround. Not that her sisters knew the reason for the reversal. Im didn't give any details about what she was looking for to her sisters. She figured they'd scoff and think she was wasting her time. She didn't hate them by any stretch, but she basically couldn't stand them. Besides, she liked that it was all her own thing—just between her and her dad, as it were.

Once her ability to sleep and dream had been fully restored, it seemed that her mind was making up for lost REM time. Her dreams were more vivid and real than ever before. And her father began to visit her in her dreams. In one recurring narrative, her father would suddenly be alive again, resurrected somehow as though he had merely been in a state of suspended animation and not ever really dead. She would, of course, be thrilled that he was alive, even though there was never any big celebration of this in the dream, as though it wasn't such a big surprise that he had essentially been resurrected somehow. She found this strange.

The one hitch in the dream was that her father would always be looking for something, which had been purged from the house, like a tool from his workshop downstairs or an article of his clothing. Imogene would feel horrible in the dream for having allowed so much of his stuff to get dumped, that she'd let her sisters do this. Still, she loved the feeling that he was actually alive, and she could talk to him again. It all seemed so real. Upon waking, she wished she could get right back inside the same dream.

Her epiphany about the Darwin book came one morning when she was lying in bed remembering a dream she had overnight. She was girl again, back in Rochester at her grandmother's house. Her father and all the adult men were sitting in the kitchen, as they typically did in those days. Talking, eating, drinking, laughing; they'd linger for hours around Filomena's 1950s oval kitchen table with the boomerang-patterned Formica top and thick chrome edging—the very kind often sought after nowadays by the nostalgic or those desiring the classic retro look.

In the old days, the women were usually outside in the yard, sitting under the massive grape arbor where Filomena grew red grapes for making jam and jelly—even wine. The ladies would sit under there on the painted green metal patio chairs with the tube arms—considered very retro-cool now, too—with the lush rose gardens sprawling in front of them, and her grandmother's huge vegetable garden off to one side, displaying rows and rows of tomatoes, squash, peppers, endive. Filomena had the greenest of thumbs.

In the dream, as always, Imogene and Maria were sitting on the floor in a corner of the kitchen playing with Lincoln logs—a favorite toy at their grandmother's—listening to the men talk. It was more fun than hanging around outside with all the Italian ladies, as they had a tendency to jabber about the girls in Italian, pointing at them, smiling and laughing. The girls never knew what they were saying. Worse, if one of the Mussomeli girls was within arm's reach, a lady might grab a hunk of a cheek between thumb and forefinger, and squeeze tightly, exclaiming how big she was getting, how beautiful she was! All of this was meant to convey affection and love, but the Mussomeli girls tried to avoid these cheek-stinging encounters at all costs.

Her grandmother was also inside the house in Im's dream. Wearing a flower-printed housecoat, she kept disappearing into the backroom off the kitchen and emerging with of a pot of this, a platter of that, always something delicious. It was all very normal, nothing out of the ordinary in the dream. But it triggered a thought in Imogene's mind. *The backroom.* What if the Darwin book was still tucked away in Filomena's old backroom?

CHAPTER 7

IMOGENE POPPED out of bed then and dashed to her computer—not stopping even for a quick pee. Brimming with anticipation, her fingers flew over the keys as she typed in her grandmother's old address on Cordova Avenue in Rochester. She remembered the number easily partly because Filomena would always blurt out the same quip.

A close friend who lived next door in her old neighborhood was named Grace. After Filomena moved to Dayton, when the family would sit down for the traditional Sunday afternoon Italian feast, Mr. Mussomeli would say, "Okay, who wants to say grace?" In response to her son's question, Filomena would suddenly pipe up and say, "Grace? Oh, she's at 227 Cordova Avenue!" She'd laugh halfway through and would barely get the full address out before running out of breath. It was her own little running joke, and everyone had heard it a thousand times, but they would still give her the obligatory chuckle because she seemed so proud of herself for thinking of this. English was by far her second language, and yet she could still make a pun.

When Imogene's Google search finally spit out a map of the address in Rochester, she breathed in quick through her nose, holding it in while chewing on her thumbnail. *There's the house...* But what if the backroom was torn down or something? When they'd driven-by the old house after her father's funeral, they'd only cruised past, slowing just long enough to get a look at the front. The tenor of the neighborhood certainly wasn't conducive to them nosing around. She knew the house itself was still standing, but she'd also seen that the grape arbor structure in the side yard was gone, and the old bowling alley next door had been demolished as well. For all she knew, the flimsily constructed backroom, an after-thought attached to the back end of the house facing the alley, had reached a point-of-no-return dilapidation and had also been leveled.

Then Imogene stopped cold.

What in the hell did it matter if the backroom was still there or not? The chances of the Darwin book actually being in there were infinitesimally small. Besides, the property didn't belong to them anymore. She certainly couldn't lay claim to anything in the house or backroom or wherever. She knew the guy who had bought the property from her grandmother had been hot-to-trot for it, presumably to slice and dice it up into multiple apartments to get the maximum in rent money. He clearly had no interest in keeping it a nice family home, and from the looks of the place when they'd driven by, he was a pretty lousy landlord. Everyone had been sad to see it all gone to seed.

Regardless, Im had to find out if the backroom addition was even still there. She clicked the Google Earth satellite view to see what she could see of her grandmother's old house, peering into her computer 500 miles away. At first, she couldn't get the proper angle to view the back of the house, but then she was able to click the pan-around arrows and zoom in. Okay, she saw the back alley and the other house on the corner across the alley—everything looking so run down. A tinge of sadness stabbed her. Then she panned a bit more with her mouse and zoomed in again.

The screen was blurry and pixilated, and she thought she might have reached the Google map zoom limit. She waited for the photo to populate, sucking in her breath again. And then, voila! She had a perfect side view of the house—and the old backroom was still there! Same little, rickety door, same gray 1930s siding, textured to look like bricks. How was it even possible? The Google Earth image showed a number of vacant lots where stuff had been torn down, and yet here was her grandmother's old house still completely intact. Even the chimney to the backroom fireplace looked basically sound. She sat there gazing at the screen. *Wow.* She was ecstatic. It's still there. *Still there!* She felt like jumping up and down with joy. Then reality began to sink in, putting a damper on her celebratory mood: Okay, so... *now what?*

Imogene had always been willing to push the envelope of her life to make things happen, work around the obstacles, cut through the red tape, and stretch the boundaries—even bend the rules—whatever it took. But now she was looking at territory that felt extremely far-flung and dicey. First, she had to hope that no one had ever tried to make a fire in the old backroom fireplace. Or that the landlord hadn't decided to seal it up with cement to prevent tenants from thinking they could roast marshmallows in there or something. Then, assuming that the Darwin book might still be in its little cubbyhole in the chimney, which was certainly a mammoth assumption, how could she possibly retrieve the thing? Clearly, going in there would be considered breaking-and-entering, and she was pretty sure that was a felony. She'd never been charged with anything... although once she had come close. Ironically, her father was the one who had saved her at the time.

It was back in her college days. Home for the summer, she spent evenings out on the town with her hometown girlfriends. Once she and her best high school friend had stopped to eat a late-night breakfast at a 24-hour greasy spoon on the way home from a long night out. It was 3 a.m.—pretty late for two young girls, not exactly sober, to be driving around downtown Dayton, Ohio. Inside the restaurant, Imogene and Lisa ordered full breakfasts, wolfed them down, went to the restroom...and then left—without paying their bill. A "dine-and-dash." It was a totally impulsive move. They'd never done anything like it before, but in that moment, the two of them seeing themselves reflected in the restroom mirror—their eyes a little wild—it suddenly seemed like a crazy, fun thing to do, just for the heck of it! In Lisa's defense, it was entirely Im's idea, though she'd not hesitated to go along.

In any event, they slipped out the back door near the bathroom, jumped in their car, and flew on down the road to Lisa's house, giddy with the excitement of having just pulled off a major heist. Neither one of the girls had ever done anything that would have put them in any legal jeopardy before. Granted, it was bad that Im was driving at all given her lingering intoxication, but the roads were deserted by four a.m., and they made it safely to Lisa's parents' house. Imogene then—and maybe it was a blessing—proceeded to fall asleep right there in the car parked in Lisa's driveway. At least she was off the road.

The next thing she remembered was Lisa banging on the car window saying that her dad had just called, and she needed to get home right away! It turned out that Imogene and Lisa's dine-and-dash attempt had one fatal flaw: Im had left her wallet on the table, naturally with her driver's license and money in it. Talk about stupid mistakes—she would have certainly made one of those dumbest criminal lists. Apparently, the restaurant realized what had been perpetrated on them, found her wallet, and called the cops. With her name and address conveniently in front of them, the police called her parents' home at five a.m. Her just-roused father, not finding his daughter at home, drove down to the city station—not in the greatest part of town either. He never gave Im the play-by-play, but the upshot was he managed to convince the cops that whatever the girls had done, they'd clearly left full payment for the meal right there on the table in the form of a wallet with $40 cash in it. In the end, Mr. Mussomeli persuaded the restaurant not to press charges. Incredibly, her father seemed to believe Imogene when she told him they'd been so tired (he never even asked if they'd been drinking), they only forgot to pay and hadn't even realized what they'd done.

While he clearly had the grounds to, her father never yelled at her. He just told her to go to bed and be more careful next time and don't ever go back to that restaurant (a condition of not pressing charges). He could have made her life miserable for a while, taking the car away or something, but he literally never spoke of it again. No admonishment, nothing. She didn't even know if he ever told her mother what happened. That was how her father was. He could just leave things alone. He didn't have anything to prove. Imogene loved this about him. It was only years later that she realized the enormity of what he'd done for her that night.

Sitting in front of the computer that morning, now armed with the knowledge that her grandmother's backroom was indeed still intact, Im wondered what her father would say. What would he do? She had no clue as to the current contents of the backroom. Besides it meant breaking-in—essentially committing a felony. It would likely have been out of the question for her father, but then again, her father would have never even considered doing a dine-and-dash. And, of course, if she did the deed and got caught, her father wasn't around to get her out of it. She wondered. How *had* she become such a bad seed?

And beyond the possible felony, her grandmother's old neighborhood was now downright scary. Her cousins had told them that it was a known haunt of drug dealers. And violent crime was apparently commonplace. If anyone caught her snooping around, some scrawny woman from Ohio, who knows where she'd end up. Besides, there was the tiny detail that she was presently at her parents' house, at least an eight hours' drive away. The longer she thought about it, the more it felt like a total Catch-22: Getting all the way to Rochester, putting herself in a risky, probably dangerous, situation, not to mention needing to commit a crime, all to possibly find out the Darwin book wasn't even there—it seemed to be the quintessential fool's errand.

Who in their right mind would ever seriously consider such a thing?

CHAPTER 8

FOR DAYS, IMOGENE could think of nothing else but getting into her grandmother's old backroom in Rochester—naturally. As crazy as it seemed, she began contemplating plans to get back to the old neighborhood and inside the place. She couldn't believe herself, but then again, a part of her wondered if it wasn't really all that insane an idea. The book could be worth so much money. It was her father's book, rightfully the Mussomeli family's property. Didn't it make sense to take a chance to try to find it? She wished she could bounce her ideas off someone, but speaking about it to anyone was out of the question. Imogene knew that the only way for a secret to stay hidden was to tell absolutely no one. *Ever.* Whether she found the book or not, she vowed to herself that she would never breathe a word about her plans to anyone. There was one exception to this:

Her mother.

As it turned out, Im knew she wouldn't need to be worried about her mother being privy to the search for the Darwin book. Her short-term memory had started to diminish markedly following her husband's death and was quickly beginning to disappear altogether. Maybe it had been failing for some time, but perhaps before, with her husband around, it had been less noticeable. He could remember things for her. Pay the bills. Keep track of stuff. Drive her where she needed to go. Imogene did recall having seen signs of her father's growing frustration with his wife, after she'd seemingly forgotten to do something or follow a simple direction he'd given her. He said things like, "What's in that head of yours anyway? Is it completely empty?" It wasn't nice, but he would have had no idea that his wife had a budding dementia at that time. Or, if he had sensed it, he would

75

have blocked this out of his mind anyway, thinking everything was probably fine. It was an optimism he carried with him about everyone's health including his own, which was as endearing as it was maddening. But he was certainly not immune to losing his patience with his wife and had done so many times toward the end.

Imogene could completely relate to the frustration of her mother's rapidly declining short-term memory. The simplest things became arduous. "Okay, mom, get dressed; let's go to the store." Within seconds, she'd have no clue what she'd just been asked to do, and might even be curled-up, back in bed completely oblivious. It was often the smallest of things that could exasperate Im, pushing her reserve of patience to its limit. Marvin had a favorite stuffed bear that was a leftover child-sized teddy bear he loved; her mother would always mistake it for something that should not be on the floor. In spite of its threadbare, chewed-up, damp-from-saliva appearance, she would constantly pick it up and place it on the couch or chair, in an apparent attempt to tidy up. The dog would then start yapping incessantly at the bear, until Im would drop it back down on the floor. No number of reminders about this to her mother would end the tiresome sequence.

That being said, Imogene knew she could tell her mother anything and it would never go any further. Out of sheer desperation, she finally shared her quandary with her. Her mom could still be quite lucid at times, at least in the moment; maybe she'd even have some good advice.

"Mom, I'm going to tell you my dilemma."

"Oh, a dilemma, what is it?" she asked with anticipation.

"So, there's this old book of Dad's I've been trying to find." That it was Darwin's book wouldn't have meant much to her, but she said, "It's the famous one by Charles Darwin; it might be really valuable—even worth a quarter million dollars."

Her mother's eyes got big. "Oh my!"

"The problem is I can't find it anywhere. I think it might still be in a hiding place back in Rochester in Filomena's backroom." She knew instantly the room to which Im referred. "So what should I do?"

Her mother, without missing a single beat, replied, "Go get it!" And there was a sparkle in her eyes that could not be mistaken. Mrs. Mussomeli, even if for only an instant, grasped the gist of the situation and was game.

When Imogene went on to ask her what she thought Dad would do, it was an immediate. "Go get it!"

Im chuckled with relief. It didn't matter that her mother might now be a little short on judgement; she had given her the go-ahead she wanted. The fact that her mom did not even hesitate for a second allowed her to feel maybe it wasn't so insane after all. It also meant that she could take her mother with her, as she knew she was going to have to do anyway.

Since she'd become a widow, it was clear Mrs. Mussomeli was no longer capable of independently taking care of herself, the house, or her dog. At least not until they found a cure for her problem, which, unfortunately, was not likely to be in her lifetime. She'd finally been diagnosed with "Dementia, Alzheimer's type." When she wasn't straight away given the dreaded "AD" (Alzheimer's disease) label, Im thought maybe it wouldn't have to get much worse. But the doctors were quick to point out that it most certainly would progress. All types of dementia in aging tend to take the same course; it sort of didn't matter what the exact label or etiology was.

That's not to say Im didn't try to decipher her mother's case...Why had she developed this condition? What could have caused it? Was it genetic? Was it likely to happen to her and her sisters as well? Im delved into all the research and scholarly reports she could find about Alzheimer's and all its known variants. She was disheartened to learn that the experts didn't yet know what caused the disease...let alone how to cure it.

But when reporting back to her sisters, Imogene had hung onto the initial phrasing so it wouldn't seem so hopeless. And maybe it wasn't. Her mother often seemed more or less like herself, just less talkative, a bit more passive; needier, and, of course, more forgetful. But it wasn't all doom and gloom. She still seemed capable of enjoying life's simple pleasures. Isn't that what really mattered?

Then, for the sake of doing it, Imogene posed the potential pitfalls of her scheme to retrieve the Darwin book in Rochester: the "B&E," the scary bad neighborhood, a locked door to the backroom. To all of this, her mother had replied, "No one has to know." "I'm tough, I can handle the neighborhood." And "You can sneak in; just climb through the window!"

"But what if the police show up?"

Her mother shrugged this off as well. "I'll take care of them."

"What do you mean, Ma?"

"Oh, I can sweet-talk them. I'll offer them sex; then they'll do anything for me!"

Imogene cracked up at this. Her mother was still the same live wire underneath it all, though joking about sex was actually quite out-of-character for her. In the past, her mother had been slightly prudish. But Im could see that along with her short-term memory loss, came some loosening of inhibitions, which out of context, could be a bit shocking. It was another hallmark of the dementia.

Then Im pointed out that they'd have to drive all the way to Rochester. Her mother again, without hesitation, exclaimed, "Oh, good! I love Rochester!"

Later, Im asked her if she really thought they should go all the way back to Rochester looking for the book.

Her mother replied, "What book? What are you talking about?" Im was obviously not going to have to worry about her mother spilling the beans to her sisters.

In spite of her mother's enthusiasm, the idea still seemed sketchy, even nuts. But given that her dad's old copy of the Darwin book was absolutely nowhere to be found in Dayton, the only possibility—if it hadn't been given away, lost or destroyed—was that it was still back in Rochester. Would her father have simply forgotten that it was hidden up in the chimney of the backroom? Back in his day, the book wouldn't have necessarily been considered particularly valuable—at least not to a non-book collector. Besides, a first edition's value then might not have been anything to write home about. There also likely wouldn't have been talk about how to know if it was a true first edition (i.e. "speceies" on page 20). Or even if there was knowledge of this, there was no internet or any other such mass dispersion of information which could have alerted her father to this fact. A quick Google search now places the book on the short list of the greatest books of all time and books that most changed the world. But back then, who would know this? Joe Mussomeli would have had no reason to be concerned about the book's whereabouts once he'd lost interest in it—as he likely had at some point.

Imogene spent a lot of time supposing this and supposing that before finally realizing that none of these ruminations were going to get her any closer to the actual book, if, in fact, it was still tucked away in her grandmother's backroom. Wow, even she could see that was a monstrous "if." She hated even the sound of the word in this context. She desperately wanted to find the book for so many reasons.

Yes, if it proved to be one of the few first editions still out there (another huge "if"), it could be incredibly valuable. But something else was driving her. Although she couldn't get any emotional distance on it at the time, it didn't take a shrink to see that the book probably symbolized her lost father and the hole he'd left in her life, which had not gotten any less gaping. Sure, she perked up finally (her sisters rejoiced, though they had no clue as to why), but she still missed him intensely. Without the Darwin book to chase, who knows if she'd have ever climbed out of the deep abyss, which had been home to her unrelenting grief.

It was not a place she ever wanted to revisit. She realized that before her father's sudden death, she had no real appreciation of what a beast the emotion of grief could be. After tangling with it her herself, she imagined she would forevermore be sensitive to the bereavement of others. The experience of the sudden loss of her father had transformed her and probably made her a better, more empathic, even more considerate person. She'd grown, as they say, and while she could see this at times, the "do-over" fantasy was yet alive and well—she would have gladly gone back in time to her more oblivious, lesser self if it meant having her father back in the world. Even for just a day.

Nonetheless, Im had mainly healed the previously festering grief wound and was now on a mission: find the Darwin book or die trying. Granted this was a bit melodramatic, but not necessarily very far off. What she was considering would surely push the boundaries more than she'd ever done before. She knew she might be putting herself in a potentially dangerous situation, legal and otherwise. Yet in those early days, plotting, weighing her options for finding her father's old copy of "Origin of Species," Imogene was energized, chomping at the bit. Any possible negative repercussions of her actions were just going to have to take a back seat. Or even a way-back seat in the station wagon of her mind.

She had not an inkling of the terrifying seismic shift that lay ahead...

Now, it was only *onward* (to Rochester)!

CHAPTER 9

THE FIRST OF IMOGENE'S many machinations about embarking on her lost-treasure hunt (why not?) involved how to explain to her inquiring (nosy) sisters why she and her mother (and by necessity, the dog) were suddenly taking a road trip back to Rochester. It hadn't been that long since they'd buried her father there. Could she say they wanted to visit the grave? She did intend to do this while in town. But she didn't think this reason would satisfy her sisters' relentless need-to-know everything about what she was doing. Their hovering, even at a distance, was annoying. She already had to fend off all of their incessant questions about her life and future. Are you dating anyone? Are you looking? Don't you want to get married? And about her career. Aren't you going to lose your job? How can you be gone so long from the University?

On the dating thing, well, whatever. But as far as her job, she'd arranged to take a sabbatical (of sorts) in Ohio once it was clear that she wasn't ready to return. She didn't tell her sisters, but she fantasized about never going back to that hell-hole. Yes, it was the next best thing to Ivy League (or so it liked to think) and considered one of the most beautiful college campuses in the country, but Imogene had never felt like a true part of the place. In all honesty, she felt like a bit of a fraud. No way was she on par with all the academics who sat around thinking 24-7 about their research and publications and going to the top of that Ivory Tower. It all seemed so meaningless to her—who really cared who had the most publications in all those obscure journals most people had never heard of? Or who had the most accolades and awards to their name? The mere mention of the "Curriculum Vitae" made her feel slightly ill. Who in the real world gave a rat's ass?

As for the marriage question, this too left Im feeling a bit unwell. Why had nearly every previous relationship eventually felt like she suddenly ended up on a dead-end street? Or was she afraid of commitment? Was she too picky? How had she never found the right guy? Or had she found him but hadn't recognize him as such? She certainly had her share of opportunities—was it the number of them that had worked against her in the long run?

Indeed, she always seemed to have choices waiting for her as soon as one relationship ended. Imogene, while certainly not perfection, was a bit of a magnet to men for reasons she had never really understood. Perhaps the combination of beauty and brains was captivating. Or maybe it was the fact that she never thought of herself as attractive. Her view of herself was still eons old. Likely a holdover from her early mustachioed days, she felt ugly half the time, even though the tiny five-o'clock shadow was long gone.

In the summer after high school, she made up her mind. She was heading off to college soon—something had to be done about her embarrassing "problem." She tried things she saw in the back-page ads of beauty magazines, promising to get rid of "unwanted facial hair"—special creams or new-fangled gadgets. And the bleaching stuff at the drugstore, though even buying it was a bit of a trauma, waiting to see if the cashier glanced up at her, zeroing in on her upper lip.

Who cared if no one else seemed to think it was such a big deal. ("It's only peach fuzz; Im. You can hardly see it!") She had enough; it was time for real action. She'd heard about professional electrolysis and found an office listed in the yellow pages. It was all the way in Cincinnati, and without the internet, there was no way to check whether the electrolysis "doctor" was even legit. But she mustered her courage and drove herself to the seedy office building in the middle of downtown Cincinnati. She never said where she was going to her parents, instead fudging shopping trips or other white lies. They would likely have been concerned if they knew what she was up to. The procedure was painful and relatively expensive, and the "doctor" was very creepy, but she didn't care. It was all worth it. She finally felt almost normal.

Still, the remnants of feeling unattractive lingered and made her inherently demure. She always tried to keep boys at arm's length so her embarrassing little mustache hairs would go unnoticed. Though it was inadvertent, it made her seem coy, even aloof. It was all fuel for the fire. What guy didn't like the challenge of that seemingly unattainable girl?

All this might have spelled imminent wedded bliss for Imogene—but it was complicated. Imogene's first real boyfriend felt like the love of her life, though he went off to college two years ahead of her. She had been that sophomore cheerleader dating the senior football player. But contrary to assumptions, her attraction to Craig had little to do with status or anything other than his utter sweetness and complete devotion to her, which felt like a warm, fuzzy blanket. Given her insecurities and long-standing anxieties, it was no wonder she cleaved to him so completely. No one had ever made her feel so loved and accepted. After college, she was even engaged to him for a while, but once she had a ring on her finger, she suddenly panicked and felt claustrophobic. She never really dreamed of the little house with the white picket fence like some girls of her era had. So what was the big rush?

She unceremoniously dumped Craig. The poor guy was like the saddest puppy on Earth. It took years for him to fully move on, not helped by Imogene's occasional cameo appearances in his life. She did love him, but it was not quite the way she imagined it should be or how she should feel. Her expectations were probably a bit off. Or maybe she had outgrown him. Either way, Imogene proceeded on to graduate school and a string of relationships, none of which ever panned out. Her track record was fairly abysmal, mostly because, with the exception of Craig, she was pretty terrible at choosing men.

Besides the recent debacle with cheating husband Ted, another boyfriend representing the nadir of bad picks was a guy she dated for years in graduate school. Sam was initially fun and breezy, if not a bit irresponsible. Imogene was happy to coast along with him by her side through the grueling days of graduate school. If she had been honest, she would have admitted she never really intended to marry him. But when a girl spends a few years with a guy, it's natural for him to expect marriage might be a possibility. Once it became clear that this was not going to happen, that he had only been a placeholder for her, Sam became unhinged, even threatening to kill himself if they broke-up. Alarmed, Imogene postponed breaking-up, hoping to gently ease herself out of the relationship over time, which resulted in the erstwhile boyfriend scenario—on and off—never a good idea, but a horrible one if the boyfriend is a bit unstable.

What Sam did next shook her trust in all men. He knew that Imogene was extremely allergic to poison ivy; any exposure resulted in her body blowing up like a balloon and days of agonizing itching. What he did with this knowledge was diabolical. He had secretly harvested some poison ivy leaf stems. While giving her a massage, he brushed them over her back and down her legs. Though she noticed a tickling sensation, she didn't suspect anything untoward. She actually loved this back-rub perk of her relationship with Sam. He never even expected reciprocation; it was all part of the glue.

The next day, her body was on fire. Her entire backside, all the way down to her ankles, was deep red and covered in bumps and welts. Cruelly, this also included part of her crotch. Still, not realizing what he had done, she allowed Sam to slather calamine and hydrocortisone cream on her back and generally take care of her in her incapacitated state. Looking back, she could see he had perpetrated some kind of twisted Munchausen by proxy on her so that she would need him to take care of her. It wasn't until days later, when she finally went to the student health center and was told it was poison ivy, that she put it all together. She hadn't been near any wooded areas, let alone any poison ivy… could it be? Once confronted, Sam finally admitted what he did, tearfully claiming he had only done it because he loved her so much and couldn't stand to lose her. Yes, she could be very bad at picking men.

In psychological circles, she might have even been seen as a commitment-phobe. She was certainly gun-shy after the experience with Sam. But Im believed she'd probably just missed the boat, that all the ships had sailed and most of the really great guys were already taken—i.e. all that was left was essentially yesterday's meatloaf. Right, the highest quality mates were usually snapped up quickly. This, however, had not always been her view.

As a girl, she'd been spellbound by fairy tales where the handsome prince or knight in shining armor galloped in to sweep the lady off her feet and make everything wrong instantly right. Also a sucker for the Harlequin romance paperbacks where the dashing man suddenly appeared out-of-the-blue and sent the girl into the throes of ecstasy, Im had gobbled these books up like candy. Of course, there were lots of fish in the sea! Why settle for the first one to come along?

In fact, she'd been proposed to a couple more times, but each time, she couldn't bring herself to say yes. Im's lack of a mate was actually a favorite phone topic for her sisters. They spent hours hashing and rehashing this sad reality, recalling some of the wonderful guys she could have married, the unanimous favorite always being Craig. *Poor Craig,* they clucked.

***

Ultimately, Im decided to tell her sisters that she and her mother were going to take a trip to Rochester because her mother's memory was failing fast, in spite of the prescribed medications. That revisiting this familiar place of the past might be beneficial, that her doctor had thought so as well. She wasn't sure she could sell it, but she willed herself to give an Oscar-worthy performance.

She dialed up Maria. "Hi Mar; it's Im."

"Oh, Im, what's up? Are you okay?" There was a tinge of alarm in her voice. Im didn't usually call Maria; it was mostly the other way around.

"Yeah, yeah, I'm fine. You worry too much, Mar!" She went on, trying to be breezy and casual. "So I just wanted to let you know that Ma and I are going to make a quick trip up to Rochester... you know, I think it'll be really good for her...."

"Wait, really? Are you sure you're up to it, Im?"

Lately, the sisters had been acting as if she was a Porcelain doll that might crack at any moment. Perhaps it was justified, but still, it irked Im. She didn't like being seen as a fragile person who had to be handled with kid gloves.

"Maybe you should wait till one of us can go with you, Im."

Ugh, no! Im absolutely did not want one of the sisters tagging along. Then she'd never be able to come close to executing her plan.

"No, Mar, I'll be fine; don't worry about it... just let me do this! Besides your family needs you home, Mar, and... you know, sooner on this might be better... the doctor even agrees..." She let her voice trail off.

"Yeah, well... I guess you're right...Okay, Im... whatever you want to do... um, I mean, just be careful, okay?"

She knew that Maria's relatively quick acquiescence was largely because she feared rocking the boat with her now. Relieved Im had finally regained a foothold in her life, Maria didn't want to risk upsetting her. While generally irritated by her sisters' obvious walking-on-eggshells approach with her, in this instance, she was glad for it. It meant they'd be less likely to interfere with her plans to go back East.

So Im convinced her sisters that a trip down memory lane would be good for their mother. Their mom had spent some of the happiest years of her life in Rochester; maybe it *would* make a difference. The little white lie was accepted; it was a go.

Soon she, her mother, and Marvin were cruising up the Ohio interstate, heading northeast, inching ever closer to New York and her grandmother's old backroom on Cordova Avenue.

On the way, she and her mother reminisced about the many trips the family had made from Ohio back to Rochester. They'd regularly driven the seemingly endless 500-mile trek in one of the wood-paneled Pontiac or Chevy station wagons they'd owned over the years. Surprisingly, in all the trips back East, they only had a problem on the road once—a sudden tire blowout. The experience had been traumatic for the six Mussomeli girls.

The exploding tire caused the car to swerve violently, requiring their father to wrestle with the steering wheel to prevent them from flying off the highway overpass. The girls screamed the whole way. In the midst of the shrieking chorus, it was amazing their father maintained enough composure to safely bring the car to the shoulder. Later, huddled together on the grassy side of the highway, the sisters cried hysterically in concert, as they were known to do. What was so terrifying at that point was anyone's guess, but none of them had ever been stranded on the side of the highway, with monstrous trucks whizzing by, their father seemingly perilously close to being plowed down by one of the evil truckers! Their measly station wagon was like a lame duck, jacked up with its hind tire disturbingly mangled, their father struggling with the lug nuts.

Ironically, Im and her mother also had a flat tire on the way to Rochester on I-70 east in middle-of-nowhere Ohio. It might have even been very near the same spot of that tire blowout in the family station wagon all those years ago. Im hoped it wasn't a bad omen for the trip.

She was glad she hadn't let her auto club membership lapse. Turned out, as she suspected, they ran over a big nail on the highway. She heard the pop and had a sinking feeling. Her gut told her to get off the highway quickly at the next exit. She didn't want a tire blowout like the one her dad had on the same stretch, stuck on the side of the road, cars and trucks whizzing by. She shuttered at the thought.

As she was pulling off the exit, she heard the rhythmic thumping of the tire having gone flat. This was all very unnerving, but she tried to stay calm. It wasn't the end of the world, though Im couldn't recall another time when this happened to her—at least not when she was the adult in charge.

She turned to her mom in the passenger seat. "Well, I think we've got a flat tire, Ma."

"Oh, we do?" She seemed unconcerned—sweetly nonplussed. In the past, she likely would have been very worried, even panicky, in such a situation. But since the dementia, everyday problems seemed to roll right off her back, seemingly unnoticed. Im supposed this might be sort of a good change—as long as her mother had someone looking after her. Im knew this was the new reality.

Still, there was something about having her mother there, with her non-rattled reaction, which was comforting. Like they'd get through it, and it'd be okay no matter what. It helped Im remember—sometimes stuff just happens.

Fortunately, a road service guy arrived quickly, but only in a regular car, not a tow truck. He did have all the tools he needed, but it turned out that the tire was punctured in a spot that couldn't be plugged on the roadside. The tire was essentially shot. The guy only put the temporary donut spare on for her and offered no further help. He didn't seem at all fazed by her growing distress at their circumstance. Every question she posed to him was met with instantaneous and clipped one-word replies. She'd barely have the sentence out and he'd already be answering her.

"So I'm going to have to buy a new—?"

"Yep."

"Do you know where I should—?"

"Nope"

"Do you think there's a tire place near—?"

"Yup."

What was with this guy? He seemed irritated that she was even talking to him. Im said, "Sorry I ask so many questions! I guess you don't like that..."

"Jus' hear same ones all day long," the guy drawled.

More than one word this time. Small victory. "Oh, yeah, yeah, yeah, well, sorry... anyway, I guess I'll figure it out..."

Pointing now, he said, "Just head up thata way and ask around. I'm sure somebody can tell ya a place. Don't really know what's 'round here."

"Right, right... okay." Im was going to have to fend for herself. She suddenly felt like such a hapless person, waylaid in life by the simplest of things.

But she did what the guy suggested and eventually ran into a woman walking along the roadside who looked like she'd lived in the little one-horse town her whole life. Yes, she knew of a nearby garage that sold tires.

She added, "They always done me right thar. Won't rip ya off just 'cause yer a chick, ha ha."

Later, back in the car with her mother, she mimicked the woman and her mother howled with laughter. "Oh, Im, you're terrible!"

Laughing felt good; why not try and relax, quit sweating it so much? Yeah, Im thought she definitely needed to try to chill out more, not worry so much, go with the flow. Trust in the universe, as they say. She thought that her father seemed to have mastered this. He used to say, "Look, Im, nothing is ever the end of the world until it *is*."

Following the local woman's directions, they soon arrived at a dilapidated auto repair shop that looked like a place straight out of a 1940's black-and-white movie. She and her mother exchanged a look and both quelled a chuckle. But they had no choice; they had to have a new tire.

The mechanics' eyes got a little bigger at the sight of the late model black Cadillac Deville, which had been Joe Mussomeli's final car purchase, less than a year before he died. He'd owned a slew of Cadillacs in his retirement in various colors, including a powder-blue one with a white hardtop and white-wall tires. Im thought that one looked a lot like a pimp's car. But the last one he owned was actually her favorite of them all. Its soft leather-covered steering wheel and cream-colored, cushy leather seats felt heavenly, and she swelled with pride and gratitude when driving the car. She knew her mother loved the car as well, though it all felt so bittersweet. The guy who really loved the car wasn't around to enjoy it any more.

In the end, the mechanics—each extremely scruffy looking, with deeply blackened fingers and filthy, ragged clothes—did take care of everything as promised. They checked all the rest of the tires, topped off all the fluids, even did a quick check on the brakes, and generally seemed to pay special attention with what they obviously thought was a special car.

The only hitch was a sudden cloudburst, drenching her and her mother and the dog while they sat in the lawn chairs outside the garage. They had to rush inside to the tiny office and wait it out. The place stank of cigarettes and burnt oil and gasoline. It was a grungy pigsty, but then why would it be anything else? Still, Im was aghast when Marvin lifted his leg and spewed out a little piddle on the leg of the desk. Fortunately, it was only a dribble since he'd already pretty much peed himself out before the rain. Obviously an attempt to mark his territory in the greasy place. Go figure.

Im apologized profusely and tried to wipe it up with a wad of paper, but the guy in there just shooed her away. "Don't worry 'bout it," he said. "This floor seen a lot worse!"

Soon, she and her mother and the dog, a little damp but no worse for the wear, were flying down the highway again in their "traveling living room," as one of the mechanics had called it. He was right; the Caddy's smooth, quiet ride and luxurious interior felt like you were cruising along in the comfort of your own home.

They lost some time, but the rest of the trip was thankfully uneventful. Even relaxing. But when they finally hit the New York State border and began to see all the blue and gold plates on cars, Imogene was suddenly bombarded by a mixture of nostalgia and dread. This wasn't just a visit for old-time's-sake as she told her sisters. She was on a mission, a fool's errand perhaps, and the enormity of what she was planning began to sink in. She was playing with fire, and getting burned, seriously burned, was a distinct possibility. Yet something propelled her forward. Like she was under some sort of spell, that turning back would have been virtually impossible. And if she was being honest, she'd have had to admit that she felt incredibly alive and energized, and she loved it—sort of. She'd always had a love-hate relationship with risk.

Imogene would be the first to say she was an odd mix. While she'd been a nervous Nelly in childhood, plagued with fears, phobias and general anxieties, there was also a dare-devil side to her that defied all comprehension. Aside from the greasy-spoon (epically-failed) dine-ndash, she had engaged in her share of risky behaviors, including routinely diving into the pool off the ten meter platform as a teenager, repelling with ropes off steep cliffs, joy-riding in a "borrowed" speed-boat with keys still in it, sneaking in the back entrance of a bar and racing off with a case of Heineken (she didn't even like beer), sweet-talking her way backstage at rock concerts, hoping to meet the band—along with a myriad of other scofflaw activities. It might have been instigated by a guy she was dating at the time, but not necessarily. Sometimes it was all Im. She realized she enjoyed the attention it brought her and the adrenaline rush. Fortunately, she'd mostly matured past her dare-devil tendencies.

Now this—though it had nothing to do with getting attention or thrills in this case. No, something else was clearly driving her...

Floating down the highway in her father's boat of a car with her oblivious mother (no clue where they were going)—and crazy Chihuahua, Imogene knew she was seriously crossing the line this time. She genuinely didn't know what she was going to do once she arrived at point "X" on the treasure map. Would she have the nerve to essentially break-in to her grandmother's old backroom? Would her dad's old copy of Darwin's "Origin of Species" book even be in there? And more importantly, would she be able to get away with it?

CHAPTER 10

DRIVING INTO NEW YORK from the West, there's a portion of I-90 that closely hugs the Lake Erie coastline, and Imogene's heart raced a little when she caught a glimpse of the tremendous, expansive deep blue water through the shoreline pines. "Look mom; look at the lake!" Her mother would then respond with an "Oh my, look at that!" This sequence would be repeated many times over, with her mother gasping at the sight of the Great Lake as though it was the first time she was seeing it.

There was something inherently delightful about how Mrs. Mussomeli's particular variety of dementia allowed her to experience so many things over and over with all the awe and gusto of it being the first time ever. For her, everything was always fresh and new, and she seemed to be in a perpetual state of bliss, which honestly seemed pretty darn nice to Im at times. Her mother could seem so utterly content. Of course, it was not always so nice for the daughter, but once Im learned to stop expecting her mother to be any different—to retain things from moment to moment, to keep track and follow directions, to realize she'd just asked the same question three times already—it took the edge off the frustration. Im got used to repeating answers to questions or reiterating a request multiple times without reacting as though anything was amiss.

When she did occasionally show her annoyance, her mom seemed so hurt and sorry, saying, "Oh, I'm such a problem; you should just put me away!" Imogene couldn't stand seeing her mother this way, for no reason other than her daughter's impatience. Im vowed to do better, to be even more patient. The innocence and vulnerability she saw in her mother squeezed her heart and led to a flood of tender feelings. She so wanted to protect her.

Yet, here she was driving her mother into who knows what? The potential treacherousness of what Im was planning to do was way past anything she'd ever entertained before. What kind of person involved her own mother in such a thing? But the thought of doing it all alone was unbearable. And really, there'd been no other way. Shipping her mother off to one of her sister's homes while she went off on her wild goose chase had been out of the question. How could she possibly have explained? Besides, while having her mother along was a bit risky and complicated at times, her mom was still a great traveling companion, especially for this particular trip. Who else could she tell all her secrets to without the slightest worry that they would be re-told to another living soul?

On the outskirts of Rochester, merging onto route 480, the loop around the city, they happened to pick up an AM station on the radio called WGY out of Schenectady. Mrs. Mussomeli immediately exclaimed, "That's where I used to sing on the radio!" Imogene had heard something of this story years back but had never really paid much attention. It had seemed like some sort of tall-tale that probably was only barely true. In fact, it was complete truth.

Little Kate Lenzio, at five years old, had indeed been a local radio star on WGY in the 1930s, after her own mother, known to be a gutsy lady, had marched her down to the studio proclaiming that her little girl could sing. Kate knew all the popular songs of the day by heart; she and her mother had sung them over and over together at home. Kate impressed enough to win a regular gig, which entailed Wednesday rehearsals and Saturday morning live broadcasts. Without a car, she and her mother would trudge to the radio station on foot over the railroad tracks. Not only was the story amazing to Im, but the fact that her mother's long-term memory remained intact was a gift she never tired of. Sure, her mother couldn't remember five minutes ago, but five, six, seven decades ago? No problem. It was the one kind aspect of what was an otherwise brutal disease.

As Imogene's mother recalled the experience from her childhood that day on their trek to Rochester, she lit up. "I must have been really talented!"

93

"Yeah, you must have been, Ma."

"My older sisters were so jealous!" she said with glint in her eye. ,

"What ever happened with all that, Ma?"

"Oh, my voice changed, and that was the end of it," she replied with a long sigh.

It was clear this had been a significant disappointment in her life. Her radio days seemed to represent a rare, happy memory from her childhood, as she could easily tick off a litany of personal woes from this time: hated by her sisters, always picked on, loner with no friends, felt ugly and unloved, spent most of her time playing alone in the attic with her dolls or reading books, got bad grades, skipped school, and dated boys from the wrong side of the tracks. And it turned out, little Kate Lenzio was even responsible for a most unfortunate accident with the Lenzio family's pet bird.

Petey was a tiny wren rescued by Mrs. Lenzio after it had fallen from its mother's nest—or perhaps it was even shoved. Petey had been born with a slightly deformed wing such that he was never able to fly. Instead, for years, he was allowed to hop around the floor of the Lenzio's tiny 1930s apartment, housing the Lenzio family of eight. Mrs. Lenzio allowed the little bird to have the run of the place, meticulously picking up his droppings as he went. The tiny creature hopped around amidst all the hullabaloo of the busy household, darting around the furniture and the feet. It's no wonder the bird was eventually stepped on. It was inevitable.

Unfortunately, it was little Kate who did this. Petey had been beloved and adored by the entire Lenzio family, and his demise was devastating for all. To have been the one responsible for the family tragedy was a particularly brutal fate.

Imogene asked her mother, "How did you ever get over that?"

Her mother replied, "I still haven't."

Yes, Kate Mussomeli's brief child-stardom on the radio so long ago may have been one of the highlights of her entire life. It was perhaps second only to the day she married Joe Mussomeli, who was her ultimate ticket out. And, of course, the births of her six daughters. Sometimes Im wondered if there had been a little disappointment with each successive birth: By the time she and Maria arrived, she imagined her father, especially, must have felt a bit let down each time he heard it was yet another girl.

Previously, whenever the Mussomeli girls would ask their mother how she and their father had gotten together, she would usually be coy and vague, brushing over the details as though she didn't really remember them. But on that long ride back to Rochester, in search of the lost book (treasure?), Kate Mussomeli was finally in the mood to tell-all.

It was in Schenectady where she'd grown up. She'd spotted him at the local dance hall called Kane's Castle, known to be a prime place at the time for meeting eligible men. Joe Mussomeli was an electrical engineer with General Electric, fresh out of school with a Master's degree. Tall, dark, and handsome, Kate Lenzio knew he was a catch. With a twinkle in her eye, she told her daughter, "I decided I was going to catch him."

She described pestering him to no end, making sure she was at Kane's Castle any time he might be there, showing up on his doorstep, or even waiting outside his apartment for him to come home from work. Then it dawned on her that being too available was probably the wrong way to go about it.

Kate suddenly made herself scarce and even instructed her mother to claim she was out on a date when Joe eventually called for her. It worked like a charm, and soon, she had a beautiful diamond engagement ring—and was marrying up. The brilliance of this playing-hard-to-get move was not lost on Imogene. Her mother had shown some real moxie back then, more than Im imagined she would have done herself in similar circumstances.

Im's mother sighed deeply after telling the story of their courtship. Tearing up, she choked out, "He was the best, Im."

"I know, Ma; I know."

Im felt her eyes welling up, seeing her mother, dog on her lap, dressed in her usual travel uniform—khaki slacks, nylon windbreaker, and short, silk scarf tied around her neck—sitting in the front passenger seat, a spot she'd occupied countless times on the same trip with her husband behind the wheel. Now she looked so small and vulnerable. Im felt a sudden, deep pang of sadness for what her mother had lost. Im had spent so many weeks consumed by her own grief. She hadn't really stopped to fully fathom her mother's.

They rode in silence then for a while, the profound loss of beloved husband and father populating their thoughts. Im fought back tears. She didn't want to make it worse for her mother. She reached out for her mother's hand, wanting to comfort her, but the idiot dog snapped at her, and she had to quickly snatch it back.

Finally, pulling off the highway near downtown Rochester, Im felt a lift. It suddenly seemed good just to be back there—in spite of everything. Mrs. Mussomeli gazed up at the Rochester skyline, glistening beautifully in the setting sun. She pointed up at the large shining statue atop one of the buildings, "Look, there's Mercury! You know, I'm the person responsible for that." This was yet another of the many Rochester stories Imogene had heard repeated over the years, the veracity of which she also questioned. But this one was mostly true as well.

Kate Lenzio had known next to nothing about the arts growing up in Schenectady on the heels of the Great Depression, but marrying Joe Mussomeli opened up a whole new world for her. They even spent their honeymoon in New York City, an entire week seeing Broadway shows, attending operas, concerts, and the Ballet. Later, in Rochester, as she raised her daughters, she became a fixture in the Rochester Mercury Ballet Company, bringing her girls there for lessons, baking sugar cookies in the shape of Ballet dancers for the bake sales, and volunteering at fundraisers. Ballet became a true passion for her at the time. She even took ballet classes herself. No doubt, she wished she had her chance to be a dancer.

Around this time, Mrs. Mussomeli found out about a statue of the Roman God Mercury, which had been confined to storage for over twenty years after its original home had been demolished. Though the statue had no direct connection to the Mercury Ballet company, she began a campaign to get the Mercury statue out of storage and displayed atop the ballet theater. She apparently came on a bit strong—as she could do about a cause—perhaps ruffled too many feathers, and her efforts were thwarted. Imogene asked what her father had thought about all this at the time.

"He said, 'that's what you get for sticking your nose in where it doesn't belong'." Im thought this sounded like her father—deadpan and probably speaking the truth.

The irony was a few years after they relocated to Ohio, they were driving into Rochester for a visit, and, miraculously, there was Mercury perched on the roof of a prominent downtown building. Although it apparently wasn't a direct result of her actions, Mrs. Mussomeli claimed she was the one who started that ball rolling, which again turned out to be mostly true.

The fifteen or so years that the young Mussomeli family had lived in Rochester seemed like golden years for her mother. Imogene thought it must have been so hard for her to leave the lively cosmopolitan Rochester scene for of all places, Dayton, Ohio.

"Did you hate leaving Rochester to move to Ohio, Ma?"

"Oh, not really, it was time to go." This, too, was characteristic of her mother, acting completely nonchalant when it was least expected.

But Im knew that leaving Rochester had been hard for everyone.

Years ago, when the Mussomeli family would make the pilgrimage back to Rochester every spring for Easter and again in late summer, the first glimpse of the familiar city landmarks would be met with cheers from the girls. The excruciatingly boring eight-hour car ride (an eternity for a kid) was finally over. Now, the highly anticipated "vacation" in Rochester—Mr. Mussomeli had been too practical to take his large family on more conventional tourist-trap-type vacations. No way was he going to foot the bill for hotels and amusements and restaurant meals for his family of eight. Besides, it was all about being with extended family and old friends. That's what really mattered.

The girls would always be so glad to be back in Rochester, partly because their parents clearly loved the city, too, and likely preferred it to

Dayton. Their greater affinity for the place, though unspoken, was obvious. For all the sisters, arriving there meant happy times ahead, visiting old friends and family who'd be overjoyed to see them. They were finally *home* again; it was where their roots would always be. Everywhere they went in Rochester, they saw people that looked like them (ethnic Italian or otherwise). There were many dark-haired, dark-eyed, darker-skinned little girls who were also a bit too "hairy" in some places—a monumental difference from Dayton, Ohio.

Back in New York State, Im never felt like she was too dark and too ethnic. And in Rochester, they were surrounded by people with names which also ended in vowels: Marticello, Petrocelli, Castiglione, Ballerini, Franciosa, Graziano; the list was endless. In Dayton, it was all Smith or Jones, Johnson or Williams. Few in the Midwest could even begin to pronounce their long Italian last name. It was regularly butchered to a pulp. And because of their name's similarity to that of an evil Italian dictator, occasionally some idiot would even ask if they were related to the infamous Benito Mussolini. Once after covering World War II in history class, some smart-assed kid asked Im if she loved Hitler, too. What the heck? The depths of dumbness in Dayton could be remarkable. Yes, back in Rochester they could feel a sense of pride in their name, which reflected their distinct Sicilian heritage.

There is actually a town in Sicily that bears their name. It is in the Caltanissetta province where both her paternal grandparents were born—less than ten miles apart—though they never met until they had each independently landed in up-state New York. Theirs was a short courtship. They were "matched" by their families, met once, exchanged two postcards, and were married a few weeks later. Things could be a bit simpler in those days.

Yes, in Rochester the Mussomelis truly fit in. For Imogene, it was always like a deep breath of cool, fresh air.

Although now that she and her mother had arrived in Rochester yet again, Imogene felt anything but comfort and happy anticipation of good times ahead. Her sense of dread was building by the second. She pulled the Cadillac into a McDonald's parking lot. She needed to think. She realized she hadn't thought through exactly what she would do once she got to the city. She did have a reservation with a small motel on the outskirts of town, but other than that, she'd made no formal plan. Suddenly, she was overcome with a wave of anxiety—and nausea. She had to get out of the car. What the hell did she think she was doing coming here? Had she truly lost her mind?

Imogene stood in the parking lot in the surprisingly balmy air of Rochester, the sun setting and the first hint of dusk starting to win over. She stayed there for a while, leaning against her father's black Cadillac, now gleaming in the final rays of the sun. A photographer she once dated called the late day sunshine "sweet light" as it gave everything a warm glow, saturating all the colors. He'd been right; it was nice.

Im peeked in at her mother, sitting patiently in the passenger seat, looking perfectly content, Marvin asleep on her lap. Her unquestioning faith and trust in Im was unwavering and total—she never much felt the need to ask her daughter what was happening or where they were going. Now on this trip of potential doom, Im couldn't help but think, *If she only knew.*

When Im finally climbed back into the car, she asked her mother if she knew where they were. They'd just driven past Mercury and her favorite skyline. She looked around and said, "No, where are we?" in her typical cheerful fashion, never concerned that about being so clueless.

Because she couldn't resist, Imogene asked her to guess. Her mother took another look around, and after a few moments considering her surroundings, she answered, "Rochester?"

This made Im smile. "Yes, Ma, we're in Rochester!" and though she still felt slightly ill, she thought maybe, at least in that moment, everything might turn out all right.

CHAPTER 11

THEY MADE THEIR way out to the little motel Imogene had chosen partly for cost (very cheap), the fact that it allowed dogs (not even a fee), location (just west of the suburb of Greece where they used to live), and partly because it was out-of-the-way and family-owned. It would be perfect for keeping a low profile (her paranoia was setting in). The motel was a collection of separate little one-room cottages, all spaced apart and set away from the office and house. They could probably avoid interacting with anyone—exactly how she wanted it. Plus, the name was comforting, "Welcome Home Motel," for whatever that was worth.

Im plugged the address into her TomTom GPS, and the British sounding male voice began to instruct them on where to go. The accent made him sound smart. Still, because she'd been led astray by the gadget before, she also had the directions scribbled down on a piece of notebook paper. She wasn't a stubbornly high-tech person—sometimes the old standbys were completely fine by her.

Heading out to the Welcome Home Motel, Im was pleased that the roads were still somewhat familiar to her, even though it had always been her father driving when they were back in his hometown. A clear, breezy, comfortably cool evening, they drove with the windows down, and she thought she could smell a hint of Lake Ontario. In that moment, it felt sort of wonderful to be on this crazy adventure with her mother, back in their old stomping grounds. There was nothing wrong with visiting Rochester again—certainly nothing illegal about that, was there?

When Mr. GPS announced, "You have arrived at your destination!" they were only a handful of miles from her early childhood home on the shore of the Lake. Yet it felt like they were hundreds of miles out in the boonies and had traveled back in time. The Welcome Home Motel looked as though it hadn't been touched, remodeled or otherwise spruced up, for decades. The place seemed to say, "Been here forever and not going anywhere."

Mrs. Mussomeli inquired, "Are we staying here?"

Imogene looked at her and winced. "Yeah, Ma."

"Oh, Im, how quaint; this is so nice!"

Imogene chuckled at this. Her mother was so easy to please, truly a rare gem who could be satisfied with whatever you gave her, wherever she was. Kate Mussomeli, though sitting on a small fortune left to her by her late husband, would never put on airs. Im knew her sisters would have been appalled by the little dive she'd found, but her mother couldn't have been happier.

Mrs. Mussomeli finally shoved the Caddy door open with considerable effort. It was heavy for someone so petite. Marvin immediately bounced out and proceeded to lift his leg in an incredibly long pee. If nothing else, the little guy was apparently blessed with a large, elastic bladder. He'd obviously been holding it in for hours.

Imogene went to the white clapboard motel office, an addition to what must have been the family home—a two-story, stucco, colonial farmhouse with Adirondack-red shutters. When she opened the door to the office, a bell jingled and a man emerged through a small passage leading from the house. He was an average-built, rugged-looking guy in jeans and a T-shirt with the Rochester Red-Wings logo across it.

She recalled her father had sometimes taken them to these minor league baseball games when they'd still lived in Rochester. But, often, Im had to stay home with Maria, who was too small to go. She remembered those moments, standing at the front picture window, watching as her father and older sisters would head off to the Redwings game, Im left behind—fighting back tears—missing out, yet again.

She almost blurted out to the motel owner that she used to go to the Red Wings games as a kid, but she caught herself. She didn't want to share too much with the guy. Given her nefarious mission in Rochester, she wanted to maintain as much anonymity as possible. She knew she was probably being overly cautious, but she didn't know what was ahead. She needed to be smart—no dumb mistakes.

The home's living area was visible beyond the motel office, and she could see a small boy quietly playing with some trucks on the carpet. The owner-guy, probably in his mid-30s, was pleasant enough. Perhaps not the chatty type, he only made some harmless small talk about the weather, asked no questions about what brought them to town, and seemed unconcerned when she said she wasn't sure how long they'd stay. Perfect.

As always, when returning to the area, the Rochester/Buffalo/Syracuse area accent was at first a tad jarring. She didn't know exactly how to describe it linguistically, but she always knew it when she heard it anywhere. It was mostly the distinct pronunciation of vowels, particularly the short "a" sound, which often would sound more like a long "a" with an extra twang in it. She thought it might have been a hybrid of a Canadian accent, but she was no expert. Either way, she was glad that no one in her family spoke with the annoying accent.

They'd moved from the area early enough that none of the sisters had fully acquired it. And Joe Mussomeli had been raised in a home where English was a second language; any Rochester accent he'd have been exposed to would have been considerably watered down. Good thing. Im found the sound of it grating. Schenectady, where Kate Mussomeli had been raised, didn't have as strong an accent associated with it, at least not such a ridiculously twangy one. She was glad that her mother too had always sounded like a "normal" person.

Once Im had the key to their own little pond-side cottage, she parked the Caddy in the spot mere steps from their door. The interior of the cottage was certainly modest at best, but it seemed clean, and the no-frills aspect made no difference to her. The bedspreads on the two twin beds were the same white chenille type her grandmother used to have. The windows were framed with ruffled, polka-dot cotton curtains and equipped with the old style, white roller vinyl shades—the type which had a tendency to violently recoil if you pulled them down a bit too far. Mrs. Mussomeli ended up causing this to happen on more than one occasion. She had a thing for always letting outside light into a room, then making sure all the window coverings were pulled closed at night. But she wasn't the least bit mechanically inclined. It ended up being a minor fiasco every time she touched the shades in their little Welcome Home Motel digs. Im never could get her to remember to stop jerking the shades down too hard, only to have them fling wildly back up, with Marvin then barking incessantly at the thing until he wore himself out.

When Im first opened the door to the cottage, she turned to find her mother no longer behind her with Marvin.

Lately, with her increasing dementia, Mrs. Mussomeli tended to roam around a bit when away from home, perhaps looking for something, or maybe she thought she ought to be watching for someone coming to pick her up. It seemed to be an extension of how she'd been all along. Mr. Mussomeli used to complain that his wife was always doing this when they were out grocery shopping. She'd leave all the actual shopping to him and aimlessly wander off. He'd be furious when he couldn't find her, circling the large store, searching, perhaps for hours on end.

Mrs. Mussomeli apparently found grocery shopping tedious and couldn't care less about the whole endeavor. She was never fussy about ingredients or the particular foods her husband purchased. If he brought it, she would cook it. And she cared even less about prices and coupons, something Mr. Mussomeli had been practically religious about. Left to her own devices, she was likely to grab the first thing she'd see, usually a more expensive choice. Her husband hated this, and if she ever did do any grocery shopping without him, he'd swear when he saw the receipt. "God damn it, look what you paid for steaks!" Mr. Mussomeli would have opted for the cut that was on sale. His wife would have grabbed eight Porterhouses without even a glance at the price per pound.

Maybe it was a residual of those shopping days with her husband, but even now, the only thing that would keep her inside when they were out shopping would be cold temperatures.

Imogene imagined the Welcome Home Motel was anything but welcoming in the dead of winter. It was probably a desolate wasteland, pummeled by the wind and lake effect snow. Rochester winters were some of the most brutal on the planet. She respected the family that owned the motel for their obvious fortitude. Who knows, maybe they closed up and escaped to Florida in the winter, though that seemed unlikely. They surely couldn't have made enough money off the motel to bankroll winters in Florida. Besides, they looked to be salt-of-the-earth types and probably loved the place, frozen or not. Later, she noticed a snowmobile inside the open garage attached to the house.

After taking their things inside the cottage, Im went to find her mother and Marvin. Mrs. Mussomeli had strolled over to the motel's small fishpond and taken a spot on the little wooden bench next to a stone wishing well and arching bridge crossing over the water. It was hardly scenic and sort of rinky-dink, like a sadly lame attempt to add some flair or atmosphere. But when Im got there, her mother exclaimed, "Isn't this nice?" It made Im smile; the smallest things could make her mother happy.

Im often wondered what her mother was thinking about in these quiet, pensive moments—moments that seemed to be gradually overtaking her days. Hours of sitting in a chair, doing and saying nothing. Whenever Im would ask what she was thinking about, her mother struggled to answer, as though her thoughts were too fleeting, disintegrating before she could come up with a response. It made Im afraid. Would her mother's brain stop working altogether one day, going into a permanent state of idling, not moving and going nowhere, a mere shell of her once vibrant self?

That night at the motel, Im and her mother seemed to be the only guests booked. There was not another car in sight and all the rest of the cottages remained completely dark. The orange neon vacancy sign blinked on and off all night. It was a little spooky, but then again, Im was relieved. She wanted them to remain essentially unseen and anonymous. For Im, it was all about staying under the radar and keeping a very low profile. She was definitely not cut out for a life of crime.

Yet in spite of growing apprehension about her upcoming mission and possible brush with a felony, Im slept soundly that first night at the motel, as did her mother and Marvin. She may have even snoozed well into the morning had a rooster not begun to crow like a maniac at the crack of dawn. Abruptly roused out of a deep sleep, Im was a bit dazed and unsure of her surroundings for a few seconds. *Where am I? And is that a rooster crowing? What the heck?* She couldn't help but laugh at the absurdity.

Even so, she languished in bed trying to come up with a game plan. They'd made it all the way to Rochester; now she had to figure out a way to get into her grandmother's backroom. She didn't think she'd have even considered breaking into the main part of the house for the book—that would have been taking it too far. But this? This was only about getting into the backroom, an afterthought, a mere add-on to the house—maybe it wouldn't even be locked. Would that really count as a B&E?

She knew the answer to that question. But she *had* to do it. To at least try to find out if her father's old Darwin book was still tucked up behind the bricks of the backroom fireplace. The thing could be worth a small fortune. And wouldn't her dad have wanted her to go for it? God, who knows, she thought. He might have said, "Don't take a chance, Im; it's too risky. It might not even be worth anything." In her mind, she could still hear how he'd have said it, in his gravelly voice, probably with a chuckle, as if to say, "Yeah, it's a nice thought, but don't risk your life over it." Her dad had always been a highly rational, sensible guy.

Suddenly, there was a wet, cold nose in her face, and she realized it was Marvin. He was a pretty smart dog. He knew that his actual mistress would not likely be the one to drag herself out of bed to take him out. Mornings had become tough for her mother, and Im wondered if it had something to do with the dementia. Even Marvin seemed to realize his mistress of all those years had become unreliable and that Im was now the go-to. But she did not feel much like budging either. The long drive the day before had completely tapped her out. She felt like she needed another entire night's sleep.

She knew though that the dog had to drop doo-doo first thing in the morning. While he could hold his pee almost forever, turds were another story. If you didn't get him outside quickly, he might just let it go. She certainly didn't want to have to clean up a mess in their motel room. She threw on an over-sized sweatshirt and went out with bare legs. Who'd be up that early? Besides, they were the only ones there apart from the family who owned the place. Their residence was a good 50 yards away. She hoped her half-naked self would go unseen.

The sun was hanging at the horizon, but the morning air was chillier than she expected. Through her chattering, clenched teeth, she blurted, "Hurry up, Marvin, you idiot!" For some reason, she couldn't resist calling him a derogatory name. As loveable as he could be at times, she thought he had to be one of the worst dogs on the planet. You never knew what his deal was going to be at any point in time. He might lick you, then bite you, then lick you again. The dog clearly had a few loose screws.

Now she was starting to shiver all over and wanted to get back inside. "Be a good boy, Marv; hurry up and do your business!"

He ignored her and took his time.

Damn Marvin anyway! Then something dawned on her like a light bulb suddenly flicking on in her head. After the ten years that her mother had owned the dog, Im had just realized that even the damned dog had been given an "M" name by her mother!

Marvin finally gave it his all, and she picked up his offering with a plastic bag she'd tucked in her pocket. She tried to be a good dog owner. She had to admit, though, there were times she'd only pretend to pick up his crap when she didn't feel like carrying a bag of poo around. Yes, it was a shady thing to do, but his turds were so tiny, what did it matter? Still, she never wanted to piss off the neighbors. To make it look authentic, she might pick up a chunk of wood or a rock in the plastic bag so it wouldn't look too empty as she went on her way. She could be rotten to the core sometimes. Now she was contemplating a felony. How had she become such a person?

Imogene spent the rest of the morning staring out the cottage window, thinking, while her mother happily lounged in bed. She used to pop up at first light in her younger days as a mother and housewife. Now it seemed she was content to stay in bed all day. This, too, worried Im. She hated to imagine her mother declining to the point of being bedridden and unable to function. It was an especially frightening thought, and Im chose to push it out of her mind.

Finally, Im ventured out of the cottage to get them some coffee and Egg McMuffins. Junk food or not, she always loved McDonald's. As a teen, Imogene worked at a nearby McDonald's. It was her first real job. Her forearm still bore a sizable hash-tag-shaped scar from when the bottom of a metal French fry basket, fresh from the hot oil bin, had accidentally touched it. It was a nasty burn, and she should have had medical attention, but the incompetent manager chose to sweep it under the rug. She was only offered ice. It was a less litigious era back then. Nowadays they probably would have called the ambulance. It occurred to her later that she could have sued the deep-pockets company. Instead, she just ended up branded for life like a steer.

While on the clock at McDonald's, a worker was allowed certain items for free depending on how long a shift they were working. Under six hours, you got a cheeseburger and fries. If you were there six or more hours, you could get a Big Mac or Quarter-Pounder with a large order of fries. Somehow it became like comfort food to Im. On this day in Rochester, 500 hundred miles away from home and contemplating a felony, McDonald's was exactly what she needed.

After breakfast with her mom, Imogene resumed staring out the window of the motel. Apparently, nothing about this struck her mother as unusual, and Im was glad for this. No reason to have her worried—not that a worry one minute wouldn't be completely forgotten the next, but still. Im did try not to act ill at ease, as her mother's mood had started to often mirror her daughter's. It must have been that without a recent memory of her own to refer to, Mrs. Mussomeli wasn't sure if she should feel happy, sad, or neutral. Imogene needed to stay generally upbeat if she wanted her mom to also be content. And if Im smiled at her frequently, she would always return one, and this, too, seemed to allow her mother to feel happy.

Im thought there'd been a psychological study about the chicken or the egg question surrounding smiling. Hadn't it been discovered that smiling, the mere physical act of it, could make a person feel a bit happier? Either way Im intended to use the approach with her mother. So far, it seemed to be working.

By noon, she figured they ought to at least go somewhere. Her morning of deliberating and staring out the window hadn't accomplished a hell of a lot. Visiting her dad's grave had been one part of the white lie to her sisters, which was actually not a lie. It would be their first stop.

Getting to Holy Sepulcher cemetery was easy. The roads leading to it had also felt very familiar for her, which was no surprise given that the family had visited the place at least twice a year since she was a kid. They'd always stop at her Aunt Geneva's grave first, as it would be a quicker visit, then they'd make their way to her paternal grandfather's, which was part of the Mussomeli family plot. (Aunt Geneva had been buried in a different location since it was expected that her grave would be a part of her own married family's plot, though sadly her grave ended up sitting all by itself among strangers.) Her grandmother had erected a relatively tall stone monument for the Mussomelis, which had a carving of the Virgin Mary on it. It could not have been cheap. Im always felt proud when she saw it.

Filomena's husband, Michael, Im's paternal grandfather, had died unexpectedly of a massive heart attack in his early seventies. Clearly, in light of this family history, heart failure had always been a significant risk for Imogene's father. But the by-pass surgery which her father had years before his death had lulled Im into a false sense of security. Surely, he wouldn't be suffering the same fate as his own father—he had heart surgery; he was as good as new! Michael Mussomeli's sudden death had come long before the medical community had figured out what was what with human hearts—at least this is what Im told herself. Her own father's heart, in her eyes, had been playing in an entirely new ballpark—one where cardiologists could field, fix, and prevent anything!

While it wasn't hard to find the cemetery, finding the Mussomeli family plot proved far more difficult. She had assumed that she'd just be able to follow her instincts and go right to it, but the cemetery was larger than she remembered. And the rows of stones all looked so similar to each other; she couldn't quite get her bearings. She recalled the family gravesite was somewhere close to the front of a section. But which? She could picture it, having been there so many times before, visiting her grandfather's grave, then her grandmother's. And now it was, ugh, her father's turn. She'd never really hated the cemetery before. Yes, it had always made her sad to be there, especially when visiting her grandparent's and aunt's graves, but somehow it still felt like a place where *other* people buried their fathers.

Im's searing grief was starting to rush back. She tried to tamp it down. She was on a mission now and had to keep her wits about her. Besides, she was hugely distracted by the fact that they'd been driving around in circles for an hour and could not find the right spot. She finally decided to go to the office and see if they could tell her where the plot was. The elderly caretaker in the old stone building housing the cemetery office was able to look it right up in his black, spiral notebook. Within seconds, she had a small map of the cemetery with a circle drawn around the Mussomeli plot. Problem solved. Why hadn't she thought about doing this in the first place?

It dawned on her then that she always seemed to be chasing her own tail in life, often missing the obvious path or solution. She vowed to turn a corner on this somehow. Although, breaking into the backroom of her grandmother's old house was certainly not going to be part of turning any corners. The foolhardiness of the situation was overwhelming to her. It mattered not that it was entirely of her own making. Like it or not, it felt like there was no going back now. What had she gotten them into?

Upon finding the Mussomeli plot, she saw for the first time the flat headstone placed over her father's grave, which had been installed by the cemetery and received free of charge from the military—just for the asking. Her father would have liked that deal. When she was first talking with the funeral director about "the arrangements," right after her father died, he'd asked if her father was a veteran. Still in a state a shock, at first, she'd reflexively said "no." Then she thought about it a second. "Wait, maybe, yes, I guess he was." Her father had served for a few years during World War II in Iwo Jima, but he'd almost never talked about this, and somehow she'd almost forgotten about it.

There were, in fact, some things around her parent's house that her dad had kept from the war—one of which was an old rifle, a Japanese Arisaka, which must have been seized from a captured guy. No one could remember the story of how her father had actually acquired it, and it was clearly too late to find out. She'd found it just sitting there in a corner of his den closet, where it had stood for years. It wasn't functional, but still her father had held on to it.

The funeral director told Im that her father could be buried with military honors if they found his DD2s, or discharge papers. Imogene thought this might be impossible, but she found them right away when she looked in her dad's old gray metal "strong box" stored deep in one of his desk drawers. Her dad had kept them for all those years with the family's birth certificates and other important papers. Imogene felt like a bad daughter for nearly failing to provide her father with the proper honors. But had he even known he would be entitled to this?

He'd always seemed to down play the veteran thing, maybe because he hadn't engaged in any combat. He was an engineering specialist—he'd interrupted college to enlist—shipped out to Iwo Jima to do technical work. He'd assisted with the radio proximity fuses for the artillery shells and instructed other soldiers on how to use them. He said he'd never launched one himself at any Japanese. Imogene and her sisters had been fascinated when they found the old war stuff around the house, like his old Army green helmet and scratchy wool, military-issue blanket. She remembered asking him if he ever shot anybody or was shot at. Of course he'd said no, and that was literally all Im could herself recall about his military experience. She only learned more about her father's actual role as a tech specialist after one of her cousin's told her about it at his funeral.

Apparently, Rochester had been a key place where the radio proximity fuses for grenades and artillery were developed and manufactured. The proximity fuse was considered a breakthrough that changed the course of the war; it meant the troops could be far more accurate in their attacks on the enemy. Before the fuse, distance to target had to be estimated and dialed in for detonation. With the radio transmitter fuse, detonation would be triggered as soon as the receiver on the grenade was within a certain distance of the target object. Hearing about all this had given Im the creeps. War was so brutal and scary.

The military honor guard had shown up in Rochester right on schedule for her father's funeral. They played taps (leaving the sisters sobbing); then the two soldiers carefully folded the flag, which had been draped over the coffin. Then, they presented the neat triangle to Mrs. Mussomeli in ceremonial fashion. It was an incredibly moving moment, and once Im had a bit of distance on it, she could acknowledge the beauty of it. At the time, she only felt sickening emptiness and sorrow.

Now the grave's headstone from the Army was the final piece, and she was glad it was there. Otherwise, it would have just been a blank grassy spot next to Filomena's grave. The stone monument marking the family plot listed the three names of the deceased: her grandfather, grandmother and father, with birth and death dates. There was a fourth listing, which had her mother's name, birth year and an open space for the year of her death. Seeing this gave Im a twinge.

Im and her sisters had always thought Filomena was being a bit morbid the way she had planned this all out, but now Imogene could see it was such a smart thing to do. All set up and paid for; it had certainly made things easier for them when their father died. And how nice that her grandmother had bought an extra plot for her son's wife as well.

In fact, it was Kate Mussomeli who had remembered about the plots in Holy Sepulcher Cemetery. The daughters had almost botched the whole thing, thinking at first they were supposed to find a cemetery in Dayton. Not one of them remembered about the plot back in Rochester. Then they worried that the cost of getting their father's body back there might be prohibitively expensive. But flying it back to Rochester turned out to be no big deal. Very inexpensive, the same as cargo—which had seemed wrong, really.

Once she and her mother finally found her father's grave that day, Imogene burst into tears. Her mother only sniffed quietly. Maybe it was the dementia, but she was rarely overtaken by the emotion of it. They stood there quietly for a while, Marvin barking in the car. *Darn him.* Im didn't know if dogs were allowed to walk around the graves. She thought it might be seen as disrespectful, regardless. Besides, Marvin would probably have lifted his leg on a grave or two.

Im felt a bit inadequate when she looked around and saw graves adorned with fresh wreaths and flowers. Why hadn't she thought of this? Actually, she knew why. They never brought anything to the cemetery back when her father was alive. She knew he would have thought it was just a waste to leave perfectly good flowers there to die on the graves. Still, a wreath of some kind that day would have been a nice touch.

When they got back into the Cadillac at the cemetery, parked in view of the Mussomeli monument, they sat for a long time. An observer would have thought Imogene, staring off into space, was immobilized by profound grief over her lost loved one. Weeks ago, that likely would have been the whole story. Now it was more complicated. Her mind, while populated with memories of her dead father, was also swarming with scheming thoughts about what had brought them to Rochester. Her mother only sat quietly, oblivious, seemingly dignified in her grief, crazy Chihuahua sleeping on her lap. But Im's mind began to race. *What now? What the heck now?*

CHAPTER 12

BECAUSE SHE COULDN'T yet bring herself to approach her grandmother's old house on Cordova Avenue—the object of her obsession and potential cause of her downfall (i.e. getting attacked by a thug, car-jacked, arrested for breaking and entering, jail time, life essentially over)—Imogene decided they should instead head out to the lake and drive by their old house. Amazingly, her mother could still rattle off their old address and phone number without missing a beat: "86 Lakeshore Drive, GL8-2139!"

In the old days, they used letters for the start of phone numbers to indicate the "exchange." Telephone exchanges referred to the central offices in a city, which served the particular phone lines, each representing about 10,000 numbers at a time. It would make no sense to use the letters this way now. Im chuckled thinking about how kids growing up today have no clue that the letters corresponding to the numbers on their cell phone's key pad originally had nothing to do composing vanity phone numbers like 800-getpizza or 800-fastcash or worse, 1-800-hotgirls.

Driving out to Lake Ontario, they didn't need the GPS guy—it was a straight shot out Dewey Avenue; Im easily remembered the way. The family had never come back to Rochester without driving out to the lake and the old neighborhood, just to see it again and say hello to old friends. It was a beloved family tradition. Back then, they'd be enthusiastically greeted and still feel such a connection, as if it was where they truly belonged.

The Mussomeli sisters loved the old neighborhood far more than the one in Ohio. It was a fun, exciting place with kids they knew in every house. In the time before hovering parents and cell phones, everyday had been a virtual free-for-all. Nobody needed to schedule play dates, and kids were allowed to stay out till they heard the dinner bell or the streetlights went on.

The same might have been true for the girls in Dayton had they moved to a "younger" neighborhood. At their new house, while it was in a nice, upscale location, they were lucky to see any kids roaming around at all. Not that it was awful, but it was a big change with mostly older couples who had grown kids, or none at all. Imogene remembered feeling as though the old Rochester neighborhood was literally the best place on Earth. They'd all be bouncing with anticipation as soon as they got close and spotted the drive-in theater they used to go to on Saturday nights, wearing pajamas, their friends' families parked nearby. Or the massive power plant with its tall flue-stacks and lines of poplar trees.

But when they'd gone back to see the old Rochester neighborhood on the day of their father's funeral, most of the families they'd known from before were long gone. And to Im, everything looked so much smaller and plainer than it'd been in her mind's eye.

That afternoon, Imogene was still numb from the shock of her father's sudden death only days before. Her sisters, though, were wildly excited to be back in their old neighborhood. They even had the gumption to knock on the door of their old house and announce who they were to the current owners. In all the times the Mussomeli's had been back, they'd never once done this. It was as though, without their father around to keep the lid on things, it was anything goes. Im might have gotten caught up in the excitement of this as well had it not been on that particular day—a day when she could feel nothing but sadness and pain. It wasn't that her sisters weren't suffering terribly as well. They just reacted differently; they had their husbands and children with them. They didn't feel themselves falling apart.

Still, when the lady living in their old house invited them in to take a look at the place, even Im couldn't resist. The new owners had knocked down a wall or two and remodeled, but some things were exactly the same:

the knotty pine in the basement (with the initials "M & M" still etched in the wood—the work of her two older sisters), the shiny, old-style turquoise and black tiles around the bathtub, the screened-in back porch built by their father. So many things looked smaller to her now, and she knew it was, of course, because she'd become full-sized—an adult.

The backyard, where so much had happened, had always seemed large and expansive to Im; it looked almost miniature to her that day. She remembered their big, white pet rabbit that used to have the run of the yard. Imogene had imagined Peter to be her best friend, in spite of the fact that he was prone to spraying her with his pee for no apparent reason. Her mother had said it was just what some boy bunnies do. She tried not to take it personally.

Having their own bunny as a pet turned out to be a cruel irony: the Italian man who lived behind them actually raised rabbits to eat. Mr. Nunziato could periodically be heard shooting some of them, presumably for rabbit stew or some other ghastly dish. The Mussomeli girls didn't even want to imagine. They would hear the squeals of the rabbits as he killed them, then see the bunnies hung up by their little ears on a line to dry. The horror of this cannot be overstated. It left all the girls essentially terrorized, particularly Imogene who feared that Peter might escape into the evil neighbor's yard and get slaughtered.

Looking back, perhaps the plethora of her childhood fears and anxieties had roots in this. Was it an inevitability given the constant state of vigilance she adopted early in her life trying to keep their cherished pet safe? She spent hours out in the back yard, watching, making sure Peter was okay and hadn't somehow found a hole in the fence and crawled through into the Nunziato's yard. The sisters imagined ways to somehow rid the neighborhood of the terrible bunny-killer: sneak into his house and poison his wine, booby trap a branch in the big tree over his patio to fall on his head, leave a puddle of marbles out his back door so he'd fall and break his back, or even bust into his house to steal his guns so he couldn't shoot any more rabbits. But they wouldn't have dared. The house seemed literally haunted to the sisters; they never went near it. Who knows what horrors might have lurked inside it? There was supposedly a Mrs. Nunziato as well, though no one had ever seen her. Maybe he murdered her in a rage, burying her in the cellar!

Imogene was the most deeply affected by the back-neighbor situation; she felt so sad seeing all the little rabbits there, innocently chewing on greens in their huts. She wanted to go open the doors so they could run away, but she knew Mr. Nunziato would only catch them again in the yard, and who knows what he'd do in retaliation. He knew they had a pet rabbit. She actively avoided going to the far corner of their backyard, the spot nearest the Nunziato's bunny huts. They sat just over the fence. Seeing all the rabbits' little pink eyes, knowing they could be slaughtered any day, made her stomach turn. Life seemed so terribly cruel.

After touring their former house in their old Lake Ontario neighborhood that day of her father's funeral, the others went outside to linger and chat some more. Imogene hung back. She wanted to look again at the half-story addition over the garage, which her dad had built himself. They'd needed the extra space back then for more bedrooms. She was only about four-years-old at the time, but she would sit for hours watching him work—stretching the tape measure, sawing boards, hammering in all the nails that looked like straight pins in his large hands. She remembered being practically glued to him back then.

Her father must have known that she was lonely. He used to take her along whenever he went to the hardware store or to get groceries. Im thought she must have been a pest, but he never tried to get rid of her. Her four older sisters, being the perfect set of pairs, had no use for Imogene, who was the unwelcome fifth. Until Maria caught up, Im was the odd one out, naturally. Her father must have seen this.

On that day they'd buried her father, Im sat down on the top of the stairs leading to the addition he'd built, the very same steps she watched him build—a flood of memories drenching her. Being back in their old house in Rochester, where she spent the first seven years of life was wonderful and awful at the same time. The recent loss of her father began to overwhelm her. She covered her face and sobbed uncontrollably, breaking down right there—in somebody else's house. She looked up and cried out, "Daddy, where are you?"

A deluge of recollections, recent and remote, raced across her mind then that day of her father's funeral. It dawned on her that she used to sit on the same stairs with a clear view of the driveway, waiting for her father to turn in, arriving home from work in the late afternoon. In the last half year they'd lived in Rochester, he wouldn't be home until Friday nights since he'd spend the entire week in Ohio at the new job location. This was before the rest of the family made the move. Sitting there, that day of her father's funeral, Im felt like that same little girl, waiting for her father— her one true pal in the family—to come home. It was too much. She had to get out before someone found her there, literally unraveling.

Now, months later, she and her mother again drove down their old street to lay eyes on what was once their home. Im got a warm feeling just seeing it. Her mother sighed deeply and got a wistful look that spoke volumes. The deep burgundy brick, the built-in flower boxes, the two windows of the addition sitting right over the garage door like eyes above a wide, grinning mouth all seemed to say, "Yep, it's happy-go-lucky here."

Of course, Im didn't even consider stopping to get out of the car this time at their old house. She was too on edge for any such thing. Her anxiety level had started to shift into overdrive. Besides, she had to keep that low profile, not call attention to herself back in the old neighborhood— preserve her "deniability" should there be any trouble with her scheme on Cordova Avenue.

Imogene, her mother, and Marvin then slowly cruised up and down the streets that used to house all their best friends, her mother pointing excitedly, naming the families who had lived in each house. Finally, they drove down Edgemere road, which closely hugged the Lake Ontario shore. Im suddenly realized the road was perfectly named, since "mere" means "lake" in Old English. The Lake actually looked more like an ocean than a lake—infinitely huge with no end in sight in any direction.

"It so gorgeous," she marveled to her mother. "I can't believe we used to live right here." Her mother just smiled and nodded, and a glazed and dreamy look settled over her face. How could they have ever left such a place?

But Imogene wondered how she would have turned out if they hadn't moved to Ohio when she was so young. She'd heard that a number of the neighborhood kids had gotten into trouble with drugs and petty theft. Maybe it was good they left when they did; the Mussomeli girls had all basically turned out okay. *So far.*

Yet, for Im and her sisters, Rochester would probably always feel like a charmed place, sadly lost to them when they were so roundly uprooted and transplanted to Ohio. It occurred to her, now that she was about to embark on a life of crime (naturally, her mind had exaggerated this to the nth degree) that maybe she was simply getting back to her Rochester roots. Or better yet, fulfilling her Sicilian promise. She was beginning to get very dramatic the closer she came to playing it all out: brazen backroom break-in, grabbing the loot (old Darwin book), making a squeaky clean (or botched) getaway, not getting caught (or getting pinched and thrown in the slammer).

They parked at a spot along Edgemere and sat for a while on a bench overlooking the lake—Im, her mother and the dog. Being there stirred all kinds of intense feelings for Im, both good and bad, mixed together in a delectable, yet slightly toxic soup. She felt her emotions darting within, her nerves getting pulled in every direction—frayed and stretched thin, like a guitar string about to snap at any moment. Her intentions for being in Rochester at all hung over her like a storm cloud. She could feel the pressure building.

Sitting at the shore, they could hear the waves rhythmically slapping the rocks. The air was surprisingly balmy for Greece, New York that fall day. Yet the wind was brisk enough to produce a smattering of whitecaps as the swell approached the shore. It felt magnetic and alluring, even calming. But Im knew this was deceptive—one could easily be overcome by the waves and flung into the jagged rocks along the shore like a rag doll. Swimming at their neighborhood's shoreline had never been allowed.

Yet, they only had to venture a mile or so down Beach Avenue to get to Charlotte Beach, a favorite place for the whole family, full of happy memories for Im. Being there at the lakeshore again made her pine for the days when they'd lived in such a magical location, a beach nearly on their doorstep and breathtaking beauty all around them. Whenever the family returned to Rochester and drove out to the old neighborhood in Greece, Mrs. Mussomeli would always exclaim, "Oh, look, there's the Lake!" at the first sight of it through the trees. No one ever tired of seeing it.

There with her mother, quietly watching the water, Im began to feel mesmerized. Even Marvin, perched on her mother's lap, was silent, not even yapping at the birds swooping down near the shore. Im could remember being similarly awed by the lake as a little girl, how she and her sisters would look out as far as they could see, imagining they'd spotted Canada. And how happy she'd been when she'd ridden her bike down the long lakeshore hill for the first time, all by herself. Still, in that moment decades before, the vastness of the lake in front of her had left her feeling vulnerable and small. The world was so huge and full of potential, yet rife with perils, too. She was just a tiny speck of a girl; who knew what would happen to her in the future…

The longer she and her mother sat there at the lake that day, the more glued Im felt to the spot, as though everything would be okay if only she could just stop time and stay there forever.

Or at least until she could figure out what to do—

She asked her mother, "Should I try to find the book in Grandma's old backroom?"

"What book?"

Imogene didn't really expect her mother to remember. She'd asked mainly to hear herself say it again.

"You know, Ma, the old book dad had as a kid that I can't find—the one that might be really valuable. I think it could be stashed up inside that old brick fireplace in Filomena's backroom."

"Why do you think it's there?"

"Because I can't find it anywhere, and I found an old notebook of dad's that showed that's where he used to put it—like a secret hiding place. It was way back when he was a boy, and he and Tony had a little club or something. I don't know...it's probably not even there."

Her mother seemed to be considering all this—she could usually hold onto an idea for a few minutes. "Is it really that valuable?"

"Could be, Ma, like even a quarter million bucks. But it might not be worth anything. I don't know."

Imogene wondered how many more times they'd have this same conversation, as if it was for the very first time.

"Well, if it's that valuable, you should go get it!" Her mother chirped.

Of course, this was exactly what Im wanted to hear. And suddenly she felt better, slightly emboldened, even justified. But she knew this would be short-lived. How could she have any real faith in her mother's judgement? The advice she desperately wanted was her father's. He always knew the right thing to do, and it usually panned out to be the best move. Her heart sank.

"Dad, please, help me, tell me what to do!" she said aloud.

Her mother looked at her and smiled sadly, shaking her head sympathetically.

"Oh, my God, Ma, I miss him so much!"

Without a word, Mrs. Mussomeli put her arm around Im's shoulders and gently held her. Im knew she'd probably already forgotten about the book and her daughter's dilemma. Still, it felt nice to be soothed by her mother.

Eventually, the sun started to go down, and Im realized they hadn't eaten since their Egg McMuffin breakfast. No wonder she was feeling so low. Maybe food was the answer. She scolded herself for having let her mother go so long without a meal. What kind of person had she become, neglecting her own mother?

She decided they should try to find the old "Hot House" where the family used to go on those rare occasions when they would go out to eat.

It might have been true for most large families, but they almost never went out to restaurants. This was also pretty much doctrine for Italian families. Few eateries would give you the massive amounts of pasta, cooked the perfect al dente, along with a mound of authentic Italian sausages and meatballs like you could make at home.

The Hot House restaurant was only about a quarter mile down the road, and a block in from the shore. It turned out to be virtually unchanged from the old days, same rustic wooden tables and benches, same strung patio lights, same menu. The only new thing was a big neon sign that read, "The Original Hot House, Greece, New York, est. 1935, third-generation family-owned." It had bright orange flames along the bottom, kissing the letters. She remembered as a kid insisting on a plain hamburger, nothing on it but ketchup. Now she and her mother both got juicy Italian sausages smothered with peppers and onions. She got Marvin a plain hot dog, no bun. She felt bad giving the dog people food, but she knew he had to be starving.

With food in her stomach, Imogene began to feel slightly rejuvenated and figured what she needed was a good night's sleep. She'd deal with the Cordova Avenue question in the morning. Right, she'd think about it tomorrow—tomorrow was another day!

CHAPTER 13

WHEN THEY ARRIVED back at the Welcome Home Motel, there was another car parked in front of the cottage right next door to theirs, and Imogene cursed the motel owner for not spacing the guests out a bit more. They certainly didn't have to be right next to each other, did they? She was not in the mood for chitchat or hobnobbing. She made sure that they exited the car quickly and scooted inside before their new neighbor had a chance to step out. Imogene knew that if she was going to be social at all, she should do the right thing and call her cousins who lived in town.

It would be horrifying to run into them by chance. But Rochester was a big place; she wasn't really worried about that. Besides, she was the quintessential think-on-your-feet-and-do-some-quick-white-lying sort of person. Not that she was proud of it, but she'd come to rely on this ability in her life and could slide into a harmless ruse, instantly and seamlessly. She knew this would have rendered her very untrustworthy in the eyes of many. But she rarely, if ever, got caught, and besides, for her, it was the best way to avoid unpleasantness and hurt feelings. She thought of it as social diplomacy, a valuable skill she believed more people should practice—the grease of the social machine.

Regardless, Im had decided long before she crossed into New York State that there would be no calling on old friends or relatives. It was all she could do to make pleasantries with strangers; she certainly wasn't up for any real socializing. All she wanted was to get into her grandmother's old backroom and get the hell out of town. And she was starting to have major doubts about whether she could even go through with it. Just the idea of driving down Cordova Avenue to get a look at the place—okay, "case the joint"—left her practically nauseous. She realized now that the plan, which had them in and out of town within a day or so, was probably not happening. She was going to have to take her time and work up the nerve.

That night, as Imogene lay in bed, her mother and Marvin sound asleep in the next, she quietly contemplated how she might accomplish her mission, the sole reason they were 500 miles from home in a sad, little motel room. She tensed up merely thinking about the deed. As much as she hated the idea of going to the old neighborhood at night, she knew that cover of darkness was going to be crucial. The last thing she wanted was to be noticed, let alone while she was breaking into her grandmother's old house! The thought of it left her completely unnerved. Finally, she resolved that she first needed to "case" the place. Baby steps. Get a good look at what she was dealing with.

Not sure if it would be a wise move or not, but she thought they should drive over to her grandmother's old neighborhood the next day. They could park on the street by Al's Stand, go in, get some lemon ices, and take a walk down Cordova Avenue toward her grandmother's house. They could nonchalantly pass by on the sidewalk without looking too interested in the place and then make the first right turn at the end of the block, which was maybe 50 yards further. Then mosey on down that street and turn right again into the alley behind her grandmother's house, where she could get a closer look at the backroom. They would have to be quick about it so as not to attract unwanted attention, yet not so hasty as to arouse suspicion.

On second thought, she imagined that she might have to leave her mother and Marvin in the car because the three of them would likely be too much of a spectacle. Plus, she didn't know if her mother would be apt to spout random exclamations if she recognized the house or the street, drawing yet more attention. But then again, Im knew that her mother might even decide to get out of the car on her own and walk around if Im was gone too long. That would be even worse.

She had learned this the hard way a few times. Imogene would say, "Mom, stay here for a few minutes while I run in and get something. Don't get out of the car, I'll be right back!" Usually her mother stayed put, but if Im was a bit delayed, she might come back to an empty car, her mother nowhere in sight. Most of the time, Im would find her right away, more or less nearby. But there were occasions when it would take a long time. Im would dash around frantically searching for her. She'd have to run inside the places her mother might have disappeared into—possibly in search of her absent daughter, but who knows. There was often no obvious rhyme or reason to where Mrs. Mussomeli would end up.

"Have you seen a little old lady?" Im would anxiously repeat, until suddenly there she was.

She might eventually find her mother inside a store resting on a bench or in a different doctor's office waiting room, just sitting there quietly, hands crossed in her lap as if she was supposed to be there. As if she was waiting for someone to come and collect her, always appearing perfectly content.

Mrs. Mussomeli wouldn't be able to recall or explain why she'd gotten out of the car or walked out of the building, even though she had promised not to. She would always be clueless, and then sorry for having caused Im so much worry. She'd chastise herself for being "such a problem." Im had to resist getting angry with her. She knew her mother couldn't help it.

Im was beginning to better understand her mother's brain condition. Wandering was a hallmark of the disorder. Im wondered if those afflicted were responding to an internal impulse to go looking for something or someone familiar. Or that wherever they'd find themselves, in the moment, they'd always feel a bit lost. Either way, searching, i.e. wandering, would be a logical response.

Recently, her mother had flown to Chicago on her own to visit her oldest daughter and family—something she'd often done in the past without a hitch. The airline ticket had been bought long before her husband's death. She'd insisted she should go as planned. But when Imogene went to the gate with a special family escort pass to collect her, Mrs. Mussomeli was nowhere in sight. After a lengthy and increasingly panicky search, she finally turned up all the way out at the front of the terminal. Some well-intended airport employee had assumed that, because of her age, she might want assistance and put her on one of the golf-cart-like transports. Always agreeable, Mrs. Mussomeli had gone right along without a thought—how nice to ride in the cart instead of walk.

Following this, Imogene sent away for one of those medical identification bracelets. It had Im's cell phone number on it in case her mother ever got lost. Or rather, if the daughter ever lost the mother. Imogene had the bracelet engraved with the words "Memory Impaired-Call family" along with her phone number. It was a bit of a problem at first, as her mother would take the thing off when she went to bed and not put it back on again, no matter how many times Im asked her to "please leave it on all the time!" Lately, her mother had finally begun to just leave it on her wrist. But occasionally she would look at it, pull it closer, and read out loud, "Memory impaired? Call family? Me? What does that mean? I'm not memory impaired!" It was hard not to chuckle at this. When Im would say, "Yeah, Ma, your memory's not so hot anymore," she'd just shrug and say, "Yeah? Oh well, who needs it."

Finally, after considerable deliberating back and forth with herself, Im decided that the best thing to do was to drive down to Cordova Avenue in the morning and see her grandmother's old house without getting out of the car at all. She hoped this would lead her to formulate a good plan. Though part of her felt like she was kidding herself thinking that she'd ever have the guts to actually go through with it. She vowed to muster the courage—or foolhardiness.

The darned rooster woke her up again early the next morning. At least she didn't have to worry about wasting half the day sleeping. Of course, with no internet, she couldn't get online and study the Google Earth shots of her grandmother's old house, as she might have been compelled to do. Probably just as well since she already spent hours doing this back in Ohio, particularly the images of the backroom. She zoomed in and out, panned around this way and that, grabbed a magnifying glass and got her nose up close to the screen, trying to make out any possible details.

The way she looked at the Google Earth images repeatedly was clearly obsessive and irrational. They were the same ones she'd seen umpteen times. It was always exactly the same: same blue car in the alley parking area behind her grandmother's old house, same weedy grass with big bare dirt patches, same junky metal trash cans out back. There wasn't going to be anything new, but at home in Ohio, 500 miles away, she hadn't been able to stop herself from checking and rechecking.

Im had been sorry to see the Google shot of the yard, a place which had once been her grandmother's pride and joy. She hated to think how her grandmother would have felt to see it now. So run down and neglected, it was like a forgotten wasteland. In the old days, there'd been a gorgeous rose garden and a lush vegetable garden, with neat rows separated by narrow cement walking paths, which her grandfather had put in before he died. Maybe that was how they liked to do a garden in Sicily, so you wouldn't have to walk in the dirt and mud to tend to it. Hadn't Im seen something like this in the Godfather movie—that scene in Sicily where Marlon Brando's Don Corleone, coffee cup in hand, dramatically falls dead from a heart attack while walking the paths of his garden one morning? Michael Mussomeli's heart attack had happened as he was starting his car one morning, in the little garage next to their vegetable garden.

The young Mussomeli girls all loved running up and down the paths in their grandmother's garden. Sometimes they played tag, but Filomena would usually come out and put a stop to that. She didn't want anyone knocking down one of her tomato plants, trampling on the lettuce, or squishing the squash. It was amazing that all of this existed in such an urban environment. Cordova Avenue was right in the heart of the city, which is probably why it was now so downtrodden. So many inner cities had gone the same way.

The Google Earth images hadn't shown any trace of Filomena's wooden grape arbor or pear trees either. These were also marvels to the Mussomeli girls, though if they ever tried a grape off the vine or bit into a pear from the tree, they were always sorely disappointed. The grapes were very sour with tough skins and nasty, big seeds, and the pears were rock-hard. The fruit was never meant for occasional snacking. The grapes were used for making red wine and grape jelly, the pears for canning in Mason jars. The canned pears were a favorite of Imogene's, and she wished she could somehow replicate them. She often pined for her grandmother's canned pears over the years and still remembered finding the very last jar in the pantry years ago. Tart, sweet, and a little crunchy, they were heavenly. Perhaps she exaggerated the wonderfulness of the pears in her mind, but nostalgia is like that. That was perhaps the beauty of it. Still, she'd be thrilled to yet have a stash of her grandmother's canned pears.

There *was* one plus about the current dilapidated nature of what was once a vibrant Italian neighborhood. With so many places boarded up, vacant or torn down, it might be easier to sneak around there at night and get into Filomena's backroom unnoticed. In the old days, even at night, there'd be people strolling around, sitting out in their yards, lingering on their porches. Now the only people milling around would likely be thugs and criminals, which, of course, could be a whole other problem for Im and her grand plan.

One particular Google image had captured a small group of people, standing around a picnic table in the next yard over from her grandmother's old house. This was a vacant lot in-between where a house had been torn down. In fact, the razed house was the one that Im's father had been born in, with the front portion serving as the family store. At some point after the kids were grown, the Mussomeli family sold the business and bought and moved into the larger house right next to it. They had done very well for a couple of Italian immigrants, each arriving at Ellis Island with nearly nothing to their names.

The people in the Google image looked like normal working-class men and women, both white and non-white. Im had zoomed in as far as it would go, and then she spied one more thing: a big, black and white dog, which seemed to be running free in the unfenced yard. Was that a Pit Bull? What if the dog was out when she decided to make her move? And how many other dogs might there be around? What if people there kept vicious guard dogs because the neighborhood had gotten so dangerous?

Dogs or not, Imogene knew it was going to be touch and go at best on Cordova Avenue. Hence, the perpetual knots in her stomach that made food taste like cardboard and left her intermittently nauseous. She was glad that her mother was so completely oblivious and did not have to suffer any of that crap. Though Im knew it was all entirely of her own making, she felt like the epitome of the moth to the flame. In spite of her many anxieties and fears in childhood, as an adult, she had often been willing to push the envelope of her life when the situation called for it. Now it was all leading to this one moment of truth in Rochester, New York, a place which had always held only warm, happy memories for her.

All of that would change in an instant if things went bad. And if that happened, who knows what might transpire, not to mention that she would never again have only those lovely memories of her grandmother's house, which she truly cherished. She knew herself well enough to know that those warm feelings would forever be tainted and displaced by cold, awful ones.

Im felt compelled and repulsed at the same time, yet completely unable to turn back. Some moments she imagined the whole thing might be doable, maybe even a piece of cake. She could picture herself slipping in the window of the backroom like a cat burglar and leaping off with the loot. But quickly, she'd vacillate to the complete opposite thought and feel overwhelmed by the madness of it, wondering if it would be smarter to just cut her losses and forget the whole thing. She still had a chance to get out unscathed in any way. But then again, she knew the train had already left the station.

CHAPTER 14

THE SECOND MORNING at the Welcome Motel in Rochester, Imogene wouldn't waste any more time lollygagging around, imagining this or that or the other thing. She bit the bullet and loaded her mother and the dog into the Caddy first thing. After putting the Cordova address into the GPS, they crept slowly out of the parking lot. It was barely seven a.m.

Here goes.

Making their way from the outskirts of Greece toward downtown on Dewey Avenue, they passed Holy Sepulcher cemetery again. She decided they should go back there once more before they headed home to Ohio— that is, as long as she wasn't incarcerated. This terrifying and overly catastrophizing thought made her wince and blurt out, "Oh, my God!" to which her mother just looked at her and patted her arm reassuringly. It was her habit now any time Im appeared to be in acute distress.

Apparently, she'd become accustomed to her daughter's random surges of emotion and crazy outbursts, seemingly coming right out of the blue. Mrs. Mussomeli never asked what was wrong, apparently accepting that this was the new normal. Although she'd likely have said her daughter was perfectly happy and that nothing was amiss if anyone had inquired about it. In Kate Mussomeli's world, all cares and concerns would be inherently fleeting. Yet Kate had not always been so carefree. If nothing else, her particular dementia had created what seemed to be unparalleled bliss. For Im, this made the glass half-full, rather than half empty. Once when Im asked her mother what made her happy, she cheerfully replied, "Everything!"

As they got closer to the city and her grandmother's old neighborhood Im found a McDonald's, and they went in for another Egg McMuffin breakfast. Their recent diet wasn't going to win any prizes for nutrition, but that was the least of Imogene's worries. Besides, her mother would always devour anything her daughter put in front of her and seemed to especially enjoy the meaty fast-food fare—even though Mrs. Mussomeli still liked to see herself as a vegetarian.

Whenever Im asked her what she wanted to eat, she'd immediately proclaim with much animation, "No meat, I'm a vegetarian!" This had not been true for years, but her mother was perhaps sometimes stuck mentally in a past decade. In this case, it would have been in the 1970's when the vegetarian thing was more or less true for her. Back in those days, she went through a number of phases, one of which was a health-craze that included daily yoga and a no-meat diet. Recalling these things about her mother gave her a sad pang. Kate Mussomeli had been something of a marvel in her day. It was hard to accept what was already a steady decline.

"Tonight we'll go get some nice Italian," Im said aloud to her mother.

"Sounds good!" Mrs. Mussomeli replied brightly.

Well, maybe. Imogene still had to figure out exactly when she would implement the Cordova Avenue plan.

She and her mom hung around the McDonald's for a while drinking coffee, periodically checking on the dog in the car. There had been a day when her mother wouldn't even eat inside at a restaurant when Marvin was waiting in the car. This made traveling with the dog a challenge. Mr. Mussomeli used to curse the dog because his wife would be sitting out in the car, while he had to wolf down his lunch alone inside. Eating in the car was next to impossible because the dog would repeatedly try to snatch your food. If you attempted to stop him, he'd growl and nip at you.

Of course, it wasn't the dog's fault that Mrs. Mussomeli had been so obsessive and protective of him, essentially allowing him to call all the shots. She simply had a huge soft spot for animals, especially pathetic ones, and she tended to be overly lenient with all of them. For her, they could do no wrong. Mrs. Mussomeli would say, "What do you expect? He's a dog!" Or if the cat was scratching on the furniture, she'd say, "Leave her be; she's just trying to sharpen her nails!" And because she had a penchant for taking in stray cats, even feral ones, the family sometimes had four or five cats at a time. Just keeping up with the litter boxes had been practically a full-time job, and Mrs. Mussomeli had done it all herself. She never asked her daughters to do such chores. This had been her way, not asking for help when she thought something was her responsibility.

Now it was only Imogene who would even think about checking on the dog while they were in the McDonald's that second morning in Rochester. The reality was that most things had become out of sight, out of mind for her mother. But, even though dementia was robbing Kate Mussomeli of a lot, Imogene was determined to make her mother's life the best it could be. She knew her father would have wanted this for his wife. Using the large nest egg he'd left to put her in a facility would surely have made him turn over in his grave. Besides, Im knew if she put her mother in a place like that, she'd shrivel up into only a vague trace of herself and likely be gone within a year, or maybe worse, persist on and on in some sort of vegetative state. She was not going to let this happen to her mother. Not in a million years. It would have gone against everything her father had believed in so deeply. A person was supposed to take care of their family, especially their parents, no matter what.

Finally, around nine o'clock Im thought the morning rush-hour traffic should have died down enough for them to easily make their way to her grandmother's old neighborhood. Perhaps most of the people living around Cordova Avenue would be off to work. That's assuming most had jobs, but that might have been a stretch. All she really cared about was that the neighborhood wouldn't have too many people hanging around, peering out windows and noticing a black Cadillac with out-of-state plates lingering there.

They left the McDonald's, climbed back into the car, and drove to the corner of Cordova Avenue where the lemon ice stand was. Her grandmother's house was too far away to see it from there, but she pulled off to the side of the street and put the car in park.

"Okay, Ma. This is it. Here we go."

Her mother raised her eyebrows and smiled at her, not knowing what "it" was, but she was always game for whatever her daughter wanted to do. Im took a deep breath, exhaled, and shifted the car back into gear. They crept down the street as slowly as she thought she could get away with. Her grandmother's house looked pretty quiet. It made her sad all over again to see the place in its current state.

It was barely a shadow of what it used to be. Once a veritable show place among the modest homes in the neighborhood, there'd been well-tended flower boxes along the front picture window, carefully trimmed hedges, and rows and rows of beautiful rose bushes throughout the yard. The property was almost unrecognizable now with overgrown weeds, half-dead bushes, and random trash strewn all around. And the lawn—what was left of it—was all beaten down to dirt. Im remembered that her grandmother's lawn never even had a weed. Lush and deep green, the girls all lived to run across the soft turf in their bare feet.

Her grandmother also had always kept nice drapes in the front picture window; now there was only a venetian blind hanging crooked, half up, half down, with missing and broken panels. It looked so neglected and awful. The house seemed to say, "Definitely seen better days." But at least the house was still standing and didn't have boarded up windows like so many others on the street. Nearly half the other houses looked vacant. Some of the parked cars even had broken out windows stuffed with cardboard, along with flat or missing tires. The street was full of potholes, and the curbs and sidewalks were crumbling badly. Clearly, the city had given up on this neighborhood.

Imogene pulled the car up and idled right in front of 229 Cordova, wondering if her mother would even realize where they were.

"Hey, Ma, look," she said, pointing at the house.

Her mother appeared confused at first, then said, "Oh, are we in Rochester? Is that Filomena's house?"

The fact that she even had to ask if they were in Rochester was not a great moment, but at least she recognized the house—even in its dilapidated state.

"Hey, where's the store?" she asked suddenly.

Her mother was referring to the store that her in-laws had owned once, which had later expanded to be a full-fledged Italian bakery after they sold it to another Italian family. "The store" next door became a popular bakery and take-out pizza place and was another of the perks of visiting their Mussomeli grandmother on Cordova Avenue. The aroma of freshly baked bread had been stupefying. All the sisters would "oooh" and "aaah" excitedly as they climbed out of the station wagon, sniffing deeply to inhale the savory scent of the bakery, knowing that their grandmother would have a fresh loaf of the store's crusty Italian bread waiting for them on her kitchen table, sliced and ready to slather with soft butter.

Of course, there were no whiffs of anything good now on Cordova Avenue. Next to her grandmother's old house was only a sad-looking vacant lot, dotted with broken furniture, abandoned mattresses, and other rubbish. The contrast was shocking.

"Oh, no, it's all gone!" Im's mother exclaimed, obviously lamenting that the beloved place had been razed. Then, "That was the house where your father and I lived when we first got married, before we built the house out at the Lake... it's been torn down... oh my!"

Clearly, she had no recall of having already seen this when they drove through the old neighborhood right after her husband's funeral. It was one of the heartbreaks of her dementia. Each time she was reminded of a loss— something she'd forgotten because it had been in the relative recent past— she'd feel fresh grief all over again, as if it was the first time she was hearing it.

This happened whenever she would be reminded of how her youngest brother had died suddenly the year before. Mrs. Mussomeli would not remember that he was dead and would say, "Oh no, did Ben die? Oh no, when? How? Oh no," and then she would start to cry. This reaction usually dissipated in a few minutes, but Imogene had begun to make adjustments, censoring and avoiding certain topics. She hated to see her mother so upset, even if it was only short-lived. Fortunately (sort of), she was able to recall that her husband was gone, and they didn't have to revisit this anew all the time. For Im, going over this news again and again would have been excruciating.

They couldn't quite see her grandmother's backroom from the street in front, so Im slowly rolled on down the block, made the first right turn, then turned right again, and drove down the alley behind the house as she planned. She didn't dare stop, so she just crept very slowly, trying to take in the view from the back alley as best she could.

The empty space afforded by the vacant lot adjacent to her grandmother's old house was somewhat comforting. Less chance a neighbor would notice someone prowling around later. There were a couple of fire escapes on the side of the house that must have been installed for code reasons, which told her that the place had been chopped up into separate units. Wait, what if the backroom had been made into a little apartment? It would have been ridiculously small and incredibly cold in winter, but she wouldn't have put it past the slumlord owner to do that. Though only a rough add-on to the house, the backroom had been connected by a door to the kitchen. Who knows what it was being used for now? She hoped it was not occupied.

Breaking into a more or less unoccupied storage room felt a lot better than if it was someone's abode, not to mention the fact that she might encounter someone in there. Wanting a better look, she decided to go ahead and shift the car into park and act like she needed to check one of the tires. Once outside the car, she made a production of kicking the back tires. Then she pulled some trash out from the car, walked up to the garbage can next to the backroom, and dropped it in. She needed a quick look up close to make sure the room wasn't actually being lived in. She could see boxes and junk stacked up inside, and there were no curtains on the windows. Okay, not a living space.

She was also relieved to see the brick chimney still intact. Hopefully, the old fireplace inside would be untouched. Wasn't that possible? If no one lived in there, it could have been left alone for many years. Unless the book wasn't even still up in there. Then, of course, it didn't matter, and she would have been risking her life and liberty for absolutely nothing. Imogene pushed that thought out of her mind. She'd come this far. She had to go through with it.

She moseyed around to the other side of the backroom, acting as nonchalantly and blasé as she could. There was a window on that side of the structure facing the vacant lot with the picnic table, where she'd seen the people hanging out in the Google image. She figured if she could jimmy the window open, it might be the best possible way in. Even if the side door happened to be unlocked, going in that way seemed too conspicuous and risky. Someone inside might hear the door opening. Besides, she noticed there was an overgrown bush partially blocking the view of the side window, better for slipping inside unseen.

She also spotted a doghouse in the backyard of a home across the alley, but she didn't see a dog anywhere. And no sign of the dog at the adjacent house she'd seen in the Google Earth image either. Still, this all made her very nervous. What if there were dogs that were prone to barking at even the slightest sound? Especially at night. Dogs can have incredible ears.

As if prophetic, a dog suddenly started yapping, in the fast way a dog does when it is agitated. *Oh no.*

Im figured it was high time to get the hell out of there. She scooted back to the Caddy and hopped in, her mother and Marvin waiting. Of course, Marvin had started yipping frantically, having heard another dog barking.

"Marvin, shut up! Stop barking!"

"Don't yell at him. He's a dog! He's supposed to bark!"

"Criminy, not now, Ma! Shut the hell up, dog!"

"Don't yell at him! He's only trying to protect us!"

"AAAH! Stop it, you idiot dog!"

Mrs. Mussomeli clucked her tongue in disapproval.

Without losing another second, Im shoved the car into gear and hit the gas, Marvin still yapping wildly at the back window. She exited the end of the alley and took off down the main road, hoping that she hadn't already aroused suspicion. She was feeling almost ill with anxiety. Just that drive-by had left her heart pounding and her stomach flipping. And the barking dog! How the hell was she going to go through with her scheme?

It was only about ten a.m., but Im already felt spent. She decided to drive back to the motel and try to regroup. She could feel herself starting to unravel. On the way back, she picked up Subway for her and her mom. Tuna fish subs. Somehow this kind of sandwich always made her feel better. She remembered her mom making tuna fish sandwiches for her in their Rochester kitchen when she was little. And it's what her maternal grandmother always made for lunch when they visited Schenectady. Her tiny kitchen there with the little vintage turquoise refrigerator and mini lunch counter and stools was a favorite place for all the Mussomeli girls. Her Schenectady grandmother was long gone, and Im felt a deep ache of longing just thinking about her, but she shook it off. She had to stay focused on this day in Rochester. It was do-or-die time.

After lunch, at the little round table in their motel cottage, Im was still feeling tense and fuzzy. It was as if the stress created a sort of static in her brain, impairing her ability to stay sharp and rational. She desperately needed a nap. Her mother was always glad to lounge in bed any time of day, so they all hopped into their beds. Imogene tried hard to sleep, but her mind was racing too much. She ran through everything, rehearsing a plan for Cordova Avenue:

1. Go back at dark, but not so late that any little noise would arouse suspicion—or get a dog barking. 9:30 - 10 p.m.?

2. Dress in black clothing, take her small string, cinch backpack so she'd have somewhere to stash the book if she found it, and also her little pen light. Wear good shoes for running, just in case.

3. Park the Caddy in the gravel parking area off the back alley, so she could readily slip right back into the car and take off.

4. Next, quickly sneak up to the window, try to stay behind the bush, and see if it could be opened. If not, go around to the other side and quietly try the door, then the other window on the door side. If no dice for either, then obviously, game over.

5. Assuming she got in, use her pen light only sparingly to get oriented, then make a beeline for the little stone hearth. Reach up in there and see if she felt anything. If so, grab it, dump it in the backpack, and get out. If the window had been very difficult to come in through, consider slipping out the door instead of climbing back out. Either way, make a run for the car.

6. Get the hell out of there!

Imogene played all the different scenarios in her head over and over. She wanted to be ready so she could instantly make plan adjustments if needed. Too much time thinking might sink the whole thing. She basically spent the afternoon pondering, playing it over and over in her mind, rehearsing every move.

She wanted to put it off for another day, but she knew there was no point in procrastinating. She would also have liked to wait for a rainy night or something to decrease the chances that people would be hanging around outside, but there wasn't a hint of any rain in the forecast—only a big high pressure lingering over western New York State. Ironic, little Im would have been rejoicing, but adult Im was only thinking, where's lousy weather when you need it?

Finally, at about six that afternoon, she decided. It was on. First, she'd take her mother to dinner. Not that she expected to be able to eat a morsel. And though she felt like locking Marvin in the motel, she knew he'd probably bark incessantly the whole time; they had to take him along. She didn't want to push her luck with the motel—they weren't even charging for him.

She found a family-owned Italian restaurant right off Dewey Avenue where they could park and still keep an eye on Marvin. Her mother wouldn't get out of the car without that assurance, even though once they were inside, she forgot all about him. Dressed all in black, Imogene wondered if she looked like she was in mourning, or worse, like the would-be burglar she was about to be. But no one seemed to notice them at all. Besides what would a burglar be doing casually eating dinner with her elderly mother in a restaurant? Of course, Imogene couldn't relax at all. The food was authentic and good, but she could barely swallow a bite of the baked ziti she'd ordered. Her stomach was as tight as a drum. Fortunately, her mother contentedly ate all her Eggplant Parmesan. It was her standard order any time she ate out Italian (yes, the vegetarian choice). Im knew she was being melodramatic, but it felt somehow like the last supper.

It was only eight o'clock when they finished the meal, so she decided they could head down to Cordova Avenue and get some lemon ices at Al's. It would give her a chance to drive by the house again to see how things looked—check to see if anything was going on. Fortunately, when she got there, things looked pretty dead. There was only one compact car parked out back. She thought maybe the place wasn't even fully rented. Though, clearly, it wasn't vacant either. Imogene knew she'd have to be extremely careful and stealth as she made her attempt to find the Darwin book in the backroom. Her one and only attempt. She vowed to get out of dodge after one try.

She was feeling so tense, Im wondered if maybe she should have instead tried to contact the owner and see if he would allow her to go into the backroom, saying something like there was a family memento in there. But she'd already hashed and rehashed that idea. It would have likely backfired and killed any chance to recover the book. Why would the owner have ever been willing to allow her to go into any part of the house without any questions asked? Any contact with him at all would have also made it too risky for her to try and sneak in there to get it on her own later. And if she did find the book with him present, why would he ever let her walk off with it? He was the owner, he'd have every right to lay claim to it himself—the cat would have already been out of the bag, never to be put back in. Approaching the owner had really never been a viable option. Her cat burglar plan was the only way.

CHAPTER 15

THE LEMON ICES from Al's Stand were delicious. In spite of being a complete wreck, her palate could not resist relishing the delectable treat. The bright-white concoction had the consistency of finely-shaved, moisture-dense snow and would instantly melt on your tongue to a scrumptious, sweet liquid, gently trickling down your throat. The tangy citrus taste conjured up an avalanche of fond childhood memories and happy days gone by. She missed that simpler time, when her family was still whole, when she was only a kid without any real problems and responsibilities. When her father was alive. Like the Lemon Ice on her tongue, any remnants of innocence had melted away that day her father suddenly died.

Still, the lemon ice, light and luscious, had a bit of a calming effect on her. She turned to watch her mother eating hers. Because of Marvin, Mrs. Mussomeli had to hold the cup and spoon up high, out of his reach. But she never scolded him for lunging for it or told him to get away. Of course not.

After the Lemon Ices, Imogene drove over to the other side of the neighborhood where there was a little park. Adjacent was the Catholic Church her grandmother and lady friends would walk to for mass every Sunday morning and throughout the week—even in the snow. Her grandmother, in her fur-lined boots and long black, lamb's wool coat, would trudge there on foot. Someone in the group of women might be clothed in all back garb, mourning the loss of a family member. In those days, a woman might feel compelled to wear black for up to a year, especially if she'd been widowed. Im figured these traditions provided comfort and even facilitated the grieving process. These long-lost customs gave a time frame and structure for grief; a person just had to plow through it.

For Filomena, attending mass frequently was a mainstay of her life—whether in mourning or not. Imogene envied the rock-solid faith her grandmother had her whole life. What a comfort it would be to have that. Im wanted to go inside the church, but she figured it would likely be locked up. Besides, she didn't want to attract any attention. She was probably being too paranoid, but she wasn't going to take even the slightest chance. She also thought that if she went into the church, she might lose her nerve for what she was about to do. It wasn't exactly a mortal sin, but it certainly wasn't good behavior, and she couldn't stomach the idea of going directly from church to more or less committing a crime. Wouldn't that be practically sacrilegious?

At nine o'clock, it was mostly dark, but she thought it wasn't quite late enough. She decided to drive to the nearby McDonald's and get some coffees. Mrs. Mussomeli was always up for a cup. Imogene felt like she had too much adrenaline pumping already, but sometimes, she found a little caffeine actually helped her focus. Maybe that meant she was a little ADD. Who knows, she'd been a tad off in so many other ways, why not that too?

She got her mother a black coffee and hot cherry pie and herself a coffee latte with heaps of sugar. Her mother relished saying that her coffee had to be black. Im would tease her and say she was going to add some cream and sugar for her. Her mother would exclaim, "Then I'll pour it on your head!" The two of them always got a good laugh out of this. But there would be no joking tonight. Everything felt too serious for that.

They sat in the parking lot for a while then, drinking through the lids of their Styrofoam cups. Wanting a little encouragement, Imogene asked her mother, "So Ma, should I go try to find Dad's old book in Grandma's old backroom?"

She thought her mother would not know what she was talking about, but surprisingly, she responded instantly and with enthusiasm. "Yeah, go get it!"

"But, Ma, what if someone catches me? I could get arrested."

"Oh, what the heck, take a chance!"

Although Imogene figured her mother might say this without really thinking about it, the reply still gave her a small boost.

"Okay, Ma, I'm going to go for it."

Her mother smiled gleefully, "Good!"

At 9:30, Im started the Caddy and slowly pulled out of the lot, knowing that she was getting to a point of no return. As she got closer, she started to feel calmer. At least she was going to get it over with, one way or another.

There was a light on in the downstairs of her grandmother's old house, but it was all dark upstairs. She hoped whoever was home would be either sleeping or blaring the TV. She didn't see any sign of the neighbors or their dog out in the yard. Rounding the corner, Im slowly inched into the alley. Although she would have liked to leave the car's headlights on, she decided she better turn them off. She parked and then realized the lights were going to stay on for a bit, like they always did in. They were programmed to go off by themselves at the right moment, presumably after you had a chance to exit and get to your destination.

The Cadillac was designed so you didn't have to think. Her father had actually been involved in the engineering of many of these special automobile features. Several brass-plated wooden plaques lined a top shelf in his den, naming him as patent-holder.

Once when riding in the car with her father, Im complained when the air-conditioning fan didn't come on strong right away. It would only gradually, gently increase its intensity. At the time, she'd been feeling miserably hot, and wanting the quick blast of cold air, she blurted, "What wrong with this dumb thing!" Then her father said, "Actually, I designed it that way, to have that delay, so it wouldn't slam you in the face with stale, warm air." In fact, it *was* a nice touch. Imogene instantly regretted acting so bratty and impatient, opening her big mouth, and being critical. But how was she supposed to know he'd designed the darn thing? Of course she never said, "Oh, sorry about that, Dad." She was her young, dumb self, not appreciating her father at all.

Now she was wishing the headlights of the Caddy would blink off faster, too. Since they were automatic, she didn't even know where the on-off switch was. This was lousy planning on her part. She frantically looked for the switch and finally found the knob to click off. She hoped she'd be able to put them back on later. Since everything was automatic on the car, if you messed with one of the controls, it was sometimes hard to get things back to normal. Surely the owner's manual would have explained how everything worked. Her father used to say it was important to take time to read a car's manual. Naturally, Im had never bothered to do this.

Finally, it was time to make her move. When she slowly opened the car door, the dome light suddenly flicked on and she cursed it, quickly shutting the door. She waited a second then, to steel herself for what she was about to do. She glanced at her mother who had Marvin on her lap. Their eyes met, and she put her index finger up to her lips, signaling for her to stay quiet. Im pushed the door open again and darted out of the car.

Thankfully, the alley was deserted. She immediately dashed over on tiptoes to the backroom and quickly ducked behind the bush under the side window. Her heart was pounding out of her chest, and she realized she was holding her breath. She leaned her back up against the rough, old siding of the place, closed her eyes, and inhaled deeply. Then she flipped around, faced the wall under the window in a crouch, and reached up from below, grabbing the bottom of the wooden window frame. Some of the flaking paint chipped off, flecks getting into her eyes and mouth. She quickly rubbed at her eyes and spit wildly. The paint was probably half a century old and full of lead.

Im tried to get the old window to lift up. It wouldn't budge. She was going to need to stand up while she tried to pry it open to give her some leverage. At first, it seemed either stuck or locked, but then she felt it give slightly. With another shove, it burst open! She quickly hoisted herself up and crawled in head-first, basically rolling the rest of the way inside. She landed on top of some paint cans, tensing up as she fell in, trying to absorb the brunt of the fall to avoid making a big thump. She was mostly successful in muffling the sound, but her right side had taken a beating. She grimaced, willing herself not to make a sound.

Even so, if someone had been in the adjoining kitchen, they might have heard something as she slid in through window, so she froze, holding her breath and listening for signs of anyone stirring in the house. Silence. So far so good. She flashed her pen light for a couple seconds and saw the room was full of maintenance items, building supplies, and lots of random junk. She made out an old white porcelain toilet, too. Then she looked to her right and saw the fireplace hearth several feet away, exactly as she remembered it.

She crawled over to it, too afraid to stand up. Then she squatted on the hearth and reached her hand up into the chimney. She had to plunge through cobwebs, and who knows what else. It was gross, but she didn't even flinch. Spiders and disgusting debris were the least of her worries at that moment. She felt all around under the edge of the opening for where something could be wedged. There was indeed a little ledge, just like her father's boyhood journal had shown. But there was nothing on it. All sides. Nothing. She tried again, sticking her arms all the way in and up, her shirtsleeves getting coated with dirt and gunk.

And it hit her—like a ton of bricks: the book was not up there. It just wasn't there. *Game over*, Im thought. Her heart dropped like a stone. *Oh, my God!* Why in the world had she ever thought she would actually find the book here? She was such an idiot! *Yep, delusional.*

Then it occurred to her. Maybe the book had been up there but had eventually fallen down with the passage of time and the work of gravity. She felt around inside the fireplace hollow. There was a heap of junk and muck in there. Crumbling logs, crumpled newspapers, sticky spider webs—generally revolting gunk and crud. She forced herself to dig into the nasty rubbish pile. Then her hand hit on something solid. She had to stick her head halfway inside the fireplace to grab it. Caked with dust, the small rectangular thing was wrapped and tied up with twine. She briefly shined her pen light and could make out a faded blue-checkered pattern, just like some of the oilcloth table coverings Filomena had made.

Oh my God, this could be it, she thought. Without losing another second, she thrust the thing into her backpack and cinched it closed. She didn't want to take any more time trying to see exactly what it was. If it wasn't it, so be it. At least she tried. Now she just wanted to high tail it out of there. For a split second, she thought about trying to slip out the side door but decided against it—someone might hear the door opening. So she made her way back towards the window she came in and was about to make her escape when she heard it.

A creak of the kitchen floor—she recognized the sound instantly. Her grandmother's old floor sounded exactly the same even after all those years. And then, the door connecting the kitchen to the backroom slowly started to eek open, only a smidgen at a time, as if someone was trying to be very quiet and sneaky about it.

Imogene froze, her heart exploding out of her chest. She quickly crouched down behind a stack of boxes, trying not to make a sound. Peeking over the tops at the kitchen door as it edged open, she could feel her eyes bulging out of their sockets as she tried to see in the dark.

What happened next made it nearly impossible for her to breathe—every fiber of her was pulling tight, about to snap. Someone was creeping into the backroom! *Okay, this is it. The jig's up,* she thought. Someone had heard her in there and was coming to nab her. But... why was the person moving so stealthily?

Then, flick—the flame of a lighter illuminated a face. It looked like a young boy, a teen, maybe. Using only the glow of his lighter, he quickly moved toward the corner of the backroom, opposite where she was hiding. She could hear him rustling around for something and heard the crinkle of what sounded like a plastic bag. Next, the boy sat down on something—the old porcelain toilet!—and she heard what sounded like the opposite side window being inched up next to him. Then she saw a tiny orange glow, the tip of something burning, and she realized the boy had just lit a joint or something... *What the hell?*

The following minutes ticked by more like hours for Im. The boy—who looked to be about 13 or 14 years old from what she could tell in the dark room—sat puffing on the joint, taking deep pulls, holding the smoke in, then exhaling out the open window, like a pro. This kid had obviously been smoking dope for a while. In the cramped tiny backroom, Im felt slightly sickened by the haze. She tried to keep her breathing shallow. The last thing she needed was a second-hand smoke, contact high!

Before the boy could finish, the kitchen door suddenly blasted open and there, backlit in the doorway, was the silhouette of what appeared to be a tall, heavy set woman. Looking formidable. The mother?

What happened next would have had Imogene laughing, had she not been an intruder hiding in someone else's house. Light from the kitchen now streaming in, the sizable woman stormed into the room, arms jabbing, pushing aside anything in her path, while the kid frantically tried to stash his pot. She yelled, "Darnell, what ta' hell you doin' back up in there! I smell that pot you is smokin'! Don't you think you can hide it now. Where is it? Don't you be droppin' it out that window. You gonna set this whole place on fire! What the hell I'm gonna do with you? You is gonna be the death of me. You is. I tell you this is the last time, Darnell!"

During the rage, she was slapping Darnell on the side of the head, punctuating her every word—not hard enough to injure him, though he shrank away as though her touch was molten hot. One can imagine these as moments a misbehaving teenage boy hates: being dressed down by his mother. The kid who thinks he is so cool and invincible is utterly powerless against his scolding mother. She grabbed the baggie with the pot and said, "I'm gonna be callin' your father 'bout this to-night! Yeah, your father's gonna be hearin' 'bout this! I told him you wasn't gonna amount to nothin' just like him. An' here's the proof. Whatchu gotta say for yourself, Darnell? Huh, what? Nothin'? Yeah, you is nothin', that's for real, boy!"

The woman then proceeded to drag him out of the backroom by the ear, while he wailed, "Momma, no, I'm sorry. I wasn't doing nothin'! Ow, ow, Momma, you're hurtin' my ear!"

The kitchen door slammed behind them, and she could hear more muffled ranting as the mother was apparently banishing the boy to his room. Im breathed a soft sigh of relief. *That was close!*

She steeled herself to try again to make her getaway. She wanted to wait a bit to make sure the dust had settled, but she was seriously petrified now and feeling compelled to get out while she could. Besides, she could hear the mother yelling at the boy toward the front of the house, probably far enough away that she wouldn't hear any sounds coming from the backroom as Im tried to exit. It was time to make a break for it.

She quickly shuffled to the window she entered through and carefully climbed out, trying hard not to make any noise. But it's tricky to drop out a window without a bit of a thud. She half-landed in the shrub. She froze, straining to hear any indication she'd been detected. Silence. *Good.* Finally, she slowly eased the window shut. She was about to emerge from behind the bush to make a dash for the Caddy when she heard the woman's ranting voice again—this time loud and clear, just around the corner of the back of the house.

She screamed, "What the hell you think is gonna happen to that boy when he got a no-good father like you? When's the last time you even laid eyes on your son? And you is late with the child support again this month. Did ya lose your job again?"

The mother was obviously having a heated cell phone conversation with her son's father. She was pacing in the yard now, along the back of the house. Maybe she wanted to be out of hearing range of her son, or maybe the cell towers didn't give her a strong signal in the house. Damn the cell phone anyway. Now what was Im going to do? She was trapped yet again.

She was horrified when the woman even walked right near where she was hiding, so close Im could see she was still wearing her pink, fuzzy house slippers with cat's eye decals beaming right up at her. All Im could do was stay absolutely still, squatting there against the house, feeling more panicky by the second, listening to the woman's conversation, which was escalating to a higher and higher pitch.

Then Im heard the woman abruptly say, "Oh, hey, I'm gettin' 'nuther call—I gotta go, but I'm gonna be callin' you back. This ain't over,

Derek!" Next, a beat, and her tone became instantly cheery. "Hey, girl, whatcha y'all been up to tonight? Y'all goin' out or what?"

With this, the woman made her way back around to the side door of the house, and Im heard it open and shut. She was taking the call back inside. So she *was* trying to spare her son from overhearing the conversation with his father. At least she cared that much. Although it certainly sounded like she was making plans to head out for the evening, leaving the boy now to his own devices. It couldn't be nice growing up in such a circumstance. Absent father, barely-there mother. No wonder he's doping it up. Im wished then that everyone could have had the kind of parents she had, the advantages she was born into. Even so, look at her, breaking into a house and trying to slither off, now essentially a criminal herself!

Wasting no more time, Im popped up to get back to the Caddy, waiting patiently for her in the alley. There was a spring in her step as she began to feel elated at the thought of having done what she'd set out to do. She was too hyped up in the moment to fully grasp how close she'd just come to disaster.

All she could think about was that she was only a few seconds away from being safely back in the Caddy, driving away, and finally home free! Yes, she'd been saved by the skin of her teeth, as they say.

Then she noticed something behind her. Distinct shuffle of footsteps. *Oh no, what now?*

The steps she heard sounded light and quick; it wasn't likely the mom living in her grandmother's old house, deciding to come after her. She thought about darting quickly to the car anyway. But she held back. She didn't want to overreact and cause a scene, arouse suspicion and possibly create a bigger problem. Instead, she put her head down and tried to mind her own business: *Stay cool, almost there.*

Then only feet from the car door, she felt a tug on her backpack, now holding what she hoped was her father's old copy of Darwin's book. She spun around.

In the dim glow from the corner streetlight, she could make out a man. Skinny, white guy, with long greasy hair, pock-marked complexion, and sunken cheeks. He was wearing dingy-looking clothes, which hung off him. He looked like a total creep.

"Hey, wha's yer hurry?" he drawled.

"Um, just getting back in my car," Imogene replied, her voice catching in her throat.

She wanted to kick him and run, but she was afraid to make him angry. He looked high, probably a drug addict—maybe even a Meth head. Imogene had seen enough documentary films on methamphetamine addiction to know what someone afflicted with this condition looked like. And she knew they could be violent and desperate. She had always felt oddly compelled to watch the television programs about this extreme substance abuse. It was so shocking. The before and after pictures of these pitiful people were horrendous. The guy standing in front of her would definitely fit the bill for an after photo. Im could feel her heart beating out of her chest.

"Wait, wait, hol' up now, jus' wanna talk to ya."

She tried to ignore him and keep walking, but he maneuvered himself in front of her. She attempted to get around him.

"Hey, wha's yer problem? Ya deaf?" She didn't answer.

Then, he put himself in between her and the Caddy. When she tried to open the door, he brought his leg up and held it shut with his foot.

"Look, I'm from out of town. I got turned around, I thought this was my grandmother's house. I'm not trying to be mean. I'm… just nervous…"

The guy looked at her, and she thought for a minute he was going to let her go.

There'd been an incident in her past, which made her think this could happen. It was when she was in graduate school, driving home for Thanksgiving. Alone, in the first car she'd ever owned, she didn't have a care in the world. When she thought back about the car now, she always felt a twinge of guilt. She knew that her father had objected to her choice because it was Japanese, not an American-made car. While Mr. Mussomeli was patriotic, this had more to do with the bottom line and the fact that he worked for an American car company and held mountains of stock in it. Rarely dissuaded when she had her heart set on something, Imogene had insisted on getting the import car anyway.

It was a little blue Honda hatchback, and at the time, the Japanese companies had a lock on the small-car market. Their compact cars were better made, more reliable, just *better,* Imogene had declared. She was paying for it entirely out of her savings. Why shouldn't she get exactly the car she wanted? It was impressive that she'd amassed such a heap of cash at such a young age, but she was thrifty and a saver. Not all of the Mussomeli girls were this way... only her oldest sister had also been able to buy herself a car fresh out of college.

In the end, though not thrilled about his daughter's decision to buy the foreign car, Mr. Mussomeli nonetheless went with her to the car lot to make the purchase. He wanted his daughter to be happy. That was his real bottom line. He was in fact a master at such car negotiations and got Im a far better deal than she'd have done on her own. She was ecstatic.

So grad-school Imogene had been heading home for the holiday in her cute little blue Honda when she had to make a pit stop for gas, venturing off the highway to find a station in a small town. The area did look a bit seedy, but her gas tank was nearly empty; she was more afraid of running out of gas than anything else. Turned out, there *was* more. As she was returning to her car after making payment (this was well before the pay-at-the-pump days), a tall, scruffy-looking guy approached her. He commented on her beauty and called her darlin'. His accent suggested a fairly recent migration from the Appalachian hills. The guy began to ask her where she was headed "all by her lonesome" and wouldn't she like some company? Imogene immediately tensed up. Head down, she continued on toward her car, but suddenly the guy was right there leaning up against the driver's side door. He took a drag on his cigarette and looked her in the eye.

He said, "What's up with you? You think you're too good for me?"

Instantly, something kicked in for her. She knew she probably had only seconds. "No, not at all...you seem like a great guy... Really, it's not you... it's... see... it's me. I just have a bad personality..." The guy. gave her sort of a confused smirk at that point. Imogene decided to go with it "I'm an agoraphobic, see. I can't help it... really, you're better off without me... I'm a mess. I can't deal with anything."

He looked her in the eye then, squinting through the cigarette smoke as he exhaled. Seconds ticked by. Imogene was petrified. The place was deserted. She was a sitting duck. He seemed to be considering what she said. He likely had no idea what an agoraphobic was. But he didn't ask— probably didn't want to appear as dumb as he obviously was.

Then, just like that, the creep took one more deep pull on his cigarette, tossed it off to the side, and stood upright. He took another long look at Im, shook his head, and said, "Yeah, well, whatever," and sauntered off.

Telling the tale later, everyone thought she'd been very lucky and reprimanded her for not being more careful about where she stopped while traveling all alone. Im rarely gave it another thought. She figured she could talk her way out of anything.

Now in the alley behind her grandmother's old house in Rochester, the situation was eerily similar to that time at the gas station. She thought maybe, just maybe, she'd get lucky one more time. But then the menacing guy grabbed her ponytail and started to drag her away from the car. She let out a scream, but it was instantly muffled when he covered her mouth with his grubby hand. She began to bite him but thought better of it. What if he had AIDS or Hepatitis B or something?

It may sound cliché, but she did experience that life-flashing-before-your-eyes moment. For Im, it felt like time in the present stalled to a stop, while her mind seemed to be simultaneously everywhere and nowhere at the same time. And then she was instantly snapped right back and thought, *Okay, so this is it for me. Sad, pathetic ending to a basically sad, pathetic life.*

In the next moment, Imogene saw the Cadillac dome light flick on while her mother tried to push the car door open. Kate Mussomeli stumbled as she tried to rush out of the car to help her daughter, who she saw was being horrifyingly and violently assaulted by a thug.

Suddenly, there was a streak of honey brown as Marvin leapt past Mrs. Mussomeli and dashed over to Imogene. The dog's instincts had obviously been tripped by the brutal scene. Marvin was insanely protective and had shown himself on many occasions to be utterly fearless. True to form, he viciously attacked the guy, growling and biting at his pant legs. The guy yelled, "Fuck!" and tried to shake him off, but Marvin had a tight grip on his low-slung, baggy pant leg. He was wearing his trousers way down below his butt, as had become the fashion for a certain type of guy.

Apparently, as the story goes, this "style-trend" originated in prisons where the inmates were not allowed to have belts. When they got out, wearing pants slung-low and beltless was meant to show support for their "brothers" still on the inside, or maybe they just preferred the look or feel of it. Either way, the trend spread far beyond the prison population and had reached ridiculous extremes—case in point, the pants of the moron who was assaulting Imogene.

Then something truly amazing happened. All of the sudden, the guy's pants were down to his ankles. Naturally, the guy tripped over them and fell, essentially on his face, letting go of Imogene in the process. Marvin had brought the pants—and the guy down! At the same time, there was a "clink" on the pavement. A knife. The guy must have had it in his pocket. Marvin just kept trying to bite the guy, and then the dog even bit Im as she quickly scooped him up. Typical. Still, she could have kissed him in that moment.

She noticed the knife glint in the streetlight and on impulse, kicked it off into the weeds along the alley. She heard the guy, apparently still struggling with his tangled pants, yelling behind her now, "You fuckin' bitch! I'm gonna fuckin' kill you, you fuckin' bitch." Im stumbled off to the Caddy, her mother half in, half out of the car. She hurled the dog over the driver's seat to the back, yanked her mother in as best she could, started the engine, and stomped on the gas pedal. But her mother's passenger side door was not quite latched, and it flew open. Im hit the brakes hard, and the tires screeched.

Some lights flicked on in a house nearby, and at least one dog started barking like crazy. *Oh my God, we have to get the hell out of there!*

She screamed, "Shut the door, Ma," and somehow her mother managed to grab the handle and pull it shut. In the darkness, Im couldn't tell if the creep had gotten up and was chasing them or not. She floored it hard, squealing the tires as she made the turn out of the alley. She prayed no one had seen or heard anything. All she needed now was a police car racing up because a Good Samaritan had called 911 about a woman getting attacked in the alley.

Imogene kept driving, without even knowing what street they were on or where they were going, just mindlessly trying to put distance between them and Cordova Avenue and the guy in the back alley. Her mother was silent, staring straight ahead. Im hoped she was okay.

"Oh my God, Ma, are you alright? Did you see that creep back there? Oh my God! He had a knife!"

Her mother seemed confused, a bit dazed, and Imogene wondered if she really knew what had just happened. Probably not, which would have been for the best anyway, but her mom did look frazzled and upset. If nothing else, the sting of the terror was probably lingering. As for Marvin in the backseat, he seemed no worse for the wear. Actually, the dog was now basically the hero. She wanted to stop and give him a big hug, but she'd learned the hard way never to do this. The dog was so deranged that any direct physical affection, even from her or her mother, would invariably lead to a snarl and nip. In general, she happily kept her distance. But nuts or not, his protective instincts had saved her. For that, she had to love him.

At some point, after driving for a while without thinking of exactly where they were, she pulled into a Wendy's and asked her mother if she wanted a Frosty. She always said yes to this offer. Inside, Imogene went to use the bathroom and saw herself in the mirror. She was a hot mess. Her hair was half in, half out of her ponytail and all tangled, with bits of leaves and miscellaneous crap in it. Her face was smudged with dirt, and her clothes were covered in paint flecks and bits of cobwebs, dead bugs, and random muck. She tidied herself up as best she could, grabbed the Frosty, and joined her mother and Marvin in the car. She handed her mother the Frosty. Her face relaxed, and she seemed perfectly content, smiling as she steadily slurped spoonful after spoonful of the creamy chocolate concoction.

Imogene glanced in the back seat at Marvin lying there, obviously a little pooped after all the excitement in the alley. She felt like she needed to give Marvin something, too, considering what the dog had just done for her. She went back into the Wendy's and got a small single hamburger. After taking a few bites herself (she'd barely been able to touch her dinner earlier), she pulled off the meat and gave it to the dog. He wolfed it down eagerly, then looked at her with his huge, brown bubble eyes, asking for more. "Sorry, that's it, Buddy."

Imogene plugged the motel address into the GPS. The travel time was about 45 minutes, so her aimless driving had taken them off in the wrong direction, but she didn't care. She'd simply wanted to get far away from Cordova Avenue. She felt the lump in the backpack on the seat in between her and her mother. It felt like a book. It *had* to be the Darwin book, or at least some book. She couldn't believe she'd even retrieved something out of the backroom. Deep down, as much as she hoped to find something there, she knew it was a long shot. She was glad that the landlord was not a neat freak and that he hadn't sold the place in all those years. It was pure neglect that had allowed it to still be in there.

By the time they finally pulled into the Welcome Home Motel, it was well after midnight. Once inside their little cottage, Im put the backpack on a chair next to her bed. She wasn't ready to open it up and look at it yet. She preferred to go to sleep believing she had indeed found the "treasure."

Her mother and Marvin were fast asleep as usual soon after they climbed into bed. Her mother usually fell into slumber the instant her head hit the pillow. It was a beautiful thing. But Imogene felt so incredibly grungy, there was no way she was getting into bed without taking a long, hot shower. Fortunately, the cottage's water heater was adequate, and she'd avoided the dreaded cold shower she had sometimes encountered at budget hotels. Standing under the warm stream was heavenly. She watched as all the gunk rush down the drain. The old metal showerhead looked like it might have been original to the time when the tub would have first been installed, decades and decades before. In fact, the plumbing and tub reminded her of the kind she'd seen in Hitchcock's classic horror movie "Psycho."

Naturally, her mind flashed to the film's bloody shower scene when the woman on the lam is attacked by Norman Bates, and her blood can be seen spiraling down into the tub drain. Im was instantly spooked and threw back the shower curtain, just to make sure she was alone. She knew she was being silly, but after being attacked in the alley, she was feeling anything but secure. She realized, with Marvin's help, she just dodged a serious bullet, or more precisely, a dead-serious knife. In fact, it was a knife, mercilessly slashing again and again, that had ended the life of the woman in "Psycho."

The isolation of the motel, which had been an attraction and comfort to her at first, now left her feeling vulnerable and defenseless. She and her mother and Marvin would be toast if anybody wanted to mess with them. She checked the door lock, made sure it was chained, and said a little prayer. Not that the old chain lock would hold up to being kicked in, but it was something. She said another silent prayer thanking God for keeping her and her mother safe, and climbed into bed.

***

The next day, when the rooster woke her up for the third morning in a row, Imogene did not feel rested at all. She realized she'd only slept five hours or so. She needed more sleep, especially if she wanted to make the eight-hour drive back to Dayton. Lying in bed, she noticed that every muscle in her body felt sore and bruised, which was no surprise given what she'd been through the night before. Fortunately, her mother and Marvin had slept right through the rooster's crowing. Imogene rolled over and willed herself to fall back asleep. She knew she was completely exhausted, though her mind would not turn off. A million different thoughts raced through it, her brain probably still coursing with adrenaline.

But a few hours later, she woke to Marvin's cold nose in her face. She was relieved that in spite of the yet pumped-up state of her mind, she had somehow been able to fall back into a deep sleep. She found herself feeling restored and ready to deal with the day—the day after she'd done something either very dumb or very smart.

After quickly taking the dog out to do his morning business, she sat on the bed with her cinch backpack in her lap. Her mother was only half-awake. Part of her resisted even looking inside the pack. What if whatever was in there wasn't the Darwin book? She'd be crushed. If she waited until they got back home to look, at least during the long drive home, she'd be able to revel in having found the lost book.

Finally, she decided on a compromise; she'd unwrap it just enough to see basically what it was, then rewrap it and wait to fully examine it when they got home. Besides, weren't you supposed to be wearing white cotton gloves when you touched an old book? That's what she'd always seen them do on PBS's Antiques Roadshow.

She carefully took the bundle out of the backpack, placed it on the little round table in their room, and pulled at the twine. It was so old, it broke easily. The oilcloth had a thick film of grime on it, but the thing inside had been rolled up in layers of material. It would have been pretty well-protected for all those years in the backroom. Using the oilcloth was a brilliant choice.

As she unrolled it, the inner layers of the cloth still retained the original color, a royal blue and navy, overlapping checkered pattern on a white background. Her father would have been able to find plenty of the cloth where his mother stored it in the backroom. Filomena always had tons of extra fabric in there, leftovers, waiting for a new use. She used to make matching dresses for her six little granddaughters from her stash of material, adorable little printed shifts with a single zipper down the back. Imogene remembered a lavender, flowered one she wore day in and out. It'd been stashed in a box in the basement for many years. Where was it now? Her sisters had probably dumped it in one of their grand purges.

Finally, she peeled the layers back to reveal what was indeed a book. It had a dark green cloth cover, with gold letters on the binding that said, "On the Origin of Species—Darwin—London—John Murray." She let out a little gasp, and her hands flew up over her mouth. She gasped a few more times, shaking her head. She almost cried. The book was in great condition from what she could see with her amateur eyes. Alright, she'd seen enough. She didn't want to touch any of the pages in case it was in fact a valuable copy.

She carefully wrapped it back up in its well-worn oilcloth coat and folded a copy of yesterday's Rochester Gazette around it for padding. She stood for a moment feeling the weight of it in her hand, breathing in the moment, then stuffed it back in the backpack. She turned to her mother, wanting to share the moment, but she'd slept through the whole thing. Kate Mussomeli had become an incredibly sound sleeper, unlike when she was younger and would spring up at the slightest noise—it came with the territory as a mother of six. The dog was perched on the small of her back, his usual sleeping spot. Blinking, wide-awake, his bulgy-round-like-saucers eyes stared back at her. She couldn't help but grin at him.

"Marv, let's go home."

PART II

CHAPTER 16

DRIVING BACK TO OHIO, her mother riding shotgun, with the devil-turned-hero-dog snoozing in his favorite place—her lap—Imogene couldn't help but smile at the happy pair. Marvin was not your typical lap dog, and her mother certainly wasn't the typical "shotgun." Imogene had used the term many times (as in "I call shotgun!") when entering a car with friends or her sisters, knowing this meant, if you say it first, that you get the front passenger seat. She never thought about the meaning behind the term until some guy she was dating had taken it upon himself to explain.

The seat was called shotgun because in the old days, like in the Wild West, that person was meant to be the "shotgun" on watch and ready to shoot at anyone who happened to be threatening the stagecoach. Or, if you were in fact the bad guys, the "shotgun" would be on the lookout for the law. Imogene had to chuckle now thinking about her mother sitting shotgun the night before, in the back alley of her grandmother's old house. In a sense, the term hadn't entirely been a misnomer—only instead of a bullet, it was her crazy Chihuahua that shot out of the waiting car. The pistol of a dog had been the ultimate shotgun, saving them all from who knows what horrible fate. They'd nearly been done in by an evil low-life, sprouted up from the seedy streets of Rochester.

Imogene was still stunned by what had occurred the night before, how close they had come to disaster. And how incredible it was that she'd actually gotten into the backroom and found the treasure she'd been after. What were the chances? She couldn't get over it. The old Darwin book was still there, exactly, well, approximately, where her father must had left it so many years ago. She couldn't believe her luck.

Im used to allow herself one lottery ticket a week. A dollar for a week-long dream seemed like a good bargain. It translated into many blissful daydreams, imagining what it would be like to hit the huge jackpot. Now as she drove away from the place of her birth, heading home to the heartland of Ohio, on I-90 out of Rochester, she felt like she finally might know something about the experience of finding out you have that winning lottery ticket.

Suddenly, she felt as light as air and couldn't stop smiling. Her mother seemed to be enjoying it all as well. Yes, she was only mirroring her daughter's emotions, but that's certainly not a bad thing if the feelings were elation and glee. Whenever Imogene mentioned the incidents of the night before, which she did often in the afterglow of her good fortune, her mother would react with a look of amazement, shaking her head as if she too couldn't believe it. While her mother probably had only a fuzzy memory of the events, if that, Im hoped there was a part of her that truly understood and was genuinely sharing in her joy.

Her mother was a great companion in many ways, but being with her often left Im still feeling utterly alone. Given Mrs. Mussomeli's disappearing short-term memory, it was usually impossible to reflect on recent happenings, discuss the news of the day, or talk about a movie they'd just seen.

Recently when walking out of the cinema, Im had said, "Wow, wasn't that a good movie, Ma?"

She had a blank look on her face, and Im got a sinking feeling. Her mom replied sheepishly, "Oh, Im, what did we see again?"

It was a hard reality to accept, so Im savored those moments when her mother did seem to have some modicum of recall about things. Maybe it was only crumbs, but it was something.

The type of dementia her mother was facing could be a very cruel disease. It is known to slowly, over time, essentially rob loved ones of their afflicted family member, leaving just a hint of the person they once knew. But Im was determined to keep her mother as connected to the world as possible. Stimulation, exercise, medication—whatever it would take. She knew in her heart it was what her father would have wanted, a family member caring for his wife, not strangers. And Im knew this would be the key to preserving her mother's hold on any sort of meaningful life.

Despite Im's elated mood that morning, leaving Rochester had not been without its challenges, at least on an emotional level. At first, when checking out of the motel, the owner, only making conversation perhaps, had suddenly become chatty and asked what had brought them to town. It was an innocent question, but due to her overly-frayed nerves and paranoia about the previous evening on Cordova Avenue, Imogene felt her face turning red and her mouth going dry. The guy, who looked like the most ordinary, plaid-flannel-shirted dad on the planet, wasn't prying or being suspicious. But Im had to struggle to stay composed, telling him they'd been in town to visit some relatives, that her family used to live in Greece. It was all she could do not to start blabbering on and on as one has a tendency to do when telling white lies. Her anxiety levels were spiking. It was just her guilty conscience spooking her. Justified or not, technically, she had committed a felony.

Then, as she was mapping the way to head home, she remembered her intention of going to her father's grave at Holy Sepulcher Cemetery one more time. But the cemetery was only minutes from her grandmother's old house. The idea of getting that close to the "scene of the crime" made her feel panicked all over again. The guy in the alley had said he was going to kill her. The words still stung her. No one had ever said that to her and actually meant it. Such an awful creep, she didn't ever want to see him again.

Chances of running into the guy were miniscule, yet she sat for a while in the motel parking lot, running paranoid scenarios through her mind. What if someone had seen something the night before and happened to be near the cemetery, spotted them and called police? Or what if her alley-attacker happened to be walking the streets around there looking for her? The utter preposterousness of this line of thinking finally sunk in, and she decided it was ridiculous not to make that last stop at the cemetery. Who knows when or if they'd ever make it back there?

Imogene gulped down her anxiety and drove over there. The stop was quick and business-like—no tears, no silent contemplation—she was far too distracted by her urgent desire to get the hell out of town. They stood for a few minutes at the Mussomeli plot, and she spoke to her dad in her head. *Sorry to be so rushed, Dad, but I'm a wreck.* She imagined her dad's reply. *Stop worrying, Im. You just think too much!* She hoped he would have been okay with what she had done; he'd been a guy with high moral standards after all. Would he have been proud of her or appalled?

When she thought about herself compared to her father, she felt way below him on the integrity scale. Not that she was awful, but somehow she turned out to be a person who would occasionally bend the rules to get what she wanted. Even she had to acknowledge that she'd far outdone herself with the Cordova Avenue Caper (at some point since pulling it off, Im began referring to the incident this way—her mother always got a kick out of the sound of it).

After the cemetery, they made a beeline for the highway going west, but in her haste, Im had forgotten to plug anything into the GPS. They ended up taking some wrong turns and finding themselves in the seediest of neighborhoods—even worse than Cordova Avenue, if that was possible. At a traffic light, a guy with matted hair, a hideous scraggly beard, and a filthy, old overcoat, walked right up to their car and began thumping on the window, apparently wanting a handout. Imogene couldn't even tell for sure what he was saying because she willed herself not to even look at him—staring straight ahead, begging the light to turn green. Her mother was confused and asked Im what the guy was doing. Of course, Marvin was barking wildly, violently lunging at the window, basically going insane. Im, too, felt like she was going to snap.

After what seemed like an eternity, the light switched, and Im floored it. Her mother's eyes got big, and she said, "Im, not so fast!"

Once they'd finally found their way to route 490 out of town, Im was so unnerved, she didn't even want to stop for breakfast until there were many miles between them and Rochester. She hoped that Rochester and

Cordova Avenue wouldn't forever feel tainted to her after what had happened. Yes, it had worked out okay, maybe even great in the end, but Imogene had a way of being haunted by highly-charged, negative experiences. This had been true for her entire life, and frankly, she was sick of it. Why couldn't she just bury stuff the way it seemed so many other people could?

For example, she couldn't drive through a certain stoplight in her hometown without thinking of when she'd made a wrong left turn—only illegal because it was one minute past 4 p.m.—and had to pay a large fine for it. Or, even more ridiculous, she couldn't make a green salad without her mortification popping up about when she'd made a salad for the Homecoming couples' dinner party she'd attended with Craig. One of the boys there, while attempting to eat the pitiful, soupy thing composed of tiny bite size lettuce pieces (ever the overachiever, she'd gone overboard tearing the greens and naively added the dressing far too early at home) sarcastically quipped, "Nice salad, Im." No matter that it was decades in the past, she couldn't tear a piece of lettuce without the unpleasant memory springing up to haunt her.

As much as she wished to, Im could never prevent the unwanted thoughts. At her university job, she had a psychologist colleague who'd done research on this sort of "thought-suppression." He'd proven that the harder you tried not to think about something, the more you would end of thinking of it—like if you are told not to think about a white bear, it's practically all you will end up thinking about. This was labeled an "ironic process" because, while one part of your brain is trying not to think of the thing, another part is constantly checking to see if you are doing what you are trying to do (i.e. not thinking of the thing), which, in the process, then brings the thing right back to mind. Dumb brain.

Imogene figured she had one of the dumbest, smart brains on the planet because she was pretty awful at ever not thinking about something she wanted to forget. This had sometimes been so agonizing that she wondered if being afflicted with a memory disorder might not have its perks. It was only a fleeting thought; she certainly hoped she'd never get the memory-robbing brain disease her mother had. But still, at least her mother wasn't plagued with nagging or haunting memories as Imogene so often was.

Being able to forget emotionally charged memories was different than denial. Imogene was pretty good at using this defense, which was more of an unconscious maneuver. For some reason, those with very "dumb" yet "smart" brains were often good at denial, almost as if their brains were wired to protect them from particularly upsetting stuff. Like when she had regularly denied to herself that her father was even close to reaching the end of his life—even though he was in his eighties and had a strong family history of sudden death by way of cardiac failure. Yes, denial had always been Im's secret friend.

As they neared Buffalo on I-90 west, Imogene was actually beginning to relax and feel proud of herself for pulling off the Cordova Avenue Caper or the Backroom Heist (she enjoyed coming up with these nifty monikers). She was even starting to see the humor in the back-alley hoodlum's epically failed attempt at doing whatever he had planned to do to her. What a dumbass. Wearing pants sliding down his rear had clearly come back to bite him in the butt (pardon the pun, but that one is totally intended). It must have been a hilarious sight: wildly aggressive, nine-pound brute of a dog, attacking and pulling down the drawers of would-be assailant, who then becomes completely incapacitated by his own pants now wrapped around his ankles. Score one for humanity.

Mrs. Mussomeli never failed to find it absolutely hysterical each of the half dozen times her daughter related the story on the drive home to Ohio. Without any apparent recollection of it, Imogene could give her the play-by-play over and over, and she would always be rewarded with squeals of laughter from her mother, who for all intents and purposes, was hearing it for the first time. Dementia be damned, she never tired of getting a fresh laugh out of her mother.

Eventually, Im decided they ought to stop in Buffalo for some food. She didn't want to yet again practically starve her mother because of her own jitters and shenanigans. Though the place was famous for them, she had no interest in getting Buffalo wings, which she found to be mostly thick, deep-fried breading, greasy chicken skin, and only miniscule amounts of meat. For the longest time, probably like many other people, she thought Buffalo wings were buffalo meat, which was admittedly silly. She finally learned from a guy she'd dated, who happened to design chicken-chopping machines, that they were in fact just chicken wings named for the city of Buffalo where they had originated—Buffalo, home of the brilliant food innovation with nearly no nutritional value at all. Right, they opted to get some nice deli sandwiches instead.

The rest of the long road trip home to Ohio was more or less routine that day, save for some brief moments of panic involving another temporary disappearance of her mother. It happened at a rest stop. She'd left her mother for only a minute while she used the restroom. Her mom had been standing in the nearby grass with Marvin on his leash. But when Im returned, her mother and Marvin were nowhere in sight. She knew her mother wouldn't wander far—there was a roaring highway out there that she'd never go near—but what if someone had grabbed her? Her mother seemed so utterly vulnerable in every way since her father had died. Of course, anyone would likely be sorry if they ever tried anything funny given Marvin's penchant for protective aggression. But yet, she worried that her mother might not recognize that some person who approached her was potentially dangerous. It was very much like how a parent would worry about their child, as in, "Don't talk to strangers."

Yes, the daughter knew that she and her mother had essentially reversed roles; it was part of the terrain of dementia and AD. This had been strange for Im at first; now, she was not expecting anything different. She'd found making this adjustment in her expectations was the key to not feeling constantly disappointed and frustrated by her mother.

Having to search for her mother and Marvin at the rest-stop *was* vexing, but at least her mother was still alive, still a part of Im's life. After the sudden loss of her father, Im knew to be grateful for this.

Eventually, Imogene spotted her mom and the dog way off in the distance at the edge of the woods abutting the rest stop's grassy area. Her mother had a maddening tendency to let the dog lead, letting him take her wherever his little Chihuahua heart desired. And they could move so fast. He'd taken her well off track, as he'd done many times in the past back home. Mrs. Mussomeli had even once been picked up and returned home by a concerned neighbor, who had recognized her as she was walking along the road with Marvin, a half mile away from home. If Imogene ever scolded her mother for not controlling the dog on these occasions, she'd just say, "I let him go wherever he wants." Mrs. Mussomeli always defended Marvin no matter what he did. Whenever Imogene yelled at the dog for barking or snapping or leaving a turd in the house, usually with the inclusion of a derogatory term like, "asinine idiot dog," her mother would immediately admonish her and say, "You leave my dog alone!" or "Don't talk to my dog like that!" It was ridiculous to Im. The dog was a complete menace, yet in her mother's eyes, he could do no wrong.

Only now, Imogene had to catch herself. Marvin had possibly saved her life. She might have to reform and refrain. This was not going to be easy, as she'd grown accustomed to blowing off a lot of steam with her verbal onslaughts toward the dog. If Im happened to be careless and do something on the don't-unless-you-want-to-get-bit list, she'd spew multiple profanities at him, revealing a potty mouth that would rival a sailor's, as they say. Her mother would be aghast. "Watch your mouth!" or "You are so bad! I didn't raise you that way!" Imogene would say, "I know, Ma. I'm rotten, but that dog is an asshole."

***

Arriving back home at her parent's house in Ohio was a wonderfully welcome relief. Imogene felt like she'd been through a war. Every muscle in her body still felt sore in spite of popping several ibuprofen tablets. She ended up sleeping for twelve hours straight. Her mother and the dog seemed equally exhausted. When she finally dragged herself out of bed the next day, she felt strangely unsettled. She realized it was because she hadn't yet even so much as touched the Darwin book since that morning in the Welcome Home Motel room, the day after she'd snatched it from Cordova Avenue.

It felt like her magical, little bundle of hope. The book had survived an eon, wrapped in its cocoon of oilcloth, tucked away in the old fireplace of Filomena's backroom, ultimately retrieved by its rightful owners in the most unlikely circumstances, and then only narrowly making it out of the clutches of a back-alley thug! When she thought about it, she got a shiver and a little anxiety pit in her stomach. The enormity of what she had done, how close she'd come to disaster, and the thought of what she might now possess left her feeling slightly dizzy. She decided she wasn't going to even touch the book again until she had found the right kind of gloves to wear. She was terrified of ruining it somehow, even though she had no idea yet if it was, in fact, a first edition, or furthermore, one of the very rare ones.

Im started rummaging through her mother's dresser drawers—her mom kept practically everything—she was bound to have a good pair of white gloves. There was a time when gloves were an essential fashion accessory. While first used for practical reasons, gloves later became an important representation of social class and style. In the modern era, they were most often worn by ladies wanting to add a touch of elegance to their evening attire. Kate Mussomeli, in her day, was actually quite the fashion plate. It was well in the past, but Im still found many remnants of this among her mother's things. She felt a stab of longing for the days when her mother was still mentally sharp and concerned with her appearance and fashion. Now Im had to prompt her mother to even get dressed for the day. In the old days, she liked to wear cute one-color outfits and carefully matched clothing. If left to her own devices now, she was apt to mix plaid with polka dots.

Imogene did find a mound of gloves in her mother's top bureau drawer, in all sorts of colors and fabrics. She decided to do a quick Google check to see exactly what kind of gloves would be best for handling an old book. Much to her surprise, she found out that, in fact, there are no kinds of gloves that are best for this! It is apparently a myth that you should wear white gloves of some type when examining an old book. Due to lack of dexterity when wearing gloves, you are more likely to tear a page and do more damage than good. And besides, if you have clean, dry hands, they are probably cleaner than gloves anyway. So maybe the guys on Antiques Roadshow were just wearing white gloves for dramatic effect!

Given this new information, Imogene realized there was nothing stopping her from going ahead and looking inside the Darwin book. Why did she still feel so hesitant and nervous then? She knew she was simply putting off that moment of truth when she'd find out if she had gone to all that trouble, risking her life and liberty, for an ordinary, nothing special copy of Darwin's "Origin of Species" worth maybe ten bucks on Ebay. That would obviously be a bummer, and she was not feeling ready for this possible reality and subsequent letdown. It was sort of like how she would be with a lottery ticket. She might hold off on checking her numbers until well after the newspaper had arrived, just so she could temporarily maintain the fantasy that hers was in fact that 100 million dollar winning ticket. In this case, the possible value of the book wasn't quite on par with that, but she figured it was probably the closest she would ever come to hitting a jackpot.

CHAPTER 17

IT WAS EARLY EVENING before Im finished the returning-home-from-a-road-trip routine. She'd unpacked their bags, done some laundry, gone through the accumulated mail and newspapers, went to the grocery store, took a long walk with her mother and the dog, and made a light supper—hotdogs and baked beans—one of Mrs. Mussomeli's favorite meals. Marvin got his regular food; the special people-food diet was over, regardless of his heroism.

Im also dutifully informed the sisters that they had made it home from Rochester, safe and sound, by putting in a call to Maria. This meant the rest of the sisters would know this, too, within the hour. If you've told one sister, you've told them all. But Im felt guilty, fudging nearly everything about the trip. "Yeah, we just relaxed, drove through the old neighborhood, spent time out at the Lake, ate at the Hot House, got Lemon Ices, visited Holy Sepulcher a couple times." Yada, yada, yada.

Im ended up having to make an excuse and cut the call short when Maria started asking more questions. "Did you go down to Cordova Avenue?" "Did you see the cousins?"

Naturally, Maria would ask these things, but Im couldn't bear to make up extra details about the trip, basically lying even more than she'd already done. In fact, she wanted to spill the beans and tell Maria all about what had happened, how she'd found their dad's old book, how crazy it all was. It would have been nice to share it. But she vowed to keep it all to herself. It was the only way. Her sisters might get upset at what she'd done, the risk she'd taken, the danger she'd put both herself and their mother in. For all that, they might even scoff at whether the book had even been worth all the trouble, saying something about how she was always collecting and holding onto worthless junk. Im didn't want to hear any of this. Besides, they could end up being right. That would stink. She hadn't even inspected the book yet. Who knows, it might not be anything special at all. Finally, it was time…

Im completely cleared her parent's dining room table, one of the first items of furniture they'd purchased once they'd moved into their brand-new house in Dayton. It was now a vintage colonial-style dining set made of cherry wood with spindle barrel back chairs and a brightly, polished cherry top. Mr. Mussomeli had made an extra leaf for it to better accommodate extended family dinners when out-of-towners had made the trek to Ohio. He'd sit at the head of the table, looking incredibly happy to have a full contingent, lording over a spread of antipasto, ahead of the Italian feast: "Mangia! Mangia!" he'd chant.

There was also a matching cherry hutch which had housed all kinds of miscellaneous items besides dishes: trinkets, cards, dice, old postcards, matchboxes, costume jewelry, marbles, random monopoly pieces, key chains with old keys to who knows what—you name it, it was in there. As a kid, Imogene would sit opening all the drawers and exploring the fascinating contents.

Completing the set was a tall china cabinet that had once held all of Mrs. Mussomeli's prized china, the dishes only let out for special occasions. Unfortunately, nearly all but a few were gone.

It happened when Mr. and Mrs. Mussomeli were away, traveling overseas for the first time. Upon return, they found a mountain of china pieces on the dining room floor. It looked like the aftermath of an earthquake. But there'd been no quake. One of the cabinet's top shelves had somehow collapsed, pancaking down onto the lower shelves. Most of Mrs. Mussomeli's beloved china dishes were in a heap, completely shattered. Imogene imagined how terrible it must have been to come home to such a thing. Especially because the truth was that her mom had stacked far too many dishes on the top shelf. It was essentially an accident waiting to happen, inevitable that the shelf would eventually fail under the weight.

In all frankness, it was not unusual for these sorts of mishaps to occur around the Mussomeli household. It'd always been Kate Mussomeli's domain, and she'd had a way of being haphazard. Maybe it was because she'd usually been in a hurry to get things done; as a busy mother of six active children, it was probably the only way. Or maybe she had too many other things on her mind and couldn't be bothered with mundane household details. It probably was a little of both.

On that evening, after their return from Rochester, Imogene called her mother into the dining room for the unveiling of the Darwin book, so to speak. Im wondered if her mother ever thought about the mishap with her china, if she was haunted by such things the way Imogene was. But she looked perfectly serene and content as usual. If she ever had dwelled on it, the thoughts seemed long gone, along with so much of her memory.

Her mother sat in the dining room chair, upright and expectant, though she had no clue what she was waiting for. Still, she was always a good sport, ready and willing, and unperturbed by her lack of information. In preparation, Im had laid down some newspapers on the table to catch any debris that might spew out as she unwrapped the book. It hadn't seen the light of day in many decades. Who knows what might be lurking in its folds? She had her laptop at the ready, sitting open next to her, displaying photos she'd found online of the contents page of a first edition of the book. She began to pull the fabric wrapping away.

Then, there it was.

It felt a little strange to be seeing it now plain as day, sitting right there on her parents' dining room table. The binding and cover did look like it was supposed to, with only the gold printing on the spine. It was actually in excellent condition with only a tiny bit of wear on the corners, and was still a fairly deep, emerald green color. Her heart was thumping, and her hands were trembling slightly as she gingerly opened the front cover.

"Here goes, Ma!"

Mrs. Mussomeli gave her one of her yes-isn't-this-exciting smiles, as though she knew exactly what was up.

The title page was naturally a bit yellowed around the edges, but without any tears. It read:

ON THE ORIGIN OF SPECIES BY MEANS OF NATURAL SELECTION or the PRESERVATION OF FAVOURED RACES IN THE STRUGGLE FOR LIFE. BY CHARLES DARWIN, M.A., Fellow of the Royal, Geological, Linnaean, etc. Societies; Author of 'Journal of Researches During H.M.S. Beagle's Voyage Round the World.' LONDON: JOHN MURRAY, ALBEMARLE STREET. 1859.

1859. 1859. Imogene kept reading it again and again. "Oh Mama, I think it's a first edition!" She jumped up, hugged her mother, and ran around the table, bouncing up and down like a little kid about to get ice cream. "This is so amazing. This is so amazing. This is so fucking amazing!"

"Watch your mouth, Imogene!"

Then her mother sprang up, too and danced around with her daughter. Marvin started yapping incessantly as he always did over the slightest commotion.

If it was a bona fide first edition, it would be worth at least something! Imogene knew, though, that to be rare and extremely valuable—like north of a quarter million dollars—it would also have to be one of the 1,250 books, which came out of the very first printing. And to be one of those, it would need to have the word "species" misspelled on page 20. Just having the title page say "1859" was not enough because there had been a second large "first edition" printing, which was also given the publication year of 1859, though it was run after Darwin had made some revisions and corrections to the actual first edition—namely, correcting the misspelling of the word "species."

So it was on to page 20. Imogene was over her nerves by now and wasn't about to put it off for one more second—she had to know, once and for all. A faint musty smell wafted up from the pages as she carefully turned them one by one. She was pleased to see that the pages were clean, without dirt, or worse, bugs. She'd had enough of those horrid slithery bugs that sometimes scurry out of the pages of very old books. They were so fast, you could almost never squish them before they'd disappear into a crevice. Just the thought of these tiny menaces made her gag.

Sitting there at the dining room table, back straight, feet firmly on the floor, she arrived at page 20 of the Darwin book. Slowly, she scanned down the page. She'd found reliable sources on the internet that instructed to go down to the 11th line of text on page 20, and if the word "species" is spelled "speceies" then you have an actual first edition. She realized she was holding her breath.

Then...there it was, that gorgeous, wonderful, fantastic, beautiful typo: "s-p-e-c-e-i-e-s." Imogene screamed, startling her mother who gasped and looked instantly frightened, while Marvin began to bark even more frantically than usual. "Oh. My. God." Im's eyes were like saucers as she looked at her mother, "OH. MY. GOD!" Imogene could not contain her excitement. She was way beyond being over the moon. She was soaring way off toward Mars.

Her mother kept saying, "What? What is it, Im?"

Finally, Imogene sat down at the table, the old book sitting in front of her. "Ma, this book right here, it's worth a hellava lot of dough (she couldn't resist falling into the vernacular of perhaps a Mafioso). I mean, *A*-lot. Mucho, mucho!"

Her mother's eyes got big then, too, and she said, "Oh my, how much?"

"I don't know exactly, Ma, but it could be a quarter of a million or even more. It's in great condition. Who knows!"

They both sat there for a while then in the dining room, surrounded by all the familiar furniture and objects of the room. But for Im, it was surreal. Her thoughts were racing. What to do next? How does this work? Did she need a lawyer? The more she thought about it, the more she wanted to take some time to let it all sink in, not make any moves till she had time to properly mull everything over. She didn't want to tell a single living soul about it yet. She was too paranoid for that. She didn't want to take *any* chances. This is how she always operated when she thought the stakes were very high—shut up and lay low. Very low.

It occurred to her that the Darwin book discovery called for a celebration. Why not pop a bottle of champagne to mark the momentous occasion? She went to her father's small living room bar built into the tall walnut hutch and found a bottle of champagne from her father's stash. He always kept at least a bottle or two on hand, in case there was a spontaneous need for celebration. It was sort of old school, but charming. When you had six daughters, you never knew when one might come home and announce an engagement—or better yet, a baby on the way. Learning of the news of another grandchild in the making never failed to send her parents into paroxysms of glee. Im felt a pang whenever she thought about how she herself had not brought this sort of joy to her parents—and now never would for her late father.

Im had her mother go sit out on the back patio, and she brought out two flutes and the bottle of bubbly. She made a big production of popping the cork and filling their glasses. Her mother loved it. Kate Mussomeli had always been game for an impromptu celebration, legitimate reason or not. Then, mother and daughter sat quietly, watching as the sky turned a beautiful, bright salmon in the west, sipping the champagne, and thoroughly enjoying the moment. Mrs. Mussomeli always loved a good sunset. Im sat breathing in the balmy evening air.

She felt good. Really good, like she'd turned an important corner. Only weeks before, she'd been at what felt like the nadir of her life, suffocating in her grief and without even a glimmer of hope for the future. Now here she was, feeling on top of the world. Yes, she still missed her father immensely, but somehow, having found the treasure, *his* treasure, it all finally felt somewhat okay. Perhaps, *yes, perhaps,* even how it was meant to be.

Imogene began to chatter on then. She was so excited. She wished she could tell someone, but this wasn't an option. No, first she needed to find a good hiding spot for the Darwin book until she figured out what she was going to do with it. She was more or less thinking aloud, knowing that her mother would be clueless as to what she was jabbering about.

Im needed to come up with a place to stash the book where no one would ever look... just in case anyone decided to ransack the house. Of course, this was highly unlikely given their nice, safe neighborhood, but still, she wanted to be doubly sure nothing would happen to the treasure. She remembered once hearing a tip about hiding valuables in odd places where no one would ever think of looking, like tucked in Tupperware in the freezer or in a pan of kitty litter. There was actually a big tub of unused cat litter stored in the garage. It could be a good alternative to rock salt, so she'd stuck it in there after her mother's last cat had kicked the bucket, the summer before.

Im felt sort of guilty that she'd been mostly happy then not to have to put up with cleaning the smelly litter box any more. Her mother had, in the old days, been fairly obsessive about keeping her cats' multiple litter boxes free of cat poop or urine. When clumping cat litter was invented, it was an improvement, but it made the scooping process constant and never-ending. But Mrs. Mussomeli's litter-box-fastidiousness had gone by the wayside, most likely due to the budding dementia. Im had had to take it over, or it wouldn't have been done at all. Still, hers had not been a fastidious approach by a long shot. The stench she encountered was eye-watering.

In fact, Imogene had her own beloved cat once, and when the cat died, she was so devastated that she swore she'd never get another pet that would only die on her one day. She clearly wasn't ever very good at dealing with loss.

Im's cat was one she acquired surreptitiously when she was a laboratory research assistant. As a college student, she'd been working for a lab, which was using cats to study human motion sickness for NASA and the Air Force Base. Along with inventor Patterson, the 'Base' located in Dayton bears the name of the city's most famous sons, the Wright Brothers. Yep, good ole' Dayton, Ohio can lay claim to being the birthplace of flight, and it milks it every chance it gets. And why not? The Wright Brothers were clearly legendary, and Dayton doesn't have much else to brag about. In 1932, the city also had the good fortune of being selected as the site of the U. S. Air Force

Museum, which is adjacent to the Air Force Base. Ever since, both have proven to be boons and lifesavers, especially during tough economic times. Yes, Dayton owes a lot to Wilbur and Orville.

As for the Air Force and NASA research using felines, it turns out a cat's vestibular system is remarkably similar to that of humans. Imogene tried to tell herself that it was important research, put to good use to help astronauts and pilots with motion sickness in flight, but she hated what they had to do to the cats. Not only did they have to put them through motion sickness trials to induce the awful malady, ultimately measured by number of vomiting episodes, but they also did brain surgery on the cats. Each would have a tiny cannula or tube implanted in their brain and cemented in place for injecting drugs directly into their little heads.

When Im was about to graduate college, she'd fallen in love with a cat in the lab. It was a petite female with a pale gray and peach, muted calico-patterned coat and two different color eyes, which seemed to have a way of connecting directly with her soul. At least, that's what it felt like to Im. The cat had a temperament unlike any cat she'd ever known before— docile, extraordinarily friendly, instantly attaching herself to people. The cat was even happy to go out for walks on a leash. Whenever Imogene visited the "cat room," the little gray calico she named "Sylvia" would suddenly leap up and run to the door of her cage. Granted, becoming attached to a lab cat was not a very sensible thing to do, especially if you were a big softie when it came to animals. The year Im spent working there was excruciating. Looking back on it, she wondered why she ever let herself be a party to any of it.

By the end, rescuing Sylvia was one small thing she could do to assuage some of her guilt. Saving one was better than none. Certainly, co-opting the cat was against all the rules, but Im had rationalized that the cat would hardly be of any use to the lab anymore because the cannula apparatus, which had been implanted in her brain, had accidentally fallen out. The plug had started to come loose because the cat had a way of scratching at it with her foot. One day, the thing just popped out. Im thought this had to be fate: the thing falling out made it impossible to confirm its placement with a dye during brain perfusion. This was a gruesome part of the research protocol that involved replacing the cat's cerebral spinal fluid with formaldehyde through the implanted tube. Yes, horribly, the cat would have to die in the process. Imogene always refused to be a part of this sickening procedure. Still, it made her despise herself even more later for ever having been involved in the feline research at all. She winced whenever she reflected back on this time.

In the end, when it came to Sylvia, she couldn't bear leaving her there to be killed. Eventual euthanizing of every lab animal was the federal regulation, intact brain implant or not. Im was not going to let that happen to Sylvia.

In an act that might be construed as one tiny gesture to make up for all her complicity in the lab's crimes against the animal world, Im hid the cat under her coat one day and quietly walked out. She essentially stole her. She never knew if they missed the cat or not. She felt sure that some of the guys she worked with would have figured it out, but maybe they decided to look the other way. They weren't bad guys, just hard-core scientist-types. Her brash seizure of Sylvia was yet another example of Imogene's basic scofflaw tendencies. She could be unstoppable when she made up her mind to do something, especially something that would right a wrong—in which case, the rules simply did not apply.

Sylvia, the former lab cat, had a number tattooed on the inside of her ear for identification purposes, which would forever brand her as contraband in her "civilian" pet life. Visits to the veterinarian brought much anxiety for Im, fearing that the vet would see the tattoo, realize what she'd done, and contact the authorities. This never happened, but the possibility lingered in her mind.

But mostly, Imogene worried that Sylvia would have a shortened life span given all that had been done to her, but the old girl lived to be nearly 20 years old. This was practically off the charts for a cat. And up until the end, the cat was spry and nimble, such that, like with her father, Imogene had secretly nursed the completely irrational fantasy that the cat might live another decade. When Sylvia died suddenly one day (obviously of old age), Imogene was completely inconsolable for months. Her boyfriend at the time tried to be sympathetic, but finally had enough and escaped the girl who couldn't get over her 20-year-old dead lab cat.

Eventually, while sipping celebratory champagne with her mother outside on the patio that evening, after discovering her father's book was indeed the real deal, Imogene settled on a hiding place for the potentially very valuable Darwin book. She would stash it in the tub of cat litter in the corner of the garage. The 40-pound pail would be deep enough to bury her treasure in, which she planned to carefully triple wrap and seal in plastic with duct tape. No burglar would ever dig into a bin of cat litter looking for loot. It was the perfect hiding spot.

Once she'd decided on this plan, Imogene and her mother did a final toast out on the patio as the stars began to twinkle: "To the young Joe Mussomeli, Charles Darwin, the backroom, Marvin, and very baggy pants!" Though this list of things to toast didn't make sense to Mrs. Mussomeli, she gladly raised her glass. Life was finally looking up again. Imogene thought her father would have been pleased.

The next morning, Imogene woke up at the crack of dawn, anxious to take care of safely hiding the Darwin book. Until it was completely secure, she couldn't truly rest. She found a box of some of her grandmother's old fabric. Yes, the Mussomelis did not often discard things. Imogene was pleased to find a big piece of red and white paisley printed fabric. It was a material like oilcloth with a felt backing—perfect for wrapping the book. She slipped the wrapped book into a doubled plastic bag and sealed it up completely with duct tape. Then she crept out into the garage and shoved it way down into the clean cat litter. Once it was smoothed over, no one would ever imagine that there was buried treasure in there. Imogene felt very satisfied with her cunning and cleverness.

Sure, maybe she'd always been the odd-ball, the "not-so-great-outlier," but now, perhaps it was going to pay off in a very big way. Her sisters would never have accomplished such a feat as this. Imogene was floating somewhere up on cloud nine or even ten. It was such an amazing contrast to where she'd been just weeks ago, nearly unhinged by grief over her father's sudden death. The world had seemed to her then like a dreadfully dark place not worth living in. Now, at least, something good might come of it all.

***

Little did she know that what was coming was actually not going to be something good. No, Imogene Mussomeli had not finally made it out of the woods. She was, in fact, about to step into a place far darker and desolate than she'd even encountered before, leaving her desperately feeling around for an exit like a blind person. And this time, she might never find her way out.

CHAPTER 18

LATER, WITH THE DARWIN book securely hidden away, Imogene researched online what the book could be worth. She didn't plan on actually tipping her hat to any local dealers about what she had yet—who knows if they could be trusted. This was all new territory for her, but she figured the safest avenue might be to contact someone at one of the high-end auction houses via email, where she would not have to give her identity. She felt slightly shady doing this, but she'd heard people in this business can be very slick—not always the epitome of integrity.

Both Christie's and Sotheby's in New York offered free valuation estimates, but Im decided she'd contact Sotheby's since they had offices around the world, especially in London. Darwin being a Brit, she imagined the English would be highly interested in her Darwin book.

Finding out that Sotheby's required photos, she kicked herself for not realizing this before she buried the book in the kitty litter bin. It was a pain to do, but Im dug it up, took multiple photos on her digital camera, including the crucial pages, and then carefully went through the process of wrapping and hiding it again.

She uploaded the images to her computer, then tackled completing the estimate request form. They asked for name and address, but only the email field was starred as mandatory. She set up a new email account to use on Yahoo solely for this purpose. She didn't list her name or address on the Sotheby's form, and filled in the rest of the fields with "anonymous" or "prefer to leave blank." In the comments section, she apologized for doing this, but said that she had only just found the book, which had been her father's and stored away unbeknownst to anyone for years. She explained that she didn't know if she even wanted to sell it and was nervous about any attention, at least until she had consulted a lawyer.

Imogene hesitated before she hit the send button—was she really ready to start this ball rolling? Even if she didn't sell it right away, the cat was about to be let out of the bag, and this made her nervous. She took a deep breath and pushed the key; up popped the words: "Your message has been sent!" She felt better once it was done. Now she could just wait. The Sotheby's website stated it could take several weeks to hear back from them. Good, it would give her some much-needed breathing room.

It was a surprise then when she checked the Yahoo account a couple days later, expecting to find only spam, but instead found a reply from Sotheby's. *Wow, that was quick,* she thought. The response was from a George Wexler, Worldwide Chairman of Books and Manuscripts. He sounded like a big wig. Her fingers were trembling as she navigated through to read the email. What if he told her she'd been mistaken and that the book was nothing rare at all? After all, no expert had yet laid eyes on the thing, and she was relying on her own ability to understand what was what. Maybe the articles on the internet weren't necessarily accurate. (Inaccuracies on the internet, *fancy that.*) For all you know, the experts laughed at people like her who thought they knew something or had a prized thing. But she realized if that was the case, she probably would not have received a response from the apparent head honcho. Someone must have thought her situation worthy of close attention. She could feel her heart quicken with excitement. She took a deep breath and clicked to open the email.

The message from Mr. Wexler was unequivocal: The information she had provided, if it was truthful and faithful to reality, would indicate that she had a very rare first edition of Darwin's "Origin of Species," which could sell at auction for an unprecedented amount. He also said that he would very much like to inspect the book. Would she be interested in setting up a meeting? If travel would be difficult, he offered to travel to meet with her himself.

An unprecedented amount! Imogene was stunned by this development. What exactly did this mean? She didn't even know how to respond to the guy. She hadn't been expecting such a pointed and individualized reply from such a person...and so quickly. What the heck? She sat staring at her computer screen for a long while, transfixed by the email in front of her.

Finally, she decided to Google this Mr. Wexler to see if he was the real deal. Skimming through what popped up, she concluded the guy was the genuine article. With Sotheby's for over 40 years, responsible for numerous high profile, record-breaking sales, head of the books department for decades, this guy likely knew what he was taking about. He also looked approachable and nice, sporting a full head of thick, white hair and a kind, calm-looking countenance.

Standing up and dancing around a bit, Im chanted, "Yes! Yes! Yes!" pumping the air with her fists. Marvin, who had been lounging on his favorite chair nearby (the one which was nearly worn through on the seat from his manic scratching, as if he was digging there for a bone) started yapping wildly at her. Her mother then came into the room and laughed joyfully at her hijinks, accustomed to these seemingly nonsensical outbursts from her daughter.

Im told her what was going on, though she knew she'd have to repeat the explanation to her countless times. Oh well, no matter, not much was going to bring Im down this particular day. Besides, telling this over and over would only add to her glee.

Eventually, after several hours of mulling it over, Im decided to look into a safety deposit box. Yes, she had felt that the hiding place deep in a vat of kitty litter was innovative and shrewd, but she realized that a bank vault would be more secure and worth the expense. She called a nearby bank and found out that she could rent a medium-size safety deposit box for about $50 a year. That was even less than she expected. It felt like the thing to do. Why not just do it now? The sooner the better, she figured.

As for a reply to Mr. Wexler, Imogene didn't want to seem rude and not respond at all, so she sent a brief message thanking him very much for his quick response. She told him she would write again in a day or two after she had a chance to think things through. It was all too much for her. She needed to buy some time.

Since it was only mid-afternoon, Imogene decided there was still time to go rent the safety deposit box and have the book secured by the end of the day. The thought of doing this calmed her a little. She realized that having the book at home, no matter how ingeniously she'd hidden it away, must have been making her more uneasy than she realized. Yes, locking the rare book up at a bank felt like an important thing to do right away.

Imogene got dressed and ready to go—she didn't want to look shabby for this event, but she didn't want to overdo it either and look like she was trying too hard to impress; khakis and a basic white T-shirt seemed about right. Then Im went out to the garage to retrieve the book. The clean kitty litter was still pretty disgusting to handle with bare hands. So dusty and gritty, it tended to get under your nails and leave a film on your skin, so she put on a pair of gardening gloves before digging into the bin. Reaching deep down in, she had to feel around for it as she had made sure to place it close to the bottom. Her hand hit the bottom and she swiped over to grab it, then swiped across again. She wasn't feeling it.

Wait, where the hell was it? It had to be there; she must just be missing it. Suddenly, she felt the blood rushing to her face, her eyes water, and an intense sense of dread and panic creeping in. Without another thought, she turned the bin on its side and dumped the contents on the garage floor. Her mother, having heard the commotion, stood in the doorway connecting the garage to the house.

There was Imogene, a mound of cat litter in front of her on the floor. She was on her knees now, frantically sifting through the mess. She glanced up at her mother, whose expression was one of concern and puzzlement, clueless as to why her adult daughter would be thrashing around in a pile of kitty litter in the middle of their garage floor like a nut.

Finally, Imogene realized the book wasn't there. Not there! She threw the gloves down and sat back against the wall of the garage, holding her head in her hands, stunned. All she could do was repeat over and over and over again, "Oh my God, oh my God, oh my God!"

Mrs. Mussomeli, always affected by her daughter's moods, looked upset, "What happened, Im? Are you alright?"

"Oh my God, Ma, the book is gone! The book is gone! How can it be gone?"

Mrs. Mussomeli went to her daughter then, who was still on the floor holding her forehead as if in severe pain. She stood next to her silently, patting her gently on the top of her head. She didn't even ask what book. Kate Mussomeli had gotten used to not knowing the details of things and was not vexed by this. She really didn't care about such things. But she cared deeply about her daughter and was concerned that, for whatever reason, she was in great distress.

CHAPTER 19

NATURALLY, THE SUDDEN disappearance of the Darwin book was a hugely, unhappy development. It threw a major monkey wrench in Imogene's grand plan. For the rest of that afternoon and evening, she was in a daze—a fog of confusion, anger, and despair. How could the book have disappeared into thin air? She felt that's what had to have happened, yet she knew that there was only one actual way that the book was not in the bin of cat litter in the garage. Someone had taken it. But who and how? How could anyone have possibly known that she even had the rare book? She'd told no one besides the Sotheby's guy. He didn't even know her name or where she lived. Besides, even if he had somehow found her—which was virtually impossible anyway—he or anyone else would never have known precisely where to look, given how brilliantly (?) she'd hidden the book. It just didn't make any sense.

Imogene even imagined that maybe she was losing her mind; maybe she had suddenly been stricken with the same short-term memory disorder her mother had. Was that conceivable? Or maybe there never was any rare book and she dreamt the whole thing up. Could she have entered into some sort of emotional twilight zone, brought on by the trauma of her father's sudden death?

A quick check of her digital camera proved the book had certainly existed. The pictures of the Darwin book were right there. Plain as day. Okay, so she hadn't completely lost her mind. Maybe just partially? Could she have only thought she returned the book to its hiding place after snapping the photos a few days ago? That, in fact, she had put it somewhere else during a momentary fugue state? What the hell was going on?

With no other alternative, Imogene commenced a thorough search of the house, car, and garage. Her mother asked her numerous times what she was looking for. Im just said, "That book, Ma, Dad's book, the one we found in Rochester." She'd reply with an "Oh." Clearly, she did not recall, but as usual, she expressed that she cared and understood how important it was because she could see it mattered so much to her daughter. This was a tiny comfort, but Im was such a hot mess. Nothing was going to help her feel better until she found the book.

Eventually, she resigned herself to the notion that, regardless of how unlikely, somehow a person had known about the book and had known exactly where to find it. There was no other worldly explanation. She wasn't one to entertain such causes for things. No, some human had stolen her treasure, and she was going to figure out who, how, and what the hell had happened! She felt like screaming at the top of her lungs; the frustration was agonizing. She was beginning to feel nauseous.

Imogene spent the rest of the evening wringing her hands, yelling out, "Oh my God!" to no one but the air, throwing herself head-first onto the bed, and pacing up and down the hall. Her mother could only watch helplessly, her eyes filled with worry, her forehead deeply wrinkled in concern.

That night, Im tossed and turned fitfully, sleeping very little at all. She woke in the morning with a headache and a heavy sense of something being very wrong. It was the same foreboding feeling she had every morning right after her dad died, when she would wake up and feel like something was wrong without knowing exactly what for a second or two. Then she'd remember the wretched fact that her father was dead.

Now she was experiencing those same feelings of devastation all over again. The whole thing was appalling. And how could she even try to get help from the authorities? She couldn't imagine going to the police, given what she had done to get the book in Rochester. Besides, what could they possibly do? They probably wouldn't even give it the time of day. She was sure she'd come off like some hysterical, delusional women who had more than a few screws and bolts loose. They might even put her on a master list of people to watch in the community. No, she certainly didn't want to be blipping on anyone's radar. She was determined to solve this one on her own. *Somehow.*

What she needed was a long, hot shower so she could try to meet the upcoming day. Imogene always loved standing under the shower stream; it was so relaxing. Still, she'd usually resisted doing this because she felt guilty wasting that much water. Mr. Mussomeli used to fuss at his girls over their lengthy showers and the elevated water bills. And he was also always walking around the house turning off the lights that the girls had carelessly left on in unoccupied rooms. Although contrary to what is in vogue nowadays, Mr. Mussomeli wasn't doing this to help conserve energy and preserve the environment. He was basically concerned about his bottom line: how much money was senselessly getting drained off for utilities—even if it was only pennies. Living through the Great Depression had left an indelible mark on him.

But today, Imogene needed to waste water; she was a complete mess. Not that her mess was the kind soap and water could exactly help, but a nice long shower might at least be restorative. It had sometimes even led to mental clarity for her in the past. She had her share of shower epiphanies.

After a good twenty minutes, a new thought did pop into her head from somewhere in the recesses of her mind: Preston Wyles. He was their closest neighbor in terms of physical proximity, though she didn't know him well. He'd bought the little old lady Kissell's house next door to her parents' place long after Im had already left home, but he'd added his own touches. A couple of Lady Godiva statues sat on each side of the front door along with another voluptuous female statue perched over a hot tub in the backyard. The place now seemed to say, "Wild parties and bachelor-pad debauchery happen here."

Preston was at least a decade older than Im, and she'd never really given him much thought. She'd sort of wondered what kind of circles he ran in. Certainly nothing like that of her colleagues back at the University, not that she was turning up her nose. They'd actually had a number of friendly encounters, and he'd seemed alright. Their driveways sat right next to each other in such a way as to be essentially conjoined; there were plenty of opportunities to run into each other coming and going. There'd usually be greetings exchanged, which would occasionally flow into small talk—nothing consequential, mostly chats about the weather or cutting the hedges or whether a tree needed trimming.

Preston had been very nice after her dad died, though it didn't seem he and her dad had ever been especially close. What had struck Imogene most about him was his sort of swagger, for lack of a better term. He wore an ostentatious, thick, gold chain around his neck, large gold rings with tiny diamonds on each pinkie, and a massive blonde, Donald-Trump-style comb over. The desperate hair maneuver made him seem sort of pathetic. Why couldn't guys just go bald gracefully?

Preston spoke with a lazy, thick southern drawl, which Im had found slightly appealing, in spite of the rest of the package. Regardless, she mostly found him sort of too slick and a tad on the slimy side, though she hated to judge him solely on his looks. He had apparently been a mildly famous racecar driver in his day, though she'd herself never heard of him. He owned three vintage Corvettes—metallic silver, deep sable-brown and bright orange—which he kept in the large second garage he'd built on the property when he moved in. This addition crowded the space between the two homes' adjoining backyards, but even Im could see it was worth it. The cars were absolutely beautiful, in mint condition, and in all honesty, she had lusted after them.

In general, Preston struck her as one of those throwback kind of guys, looking like he'd just walked straight off a 1970's B-movie set. Not exactly her type. But Imogene could tell that he found her attractive; he'd invited her over for drinks on more than one occasion. Although she had always made an excuse, she'd never totally shut him down. He had an air of confidence and danger about him, which Im had always found appealing in a man, even though she knew this was not a good thing.

Of course, this was in keeping with the fact that she'd never been terrific at picking men, and usually fell hard for the wrong ones—in spite of herself. She was trying to chalk the horrible internet Ted episode up to her instincts having been all fouled-up, given her grief-stricken and desperate state, but Ted was a perfect example of her flawed selection skills and weakness for bad boys—even if they wore sheep's clothing.

Im had a tendency to pass up the best guys, going instead for the ones that felt more exciting or challenging. Preston would have easily fit in the latter category while in his prime, and such things never completely fade in a person. He still had something—sex appeal maybe?—though Im didn't find him especially attractive physically. He was definitely starting to show his age, and perhaps the effects of past hard living. He had a fairly hefty paunch, and his skin looked weathered and leathery. *And that comb-over.*

Preston was clearly no longer any prize, if he ever had been one. Im had found it easy to keep the upper hand and fend off any overtures he made, while still keeping him interested enough. She enjoyed the attention of men too much to slam the door in his face. He seemed kind of fun, and then there were those 'Vettes. She loved sharp, flashy cars. But she was disgusted to see that he was a smoker—cigarettes. For Im, this was an absolute deal-breaker. She thought smoking was grotesque. In fact, she was a bit of a nut about second-hand smoke and loved the fact that smoking had finally been outlawed in most public places.

What she hated particularly was to see little kids stuck in cars with parents who were smoking, with the windows shut or only barely cracked. This was truly criminal in her book. But you can't really do a thing about parents doing this to their kids. She found this out the hard way once when she saw a young woman smoking like a chimney with her little toddler daughter in the back seat, not even one open window to give the little girl some fresh air. Imogene, idiotically, followed the woman into a store parking lot and then jumped out of her car. She walked right up to the car with the smoker mom and her toddler inside and said, "You know, you really shouldn't smoke with your young daughter in the car."

As soon as she'd said it, Im knew it had been a mistake. The woman instantly started yelling and swearing at her. "Who the fuck are you? Who the fuck are you? Mind your own God damn business before I fuck you up!" The woman looked like she was about to jump out of the car and slug her. Im just slunk away feeling like a complete dumbass for thinking the trashy woman would actually listen to what she had to say and further, take heed. It was a ridiculous thing to do; she could have no impact on a situation like this, but it was just like her to try. Needless to say, Preston puffing on cigarettes pretty much put him out of the running for her—not that he was ever really in it.

After her long shower, she put on her thick, white terry-cloth robe and sat on the living room couch, thinking, trying to process it. Did Preston sneak in and take the Darwin book? Could he have heard her talking about the Darwin book? How else could he have known about it? Then it hit her. That evening, on the day after they returned from Rochester, she and her mother were sitting out on the patio, sipping champagne. Im had been basking in the glory of having pulled off the Cordova Caper, the Backroom Bust, what have you. She was speaking excitedly about it, without a thought about anyone possibly overhearing her.

What had she exactly said to her mother while they were outside that night? She remembered spouting off about the book's potential value, throwing out some astronomical figures. "Could be half a million, Ma! Or even more!" How loud had she been talking? Was Preston out that night? She had seen him tinkering around in his extra garage, which sat only yards from their covered patio. Friends told her she had a habit of talking rather loudly. She always said it was because she was Italian, so she couldn't help it. This was more or less true. She really never knew she was being obnoxiously loud until someone pointed it out to her. And then she always felt like a shushed kid—a dunce.

Now she wondered, could her stupid big mouth have allowed Preston to eavesdrop without her even knowing it? She tried to think back. He could have been there in his garage, out of sight, yet listening to every word. A hedge served as a barrier, giving a sense of privacy, but it was an illusion. It was all very close back there. If Preston had noticed her talking in such an animated, excited way, he might have been curious. It wouldn't have been difficult to hear everything, including when she told her mother all about her ingenious plan to hide the book in the big bin of kitty litter in the garage, where *no* burglar would ever dream of looking. Im had been so proud of herself for coming up with the plan and had said it out loud more than once, needing to repeat herself as usual when talking with her mother. *How could I have been so careless? Such an idiot,* she thought.

Had she even checked to make sure that the outside door going into their garage was locked? It even faced his house. She'd have never seen him creep in there, especially if it was dark. Or if he happened to be watching her leave—they did go to the grocery store the other night—he'd have had free rein. Wasn't that side garage door always locked though? It was supposed to be, but it could have easily been left unlocked by the last person to use it.

Imogene realized that she'd been lulled into a false sense of security by what she considered to be a virtually undetectable, uncrackable hiding place. She hadn't even worried that much about prowlers in there—they'd never have thought to dig in the cat litter. That is, unless the thief had heard it straight from the damned horse's own loud mouth. Im knew she was making a huge assumption, and yet there wasn't an alternative explanation that was even in the realm of possibility. It had to have been Preston.

She decided to go out and check the side door to the garage. She tried to appear casual as she went over and checked the doorknob. It sprung right open. It wasn't locked. *Shit!*

Imogene spent the rest of the morning in a state: rubbing her forehead, covering her face in her hands, yelping out as if in pain, and convulsing in exacerbation. She was seething. The book belonged to her family! She'd been so thrilled that she found the lost treasure. She risked everything to get it back. She imagined her dad smiling down on her, so proud of her. How could that slime ball next door have been so evil? And what was he going to do with it? When exactly would he have taken it? It could have been anytime in the last few days. If he'd been careful, they'd never have heard a thing. And because Marvin practically barked at a pin-drop, they'd long ago stopped reacting to his crying wolf.

Now she began to feel a new sense of dread. What if he'd already taken it somewhere else? She imagined he would be thinking of how to secure it. Was he planning to cash in on it right away? He probably could pull that off on the black market. No one would ask any questions. Im would never know what happened to it. And even if it eventually showed up in the news, how could she ever lay claim to it? She couldn't. Simple as that.

Imogene wanted to just barge over there and demand he return her book, but of course, he would only deny having it. Then he'd know she was onto him and surely run off to stash it in a safety deposit box or who knows where. She thought he had a lake house somewhere. She'd never be able to track it down if it left his home next door. It dawned on her that if she had any chance of getting the thing back, she was going to have to act fast—as soon as humanly possible!

Playing it out in her mind, Imogene figured he may have only grabbed the book a day or so ago. Preston owned and ran his own business, of some sort. She thought it might have been construction, but she wasn't sure and had never wanted to show too much interest by inquiring. Whatever it was, he worked long days. She could usually see him watching TV on his couch in the evenings—he often had the blinds open—reclining in his easy chair with his white-stocking feet propped up on his coffee table, sipping on a beer. Maybe given his work schedule, he hadn't had time to do anything with the book and had only stuffed it away temporarily, somewhere in his house until he came up with a plan for it. She could only hope.

In truth, Im really didn't know enough about Preston to feel any confidence in her dark suppositions about him. She could be way off base. But something told her she wasn't. Although Im knew it was a bit far-fetched, he seemed to be the only person who could have conceivably had the knowledge and opportunity to do it. The book did not walk away on its own.

Where to turn? Well, of course, the internet. Imogene spent the next couple of hours scouring the web, searching every possible corner for any background information on Preston Wyles, which might hint at a criminal nature. Something that would indicate he was capable of the kind of despicable behavior of which she was suspecting.

Being an amateur, her sleuthing was not particularly sophisticated. Her first Google searches turned up next to nothing. The guy really didn't seem to have a big cyber footprint, which didn't surprise her. He had not struck her as an especially posting-stuff-about-himself-online sort of guy, nor did his work (whatever it was exactly—now she'd wished she had been more inquisitive) likely lead to much internet exposure. He was of that generation that had no inkling of the cyber world to come. Some his age hadn't fully jumped on the bandwagon yet. Although whatever his business was, he obviously did well for himself, internet exposed or not, having two garages full of Corvettes.

Interestingly, evidence of his supposedly notable racecar career was nowhere to be found. Figured. Of course, it had been decades before, and perhaps this history wouldn't necessarily turn up online; lots of stuff wouldn't. One would have to do deep newspaper archive searches for a lot of older information. Either way, she imagined his accounts of his big-shot racing days were likely overblown. If nothing else, he was probably a braggart.

After spinning her wheels for a while, getting search results with the text grayed-out indicating she'd already clicked on the links, she decided to see if he had a mug shot. Finding this would at least give her something. But nothing at all popped up for Ohio. She began to wonder if she might be wrong about him. Then she recalled something about him having moved to Ohio from Kentucky, so she looked for a mugshot there.

Lo and behold, on almost the first click, there, staring back at her on her computer screen was a younger, scruffier-looking Preston Wyles, with longish, blonde hair, clearly receding at the time, and a massive Fu Man Chu mustache. She'd always felt that you couldn't trust a guy sporting a Fu Man Chu. His expression in the image seemed to be one of perturbed resignation.

Maybe he hadn't really done anything much. A mugshot only means an arrest. She scanned down to read any details listed or court records. The arrest had been nearly two decades before. The charge had been insurance fraud and criminal conspiracy to commit theft! Im couldn't quite decipher everything it said in the records, but it appeared there had been a plea and perhaps probation and a fine. She tried to find some sort of inmate or penitentiary records, but she kept coming up with dead ends. It looked like she could pay a fee to get a full criminal background, but she thought it would be a waste of money. She'd already found what she was looking for; she didn't need a detailed report to tell her that the guy had been a criminal.

She caught herself again doing the obsessive repeat searches, which could and had eaten up hours of her life. She had enough already. She'd answered the question. The guy had a record and had clearly engaged in some serious criminal behavior in the past. Maybe he moved to Ohio to start over... maybe he was reformed. But then again, maybe not. The arrest record only indicated that he'd gotten caught at least once. Who knows what else he'd gotten away with or was still getting away with? All those years, her parents were living right next door to a felon, and they apparently had no clue!

How could she have been such an idiot? Talking so openly and loudly outside that night with her mother, celebrating with champagne, giddy with her great coup. She had such a low tolerance for alcohol, she'd felt tipsy after just one glass. She hadn't been thinking that she had to be especially careful of how loud she was talking. She didn't think that they had a felon—a virtual low-life— living right next door. Had she known, she certainly wouldn't have been spouting off about the very valuable rare book she had in her possession, even throwing out figures of its possible worth. And then to have announced her "perfect" hiding place so triumphantly. Hell, Im had practically handed the fink her treasure on a silver platter. Granted, she never thought someone would be eavesdropping, let alone someone with a criminal history. But still, she should have been more careful. With all her good fortune, she'd gotten carried away. Complacent and careless.

She decided not to waste any more time fleshing out the details. Preston Wyles was basically a common criminal—or at least had been in the not-so-very distant past. Certainly, he was capable of stealing the valuable book. Here was a golden opportunity right in front of him—how could he resist? It might have even been an impulsive thing. Maybe he saw them leave the house and decided to try the side door of the garage, found it open, and then...well, he probably figured they deserved to have it stolen for leaving it so vulnerable. Yeah, she imagined that's how someone like him would think. Blame the victims.

Imogene went to find her mother. She was sitting quietly in the living room in her usual chair, Marvin snuggled on her lap looking angelic (looks can truly be deceptive). Im settled in on the sofa, lying on her back, staring up at the ceiling in silent contemplation. Her mother was content just to be there, keeping her daughter company, glad she'd apparently calmed down enough to stop pacing the house.

In an epiphany of sorts, Imogene concluded that her only hope of recovering the book, her book, *her father's book*, was to act right away. Not lose another day, hour, or minute. She had to come up with a plan. Fast.

Preston was currently at work, but she didn't dare try to sneak in the house—he kept it locked like a fortress and had an alarm system in place, armed whenever he was out. He'd told her about this one day when they were chatting in the driveway, explaining that he once had his house broken into. He seemed obsessed with the possibility of being burglarized again. Maybe that should have alerted Im: a person's worries about what other people might do to them are often projections of their own inclinations. He did have a criminal history, for God's sake! She had worked herself into a frenzy. She felt like she was on fire, every part of her vibrating. She was furious.

Okay, think, *think!* What could she do? She felt utterly powerless and defeated, with no recourse. *Damn it.* How could this be happening? What the hell was she going to do?

Suddenly, another epiphany—*sex*—the one arena where she had the upper hand with Preston Wyles. Imogene didn't exactly love the idea of using this to manipulate a situation, and she could honestly say she'd never physically done so—as in actually performing sex acts in exchange for something. But there are definitely a lot of shades of gray when it comes to how sex plays into what goes on between people. It could certainly have a big impact on the dynamics of social interactions, especially power plays and negotiations.

Imogene was sure that many times in the past, her life had benefited indirectly from her sex appeal. Men had always responded to her, and she usually took advantage of it. This never struck her as unfair. Why not capitalize on her natural assets? It was just how the world worked. She'd always taken this for granted and rarely, if ever, stopped to consider the injustice in it—that by virtue of her "good-looking" genes, she'd always had an unearned edge.

Although now with her increasing age, she was starting to notice that the power she once held with men was on the decline. She was not looking forward to the day when she would no longer enjoy the perks of being attractive to men. Like so many young people, Imogene had allowed herself to deny the reality of what aging would look like for her. In her mind's eye, she'd always look the way she did now.

It bugged her especially that there was such a double standard for men and women. Men often grew more distinguished with age, while women only had to look forward to growing more frumpy, shriveled, and droopy. Fortunately, Imogene had not drooped just yet, and she planned to use every part of her perkiness to remedy the travesty, which had been perpetrated on her by the horrible rat, Preston Wyles. There was no innocent until proven guilty in this case. She knew in her gut that he had stolen the Darwin book.

Imogene was desperate to get inside Preston's house to search for it. And she was praying that Preston had not decided to stash the thing elsewhere. If he had done this, then she was royally screwed—she'd never get the book back. But Preston was a busy-enough guy. His pattern was that he came home from work, pounded back a beer or two, watched TV, and crashed. At least that's what she had surmised over time. Isn't it possible that he snatched the book but hadn't had a chance to do anything with it? She also hoped that he was arrogant and chauvinistic enough to assume Imogene would never suspect him or have the wherewithal to be a real threat to him. He could easily be thinking that he had plenty of time to dispose of the book and cash out before Imogene knew it was gone or ever suspected him.

In fact, this would have to be part of her strategy: pretend like everything was fine to keep him thinking that she was oblivious, that she had no idea the book was missing, that he had nothing to worry about. She was going to have to steel herself to play it cool and not show any distress when she saw Preston next. But the big question, how was she ever going to be able to get inside his house and search around for the book without him knowing?

The options were not great. She imagined herself seducing him and convincing him she was into bondage, which included tying him up. But this just seemed insane, and she thought that even he wouldn't be dumb enough to fall for this and not realize that she was up to something. Besides, there was no way he'd believe she would suddenly go from zero to sixty with him in an instant, right out of the blue, without any ulterior motive.

It had to be something more subtle. What if she found a way to drug him? Incapacitate him just long enough to search his house? Wasn't there a date-rape drug that would put a person out while the other person had their way with them? She thought it was called Rohypnol. She hated to think what had been perpetrated using the stuff. Such a horrendous and disgusting thing, but the world had a lot of nasty freaks in it. It made her feel slightly ill to realize she was even considering using the drug herself on a person. Assuredly, her purposes would be very different, but it felt creepy all the same. Regardless, Imogene certainly didn't have any of this drug on hand.

Even if there was a way to get it somehow, she'd never get it by the time Preston came zipping up his driveway from work that evening.

Then it occurred to her. She still had the mountain of medication that her doctors prescribed when she had been completely incapacitated by grief and depression following her father's death. If she could figure out what to give Preston and how much, maybe she could slip it to him and put him out long enough to search his place and find the book. Lots of big "ifs" in this scheme, but the more she thought about it, the more it seemed to be the only feasible option. It might not work—she might not be able to find the book—for all that, maybe he didn't even have it any more or had put it someplace where she'd never find it. Imogene knew all of this was likely true, but she resolved not to go down without a fight. She'd gone through too much to get the book. It was worth a ton of money. It belonged to her and her family. She wasn't going to allow some washed-up, low-life playboy get away with stealing it.

She took an inventory of her war-chest of pills. She thought the doctors were idiots to have kept prescribing so many potentially lethal medications in such colossal quantities; she could have offed herself many times over with the stash. She'd ended up with lots of unused pills because nothing would ever work, or she'd experience terrible side effects and have to stop the medication. Entire bottles of pills would go practically untouched, only to be replaced by another, and then another and so on.

Imogene thought the best bet for her purposes would be a fast-acting soporific of some sort. She did have a variety of these, prescribed when the insomnia set in shortly after her father's death. In just the right dose, one of these might do the trick. She only wanted to put him to sleep for a while, long enough for her to rummage through his house. Of course, she'd have to figure out a sure way to get him to ingest it. This all felt like an impossible task, but by now, the adrenaline was pumping through her like white-water rapids. She was determined to do something to try to recover the Darwin book, no matter how much of a long shot it was.

Her mother had spent the day napping and reading, this and that. She was happy to pick up whatever book was nearby, even if it was the same one she'd already just finished. She never seemed to realize this. Like always, she was content and worry-free. Im would have liked to ask her opinion on the situation, but she couldn't really appreciate how important it was for her to get the book back. At this point, she'd probably tell her daughter just to let it go. Besides, Im didn't want to waste a second explaining things over and over to her mother. It was already early afternoon; she had to be ready by the end of the day.

Im researched online which of her leftover medications would be the best candidate for safely putting Preston to sleep fast. Some of the pills she'd been prescribed were definitely dangerous in high doses, but the minor tranquilizer Xanax was considered safe. All the information she'd found indicated that, while Xanax was addictive, it was almost impossible to overdose on it alone. As it happened, she had plenty of Xanax on hand. The only danger came when mixing large amounts of it with alcohol. If she went with it, she'd have to hope Preston didn't have much alcohol in his system. When she had used the medication herself, it had helped to calm her down quickly—needing only fifteen or twenty minutes to take effect. She remembered the drug making her feel very drowsy and loopy. A moderately, larger dose should work to put Preston out in short order.

Obviously, she wanted to give him enough, but not too much. Everything she read said that you'd have to take handfuls before it could ever kill you, and even then, it might not. The doses listed for the drug were not meant to induce sleep, but it seemed sleep would likely occur if one took, say, three to four times the amount prescribed. She had a stash of 1mg pills. The bottle said to take one pill for anxiety as needed, not to exceed eight pills in a 24-hour period. Imogene recalled that even one pill made her feel sleepy. The one time she had taken two, she ended up dozing off in no time. Preston was tall and probably nearly twice her weight. She thought three pills should have the same effect on him. But then again, she was very sensitive to medication. She decided she could safely give him four pills, and it should induce sleep fairly rapidly.

But how the heck was she going to get the pills in him? This was no small quandary. The whole proposition was going to be very dicey, to say the least.

Everything had to line up perfectly in her favor for the plan to work, and she had to be very careful because anything too far out of the ordinary might tip him off. Im hoped that his ego would lead him to think that her sudden attention was due to his animal magnetism, and not any other agenda.

All indications were that Preston did indeed have a rather sizable ego and may think that she'd finally seen the light and was into him. The only problem was the timing, coming on the heels of his presumed heist of her treasure. She was going to have to play it just right. She had a plan for that. But first, she needed to figure out the mode of delivery for the soporific.

Im and her mom were often sitting out on the patio in the early evening when Preston rolled in from work. What if they were out there drinking smoothies or something? She could offer him one. Would this make him suspicious? She could disguise the bitterness of the pills if they were well-ground up and put in a fruit smoothie, especially if she also put some bananas in it. Bananas could mask anything. She'd make it non-alcoholic, but act like she'd spiked it a bit. More likely, he'd want to drink it, and if he did taste something funny, hopefully he'd assume it was because of cheap vodka or gin.

She could act like they were trying out their new smoothie machine for the first time. They'd had it for a while, but he'd never know that. She could pretend like they were celebrating some good fortune, without saying what it is. If he asked, she would be coy and say that it was something she couldn't talk about yet. This would hopefully put him off the notion that she had discovered the book missing and was up to something. She'd pour on the charm, act all seductive, wear something low cut—he'd never think she would be acting this way to him if she knew he'd ripped her off. The hitch was that all this had to take place at his house so she could search for the Darwin book, after he'd conked out from the Xanax.

Wow, even Im thought it sounded far-flung and highly unlikely to work. But what else was there to do?

By five o'clock that afternoon, Imogene had everything ready. She'd crushed the Xanax pills into a fine powder, had run out and picked up fresh strawberries and bananas to make the smoothies, and had it all laid out on the countertop, ready to go. Right before seven o'clock, she would make the smoothies in the machine, pour out enough for her and her mother, while reserving an ample amount for one more tall glass full. This would be the smoothie drink for Preston. She'd throw in the Xanax powder and mix it all up thoroughly. That batch would be only his—she'd already have the non-drugged stuff in glasses for her and her mother safely set aside.

After having all her ducks in a row, Im went off to prep herself. She showered, put on makeup, did her hair, and dressed in some skimpy cut-off jean shorts and a black tank-top with a plunging V-neck, along with a black, push-up bra, lace edge peeking out a tad from underneath. Looking in the mirror, she was afraid she'd overdone it, but she knew she had to look sexy enough to get him to go along with her plan, perhaps against his better judgement. Im imagined that if the situation were reversed, she'd be a nervous wreck and avoiding him at all costs.

If she were the perpetrator, she'd have been preoccupied with her crime and overwhelmed with guilt and fear of being exposed; she would never allow herself to relax long enough to be wooed. But she knew that Preston was certainly not the neurotic sort; race-car drivers rarely were. Living dangerously, taking risks, and a high tolerance for stress surely dominated his genetics and personality. Feeling anxious or guilty over recent shady behavior? Not likely for a Preston Wyles.

CHAPTER 20

AT 6:30 P.M., Im had the strawberry-banana smoothies made and the pitcher with the concoction in the fridge. She had her mother go sit out on the patio with Marvin on the leash. Right before seven o'clock when Preston usually got home, she planned to pour the two glasses meant for her and her mother. She'd take her mother a glass, leave one for herself, then come in and mix the crushed Xanax pills into the portion meant for Preston left in the pitcher. Outside on the patio, she wanted it all to seem very spontaneous, as though she'd suddenly realized there was extra smoothie in the pitcher and would he like it? With Marvin out there, likely barking at him like a maniac, she could easily say, "Oh, I'll just bring it over there to you." Meanwhile, he'd probably want to first go inside his house, so she'd quickly waltz over there. She hoped she could manage to follow him inside, carrying the smoothie pitcher.

At seven o'clock, as planned, she and her mother were sitting out on the patio with their non-drugged versions of the strawberry-banana smoothies, the drugged stuff waiting on a little table nearby. When the clock ticked 7:05, Preston's driveway was still empty, and she started to worry that he was not coming straight home from work. It was going to be harder to pull off the scheme later when it was too dark for her and her mother to just happen to be sitting out there on the patio enjoying the evening air. The only way any of it was going to work was if it looked unplanned. Now the wait was killing her. *Preston, where the hell are you?*

Finally, at about quarter after seven, he pulled up to his mailbox like always, took a few minutes sorting through his mail, and then zipped on up the short incline. As soon as he got out of his bright red truck (massive, extended cab version), she stood up, holding the smoothie pitcher in one hand and her glass in the other and called over to him. "Hey, Preston, you want some smoothie? We can't finish all this."

At first, he sort of stood there like he was confused by her overture. Then something seemed to click in, and he said "Sure!" and started to walk toward them. Right on cue, Marvin went wild—God, he was annoying, but she had to love him for it in that moment.

Gesturing toward Marvin, she said, "I hate this damn dog. How about I just bring it to you?" And without waiting for an answer, she headed right over.

Preston was standing in the driveway. As she sauntered across the grass, she could see him look her up and down a couple times. *So far so good.*

She decided to turn on her usual chatty self. "I love this new smoothie machine we got. I could live on the stuff. Man, it really hits the spot!" Then they were both standing on his patio, her own glass in one hand, and the partially filled pitcher in the other, and she said, "Oh, wait, have you got another glass?"

"Oh, yeah, I'll get one," he said. Without missing a beat, she continued blabbering on with mindless chatter, seamlessly following him right into the house.

"Yeah, this smoothie machine was pricey, but we're kind of celebrating these days..." Then she waited.

He stopped and gave her a quizzical look. "Oh, yeah, so what are you celebrating?"

Imogene wanted to convey just the right tone with her reply— something that said, well, I want to tell you because it's so great, but I can't tell you because it has to stay secret. She said, "Oh, I can't really go into yet, but it could be big!" as she rubbed her middle finger and thumb together in the universal "money" gesture.

She tried to say this in the most natural way, as though she hadn't the slightest concern about him or that he could possibly know what she was referring to. Based on his expression—surprise, then slight confusion, followed by what looked like relief—and the fact that he didn't even try to get her to elaborate, made her think, *Guilty as charged.*

She padded behind him in her flip-flops as they both walked into his kitchen, and she began to feel giddy—maybe she was going to be able to pull this off! The kitchen was the prototypical bachelor's variety, a total mess and decorated straight out of the 1970's: brown, orange, and gold printed foil wallpaper with dark wood cabinets and olive-green appliances.

Not that she was judging. Her parents' decor next door was terribly outdated. She knew that some people, including her parents, didn't like spending gobs of money redecorated their homes. But beyond that, his kitchen was disgusting: sink stacked high with dirty dishes, empty beer cans and liquor bottles everywhere; countertops completely covered with stuff, not an inch of available space in sight.

Preston reached up into a cupboard for a glass. She was glad to see there were still some clean ones in there. She had her own glass in her left hand and the smoothie pitcher in her right, so he held the glass while she poured the rest of the drink for him and added, "Yeah, I spiked it a little just for fun!"

"Cain't argue with that!" Preston drawled. They both stood there in his kitchen for a few beats, and she waited for him to say something. "Hey, you want to go sit for a bit?"

She responded with a hesitant, "Well, maybe for a minute or two. Need to get back to my mom before she decides to wander off somewhere with Marvin. She lets him go wherever he wants. It's ridiculous!"

"We could sit outside and keep an eye on her if you want," he offered.

"Okay... well, no, it's almost dusk now. I'll get eaten alive by the mosquitoes—they love me." Then Im made a glancing gesture over at their house. "Oh, my mom won't go anywhere... we can just sit in here for a bit."

Imogene, of course, wanted them to stay in the house all along, but she didn't want to seem too eager. Following him down the hall felt surreal; being in his house at all, about to do what she was planning to do, she really couldn't believe herself. Preston's living room was the ultimate man-cave. Massive, flat-screen TV, four huge, old-style stereo speakers he'd probably had since his college days, dark brown, leather recliners with built-in cup holders and a large, gold leather sectional sofa. He chose the sofa, and she sat on a recliner. It would have been out of character for her to sit next to him on the couch. Everything had to seem normal.

Both sitting then, she couldn't tell if he'd drunk any of the concoction yet, so she lifted her glass and said, "To the good life!"

He lifted his glass and took a big swig. Then another. "Yeah, that does hit the spot!" he said.

So far so good.

Im decided to keep the chatter going so she could control the conversation, and she went on to complain about her mother's dog, how annoying he was, how she hoped he didn't hear the barking at his house too often. Preston mostly listened and fortunately continued to drink the smoothie.

At one point, he got out a cigarette and lit it. "Mind if I smoke?"

"Um, no, sure, go ahead," she stammered. God, how she hated to breathe in secondhand smoke. Obviously, she was not about to split hairs on it at that moment. In other circumstances, she might have said something snide like, "You do know that the Surgeon General has determined cigarettes cause cancer, among other things?" By the looks of his overflowing, badly-in-need-of-emptying ashtray, he obviously didn't give a rat's ass what the Surgeon General had to say about anything.

Instead, she kept right on jabbering and moved on to the topic of her mother's dementia and how quickly it had seemed to progress since her father died. Preston said something about being sorry again for her loss. She thanked him and rambled on about how hard she'd taken it, but that she was better now and that things were really starting to look up. She hoped this would again give him the idea that she was referring to the rare book in her possession, concluding that she hadn't yet realized it was gone.

Then, Preston gestured to her, "Whatcha doin' all the way over there anyway? Come on. Sit over here next to me."

Imogene had not the slightest interest in sitting anywhere near him on the couch, but she knew she needed to play along. She was a little surprised with his overt flirting and forwardness—given what she believed he had done—didn't he have any scruples at all? He certainly had a set of balls on him.

She wondered if he was even worried about her being in his house. She felt surer than ever that he had been the one who stole the Darwin book. And by the haphazard looks of his place, she was guessing it had all been done impulsively: He'd grabbed the book when he had seen the opportunity and quickly stashed it somewhere in the house, saving the planning for another day. She could see by his housekeeping—or lack thereof—that he was a bit of a procrastinator and wasn't particularly organized or careful about most of his belongings. The only things he was fastidious about were his Corvettes, which he kept in pristine condition. As much as she lusted after them, she wanted to smash the things to bits right then for what he'd pulled on her.

Im prayed that he'd hidden the stolen book away some place in the house, without giving it too much thought. He probably wouldn't have wanted to act on it too fast or go public with it, figuring holding it and keeping a low profile was the best bet. He likely knew a thing or two about how to handle "hot" or stolen goods. She wondered what would have happened if she suddenly demanded, right then and there, that he hand over the book.

Okay, Preston. The jig is up. Hand it over!

Would he deny knowing anything about it? (Most likely response.) Would he have felt bad and given it back to her? (Not in a million years.) Could she have sweet-talked him, told him she'd give him a cut when she sold it? (Yeah, right.) No, she would not be taking a chance on anything of the kind. She was going to stay the course and hope everything fell into place.

At some point while she rambled on, Preston put his arm around her and pulled her over close to him, her shoulder touching his. The stench of cigarettes on his breath was nauseating, and she nearly gagged once. She could feel herself stiffen in his partial embrace. She willed herself to relax. She knew she just had to go with it, as distasteful as it was. They sat this way for several minutes. She noticed that Preston was sweating rather profusely and breathing a bit heavy, like he was getting aroused.

The creep was probably imagining that he'd be bedding her in no time. *What a motherfucker.* Imogene desperately tried to resist pulling away from him as she sank further into the leather sectional sofa, feeling his clammy skin next to hers, surrounded by a cloud of smoke as he sucked on his Marlboro. Of course, he'd smoke this brand. She'd heard it was the standard for middle-aged, Marlboro-Man-wannabes. Im was relieved he didn't try to kiss her. She couldn't imagine enduring this.

Then she felt Preston slide his hand down under her butt on the sofa cushion and kind of cup her ass. *Oh God.* He kept trying to sneak his grubby fingers inside her shorts and up into her crotch. She should have figured he'd be one of those guys who skips the kissing phase, instead going right for it— swooping in for the kill. She'd dated guys like this who seemed to have an aversion to the more intimate, lip-to-lip contact. It was maybe too soft for their manly, animalistic urges. They are usually the jerks who don't respect woman at all—assholes who see them as objects for the taking.

Imogene felt utterly repulsed by his touch, but she only squirmed and tried to coyly brush his hand away, while she continued to jabber on about whatever came to mind, as though nothing was happening—biding her time, praying that the Xanax would kick in soon. This was not exactly what she had bargained for, but she felt she had no choice but to let it happen. He did eventually manage to get his fingers under her jeans shorts, tight as they were, and sort of poked around, grazing the opening to her vagina, then finally partially inserting his middle finger. To her horror, she could feel herself going moist, and she cursed her body for its betrayal in that moment. Im held still and hoped if she didn't respond, he wouldn't take it further. *What a creep,* she thought. He was probably feeling proud of himself for having scored so easily with her.

After several more agonizing minutes, his nasty finger still up in her, he finished his repulsive cigarette, started to yawn, and half-reclined on the sectional.

"A-a-h-h ye-e-ah, tha' drin' r'ally h-hit tha' spo'…" his voice trailed off.

Wow, maybe it was working.

She noticed his eyelids starting to get droopy, and she could barely contain her excitement. It was happening. In a few more minutes, he had shut his eyes completely. Imogene chattered on softly about how she didn't know when she would return to her job, if ever. How she thought she might need to stay and take care of her mother, that her mom really didn't seem capable of being on her own anymore, and on and on. She was afraid to stop speaking.

Finally, after about ten minutes of complete silence from him, she quietly nudged him, whispered his name, and asked if he was awake. No reply. She could hear his deep, rhythmic breathing. Yes, he was sound asleep! Her little smoothie concoction had worked like a charm. She was elated, but she had no time to rest on her laurels.

Time to get to work.

She was going to have to unwrap herself from him. His stinking finger was still inside her shorts, so she inched herself away from him as if in slow motion. Once she was clear of him, she gingerly eased herself up from the couch, trying not to make a sound, which was not easy on the soft, deep leather sectional that had nearly swallowed her up whole. Naturally, it let out loud creaks when she shifted on the leather cushions, but Preston dozed on through it.

Thank God.

Eventually extracted from Preston's and the sofa's clutches, she quietly crept out of the living room to begin her search of the place. She looked behind every stack of books, peered into any large enough containers, inside cabinets, under cushions, in all his desk drawers, in each of his kitchen cupboards—she even looked in the freezer and found typical bachelor pad freezer contents: multiple TV dinners, Stouffer's entrees, bottles of Beefeaters Gin and Absolut Vodka. She frantically looked everywhere she could think of, but found nothing. Then she went around to all the beds and looked under the mattresses. Yes, cliché, but who knows? Preston didn't strike her as particularly clever or original.

Next, she began a search of his closets and every box, bin, or bag she saw. Then in his bedroom (which was essentially a pigsty), she commenced a search of all his drawers. His bedside table drawer was full of condoms and sex toys. *How gross.*

Then she noticed something shiny and silver in the back of the drawer and gasped. A gun!

Oh God!

She couldn't remember when she'd ever seen a real live handgun, obviously loaded and at the ready. This guy was serious about protecting himself. Her stomach flipped, and she felt a bit queasy. What the hell was she doing tangling with this guy?

No, she knew exactly what she was doing. She was going to get back what was rightly hers. She couldn't run scared yet. More determined than ever, she picked up the pace. She resumed her search, yanking open the drawers, digging deep, yet being careful not to disturb anything. But it was getting late. She had to get the hell out of there before he woke up. She could feel a bit of panic setting in.

The guy has a loaded gun! Im took a deep breath. *Okay, stay calm. Focus!*

Finally, she pulled open the bottom drawer of his oak, tallboy chest. It was full of underwear, mostly tidy whities, though there were a few silky men's bikinis in there, which looked to be also from the 1970's era. She was feeling revolted having to touch them as she sifted through the deep drawer. She wondered if he'd ever thrown a worn pair out. Some looked practically antique.

She'd about had it with the underwear when she suddenly heard something crinkling at the very bottom of the drawer, like a plastic bag. She had to reach far into the depths of the disgusting underclothes, but then, there it was. A small bundle wrapped in a Kroger's grocery bag. Could this be it? Her heart was racing now, and she felt like she might faint. She looked inside the bag and saw instantly that it was, in fact, her Darwin book—he'd sloppily unwrapped it from the way she'd had it packed, then partially rewrapped it and dropped it in the grocery sack. He'd have quickly pitched the trash bag it was stored in originally—it would have been all caked with dust from the cat litter. He'd probably cursed her for making him sift through the annoying stuff.

What a jerk.

Imogene sat down then for a minute on the man's insanely large bed—was there a size bigger than a king? She felt herself falling into it and tried to catch herself, letting out a yelp. Next, loud swishing and sloshing sounds.

Oh my God.

It was a huge waterbed! How cliché—a bachelor pad with a waterbed. And it was the old mahogany, wood platform type popular back in the 70's. The hilarity of this suddenly hit her, and she snickered out loud. A huge tacky waterbed, why was she not surprised?

Floating there on her back, swallowed up in the massive waterbed, Im glanced up and noticed a large mirror mounted on the ceiling! She burst out laughing. It was just too perfect! Then she heard something coming from the man cave.

Shit!

Had she awoken the sleeping giant? Im froze and willed the bed to stop with the annoying sloshing and slapping water sounds. What if Preston came back to the bedroom and saw her splayed out on his waterbed. He'd probably think she was hot for him. But she was holding the Darwin book he'd stolen from her! Who knows what he'd do then? She held her breath, listening, straining to hear what was happening out in the other room. Silence.

More silence.

Slowly, she exhaled, waiting. Still nothing. Maybe she hadn't woken him. Maybe he'd only stirred. She knew she had to get the hell out of the house before he actually did wake up. What the hell was she thinking lingering around in there?

But she'd been literally stunned at her incredibly good fortune once again. It seemed too good to be true—first finding the book in her grandmother's old backroom in Rochester, and now being able to recover it again. It defied all logic. It was as though lightning had struck twice in the same spot in her little life. As though somebody had been scripting the whole thing from above or something. Although she knew it was magical thinking, she couldn't help but wonder if her father was lording over all this, pushing the hand of fate somehow. More likely, it was merely dumb luck that everything had fallen into place once again. Didn't she deserve a little luck anyway?

Although, her luck might be running out fast if she didn't get moving and clear out. Im carefully tried to pull herself up out of the monster bed. It wasn't easy as she had sunk into the middle.

Damn bed.

She moved in slow motion to avoid creating waves and more insane sloshing. Finally, she was free of the massive bed's clutches. Then, bag in hand, Darwin book inside, she crept out of the bedroom and out to the man cave. Thank God, Preston still seemed to be sleeping like a baby, breathing deeply, a little spittle spilling from a corner of his mouth. He looked comfortable, in more or less the same half-reclining position on the leather sectional where she'd left him. But his empty glass on the coffee table in front of him was tipped on its side. That was probably what she'd heard. He must have jostled the table when he'd shifted in sleep.

Dumbass.

Imogene despised him more in that moment than she'd ever despised anyone before. No one had ever done so rotten a thing to her. He deserved to rot in hell!

She tiptoed over to the coffee table to retrieve her own empty glass, then decided to grab his, too. She didn't want him noticing the empty glass later, prompting his little brain's wheels to start turning, making him suspicious of her. He'd be mad as hell if he figured out what had been perpetrated on him.

In one fell swoop, Im reached for the glass and, being her klutzy self, knocked it off the table onto the spongy, shag carpet. At least the hideous rug was thick enough to prevent the glass from shattering. But the clunk had caused the oaf to stir a little. Im froze stiff, afraid to even breathe. She stared at him intently, praying he wouldn't open his eyes and ask her what the hell she thought she was doing!

Finally, he seemed to settle again into a deep slumber. Time to dash out before he stirred again. She didn't bother with his glass on the floor and only snatched up her own, and ran to the kitchen for her smoothie pitcher. Then, with the plastic Kroger bag holding the Darwin book dangling off her arm, she stealthily slid open the glass patio door and slipped out. She stood for a moment, breathing a huge sigh of relief.

It was dark by now, and she hoped that her mother was safely inside and hadn't ventured off somewhere with the damn dog. Im definitely didn't feel like prowling around the neighborhood searching for them. She scooted over to her parents' house, leaping on tiptoe through the grass, already damp with evening dew. She was gloating a little inside now, realizing she'd pulled off yet another heist—of sorts.

Preston Wyles, you stupid motherfucker! You thought you could get away with stealing from the Mussomelis. Yeah, you had another thing coming.

Im was relieved to find her mom inside the house, sitting in her usual chair with the TV blaring, Marvin on her lap. Imogene always loved it when her mother would turn on the TV herself. It made her feel like her mom was still connected to the world and able to take some initiative for herself. Of course, it wasn't much, but there were too many times lately when she would find her sitting in the same chair, no TV, no book, just staring off into space—maybe for hours. This always made Im worry that she'd one day not even know who her own daughter was. It was Im's biggest fear, and she prayed earnestly that this would never happen.

Safely back inside her own house, Imogene carefully took the Darwin book out of the plastic Kroger bag. It looked fine. Nothing had happened to it in the short time it had been in the creep's possession. Thinking about it now, knowing for sure that he had, in fact, brazenly stolen from her and thought he was going to get away with it, galled her to no end. What a complete dirt-bag. How was she supposed to continue living next door to such an asshole?

She thought about how she should behave going forward when she saw him. She decided that the best approach would be to act like nothing unusual had happened at all, never speak about the book, never acknowledge anything. He wouldn't dare ask her about it, but even if he did have the nerve to confront her on it, she'd lie through her teeth. Besides, who knows when he would realize that the book was no longer at the bottom of his revolting underwear drawer? He might not check on it for days. Once he saw it was gone, he wouldn't absolutely know that she had been the one to take it. Who's to say someone else might not have been there and taken it? And he'd probably be so chauvinistic as to think she wasn't capable of such trickery. Whatever—she really didn't care what he thought. Tomorrow she would go to the bank very early and get the safety deposit box like she should have done in the first place.

Imogene did just that as soon as the bank opened at nine o'clock the next morning. She'd slept the night before with the book right next to her in bed, under a pillow. She was not about to take any more chances or waste another second. She didn't want to risk Preston discovering it was gone and trying to do something about it.

Her hope was that he'd woken up later on the couch, maybe not even until morning, and had seen that, naturally, she'd up and left. Perhaps he'd even felt a bit like an idiot for falling asleep on her, but he'd have no reason to suspect that she would have rummaged through his house while he snoozed. As she'd searched the place, she was especially careful to make sure nothing would look disturbed—which wasn't too difficult given the state of disarray in his house. Thank God, he was a slob. Besides, Preston didn't seem to be the sharpest crayon in the box. Im felt sure that she must have put him off any suspicions with her Oscar worthy performance. Cool, casual, like she was on top of the world because she thought she still had the rare and valuable book safely stashed in a bin of cat litter in her garage.

Yes, Imogene felt certain that this macho-man, washed-up playboy with a super-sized ego would have deluded himself into thinking that her overture that evening had been because he'd finally worn her down and she was about to succumb to his irresistible charm. The thought of it almost made her gag. *What a pig.*

Im sincerely hoped that the next time she saw her neighbor, it would be uneventful. She was a bit anxious about future encounters, so she planned to avoid him for as long as possible. After all, in spite of the adjacent driveways and his close second garage, their actual houses were a good distance apart. She could recall days going by when she'd not see him at all. He'd leave very early for work, and if she wasn't watching or outside when he came home, she wouldn't see him at all. She would definitely be laying low for a while.

That morning when Im went off to the bank, she took her mother with her to make an outing of it. Why not, it was another great moment, and her mom was wonderful at sharing in her happiness, even if she didn't really know the source of her daughter's jubilation. If Imogene was smiling, she would be smiling. It was a perfect (albeit, conciliatory) arrangement.

It felt so good to hear the solid, massive vault door close behind them once she'd put the Darwin book in the locked safety deposit box. The bank had a number of security procedures including a signature card, and they explained how it all worked. If someone ever got a hold of one of the keys (she was given two small keys), they'd have to know which bank to go to (there was no identification on the keys), they'd have to present her ID, look just like her, and sign her name just like she did. Im supposed someone could possibly do all this, but in reality, it was never going to happen. The biggest risk was her losing the keys to the thing, but there were ways to deal with that.

Besides, she planned to sell the book soon. This seemed like the best thing to do. It was worth something in the neighborhood of a small fortune, at least in her world, and she didn't want to sit on it so long that another rare first edition materialized, perhaps reducing the value of her copy. Clearly, it was a supply and demand game—she had the one of something, perhaps even the last of its kind, which hopefully, very many buyers would want to possess.

Imogene still had to decide how she was going to handle the issue with her sisters. Yes, she supposed they could lay claim to some of the profits, but really? They were the ones who had thrown away her dad's little old notebook. If she hadn't insisted on going through the trash bags—which they had already tied up and set out for the garbage men—and fished the thing out on her own, it would have gone to the dump. No one would have known that her dad had ever had a copy of the Darwin book, let alone an incredibly valuable rare copy. The book would have likely spent eternity slowly disintegrating in a heap somewhere after the Cordova house and backroom were ultimately torn down. Or maybe the owner of her grandmother's old house or even some random construction or demolition worker might have found it and cashed in—if they were even savvy enough to appreciate what it was.

All these things made Im feel more and more that she didn't want to say anything to her sisters at all. Why couldn't she just sell the thing anonymously through a Sotheby's' auction? Surely, Sotheby's would be willing to keep her identity a secret. She wanted nothing to do with publicity or the limelight—that would have been her worst nightmare. The idea of keeping it completely to herself made her feel a bit like a heel at times, but she vacillated between that feeling and one of triumph, even vindication, since her sisters certainly had shown no mercy in their ridicule of her resistance to throwing stuff out.

Yes, perhaps she did have pack-rat tendencies, but look what they had led to? If anything, she and her mother should be the ones who would enjoy the spoils of their efforts. They were the ones who had earned it. She could have lost her freedom over it, or worse, they could have been hurt badly or killed by that horrible thug in the alley behind Cordova Avenue.

After the bank, she took her mother out to eat at a favorite lunch spot and basked in the glory of it all. Imogene felt like a huge weight had been lifted off her. It wasn't only having the book secured at the bank, but also that she'd accomplished something which had allowed her father's sudden death to lead to something positive.

She'd had her share of accomplishments in her life, but this felt different, more organic: her father's tendency to squirrel stuff away, keeping the old notebook—Imogene being the sort not to just unceremoniously shuck it all, but to take the time to see what was there, just to honor her father's stuff. She couldn't help but feel that her father would have been proud of her. She'd been resourceful, smart, gutsy, determined and even a bit fearless. Sure, she was gloating now, but what of it? After a time when she had experienced the lowest of lows, she could finally feel that life was worth living again. She wanted to savor the moment.

Imogene was thrilled when she did not see Preston Wyles for a couple days. His truck was still parked in the exact same spot, but he often drove his other "everyday" car, a silver Camry, when he went to work. He'd just pull it in and out of the garage and enter the house from inside. What he drove on any particular day seemed random, but it was probably based on something practical like whether he needed his truck to haul something or who knows what? Maybe some days he was in the mood to feel macho, sitting up high in his four-by-four, Ford truck—*whatever*. She was just happy she hadn't run into him yet.

The whole experience made her feel more ready to go ahead and put her mother's house on the market and get the hell out of there. Who wanted to live next door to a guy like Preston Wyles? When the house sold, who knows? They could go anywhere. Im was feeling more and more like she was going to resign her position at the University. Because of the windfall that would be coming (hopefully), she'd be financially pretty well set with what she'd already accumulated during her career.

Besides, her mother clearly needed her, needed someone full-time, and it needed to be family. It *had* to be family. Putting her in a facility was unthinkable. And no hired help could take the place of the connection with a daughter. Really, Imogene was the only one who could be there for her mother. All Kate Mussomeli's other daughters had their own lives, husbands, families. She was the best choice, and she was okay with that. She loved her mother dearly and hoped that with continued loving care, she would live on and on for a long time, healthy and happy.

The thought of losing her remaining parent was too much to even contemplate. Of course, Im had learned that you never know, someone could be gone in an instant, but the idea of being parentless—an orphan—was excruciating. She still wondered sometimes what it was that had made the loss of her father so utterly devastating for her. Why it had almost destroyed her? Other people seemed to get over the deaths of their parents without the wheels falling off. Why had she been nearly unable to recover from the loss?

Perhaps it was the deep unconditional love. It's what every parent hopefully gives to their child. Imogene had always keenly felt this love coming from her parents, and she wondered if that was what made the loss of her father so unbearable. Until it was gone, she hadn't even realized how much she must have relied on this to survive in the world. In a sense, no one can give a person the kind of love that a parent can. Maybe a good husband could come close, though she had her doubts about this. Still, she hoped she might find the right guy and marry one day. She knew it's what her father would have wished for her.

Beyond that, she very much wanted to have a child herself. Being the unmarried, childless daughter had probably contributed to the intensity of her grief after her father died. She didn't have the support of a husband and family like her sisters. Her parents had always been her prime emotional support. While she still remained technically in her childbearing years, she was getting close to the end of the road on it. The tick-tock of her biological clock was becoming almost deafening to her. In all honesty, Im was beginning to panic a bit. Would it ever happen for her?

Then there were other times, especially when she was feeling sorry for herself, that she thought maybe being childless was how it was meant to be. She often saw herself as so flawed, she questioned whether she'd be a good parent, or even what sort of genes she'd be passing on. Imogene had felt so off-kilter for so much of her existence. Would a child of hers be burdened with the same thing? She wondered sometimes, from a strictly Darwinian survival of the fittest perspective, if she even measured up. If she had lived in the very early days of mankind on Earth, would she have survived to pass on her genes or would she have perished at a young age, without leaving a trace?

CHAPTER 21

A FEW DAYS AFTER she'd retrieved the Darwin book from the despicable Preston Wyles' underwear drawer, while he'd slept peacefully on his couch, oblivious of her cunning and adroit maneuvering, and with the book now secure at the bank, Imogene woke to birds chirping and a feeling that all was right with the world. She intended to look into meeting with a lawyer as soon as possible. She wanted to have all her ducks in a row before she contacted Mr. Wexler of Sotheby's again. She needed a definite plan to understand what she needed to know and what she didn't know. Im had long ago decided to be a person who did the necessary due diligence in every situation.

It was way too easy to think you knew about something when you really didn't. Imogene thought it was a sign of true intelligence to know what you didn't know—this was maybe even more important than what you *did* know. Clearly, she was ignorant when it came to the rare book world and of what exactly to do if in the possession of something extremely valuable—what had Mr. Wexler said?—perhaps even unprecedentedly so. She wouldn't share the specifics right away with a lawyer; she had to know she could trust the person. What she needed to do at the moment was get a good idea of the lay of the land and how best to proceed.

Imogene was on her computer researching local lawyers when she heard it: some sort of commotion outside, vehicles pulling up near their house, car doors slamming shut. She got up to look out the window, and her stomach dropped to her knees. There were two police cruisers in front of Preston's house with their lights flashing, and a couple of other parked cars, one of which looked familiar. She'd seen it there before—a friend or family member?—she didn't know.

What the hell? Police cars, especially with their lights going, always made her anxiety level skyrocket. She didn't know if this was the normal reaction of most people, but it was reflexive for her. She automatically felt like they must be coming for her—that something very bad had happened or was about to.

For Im, this was a familiar feeling. She'd be instantly transported all the way back to when she was a small girl, powerless in nearly every sense. That feeling she had long ago, watching big whitecap waves forming on Lake Ontario, knowing a storm would soon be gathering overhead—and that there was nothing she or anyone could do to stop it. A huge Mack truck was on the way, in high gear.

Mrs. Mussomeli, not yet out of bed, yelled to her from her bedroom. "What is it, Im? What's out there?"

Marvin, by this time, had started barking in the frantic way he did when there was really something to yap about.

"I don't know, Ma. There are police cars pulled up to Preston's house."

Imogene's first thought was that maybe Preston had called the police because he discovered he'd been robbed of the rare book—but really, would he have done that? No, it couldn't be that—he'd stolen the book from *her*; he'd never be dumb enough to call the police to come out to his house about it. Maybe they were there to arrest him for something else he'd done. After all, he had proven himself to be a thief.

Still peering through a slit in the drapes, Im saw an ambulance driving up the street towards Preston's house. But it didn't have the siren on. It just pulled up slowly. Two paramedics hopped out, opened the back, took out a stretcher, and went inside through Preston's front door.

Im could feel every fiber of her body pull tight, and she realized she was holding her breath. She covered her mouth with her hands, breathing through her cupped fingers. Her breath smelled morning fowl. *Oh God.* She could feel herself breaking out in a sweat. She stood wringing her hands, eyes transfixed on Preston's front door. After what seemed like hours, but was only about 10 or 15 minutes, the front door of Preston's house slowly crept open. The paramedics were bringing the stretcher out, one on each end, like they always do. They didn't seem to be in a big rush. Imogene could feel her heart thumping, and, for a second, it felt like time stopped. On the stretcher was what looked like a person covered from head to toe in a white sheet.

Wait... what?! Is that a bod—? Oh God, oh God, oh God. Is it... a body? Is it Preston? Oh my God, is he dead? Oh, no, no, no...NO!

Imogene immediately felt clammy and nauseous. She wanted to run to the bathroom and throw-up, but she couldn't risk missing a second of what was happening next door. She stood frozen at the window. She had to *see.*

Maybe it wasn't Preston on the stretcher at all, but someone else, perhaps someone who'd been a guest. Maybe! She wanted to go outside and ask, but she didn't know how she would react in front of the police. What if they wanted to question her? *Oh my God.* No, she decided the last thing she wanted to do was call attention to herself.

Stunned, Im continued to watch intently from behind the tapestry drape. She hoped no one had noticed her peeking out. The Mussomeli's cars were in the garage. The police wouldn't know for sure the next-door neighbors were even home. She had to lay low. She desperately wanted to know if it was Preston being brought out of the house, but she was too afraid to show herself and ask. If it was him, then there was only one conclusion that could be drawn, knowing what she knew.

She'd killed him. She'd killed a person. *Oh my God, killed someone!*

Somehow she'd miscalculated and overdosed him. She prayed that it wasn't him on the stretcher, but she knew in her heart that it must have been. That finally, she, Imogene Mussomeli, had gone too far. She'd committed murder. *Murder.*

Watching as the ambulance drove away from Preston's house that morning, in no particular hurry, Imogene knew in her gut that she was doomed now for all time. Any hope of ever leading a normal, happy life again had been completely obliterated. What she'd seen out that window had sealed her fate.

Imogene could feel herself growing woozy, her legs beginning to feel like rubber. She stumbled to her bedroom, a place she'd retreated to so many times in the past. It was the middle of the morning, but Im climbed back into her bed and pulled the covers up. Normally, her mother might be getting up soon, but if the house was quiet, her mom would usually stay in bed longer. Hopefully she would; Im needed time to try to somehow come to terms with the repulsive developments next door. Every part of her felt stretched and about to snap. Her head on the pillow felt too heavy and began to throb. When she closed her eyes, she was tormented by images of the stretcher coming out of Preston's house. She kept going over it in her mind—maybe it wasn't him—of course, it was him—no, maybe it wasn't him—back and forth, and on and on.

She screamed over and over to herself. *What have I done, what have I done, what have I done?*

It didn't matter that she hadn't meant to harm him. She was responsible. *Murder.* A cardinal sin. *Cardinal. Sin.* Her Catholic guilt went into overdrive.

How was this going to work? Would the police come around asking questions? What would they say? How would she react? Should she just turn herself in?

Moments before Im had discovered the horror going on at Preston's house that morning, she'd been on the internet checking out local lawyers to advise her on how to handle the sale of her valuable, rare book. Obviously, counting her chickens before they'd hatched. And how ironic that she'd been looking for a lawyer—only now, the search would have to be for a different kind of attorney—a criminal one. The mere thought of the word "criminal' sent her into even deeper paroxysms of despair.

She kept asking herself what she had done wrong. Hadn't she been careful? Xanax wasn't supposed to be lethal, even in big doses. Suddenly she had a thought. Maybe they'd just think he'd accidentally overdosed on his own. They'd have no reason to suspect foul play, right? But the smoothie glass? The police would find traces of the drug in there. If they put a good detective on the case, wouldn't they look at her, the next-door neighbor, perhaps someone even with a gripe of some sort against Preston? Or who knows, they might think it was a love affair gone bad.

As she lay in bed, Im became more and more paranoid. What if they dusted for fingerprints? They'd find her prints literally everywhere. How could that be explained? They wouldn't have her fingerprints in the law enforcement database, or would they? She couldn't remember if she'd ever been fingerprinted for anything that might have been entered into a database.

Then another devastating thought—what if Preston had bragged to someone about having snatched the valuable book from her? Then it was going to be all over. The police would know it was her. But maybe Preston had not told anyone how he'd actually acquired the book? He might have instead bragged about finding it at a yard sale or something. Would he have even risked telling anyone about it? After all, he had just stolen the thing from her. Maybe he would have wanted to keep it to himself, as she had done.

Regardless of all the what-ifs, Imogene was coming to another awful conclusion. How could she risk selling the Darwin book now—wouldn't Sotheby's have to make sure it hadn't been stolen? What was the procedure for doing this? If Preston had told someone (perhaps, a close friend or family member) about the book, if that person looked for it in his belongings and didn't find it, would they report it missing to the police? Would it then be seen as a possible motive for murder? For Imogene, the what-ifs were limitless and agonizing and incessant.

Now, after all she'd risked getting her father's rare book, both initially and later after Preston had lifted it, she was going to have to bury it for all eternity. How could she risk coming out with it? It could implicate her in a murder—if she wasn't a suspect already. These mental machinations sent

Im into yet a deeper state of shock and horror. It felt like an insurmountable conundrum. How was she ever going to go on?

Eventually, she dragged herself out of bed. It was noon. Her mother was up sitting quietly in her chair, dog on her lap. This is how it was. Mrs. Mussomeli would just sit quietly for hours. Imogene imagined if her mother were all alone long enough, she might eventually go find something in the kitchen to eat or drink. Although, she might not remember to feed the dog. Her daughter had taken over all of these things. Things wouldn't happen otherwise. She'd already tried to work with her mother on this, but a persistent inertia had begun to set in. Without someone directing her, her mother would usually only sit still, doing nothing. It's how the brain disease seemed to work.

On this day, Im was glad for the stillness. She was a complete wreck and was so distracted by the events that had unfolded around her, she could barely look after herself, let alone another person and a dog. But she knew she was going to have to, regardless of her mental state. They depended on her. She went through the automatic motions of giving her mother her daily pills, making coffee, and fixing her something to eat (she herself could not eat a thing). She fed and took out Marvin and popped her mother's favorite ballet, Swan Lake, into the DVD player. She hit the repeat button and disappeared into her bedroom. This would give her a few more hours before anyone needed her again. She forced herself to drink half a bottle of water, then crawled back into her bed and curled up into fetal position.

Although Im didn't expect to fall asleep, she did. It was something of a holdover from her teenage years when, after a bad day at school or otherwise, she would immediately retreat to her room, climb into bed, and escape into sleep. She can recall her parents worrying about her, but she usually would snap out of it after a few days—until the next episode. When they asked her if anything was wrong, Im would say no, that she was just tired. She never wanted to talk about what might have been bothering her. For whatever reason, she had a hard time reaching out for support, which was too bad because she often could have benefited from it.

Now, Im was in a dire emotional state, yet the last thing she wanted was to tell anyone about it. She was horrified and disgusted by what she'd done, inadvertently or not. The intense shame of it was overwhelming to her. Talking with her sisters or friends was flat out of the question. How could they possibly help anyway?

Late in the afternoon, Imogene woke to her mother sitting on the edge of her bed, the same single bed she'd slept in as a kid, the same room. It was the one place where she'd always felt safe. Im suddenly felt like she was a teenager again, hibernating in her room when things got tough, but now with a problem beyond any she'd ever encountered before. Of course, she'd had her share of mishaps and upheavals in her life, but even the worst of those things felt like a walk in the park compared to what she presently faced.

Imogene remembered a time decades ago when she had spent days in her bedroom, escaping into sleep in the very same bed. It was after she had a bad experience with a boy. She was only thirteen, and if she was honest with herself now, she would have to say it was possibly some sort of sexual abuse. Although, because she had sought out the seventeen-year-old's attention in the first place, she had never seen it that way. Mark was a big-shot basketball player at the high school, who happened to live a few streets over. Imogene had a crush on him, looking for ways to run into him, walking by his house. Sometimes she rode her bike to the park where he and a group of boys would be playing basketball. They noticed her. She had developed early and looked older than she was; she had become, frankly, a little bombshell.

She was thrilled when Mark showed interest in her, and they spent hours just talking about anything and everything. She'd never even kissed a boy when one night, sitting alone in the park, he began kissing her. It felt awkward but thrilling at the same time. Here was the boy she'd been crushing on, the boy every girl she knew including her own sisters were crushing on, and he apparently liked her. Her, Imogene! She felt special just being by his side. She never intended or expected it to go any further, but suddenly he had his hands up her shirt, then down her pants, inside her underwear. She didn't know what to do. She tried to get him to stop, pulling his hands away, but he kept putting them back. He never got her clothes off, but afterward, when she went home, alone in the quiet of her bedroom, she felt ashamed and confused. Dirty. Even though she sensed she had somehow been violated, Imogene believed it had ultimately been her own fault. Hadn't she let him take advantage of her? Yes, she'd resisted, but she still let it happen, even more or less enjoyed it—in spite of being petrified the whole time. It was her fault. She could have made him stop.

Imogene had spent hours, even days, after this happened, sulking in her room, staring off into space, feeling that her young carefree teenage life was over—that she'd never be the same innocent girl she was before that frightening night with Mark: that she was now forever tainted. One day, concerned, her mother came into her room, sat on the edge of her bed, and asked her daughter what was so clearly wrong. Im could hold it inside no longer. Although she could barely speak the words, she finally blurted it out and confessed to her mother that she had done bad things with a boy. She didn't go into detail, and in those days, even if she had, nothing would have probably ever come of it. Besides, she felt like she'd deserved it, that it was her own fault anyway. The shame of it had been unbearable, but her mother did not freak out on her; she simply listened and told Im that it would be okay.

And though they never discussed it further (nor had since), that little talk with her mom was enough to allow Im to climb up out of the abyss and get on with her life. She would always remember her mother's simple reassurance that day and what a powerful sense of relief it had provided. Perhaps the incident had left her scarred in some ways, but she'd put it in the past and learned to be more careful with boys. Still, she was the only one of her sisters without a husband. Perhaps this early traumatic sexual experience had somehow derailed her, left her destined to bad choices and unmet potentials.

Now, here was her mother sitting on the edge of her bed, just like she had done all those years before, asking her what was wrong. Again, a traumatic scenario involving a member of the male species. The irony might have amused her on another day, but of course, not on this day. Suddenly Imogene realized her mother was, in fact, the only person in the world she could tell about Preston.

She'd already told her what she had done to recover the book from his house. Mrs. Mussomeli had laughed along with her daughter at how she had outsmarted the twit. Granted, a few hours later, when Im mentioned it again, she seemed to have only a vague idea of what her daughter was referring to, but still she could hoot and holler about it with her just the same. Imogene knew that she'd never have to worry about her mother spilling the beans to anyone—she could rattle on about it all until the cows came home.

Im felt a desperate need to tell someone, anyone, about accidentally overdosing and killing Preston. Her mother was the only choice—there was absolutely no one else she dared tell. She hoped it wouldn't alarm her too much, but she had to speak about it before her insides burst. Mrs. Mussomeli listened quietly to it all. There was a gasp when Im told her that she thought Preston was dead, and her facial expression showed pained concern, but she didn't seem horrified. Im thought that she probably couldn't appreciate the seriousness of it, or even if she did in that one moment, the concern was going to be fleeting, as were all her thoughts. Besides, she knew her mother well; it would be hard for her to grasp that one of her children had become a murderer—a common criminal.

Imogene realized she could confess to her mother a million times, and she would always listen attentively, patting her on the arm, nodding in support and sympathy. Even though her mom said almost nothing, it was a small comfort for Im to get it off her chest. Her mother did say finally that she thought it would be okay, that, of course, she hadn't meant for Preston to die. That Im should just be honest and everyone would understand it was an accident.

Imogene, hands gripping the sides of her head, as if in searing pain, vigorously shook her head, "No, no, Ma, they'll put me in jail!"

Her mother reacted to this. "Oh no, they wouldn't do that would they? Well...then, let it go. It's over and done. You didn't mean it. They don't know you did anything. Just don't think about it. You can't change it."

Imogene was amazed at her mother's lucidity on the issue. It was likely deep fear for her daughter which had evoked such a clear and thoughtful response. Mrs. Mussomeli certainly didn't want her daughter to be charged with a crime, let alone incarcerated. Her solution was for her daughter to say nothing, do nothing, just forget about it. Imogene would have loved to forget it, if only she could. But her mind was her own worst enemy, and she knew herself too well. There would be no reprieve from this nightmare.

CHAPTER 22

OVER THE 24 HOURS following the ghastly development next door, Im felt like there was a dense, suffocating fog enveloping her, leaving her barely able to breathe or see. She could not even touch food. The nauseating pit in her stomach felt like it went through the floor. She had to force herself to swallow water so she wouldn't dehydrate. She kept a constant vigil on the local news waiting for a report to appear about a mysterious death on their street, and she peeped out the window frequently at Preston's house to monitor any new activity. When nothing happened, Im figured the police must be waiting for the coroner's report or toxicology results or something... isn't that the way it worked?

The lack of information led Imogene to nurse fantasies that the unthinkable hadn't really occurred. She still didn't have any confirmation of who had actually been carried out dead on a stretcher from Preston's house. Maybe it was some friend of his and not him. There'd been no obituary for Preston in the newspaper the next day, so who knows? True, she hadn't seen Preston in days or noticed any sign of life from his house, but hadn't things often seemed pretty dead over there anyway? He didn't have a dog to walk, he didn't take a newspaper that he'd creep out and snatch up in the morning, and he didn't sit out in the open air on his patio. He really did tend to hole up.

Preston never even washed his cars himself. She could tell he was the kind of guy who'd only take his cars to the upscale carwash or detailing place. He also didn't do much of the lawn and yard maintenance himself. A truckload of guys would show up at regular intervals with mowers and equipment, and his lawn often sported those little flags around the edges warning that chemicals had been applied. She kept reminding herself that days, even weeks, had gone by in the past when she would never see Preston Wyles in the flesh at all. The only way she had known he was alive was that his truck would be gone from the driveway, then would reappear parked again at some point. She never worried about him being dead back then. Right, that was before someone covered by a sheet had been transported out of there on a stretcher!

Im desperately wanted information, anything, so she could know exactly what she was facing. Had the police already ruled it a homicide? Were they going to be coming around to investigate? Would they interrogate her? Did she need to get a lawyer? The unanswered questions tormented her to no end, but she didn't dare step forward. She needed to play the role of the oblivious neighbor, an uninterested party who barely knew the dead guy, who didn't even really live there anymore, was only back temporarily to help her mother after her father's death. Her mother had legitimate reasons for being clueless, so why in the world would the mother-daughter pair next door even be seeking information?

As Im played it out in her head, it would have been easy for her to plead ignorance and act like she must have missed the police and ambulance that morning they came to Preston's. She could have been asleep or out. The Mussomeli's house was on the corner; the next nearest neighbors were across the street. Certainly, in a quiet, low-density neighborhood where people minded their own business and kept to themselves, one neighbor might not even know until it hit the newspaper that anything had happened to another neighbor, right? But Imogene wasn't sure of anything anymore. Maybe it would seem more suspicious if she wasn't inquiring about him. All of the possibilities, most of them appalling in her mind, left her essentially paralyzed. Riveted in place. Waiting for the shit to hit the fan—that moment when the police would come to her door and take her away in handcuffs.

Imogene had never been in handcuffs and couldn't even imagine enduring this torture. She was fairly claustrophobic, and even being held down in a playful way could send her into a panic. Once, as a teenager, she suffered a near anxiety attack when she and some girls had crammed into the backseat of a guy's sports car. She felt like she couldn't breathe and began to get hysterical, pleading for them to let her out right away. Even if she knew in her mind that she wasn't really in any danger, she could not rationalize herself out of the sheer terror of feeling confined.

She wondered if her general claustrophobia had roots in early experiences when playing around with her sisters, she might crawl into a tight space and be momentarily stuck. This happened when she had climbed into the square, brick cubbyhole next to their fireplace which was meant for log storage. She could vividly recall how intensely frightened she felt when she found herself wedged in too tightly, unable to get out, imagining her skeletal remains found inside there years later. Or the time she and Maria were playing around in the laundry room, and she briefly got stuck in the clothes dryer.

At some point later in her life, she'd found herself feeling the same hemmed in feelings whenever she was closed in a small space, like in the back of a crowded car or an elevator. In these kinds of situations, Imogene became acutely aware that she couldn't freely move and didn't have full control over an escape route. That was what seemed to send her into a panic. She couldn't tolerate it even for a few seconds.

Although maybe it had nothing to do with experiences at all, and maybe she was just hard-wired this way all along. Either way, the mere thought of being locked in a prison cell, by definition a place where an individual had absolutely no control over any escape route, left her stomach in knots and her heart pounding out of her chest. It felt like a vise grip squeezing her brain.

Mrs. Mussomeli, though unaware of what was eating away at her daughter, nonetheless, showed some small signs of distress as well. She didn't appear contented and happy as she usually did, and her appetite seemed off. Imogene now knew this was how it worked for people with dementia. Without any immediate short-term memory train to carry them from one stop to another—one minute to the next—they essentially lived only in the moment, and looked to those around them and their environment for cues about how to feel at any point in time. It could be a great thing, blissful even, unless the person was surrounded by negativity.

Imogene hated to think she was becoming toxic to her mother, a complete innocent in this morass. She tried to keep functioning, at least for her mother's sake, forcing herself to do everything that was required to keep her mother safe and healthy in spite of her own dismal emotional status. At least her sense of duty and commitment to family was alive and well. She hadn't fallen completely into a cesspool of self-loathing and despair, though she knew that she was teetering on the edge. It took all her energy not to simply crawl into her bed and wait to die of starvation.

That afternoon, Im decided she needed to get her mother and the dog outside for a walk. Maybe fresh air would do them all some good. They hadn't left the house since the morning when she went to the bank for the safety deposit box, which felt like forever ago, though it had been only days. So much had changed in the short interval; she felt like a completely different person.

Before the awful day—Preston-dead-on-a-stretcher day—Imogene had been feeling like she was on top of the world. She'd pulled off a feat she never dreamed she could. She'd triumphed in a high-stakes game. She felt literally unstoppable. It was survival of the fittest, and she'd been the fittest! She'd been eagerly awaiting the spoils, anticipating a major windfall when she would sell the rare Darwin book. The events of the previous weeks had taken her to hell and back...and, sadly, back to hell.

Before the awful day, she thought she might finally have turned a corner in her life. Now, after what she'd done—homicide, the worst sin possible— she felt sure that she was destined for Hell, both the living version and the dead version. While afterlife Hell had to be worse, the living version already felt like a dreadful nightmare, from which she would never wake.

How could she have become *that* person?! A doomed-all-is-lost soul? A common criminal! A *felon,* no less!

The anguish was so excruciating that she decided to allow herself to consider, at least until finding out something to the contrary, that maybe her assumptions were somehow wrong. Perhaps it hadn't been Preston under the sheet, being wheeled out on a stretcher, but someone else. It was possible, wasn't it? Or even, if it was indeed Preston, maybe because of the angle of her view, peering out the window of their house, it only appeared that the sheet was pulled all the way over his head. But maybe it wasn't and he was merely being taken out to a hospital for care and she had not actually killed him at all. Maybe!

Im told herself that until she saw his name in the newspaper, it wasn't official. Who knows, perhaps Preston wasn't dead at all. This gave her a slight sense of calm, and out of sheer desperation, she seized on this tiny glimmer of hope. Surely, it was not rational, but it was all she had to keep herself going. So she decided that she would wait for confirmation from some source: an obituary in the paper or on the internet. She'd also, in the meantime, keep an eye out in case anyone came to his house, and then she might play dumb and ask whoever it was if Preston was around, as though she needed to ask him a question. She'd seen his brother there occasionally, though she didn't know if he lived in town or not. Either way, if the situation presented itself, a casual inquiry as to Preston's whereabouts wouldn't create undue suspicion, would it?

Having come to this resolve, such as it was, Imogene allowed herself to retreat into the fantasy that all might not be lost. She and her mother and Marvin went out for a nice, long walk. It was a beautiful, bright day; the fresh air and sunshine lifted her slightly from the dark place she'd been living in, and she felt a small easing of the tension that had set up camp in her body. She wasn't fine and dandy, but she finally had the desire to eat something.

That evening, she and her mother went out to her favorite Asian restaurant in town, owned by a charming Chinese lady and her family. Im ordered her usual lemongrass chicken, rice vermicelli noodle. It was delicious—the first time in days she'd been able to enjoy the taste of the food she was shoveling into her mouth. Tucked away in the quaint restaurant with its traditional Asian decor, no windows, no hustle and bustle, Imogene felt slightly revived.

In that moment, Im promised herself she would stay strong, at least for her mother's sake, and deal with whatever might come. She was even able to enjoy her mother's adorable attempt at reading her fortune from the cookie, initially reading the wrong side of the fortune slip and announcing hers to the table (Imogene), as is the custom, "Learn Chinese...?" This was of course just the filler phrase printed on the backside of the fortune slip, along with some Chinese characters. Imogene couldn't resist chuckling. Her mother had read what she thought was her fortune with so much theatrical gusto, but her tone had lifted as she got to the last word, "Learn Chinese?!" as if to say, what the hell kind of lousy fortune is this anyway?

Her mother was truly a joy at times, and Imogene vowed not to let her personal crisis overshadow her mother's life and happiness. If the worst happened, Im would make sure that she would be well taken care of by one of her sisters, and make them pledge not to dump her in some nursing home with a bunch of strangers. Whether she could get her sisters to commit to this might be a challenge, but she hoped at least one of them would be willing to make the personal sacrifices necessary to insure her mother fully enjoyed the final years of her life. She knew it was what their father would have wanted.

Im hated herself for having brought herself to the brink of collapse and possible incarceration or worse. What were the laws in Ohio anyway? Was what she had done possibly a capital offense? In some states, there was something called felony capital murder, which was killing someone in the context of committing a felony—and that was considered a crime of the highest order. Would that apply here to her? *Oh. My. God.*

Returning home after dinner out that night, nothing had changed at Preston's house. It was all dark inside. Only the post light was on, which she knew was set to switch on automatically at nightfall. A tiny part of her had still hoped they'd come home to something that would indicate he was actually alive and well, even though she knew in her heart there was virtually no chance of that happening.

After pulling the car into the garage, she was suddenly overcome with despair, and began sobbing into her hands, her head down against the steering wheel of her father's Cadillac.

Her mother reached out to her daughter. "Oh, Im, what's the matter?"

Imogene was too exhausted to get into the whole pathetic story for the umpteenth time, and only replied, "I miss Dad."

Mrs. Mussomeli then said, "Oh, so do I, so do I, Im!" Her voice sounded weepy, but there were no tears. She never really cried about it anymore. Maybe her memory loss was a blessing in that sense. As much as she missed her husband, her tendency to live only in the moment had likely sheltered her somewhat from the grief. Perhaps dulled it a little. When something was out of sight, it could be out of mind for her, it seemed. Although her mother didn't ask about him, as in, where he was, sometimes Imogene wondered if she was always completely cognizant of the reality that he had indeed died of a heart attack and wasn't coming back.

That night became another essentially sleepless affair for Imogene. The welcome escape into sleep she'd enjoyed for a while was no more. Now it was back to that all-too-familiar pattern—she'd wake up after brief periods of fitful slumber, often in a cold sweat with her heart racing. On this night, she'd startled awake from a nightmare. Frightened and nauseous, she stumbled to the bathroom and threw up. In the dream, she was in jail, stuck behind bars, and she couldn't breathe—clawing at her clothes, tightly clutching the bars, trying to shove her head out to get air— frantically screaming for someone to please let her out.

Im knew that she was in fact so claustrophobic she might indeed expire from the sheer panic of being locked up.

Even just imagining such sent her reeling. She thought she could feel the cortisol levels of her body rising precipitously, though levels of the hormone would not be detectable via human senses alone. Still, she knew the fuzzy, heavy feeling in her head all too well, and that heightened cortisol levels were the culprit in serious sleep disruption.

Cortisol, a primary stress hormone, is a key part of the body's "fight or flight" response. A vestige from our ancestors whose stress was almost always from a real physical foe or threat, survival depended on being able to rally all available energy and focus a response either on fleeing from the threat or fighting to defeat it. The release of the hormone produces a state of heightened alertness, antithetical to sleep. Eons ago, having a strong cortisol-driven, fight-or-flight response insured survival and was adaptive, so it was selected for, as Darwin would have put it. Because the individual with a strong fight-or-flight instinct survived, that individual would have a chance to pass on genes to its offspring, including the gene for this trait.

The problem is that the stressors humans face in the present era on Earth are very often not the sort for which the release of cortisol for flight-or-flight is an asset. Indeed, this bodily response to stress is considered maladaptive and even counter productive. Yet, it is so hard-wired due to its age-old importance to overall survival—in the organic sense—humans are basically stuck with it for now. On a strictly evolutionary timetable, human beings have only been around a smidgen of a moment in the big scheme of things. This is nowhere near enough time to modify something as primal and entrenched as the fight-or-flight response.

Now, Imogene Mussomeli's cortisol-driven stress response was careening off the charts. She would have survived many an ancient predator's attacks, one way or another, but surviving a modern day crisis was clearly another story. If her cortisol levels didn't calm down, she was headed right back into an endless stretch of insomnia, which would invariably put her into the throes of a deep depression, a place she never wanted to go again.

CHAPTER 23

BY SIX THE NEXT MORNING, Imogene had given up on sleep and dragged herself out of bed to see if the newspaper had been delivered. It usually arrived sometime between six and 6:30 a.m. It wasn't there at six, so she made herself some tea and sat quietly waiting, feeling she could do nothing else until the paper came. At about 6.20, she saw the newspaper delivery person's car pull in the driveway, drop the paper, and pull out. Rarely were paperboys really boys riding around on bikes with their newspaper-laden canvas bags around their necks—or even boys anymore, for that matter. Now, the typical newspaper delivery person was an adult who maybe couldn't get a better-paying job. The Mussomeli's paper was currently delivered by a middle-aged woman in a dilapidated sedan. The new economy had definitely created a new world. Growing up today, Im would have had no opportunity to develop a crush on the paperboy bringing the newspaper with the all-important weather map. If only her biggest worry could again be merely the weather…

Im quickly ran outside in her pajamas to grab the paper. The fall morning air was crisp but not too cold. On a different morning, she might have taken a minute to mosey around the yard to see what might need doing. Her father had always tended to the large lot himself—cutting grass, trimming bushes, pulling weeds. He didn't like hiring someone for a job he felt he could do on his own. It was a lot of work, but that was his way. Her sisters used to fuss at him for not hiring professionals to make the yard more polished, but Im knew that it made him feel good to do it himself. Sure, it didn't look perfect, but he did his best, and that was really good enough. Im hoped she could continue in this tradition and at least keep her parents' place from looking like a neighborhood eyesore.

Though she supposed the most likely eyesore possibility now was not going to be the condition of the yard or house, but rather the fact that it had been the home of a murderer.

Back inside the house, Imogene placed the morning newspaper on the dining room table and unfolded it to pull out the section that would list the obituaries. Her hands trembled as she opened to the final two pages of the "Local" news section. There were two full pages of obits, some long, some short, some with photos, some without. She scanned down the alphabetized listings, quickly moving to the latter half of the list. This is where the "Ws" would be. And then she saw it.

WYLES, Preston M. Died October 15. Services pending. Foxgrove Funeral Home, Huntington, Kentucky.

Imogene immediately felt ill, ran to the bathroom, and threw up. The horror of her actions and her worst fears had finally been unequivocally confirmed in black and white. There would be no deluding herself further. She was, in fact, a murderess. Looking at herself in the bathroom mirror, she could see the whites all around her deep brown irises; the look of alarm, terror, and dismay was clear. She swished with some mouthwash and crawled back into bed. She was feeling unwell. This was not going to be a good day.

She lay in her bed for several hours, feeling lost and alone and numb and hopeless. Her mind was bursting with self-recriminations. How could she have been so cavalier with another person's life? With her own future? And all for what? Im wanted to think that it was sentimentality for her father's rare book that had driven her to do what she did, but of course, she knew that wasn't the case at all. Had the Darwin book not been so valuable, she would have found a way to let it go and chalk it up to bad luck or fate.

Like so many others before her, it was ultimately just one thing that led her down the road to ruin: greed.

Imogene tried to think through what the future might hold. The thought of a police car pulling up, followed by a knock on the door, petrified her. Should she run? But how could she? Her mother needed her. If she took her mother and Marvin and some essentials and bolted, she might only make herself look guilty. After all, what other evidence would they have that would point to her? Well, there would be the empty smoothie glass, which would have residual Xanax in it, but how would they trace it to her? Besides, Preston's disgusting kitchen was a mess of dirty glasses and dishes—would the detectives be sharp enough to pick out the one that held a clue?

Then Im remembered that she'd left Preston's stupid glass lying on the carpet in her haste! But would they even have any reason to suspect that he was drugged by anything other than his own hand swallowing too many pills? There'd be no reason to think that he was dosed without his knowledge. Still, they wouldn't find a prescription bottle for Xanax anywhere on the premises. How hard would they try to find out where he got it? If they searched the Mussomeli house they'd find a bottle of Xanax. She'd have to find a way to get rid of it, though she knew if they truly suspected her, all they would have to do is get ahold of her prescription history from the pharmacy.

Then there were her fingerprints, likely to be found on almost every surface of his house. She touched practically everything in the damn house in her search for the Darwin book, before she finally found it deep in his gross underwear drawer. But she didn't have a criminal record. Would they be able to match the prints to her? Of course, all they'd have to do is arrest her and take her prints. She'd be toast. *Oh God.*

If this, if that, would they this or would they that? The list of questions and possibilities was endless. What was the bottom line? Should she consult an attorney? That might only implicate her, make her look guilty of something. Besides, she certainly didn't want to speak of the unspeakable to another living soul, notwithstanding her mother. At least she could confide in her mother—there was no risk in doing that, a small comfort, such as it was.

Finally, Im forced herself to get out of bed to take care of the dog and her mother. Mrs. Mussomeli took one look at her daughter and said, "Im, you don't look good. Are you feeling alright?"

Im immediately broke down. "Oh, Mama, he's dead!"

"Who?"

"Your neighbor, Preston Wyles. I really did kill him. I didn't mean to, but it's true—it's in today's obituaries. Oh, Ma, what am I going to do now? What am I going to do?"

"What do you mean you killed him?"

Like always, she had little or no retention of the story Im had already told her many times. Im gave her the thumbnail sketch—she'd learned that if she kept a narrative concise and short, her mother would be able to hold it in her mind long enough to understand it fully for a moment or two and respond. Mrs. Mussomeli listened attentively, then was quiet. She seemed to be mulling over her daughter's predicament.

"Oh, Im, you didn't mean for it to happen. Just don't say a word. They'll never know it was you. Besides, maybe it's not as bad as you think it is."

"No, Ma, I did it—he's dead, and it's my fault. What the hell am I going to do? I feel sick." Imogene ran to the bathroom and buckled over in dry heaves. She felt like her insides were being forced out. She collapsed on the floor.

Her mother followed her into the bathroom and knelt next to her, gently placing her arm around her daughter's shoulders. "Oh, Im, it'll be alright; it'll be okay."

Im closed her eyes, "If only."

***

For days after she'd read the obituary, Imogene walked around in an agitated state—hyper-vigilant, jumping every time she heard a vehicle outside, running to the window to see if anyone was coming, obsessively checking the local news for any mention of a homicide investigation, incessantly searching on the internet for any information, researching the laws in Ohio to see what she would be facing. She didn't think she'd be facing the death penalty. The bizarreness of even thinking about this and asking this question in terms of her own fate was too much. Her emotional status was going downhill fast, and she knew it. She wondered if she should call one of her sisters to come and take her mother. The thought of doing this was unbearable though. How was she going to explain what was happening to her? She couldn't imagine confessing the whole thing. But then again, she knew her sisters loved her. They'd stand by her side, wouldn't they?

She went through another panic as she realized that if she was a suspect, the police would seize her computer. Even if Im deleted all her self-incriminating search histories, she'd heard that nothing was ever truly erased without a trace, that technicians could always still find it. Should she smash up her computer and dump it somewhere? No, that would be even worse probably. If she did anything like that, she'd learned enough from crime shows and her criminal law research to know that she'd also probably destroy the possibility of getting any leniency at sentencing. Really, the best chance for getting any leniency at all was to come forward, come clean, confess before they even charged you.

Imogene kept trying to imagine what her father would have told her to do. On the one hand, he had been a man of high morals and integrity, a very honest man. But on the other hand, she knew that he sometimes would try to get around some stupid tax regulation or something which had negative implications for his investments. Not that he ever broke the law, but he did do things to maximize his profits while paying the least amount in taxes. Isn't that what everyone does, though? Mr. Mussomeli was also fiercely loyal to his family and seemed to be of the mindset that sometimes you do what you have to do for your family, no matter what. Maybe he would have wanted her to go on as if nothing had happened. After all, she hadn't meant to harm Preston. What evidence would they even have against her? Besides, look what Preston had done. Maybe he deserved what he got.

Would her father have actually supported the actions that she'd taken? Of course, it had all gone bad, but part of her believed that he would have wanted her to get the valuable book back from the despicable thief. That her father would be saying she did what she had to do. Imogene wondered if he'd want her to practice Omerta—the Sicilian code of silence. Although Im knew it didn't exactly apply Omerta was that you didn't rat someone out to the police, even in your own defense. Well, maybe the code would mean that she shouldn't rat herself out.

Preston's house next door seemed completely deserted, though one day she noticed that his truck was no longer there. What did that mean? Some member of his family, most likely the brother, the only one she knew existed, must have come and driven the vehicle away. Given that the funeral home listed in the obit was in Kentucky, it must be where his roots and family were. It would explain the lack of activity at his house. Selfishly, it occurred to Im that if the family was not local, they'd be less likely to be hounding the police about finding out who was responsible for their loved one's sudden death. Imogene wanted to die herself. She knew what it was like to grieve a sudden death of a family member—now she'd inflicted this on someone else.

The worst thing for Imogene, beyond all else, was the crush of her own guilty conscience. She realized one afternoon, while she was lying on the living room sofa in her usual state of stuporous despair—mixed with occasional hysteria, mixed with periodic, calm-before-the-storm feelings—that she was sort of living the hell of Dostoyevsky's Crime and Punishment character, Raskolnikov. When this thought occurred to her, she almost laughed. She'd been mesmerized and riveted by the book when she read it after college. She'd found a paperback copy of the book in her father's little den library one summer when she was home and had nothing to read. Imogene considered it one of the best books she'd ever read. In the story, Raskolnikov does something far more intentional and heinous than what Imogene had done, but the moral dilemma in which Im found herself now was essentially the same as that of Raskolnikov. Dostoyevsky's character is a struggling young man who robs and murders a nasty old woman pawnbroker/money lender and is not even a suspect, but is tormented and nearly driven to madness by his own conscience. Ultimately Raskolnikov begins to implicate himself with all his bizarre, post-crime, guilt-driven behaviors. In the end, he confesses because it is the only way to set himself free from his personal hell. He is sentenced to eight years in Siberia.

The parallels to Im's situation were clear. Why had she loved this Dostoyevsky book so much? And how ironic, given where she currently found herself. Was it because she could see herself in Raskolnikov? That she could relate to his mental anguish because she sensed she would be the same way if ever in a similar circumstance? It was like some kind of weird foreshadowing. Here she was, it was all happening to her, the very thing she imagined would be so incredibly shameful, utterly disgraceful, and absolutely horrific when she'd read about it. She had thought that what Raskolnikov had done, taking another person's life, was the worst thing a human could ever do in their lives, and believed that the resultant personal hell would be insurmountable and ultimately not survivable. Now, *here she was*. Why had this book moved her so much? It was the one book she always mentioned in any conversation about the best books of all time.

The one-week anniversary of Preston Wyles' death passed without even one iota of news or information about his untimely demise. What was going on? The lack of any information felt almost worse than having some new information, even if it meant bad news for her. This blackout left Imogene on edge, unable to move one way or another, essentially glued to one spot in time and place.

Fortunately, she had begun to eat again, and her mother and Marvin seemed to be fine. Yes, her mood was dark and grim, but she did her best to put on a cheery facade because she knew that anything else would have brought her mother down. Her mother was a complete innocent in the situation, and the last thing she wanted to do was jeopardize her well-being. Im also wanted to take good care of Marvin. She owed him, and besides, her mother adored him, even though she couldn't pet him liberally without him suddenly snarling and snapping. When he was on her lap, which was often, she had seemingly trained herself to be perfectly still so as not to provoke him. Right, what a *terrific* pet. Yet, her mother's love for the dog was unflappable. She would vehemently defend him at every turn, regardless, and often in spite of his clear wickedness.

The depths of her affinity for the crazy Chihuahua were preposterous. Imogene had even heard her mother exclaim once, "Oh Marvin, I love you. I want to go on to doggie heaven with you someday."

Imogene did receive another email from Mr. Wexler of Sotheby's. He must have been getting anxious that she was considering taking "his find" to Christie's or somewhere else. The message was short and sweet, basically just saying that he was eager to meet with her whenever she was ready to discuss plans for her rare copy of "(On the) Origin of Species." In any other circumstances, Im would have been pleased about his pointed interest, but now all she could think of was how her greed for the book had led her down her current appalling path. And if not for Im's stubborn pack-ratishness, she'd never have even known that the book existed. She wouldn't be in her own personal black hole of guilt and utter despair. And she wouldn't be going to Hell.

Further, as she traveled down the if-only-road, Im realized that if only she'd not been so picky and stupid where men were concerned, she could have had herself a nice husband by now, a few kids, a big bustling, happy home of her own—a life. She wouldn't have had time to hang around her mother's house foraging through trash bags her sisters had compiled. No, she would have had her own family to attend to. She would have been *normal*.

In her darkest moments, the moroseness of her own thoughts would overtake her, and she would even drift all the way back to her own birth. If only she'd never been born, everyone would have been better off, and none of this would be happening to her and indirectly to the rest of her family. The shame Im was going to bring would be unprecedented in the family history. In fact, it struck her for the first time that maybe she was never supposed to be born at all. She was the only one whose birth had been complicated. True to form, she had resisted coming out the normal head-first way and instead had been in the traversed position (sideways), with her shoulder sticking out, as though she was trying to reach out to the world with her arm. Look at that, she'd been a conniving, grabby thing from the very start. The doctor had to shove her back in, re-position her, and use the forceps to yank her out. Nothing like this had happened with the births of her five sisters. It seemed she'd been the odd one out from the very beginning, innately misaligned with the world from the get-go.

CHAPTER 24

DAYS WENT BY WITHOUT any word of Preston Wyles' demise. Imogene passed the time in a cloud of worry but did her best to get on with life, in any small ways she could. Her appetite was awful, but she tried to eat enough to live. Mrs. Mussomeli, when on her health kicks back in the day, used to proclaim, "One should eat to live, not live to eat!" There was certainly no danger that Im would be living to eat any time soon. Food pretty much tasted like soggy sawdust or crunchy cardboard to her. She was essentially force-feeding herself so she could survive and have the strength to continue to do what needed to be done at home. She tried to cook decent meals for her mother's sake, but they went out to eat a lot because Im never had the energy to put forth the effort in the kitchen.

Imogene knew she was depressed, but unlike the deep depression she'd experienced after her father's death, her current state proved different. This time, instead of insomnia setting in, she found that she could usually sleep and sleep, anytime she wanted. It had taken this turn after she had found Preston's obituary and had confirmation of his death. She was surprised, but it was a gift of sorts; it reminded her of when she'd been able to escape into the oblivion of sleep anytime as a teenager, especially when she was upset.

While being able to sleep this time kept her from disintegrating as a person, it did nothing to solve her problem—which was that she was a murderess. Her self-hatred was immense and relentless. Im tried not to talk too much about it with her mother because it only seemed to upset her. Her mom would protest that Imogene was not horrible and evil and that she loved her very much. Im hated to see her mom in distress, so she buttoned up, tried to forge on in silence, keeping things afloat—going out to the grocery store, cleaning the house, doing laundry. But unless she was sleeping, she was constantly tormented by her situation.

Before, Imogene used to watch all the true crime shows on TV, especially those involving murder. She always found them riveting, and though the quality of the programming was often lousy, she would still be compelled to watch every one. Hearing about and seeing all the gory details fascinated her to no end, and she would be amazed at the depravity and stupidity of the perpetrators. How could anyone ever stoop so low as to murder another human being? It had all seemed so foreign and distant from her. Now she was someone who could actually be the subject of a Dateline crime show! The irony of it all was too much. She had become a total ruin of a person, a basket case ensnared in the teeth of something so huge and horrible and merciless—there was essentially no escape.

Even if she managed to put the reality of her situation aside for a few moments, was able to be distracted temporarily, the seismic anguish would always return full force with a jolt, reminding her that she was now doomed and going to Hell. It was not a pretty picture. She couldn't focus for a second on a good book, a TV show, a movie. Obsessive thoughts of her predicament, intense feelings of horror and dread about the future, would invariably interrupt her train of thought. Her ability to engage and interact with the world unfettered by shame and remorse was virtually non-existent.

In her now perpetual state of self-loathing, there was barely a waking moment where she wasn't in the clutches of the greedy monster of her own guilt, swallowing up every shred of even the smallest of pleasures. Practically stuporous, she'd often drift into long reveries where, reflecting back on her entire life, she would say things to herself like, "You were always a lost cause!" and "You finally got what you deserve!"

For all the devious and slightly shady things she'd done, for all the nearly illegal or mildly shady acts, for all the times she stretched the truth, scored one for "the Equalizer" in her own mind, for all the moments when she white-lied to avoid something or get herself ahead in some way, it was now brutally apparent to her that all she'd been doing was amassing a huge store of very bad karma—a gargantuan tower of impending doom that would one day come tumbling down on top of her, crushing her to smithereens. *Kaboom.* Yes, Imogene's mind could be quite dramatic. But sadly, now, it felt terribly apropos.

Going into the third week after Preston's unseemly end, Imogene felt she was approaching a nadir beyond any she'd ever known before. The slide into total despair was steep and frightening; her growing pessimism about her life was utterly blinding. How was she ever going to go on?

There was one thing that could briefly transport Im away from her mental misery: music—specifically, Beatles music. She didn't know exactly why this was the case, but she was glad for it and sat for hours listening to all their old recordings. She had the entire catalogue and knew the lyrics to every track because she'd heard them over and over since she was a little girl. The words were second nature; she never missed a one.

Imogene was very young when the Beatles first made their mark in America, and she grew up listening to all of their songs. Like all the girls back then, she fell hugely in love with each member of the group. Her first love had been Paul McCartney, and she'd wile away hours listening to him sing the Beatles tunes, gazing at the album covers with his photos. She especially loved the ones of him on the Help! Album, looking particularly adorable on his skis, red and white striped scarf carelessly wrapped around his neck.

While Im was drawn first to Paul, he was the popular choice; most girls were madly in love with Paul at the time. Her oldest sister Michaela had already "called him" so Im was pressured by the rest of her sisters to choose a different Beatle. There were only four Beatles, of course, but Maria was still too young and oblivious, and Monica liked someone from the Dave Clark Five. In the end, Im chose George because her sisters were willing to let her have him, and she grew to love him all the same.

Naturally, it all seemed so silly looking back on it as an adult, and yet the nostalgia for this earlier time, a simpler time of innocence, certainly a more carefree time, would wash over her like an ocean wave. Now, it was the one time she could still lose herself in something, even if only temporarily.

It was fitting, then, that listening to one of the few Beatles songs that George Harrison had written would prove to be a pivotal point for her. Harrison's song "Here Comes the Sun" from the Abbey Road album had always been one of her favorites. In fact, the album was especially dear to her partly because she'd won it on a call-in contest to the radio.

She and her sisters used to spend hours in the basement listening to albums or music on the radio. One station regularly had album giveaways; you'd win if you happened to be the correct number caller. The girls would dial up the station over and over on the old black rotary phone in the basement, hoping to be the fifth caller or the seventh caller or the whichever caller. Their fingers would cramp as they pulled the numbers over and over. All they'd get was a lousy busy signal, but they kept on trying until they finally heard the announcement that somebody else had already won. But one day, instead of the annoying busy signal yet again, Im heard the line ringing. Her heart skipped a few beats, and then she heard, "Hello, caller number six! You are our winner!" A few weeks later, her new Beatles Abbey Road album arrived in the mail.

In the middle of "Here comes the Sun," singing along with the chorus for the umpteenth time in her life, Im had an epiphany, and she began to sob. The simple beauty of the song, the fullness of the chords, the lovely string accompaniment, the lyrics so pure and uplifting, she knew in that moment that there was really only one way for her to go on in her life. One clear path—and she had to take it, no matter how hard it was going to be. She felt a tinge of relief having come to some resolve, and yet she also knew—it was not going to be easy.

Energized for the first time in days, and with a new sense of purpose, Imogene spent the rest of the day tidying up the house, cleaning the bathrooms, vacuuming, dealing with the mail and bills, making sure there was enough food in the house and kibble for Marvin, getting all her mother's medications in order and filling a couple weeks of her daily pill boxes. She called the Chairmen of her department at the University and told him that she was going to have to extend her sabbatical/personal leave because she was still needed in Ohio, what with her mother's diagnosis of dementia and tying up her father's affairs. He was nice, understanding, but who knows if they'd already written her off. They hadn't scheduled her to teach any of her regular classes for the upcoming term, and she had no idea what they'd done about her other administrative duties. It seemed her assistant had been able to step in for the most part, an upper level graduate student who was being supervised by another faculty member. Perhaps they'd decided Imogene was expendable. So be it. She wouldn't concern herself with any of that now.

In her recent period of intense mental turmoil, she'd neglected some things around home. She was dismayed at this, and it took the whole day to get everything the way it should have been. There were even a couple of credit card bills which were past due—something she had always been practically religious about—but she called and explained that there was a serious family illness (true, hers) and got the large overdue charges reversed. She called her sisters, too, just to touch base. She didn't say anything about anything; she only wanted to check in with them, see how things were going, make sure all was okay with them and their families. She wanted to know they would be there in case she needed them to step in and care for their mother.

Maria did pick up on something when they talked. "Im, are you alright? You don't sound good…"

Imogene had to fib. "Oh, yeah, I'm fine, Mar. Just feeling tired, and my throat's a little scratchy, might be coming down with something…or maybe it's only allergies. Don't worry. I'll be fine," she said, trying to sound cheery.

At the end of the day, she took her mother out to their favorite Italian restaurant. Mrs. Mussomeli got her usual Eggplant Parmesan, and Imogene ordered Lasagna. Im's appetite was still lousy—she could only eat about a third of it, bringing home the rest for her mother to have the next day for lunch or dinner. Im wrote "Lasagna" and the date on the Styrofoam box, and she realized how much she loved writing with a ballpoint pen on Styrofoam. There was something so satisfying about the way the pen would sink in a little as you wrote on it, gliding along so smoothly, producing the most clean, perfect mark. The surface would absorb just enough of the pressure so that the ballpoint could do its best work. She knew that Styrofoam got a bad rap because of its negative environmental impact, but she liked it and wasn't offended by its continued use in the world. Im figured some would judge her for feeling this way, but so be it. She was not a freak where this stuff was concerned. The world had a lot bigger problems, which Styrofoam had no hand in.

Imogene was amazed at her relative calm on the eve of her next move. It was perhaps simply the quiet before the storm, but either way, she was glad to finally have some clarity, that she was able to experience a small sense of peace for the first time in weeks. She was pleased that her mother seemed completely content. She hoped that the future for her would not be difficult.

She truly adored her mother and felt such a tenderness and powerful desire to protect her. Im knew that her father would have wanted his wife to be well cared for. She'd hoped to always be available to care for her mother, who was going to need a truly loving guardian. This felt like no small purpose. Yes, people could be hired, but Im knew that there was no substitute for a family member, a daughter, who wouldn't seem like a complete stranger to her mother—a random person who, each day, would seem to have suddenly appeared out of the blue in her home. Now, Im prayed that her mother would be alright, no matter what happened.

They returned home after dinner to the persistent yapping of Marvin as usual, and though she cursed him to no end, Im imagined she'd still miss him one day. Entering the house through the garage, her eyes caught sight of the bright gold and blue bin of kitty litter in the corner. She suddenly felt a lump in her throat. If she had put the rare book in a safety deposit box in the beginning, none of this would be happening. Preston would be alive and well. Life would not be a living hell. She would not be going on to Hell when she died. Yes, *if only*. But she knew she couldn't change the past; what was done was clearly done. Instead, it was time to focus on being prepared to deal with her future. She was going to need to be very strong, brave perhaps. She hoped she would prove to be made of the right stuff.

There had been a small incident, a couple years back, which supported the idea that maybe she was. Home for the summer, she and her mother would go out walking with Marvin most afternoons. As they were passing a house a couple streets over from theirs, a huge black dog came bounding over to them from his yard, full speed. He clearly had his sights set on something. The owner came chasing after him, but it was too late. In an instant, he had his jaws around Marvin's neck. Barely nine pounds, Marvin was no match for the beast of a dog, a hundred pound whatever he was—some sort of Chow mix; it would be no contest. Marvin was going to come up short in the deal and was likely to be a goner in another few seconds.

Mrs. Mussomeli stood looking on; the expression on her face was one of utter and complete horror. As much as the dog was an annoyance, Im certainly didn't want to see him mauled to death. There was no time to think. She just threw herself on top of the huge black dog, put her arms around him in a big bear hug, and yanked tight around his chest. He finally spit out Marvin, who fortunately only had a neck full of the other dog's saliva and a bloody ear. The dog's owner was, naturally, incredibly relieved that his dog had not killed their dog, that there would be no major vet bills, and that the Mussomelis would not be suing the crap out of him.

The owner said to Im, "Wow, that was really brave of you." At the time, it made her feel good to think that maybe she was a brave person after all, in spite of her childhood fears and long-standing anxieties. She never forgot what he'd said. Now she hoped it was true.

That night, after their dinner out, Im sat with her mother and watched a ballet with her. Normally, Im would just pop one of her DVDs in the player when she might be stepping out and needing to leave her mother on her own. She always hated the thought of her mother sitting in her chair, alone in the house, staring off into space. Her mom might pick up a book—she did still like to read—but she rarely seemed to cleave to a new book. Im figured that the dementia prevented her from remembering anything about what she had already read when she'd open to her bookmark. Im hated the thought of her mother being robbed of the true pleasure of reading a good book.

But Kate Mussomeli could always enjoy the ballet, so they watched the Bolshoi's Swan Lake together that night—it was her mom's all-time favorite. Seeing her mother's face light up, glowing in the reflection of the screen, eyes bright, cheeks flushed with a dreamy smile on her face. At times, she'd even gasp, "Oh my!" when Prince Siegfried did Grand Jetès across the stage or when Odette and the Prince finished a dramatic Pas de Deux. Being there with her mother that night, watching her enjoy the Ballet, felt priceless to Imogene. She wanted to remember it forever.

CHAPTER 25

IMOGENE WOKE EARLY the next morning feeling agitated, with a heavy sense of foreboding, which she knew had everything to do with the day ahead. She lay in bed for quite a while, wishing she could stay there indefinitely. She began a conversation then with God, asking for strength and guidance. Then she said, "God, are you even there? I really need a sign, please, God, just a little sign." Im knew this was probably silly. God, wherever, whatever, whoever, would not likely be obliging—it didn't work that way. She knew that the truly faithful wouldn't even ask for signs.

She finally dragged herself out of bed and went to the window to pull up the blinds. The sun was up, sparkling through the trees. At least it wasn't going to be a foul weather day. Then Im noticed something at the bottom of the window screen. A big, bright green bug was peering in at her, with its triangular head, alien-like eyes, and long human-like forelegs—just sitting there out on her bedroom window ledge. Although she'd never seen one up close before, she realized instantly that the strange, slender-bodied insect was a Praying Mantis. She let out a little gasp.

An objective observer might have seen this as nothing more than an interesting coincidence. But for Imogene, there it was: her sign, a Praying Mantis—it had to be her sign from God. Sure, an insect might seem like a bizarre choice, but really, what other kind of sign could God have sent in that moment, which would only be seen and understood by her? Anything major and glorious would be far too disruptive to the world at large. Besides that, it would have been excessive. Im didn't imagine that God tended toward overkill. No, something more subtle, even parsimonious, would be more fitting.

Overcome, Im dropped to her knees, clasped her hands together, and said a little prayer of gratitude. Her eyes welled up, and her voice caught in her throat as she said aloud, "Thank you, thank you... thank you, God!" She stayed there for a while in prayer position, eyes closed, basking in the warm feelings and sense of calm she had in that moment. Maybe she wasn't all alone after all.

She rose then and quickly dressed in a favorite pair of worn-in jeans and a soft, white American Apparel T-shirt. The particular brand of shirts seemed exorbitantly expensive, but she'd bought it cheaply at a consignment shop. She knew that part of the point of even buying one of these items was to pay the price and support "American-made," but Imogene couldn't bring herself to fork over the regular retail price. Although once she owned the brand, she could see why they could charge so much for a simple T-shirt: the cotton was the softest and most comfortable she'd ever worn. It seemed some things are perhaps worth the extra money.

Im wanted to leave the house by mid-morning, so she hoped her mother would pop-up out of bed on her own by nine or so. She wanted to make sure her mom was well situated for the day, since she didn't know how long she'd be gone. The uncertainty of it all was disturbing, but she was resolved to follow through with her plan. It was the only way she could go forward. She hadn't said anything to her mother about it; it would have only upset her, so why bother? Mrs. Mussomeli would have wanted to try to help her daughter somehow, but she could've done nothing. Better to leave her mom in the dark.

Her mother finally rolled out of bed around 9:30. By ten o'clock, Im had given her a good breakfast and had fed and walked Marvin. It was time to head out. She gave her mom a big hug, though Marvin snarled and yapped at her for doing it. Yep, you couldn't touch Mrs. Mussomeli when he was around, which used to annoy her husband to no end. Im knew the dog was only being protective, which, of course, could be a good thing, given the right context...

"I love you, Ma."

"I love you too, Im."

There had always been an enormous amount of love in the Mussomeli family, though verbalizing the words "I love you" had not been a common or frequent occurrence. They were more about actions than words. Im could tell that saying this out loud explicitly this morning had caught her mother a bit off-guard. But it was a nice moment, and Im was glad it happened.

Then Imogene climbed into the Cadillac in the garage, the same way her father would have so many times. The same way he'd done on the very last morning of his life. She had to go and retrieve the car from the shopping center parking lot the afternoon after he had his heart attack, right there inside the supermarket. He'd actually parked his car that morning in a spot labelled "Carry-out only," which was, of course, meant for the restaurant next door. She winced when she saw this. The irony of it felt so brutal to her; she certainly couldn't appreciate the black humor in it at the time. Later, she wondered if he'd not been his sharpest self that morning, parking essentially in an illegal spot. Perhaps his heart was already beginning to falter. Or maybe he'd just said, "What the hell, there's nowhere else to park; I'm taking this spot!"

Imogene sat for a minute in the garage before starting up the engine. She knew she was doing the right thing, but God, it was hard. She felt like she could hear her father's voice, how he would have sounded, encouraging her to do what she had to do. That he would support her no matter what. She pushed the button on the garage door opener, turned the key, and backed out. It was only a five or six minute drive into town. She left the radio off and drove in silence. A million things sped through her mind, but she lit on none of them. She thought about how the Cadillac had such a smooth ride; she totally got why her dad, as soon as he retired, had decided it was time he allowed himself to splurge and buy one.

Passing her old high school on the way that morning, she was amazed at how little it had changed since she and her sisters had attended—it felt like eons ago and yet, too, like only yesterday. Apart from a few things, which were her own doing, it held mostly good memories for her. It was where she met Craig. He truly was the nicest, sweetest guy—everyone thought so. If only she had married him instead of so cavalierly breaking his heart. Surely, she would have ended up happy. She'd have children, a home, none of the agony and heartache of her present situation. Another "if only." There were so many.

That day, in keeping with old times, there were even some grungy-looking teenage boys standing just outside of school property, smoking cigarettes—in the very same "smokers' spot" of decades before. It was something she'd seen so many times when her father would pull up there in the mornings. He usually dropped his daughters off at school on his way to work. These loitering boys, hiding behind the bushes, puffing on "cancer sticks" were the low lives, the "hoods." She supposed there was a different name for them today. Then she realized. She was probably worse now than any of these smoker boys, past or present. None of them likely went on to actually kill a person. She felt ill.

Finally, she arrived at the traffic light across from the police station. It was the longest one on the planet, and it was particularly agonizing now having to wait it out. Finally, it changed to green, and she slowly pulled into the parking lot, dotted with cop cars. *Oh God.*

Im parked near the back of the station, away from all the parked cruisers, including a few paddy wagons. *Gulp.* Just then, a back door opened, and a guy was being escorted out. He was in handcuffs, wearing an orange prison jump suit, and was shuffling as he walked. Im saw that he was in ankle-chains as well. *Shackles!* A shudder rippled through her. A vision flashed through her mind of herself in a tiny cell, four cement walls, no windows. No way out. How was she ever going to endure it? She wasn't strong enough to withstand captivity. She'd wither and die. Die of claustrophobia. Die of panic. *Just die.*

She suddenly felt oddly frozen in place, pinned, as if melding with the Cadillac's soft, leather seat. And she felt almost embraced then, and oddly safe in that moment. Maybe she should turn the key, start the engine, and drive away. Go back home. Pretend nothing terrible had happened, that all could be right again. She could still do this. She could! But sitting there, she knew deep down her fate was already sealed. She'd made her bed. She'd have to lie in it. It was the only way she could ever hope to continue to exist in this world.

Imogene closed her eyes, took a deep breath, and then glanced at her face in the vanity mirror. There was a distinct weariness in her eyes, along with a look of intense fear and sadness. She felt the weight of her entire life pressing on her, crushing her—it was all coming down to this one moment in time: she supposed it was the consummation of the curse…long in coming, but probably right on schedule.

She pushed the car door open. *Here goes.*

The police station was a drab, windowless, dark gray concrete structure, which seemed to say, loud and clear, "Nice things don't happen here." Not at all inviting, but then that was probably the point. The entrance was set a bit below ground level and opened into a lobby with chairs and a large, security glass window. The officer behind it, staffing the desk, looked up expectantly, "Can I help you?"

Okay, this is it. *This is it.*

"I need to talk with someone about Preston Wyles." She could hear her voice quivering.

The officer at the desk said, "Who? Can you spell the last name?"

He jotted it down on a piece of paper and told her to wait there a minute. The harsh, florescent lights made the top of her eyes hurt, and the humming sound emanating from them seemed to grow louder and louder with every second. The lobby was also freezing, and Im could feel her body tensing up, starting to shiver. Her teeth were chattering by the time a side door opened, and a guy walked toward her.

Im recognized him instantly. She'd gone to high school with him, though he'd been a grade ahead of her. A really nice guy she hadn't known well, but who had asked her out once. She'd turned him down. No surprise, she turned down most of the really nice guys who'd asked her out back then. With the exception of Craig, Imogene always gravitated toward the less-nice ones, the ones who didn't seem bowled over by her—the ones with a bit of swagger. What a flawed system, she thought.

"Imogene?"

"Yeah, hey, Jack, right?"

"Yeah, gosh, so how've you've been? Wow, it's been a long time..."

"Yeah, it has..."

"Okay, well...um, let's go back to my office."

"Yeah, sure." Im could feel her throat starting to tighten up.

Imogene followed him through the door he'd come out, which he had to swipe with a card to open. They walked down a hall lined with photos of what were probably past chiefs and town mayors. His was the office on the end. The nameplate read, "Detective Jack Lipton." She'd heard at some point long ago that Jack Lipton had become a cop, but she hadn't realized he worked for their hometown police department. She was impressed that he had become a detective. She certainly hadn't expected to run into someone she knew here. Maybe it was going to make things easier.

"So what can I do for you...you said you wanted to talk about Preston Wyles?" Jack typed on his desktop computer while he asked the question, his eyes obviously scanning the screen.

"Yes, he was my neighbor...," she waited for a reaction.

"Yeah, poor guy, looks like he never had a chance..."

"Um...never had a chance?" Im was suddenly confused.

"Yeah, I don't think the guy was married, but the widow-maker did him in. Oh, wait, it looks like there was actually an ex-wife..."

Imogene felt her face flushing, her heart thumping wildly, and sweat instantly forming on the back of her neck. "What do you mean the widow-maker?"

"Oh, that's what they call the left main coronary artery...reminds me, I need to get my cholesterol checked," Jack said with a little chuckle.

She was too stunned to say a word. Jack went on, his eyes checking the computer screen. "Sorry, I guess he was a friend? Yeah, he was basically a ticking time-bomb as they say. Autopsy report says here there was close to 100% blockage in that artery. What little I know about this stuff, it's amazing he didn't die a long time ago."

Imogene realized she had to say something, "So... so... he had a heart condition?"

"Well, yeah, I guess you could say that, but often a guy doesn't even know. Usually no symptoms, he just drops dead one day out of the blue. That's why they call it the widow-maker. Not really a survivable heart attack when it happens, I guess."

All she could muster was a word, "Oh." Then she fell silent. Her mind was in complete chaos. Preston was a ticking time-bomb? 100% blockage? There was an ex-wife? *What the hell?*

Jack filled the silence with a bit of chit-chat, not seeming concerned about her reason for being there. "So, how are all the rest of the Mussomeli sisters?"

"Oh, they're fine... um, well, our dad died recently... a heart attack, in fact."

"Oh, wow, I'm sorry," Jack said, with genuine sympathy.

He really was a good guy, another one of the boys that Imogene had nonchalantly passed up, not even giving him the time of day. He'd been attractive in high school in a boyish, slightly awkward way, but now as a man, he was very good-looking—full head of blond hair laced with a trace of white, and a smooth, honey-golden complexion.

Im envied the way a blonde person's hair could go from blonde to white, no gray stage. Her own hair was already beginning to go prematurely salt and pepper, just like her mother's had done when she was young. Im had to douse her hair with coloring rinse every few months just to keep herself from looking like an old-maid-hag.

"So, Preston Wyles...what did you want to talk about?"

Imogene stammered a bit. "Well, I just...see I was concerned... I mean, I just wondered... well, his obit didn't say much, um, I guess, well, I mean, does he have family?..." Im was clearly floundering, caught so off-guard, she could barely form a coherent sentence. "Well, see things are always dark at his house; I mean... what's going to happen to the house and everything?"

"Um, yeah, it says here he was born in Kentucky. Probably had family back there... I'm sure someone will be up here settling his affairs. So was there... I mean, do you have a question or...?"

Something was building inside Im now, like a giant volcano about to erupt. She worked to contain herself. Jack was a detective after all; the last thing she needed was to blurt out something stupid.

She had to think fast. "Well, I was feeling a little nervous—I know he has some valuable cars, and it is completely dark over there night after night... I'd hate for something to happen. Plus, it's only me and my mom next door... I guess I'm just being paranoid. Sometimes our dog starts barking like crazy..."

Jack looked concerned. "Have you seen something suspicious?"

"Well, not really. Like I said, maybe I'm only being paranoid... I took it real hard when my dad died… I think I'm still sort of shaky, you know, emotionally."

"Yeah, I hear you. My wife died a few years ago from cancer. It was really rough. Had to take a long leave from work."

The wheels were turning in her mind; she decided she had to know more.

"Jack, I guess to be honest, I was sort of worried... I mean, I saw Preston a couple nights before he died. I had a drink with him, but he fell asleep, and I just left him there asleep on his couch. I mean, now, I'm wondering if he was even okay when I left. I didn't think to see if he was really alright, you know, maybe not just sleeping... I figured he must have been really tired or something. I mean he would usually leave for work by 6:30 every morning. Does it say where he was when they found him?"

Jack clicked and moved the computer mouse. "Looks like they found him in his bed, slumped like he was in the middle of climbing out of bed or something. I guess getting up in the morning can be a prime time for these things to happen. So, yeah, I'm sure he was fine the last time you saw him. You know, these things just happen, out of the blue. Fine one second, gone the next."

"Yeah, that's pretty much what happened to my dad. But he was in the grocery store. Anyway, hey, thanks a lot for your time. Sorry to have bothered you. I just think too much I guess! But yeah, hey, it was good to see you, Jack. I'll let you get back to work."

Imogene got up then, and Jack followed, walking her out. When they got to the lobby, she didn't know what to do, so she just sort of half reached out her hand toward him, in a gesture that said I don't know if we should shake hands or hug or what.

"Hey, thanks again for your time... good seeing you, Jack... take care," lightly grazing his forearm with her outstretched hand for a second. She turned around and started to push the door open.

Then Jack called her name, and she froze. "Hey, Imogene... um... would you want to get a coffee sometime?"

She exhaled, relief washing over her. "Ah, sure... yeah, that'd be nice. Here, I'll give you my number."

Jack pulled out his cell phone and punched her number in.

"Okay, see you later, then, Jack."

"Yeah, take it easy, Im."

Im smiled brightly at him, spun on her heels, and strolled off toward the parking lot. Anyone watching would have wondered why she couldn't stop grinning. When she got into the Caddy, she could contain it no longer. Hands covering her face, she bowed her head against the steering wheel and sobbed uncontrollably. The flood of emotions left her gasping for air, the sense of relief was so intense, so all-consuming.

She felt like she'd just narrowly escaped a ghastly accident, like the person who was running late and missed getting on a flight that ended up crashing horribly. Like she was suddenly given a second chance at life. She'd woken up that morning thinking her life was about to completely collapse and implode. Now she was elated beyond belief. A million thoughts were running through her mind: she hadn't caused a man to die, she wasn't a murderess, she wasn't destined to live a life of hell on Earth and beyond. The emotional release was immense and overwhelming:

"Thank you, God, thank you, a thousand times over! I promise I'll never do another shady thing my whole life. I promise I'm going to be a better person!"

Yes, Imogene vowed that she would, finally, truly grow up.

On the drive home, she rolled down all the Caddy's windows and let her fly in the wind. The radio was blasting the oldies. Another of her favorite Beatles songs came on, "All You Need is Love," and Im sang along at the top of her lungs. She knew every word.

It was an unseasonably mild day, and sunshine warmed her forearm resting out the driver's side window. She took her time getting home, cruising the familiar streets of her childhood, well below the speed limit. Her father used to do this. He often seemed to be in no hurry to get anywhere when he was behind the wheel, as though he was savoring every moment of the smooth ride and the sights around him. Im used to get impatient as a passenger, but now... yeah, now, she thought maybe she finally got it.

The sky above was a dazzling, deep blue, not even a single wisp of a cloud in sight—it was the sort of sky that used to make young Imogene feel especially glad. It meant all clear skies and sunshine ahead, no stormy weather in sight. Yes, there was indeed a nice, big high-pressure cell hovering right over Dayton, Ohio... A picture-perfect day.

CHAPTER 26

NINE MONTHS LATER.

Im sat, her back rigidly straight, on the edge of the plush-padded seat with no armrest. Always the same sort of chairs set up for these kinds of events. Long, horizontal rows of seats, arranged closely together to accommodate a large group. Bright lights. Sparse decor. All eyes would be fixed on the front.

Her body was tense, holding tight—not able to let go—though she wasn't aware of this at all. Her mind was on so many things all at once. With her mother in the chair next to her, there was always the need for low-level vigilance. If Im wasn't keeping an eye on things, her mom might get up and saunter off to wherever her mood might take her. It would be fine if Mrs. Mussomeli were able to keep track of where she was and how to get back to the starting place, but within the last year, this ability had become increasingly absent. It worried Im, but there was also a bliss that came in tandem, and it wasn't an awful trade off. So whenever she was traveling with her mother, Im rarely ever completely relaxed. She might have left her mother with one of her sisters—they had become very helpful in this respect—but Imogene wanted her mother to be a part of this. It was only right for her to be there, too.

Im's mind also went to their little hotel in Gramercy Park, currently housing the devil-turned-hero dog, Marvin. The room was clean and nice, but small as was always the case in non-luxury hotels in New York City. Flying with the dog on the plane was no big deal since her mother's doctor had agreed he was a comfort and anchor of sorts for her mother. The airline had no objections to the letter declaring Marvin a support animal. *Ha, if they only knew,* she'd thought. Now, Imogene was hoping that he wasn't piddling in the hotel room somewhere. He had a knack for lifting his leg at anything vertical when in a new place. The tiny pipsqueak of a dog who thinks he's an alpha, determined to mark his territory. Hotel bedposts were a favorite for this.

The day before, strutting through the Dayton airport, Marvin had been quite the hit, prancing along with his snout held high and long, honey-brown plume of a tail curled, waving with every step—as if to say, "Look at me; aren't I adorable?" He certainly could fool the unsuspecting onlooker. Im would always have to say, "Yes, he's cute... but *look*, don't touch, if you still want your hand in one piece!"

The large room they were sitting in was quickly filling up. The rich mahogany wood podium loomed large up front. The adjacent display nook, a well-lit recessed alcove, looked poised, ready to receive the prized contents, the said items on the docket that day. The lots.

Any minute now.

She wondered if she was doing the right thing. Would her father have wanted this? Every time she pondered it, she always came up with the same answer: *Hell, yes.* There was really little doubt in her mind what her dad would have said. "Are you kidding? Take the money, Im!"

But she continued to struggle with the idea of letting go of the Darwin book. She knew that the book itself didn't really hold much sentimental value. Her father hadn't ever even spoken about it; he'd apparently forgotten that it even existed. Still, the book felt like a cable connecting her with her father. As long as she had the book, a part of him was still there.

She'd awoken that morning in Manhattan at daybreak, a sliver of light invading through the heavy drapes of the hotel room. She still felt that familiar fuzziness of fatigue, typical for her when traveling, but was unable to sleep any longer. She was too keyed up. It wasn't going to be an ordinary day. Lying in bed, she looked up to at the high ceiling with its detailed partitions and thick crown molding. The room was small, tiny really, barely enough space for the two twin beds. But with the towering ceilings and tall windows, the place felt less small and very old world. Truly charming. This is what made the tight, old hotel rooms tolerable, even comfortable. Still, a guest might not put up with it in another city, but in New York, it was fine. Perhaps seeing so many down-and-out people living out in the shadows of the buildings or even camped right on a street corner, just having a warm place to lay one's head felt like enough, no matter how cramped.

Walking along the streets of New York, Im struggled not to look at the homeless, the bereft, those obviously mentally ill or drug-addicted. The street people. They often had a cardboard sign balanced on the side of an empty box begging for money, usually with a phrase, written crudely in crayon or marker, about their plight: "Homeless vet," "Abused as a child," "Hungry." Seeing these people always made Imogene feel guilty for having so much. If she hadn't been born into a good family or one with means, who knows? This could have been her. She wondered if they still had parents who cared about them, or if their mothers knew where they were.

She'd almost lost her own mother that morning in the subway. They'd descended the stairs together, her mother safely by her side. Getting her through the turn-style was always a bit of a challenge. Of course, her mother wasn't used to the routine. Not that she ever could be. Over the past several months, it'd become clear that learning new tasks would be nearly impossible for her mother now. Im knew she'd have to guide her carefully. They'd been on the subway a couple times already without incident. Perhaps Im had become a tad complacent. Or maybe it was the excitement of the day ahead that had distracted her.

It happened when they were about to board the uptown train. There was the usual, sudden outflow of passengers and then the rush to get on the train. Im's mother got ahead of her somehow in the crowd. Dutifully, she followed the stream of people and got on the train. Im was following close behind when she felt her purse strap catch on something. It had gotten snared on the metal edge of a large, free-standing sign.

These fixtures were placed throughout the subway tunnels, displaying the various subway lines in bright red, blue, yellow, orange, and green. This particular sign was damaged and had a piece of its metal edging jutting out, sharp and ready to jab anybody walking by. Im tried to quickly untangle herself, but the strap was lodged tight. In her panic, she probably made it worse.

Finally, she managed to free the purse and turned to rush on the train when she saw the double-doors begin to close! She reached out reflexively hoping to catch it—she'd seen people stick their arms in-between this way and the doors would automatically spring back open. It was essential for safety reasons, naturally. But Im always thought the people who did this were braver than she. What if the door didn't stop closing and instead your arm got stuck? You'd be yanked along with the train. Falling under it, instantly crushed, sliced and diced! She could too easily picture the gruesome sight of a human body, mangled and reduced to mere hunks of flesh and bone.

Regardless, Im was ready to stop the subway door with her arm. Her mother was on the train without her! Who knows what would happen to her? Given her dementia, how would she ever find her again in New York City? But Im wasn't close enough to catch the door. She had no choice but to back-off helplessly and watch as the train raced away, with her clueless mother inside.

Im was left back on the platform horrified. Stunned. How could she have allowed her mother to get ahead of her and board the train before her? Anybody would have known this was a very, bad idea. She was supposed to be taking care of her mother. She should have been holding her hand on the platform. Now her mother was alone on the New York Subway! What was going to happen to her?

Aghast, Im stood frozen in place. Her first instinct was to run to the nearest police station for help. But what could they do? How long would that take? What would become of her mother in the meantime? She could end up anywhere. How would she ever find her daughter? She'd never remember where they'd been heading that day or the name of the hotel or

Im's cell phone number. She never called Im's cell phone. No way would she remember the number. Was she even wearing her medical ID bracelet that day? Would she know how to get help or go to the police? Would she even realize she was lost? *Oh no!*

Im began to pace, trying to think what to do, what the hell to do! Her mind was racing through scenarios, most worst-case. She tried to calm herself. Then she recalled something a cousin and native New Yorker had said. If people ever got separated on the subway, the standing rule was to simply get off at the very next stop and wait for the next train to come, bringing whoever had been left behind. Yes, this was an elegant, easy solution. The question was, had her mother ever heard this? If so, would she possibly remember and know to do this?

She knew then that the only option was to have faith that her mother would somehow know what to do—or even just follow the crowd off the train. Im looked up at the schedule. The next uptown train was to arrive in eight minutes.

Im went to the smooth tile wall along the platform. Trying not to cry, she leaned her head back, closed her eyes, and prayed. The eight minutes waiting for the train felt like an eternity. She wanted to scream. She'd been a lousy daughter, *yet again.*

Wait... no, she hadn't really. This wasn't her fault. The damaged sign had caught her. She hadn't caused that. It was only bad luck. Stuff happens. She had to stop beating herself up about things.

Suddenly, she heard the roar, and the next train blasted into the station. Im was always overwhelmed by the noise and the explosive force—the deafening screech of the train's brakes. It was inherently terrifying. The sheer power of a speeding train, it can't be stopped, it's going to obliterate anything in its path.

Finally, the train came to a halt, the doors flew open, people rushed out, and Im got on. *Please, please, Mom, be there. Please, God.*

The ride to the next stop was quick, maybe covering only five or six blocks. *Please, God, let her be there.*

Im felt the train begin to slow, her eyes reaching for a view of the next platform. *Please.* Finally, the train came to a complete stop, and the doors opened. Im was in a back subway car so she couldn't see the platform yet. She got off and began to run. *Please be there.*

The platform came into view, and she saw some people standing there... none of them her mother. Her heart sank and her stomach dropped. *Oh no.*

But ahead, she spotted a bench and a hint of a black hat. Was that her mom's hat? Then she saw her. Sitting calmly on the bench—regally almost, like she hadn't a care in the world and was exactly where she was supposed to be.

Looking up, she saw her daughter. Mrs. Mussomeli said, "Oh, Im, there you are!"

Hugging her mother tightly, Im said, "Oh, my God, Mom, I thought I'd lost you forever! I was so scared!"

"Oh, don't worry, Im; you aren't going to lose me," she said with a chuckle.

***

Startled by the strike of the auctioneer's gavel at the podium, Im jumped a little in her chair. It spoke to how tightly wound she was that day. After what she'd been through on the subway, along with the excitement about the auction, it was no wonder.

The auctioneer shouted, "Sold for $575,000!" It was the first lot. A letter signed "A. Lincoln" to Ulysses S. Grant. Imogene knew that her father's Darwin book was down toward the end of the list of lots for the day. Apparently, this is what they tended to do with some of the more anticipated items. She could feel her palms beginning to sweat. This was really happening.

Several more lots. An old copy of the "The Great Gatsby" went for $377,000, then another rare and very obscure book sold for $730,500. Im had no idea what it even was or if that was a remarkable price or not. She really knew next to nothing about the rare book world.

Finally, their Darwin book was announced. The auctioneer spoke of its merits, a very rare 1859, first edition of Darwin's "(On the) Origin of Species," how the provenance indicated it was one of the copies that Mr. Darwin may have held in his own hands. The experts had taken months to examine it. How had such a book ever landed in Rochester, New York, stashed away for decades? No one really knew. Sometimes, as luck would have it, these things just happen. Yes, the energy around the book was palpable.

The actual bidding for the book was a blur for Imogene. Everything seemed to go at warp speed. Her mother sat there getting swept up in the energy of the place, even now and then exclaiming with an "oooh" or "aaah," for no reason other than she'd noticed others reacting this way. She didn't exactly know what was going on, but it was typical for her to move with the flow and get caught up in the excitement or whatever was happening around her. Yes, it was one tiny gift of her dementia, if you will. Her mother could be so happy and blissful and carefree, no matter where she was—never a worry. Im envied her this.

Then, the final loud bang of the gavel. Im jumped again. Tears stream down her cheeks. Her mother turned to look at her, alarm and concern now in her eyes. She reached out to clasp her daughter's hand—to comfort her, not knowing what or why—it was just instinctive. The love for her daughter was constant—unwavering and eternal. Imogene squeezed her hand back.

"No, it's okay, Ma. I'm just happy. Really happy."

Made in the USA
Middletown, DE
07 May 2022

65461661R00163